PRISONER OF PASSION

The ghost of a smile crossed her lips at the irony. She had finally found a man she wanted to touch her—and he was the enemy. Ryen reached out a hand, meaning to stroke the wound on his cheek, but Bryce flinched and drew back.

"What do you want from me?"

Perhaps it was ridiculous, Ryen thought. Men never seemed to have a problem with taking what, or who, they wanted. Maybe I'm making it more complicated than it should be. He is my prisoner.

She raised a hand to touch his thick mane.

Bryce pulled back instantly. Ryen wrapped her fingers tightly in his hair, leaning into his strong chest. "You fear my touch?" she wondered in a soft whisper.

"Loathe is more like it," he said.

She could feel the lie through his leggings and smiled. "Your body betrays you."

"Step away from me, witch," he snarled.

Ryen stood on the tips of her toes and pressed her lips against his. At first they were immovable, but suddenly they parted and the hot passion he was trying to hide was released. His tongue slipped into her mouth, warring with hers . . .

Advance praise for THE ANGEL AND THE PRINCE:

"Pageantry, excitement and high adventure brought to vivid life."

—Flora Speer, author of FOR LOVE AND HONOR

"A wonderful debut, lush, sensual, and rich in history."
—Jane Kidder, author of PASSION'S GIFT

"Wow! A magnificent tale [that builds] tension till you want to explode!"

—*Affaire de Coeur*

THE ANGEL
AND THE PRINCE

LAUREL O'DONNELL

ZEBRA BOOKS
KENSINGTON PUBLISHING CORP.

To my husband Jack, whose understanding,
help, and love have given me the time to dream
and the confidence to act.
It is with all my heart that I dedicate this book to you.

ZEBRA BOOKS are published by

Kensington Publishing Corp.
850 Third Avenue
New York, NY 10022

First Printing: March, 1996
10 9 8 7 6 5 4 3 2 1

Printed in the United States of America

Prologue

France, 1410

The choir of voices ascended to the far corners of the cathedral, where sculptured angels listened with somber faces to the Latin words. Shining white marble pillars spiraled down to the steps of the great altar. At the top stair stood King Charles VI and behind him, eight small boys dressed in immaculate white robes, each holding a red velvet pillow with golden tassels at each corner. Upon every silky velvet pillow rested a resplendent sword. Above and behind the boys, golden statues of saints stretched out their cold arms in welcome and forgiveness with unseeing eyes.

The king shifted his regal stance, his gaze locked on the tall wooden doors at the back of the church. He knew eight young men waited anxiously outside, their breath tight in their chests, their palms slick with nervous sweat. Each one would enter as a squire filled with a boy's apprehension, and leave as a knight of the realm filled with a warrior's pride.

One of the banners caught his eye. It was for Ryen De Bouriez, the third son of Baron Jean Claude De Bouriez. King Charles's eyes scanned the mass of people before him until they came to rest on two men—the elder De Bouriez brothers. They were tall, even by knightly standards. Lucien was fair; his honeyed hair, blue eyes, and boyish looks were rumored to have cost more than one maiden her virtue. Andre was dark, with chestnut eyes and a heart of gold. Both were skilled warriors, and this pleased the king, for he knew Ryen would make an excellent addition to his troops. He studied the brothers closely. They shifted from foot to foot nervously; even Andre, who was usually so calm, seemed unsettled. The king frowned. Perhaps the two giants were uncomfortable with the civil surroundings and were eager to be out of the church. King Charles sympathized. The De Bouriezes were, after all, known for their prowess in battle, not their sociability.

The king glanced over row upon row of nobles in their elegant satins and velvets. The Countess of Burgundy was there. Not far from her, the flamboyant golden caul headdress of the Duchess of Orleans caught his eye. Slowly his brow creased into a frown as he finished surveying the attending nobility. Where was Ryen's father?

The choir of voices that had filled the chamber suddenly ended, their last echoes resonating throughout the cathedral until they slipped away into nothingness.

Glancing toward the trumpeters awaiting his signal in the balcony, King Charles nodded. When they put the long golden horns to their lips, the triumphant music began. All eyes turned to the heavy oak doors at the back of the church as they slowly creaked open.

Eight squires advanced down the long carpeted aisle, one behind the other.

Sunlight streamed in from the stained glass windows, reflecting brilliantly off the shining silver-and-gold plate mail of the approaching men. King Charles squinted as a ray of light shone in his eyes. He tried to be a fair man, judging all men equally, but he found himself anxious to see Ryen De Bouriez, around whom so much controversy swirled. The first time his name had reached the king's ears, it was with the capture of Castle Picardy, the feat that had earned him his knighthood. King Charles had heard the same story three times, and with each telling, Ryen's achievements had seemed to grow until they were of Herculean proportions.

Since then, the name Ryen De Bouriez had arisen time and time again in casual conversation. The man's strategic maneuvers were ingenious.

The initiates climbed the stairs to the great altar and bowed before the king, then stepped aside to form a row before their lord. As the squire preceding De Bouriez bowed, King Charles tried not to seem obvious as he peered over the top of the man's head to get a glimpse of Ryen. Finally, like a curtain being drawn, the squire stepped aside and Ryen De Bouriez was revealed to King Charles. The initiate still wore his helmet. All traces of astonishment disappeared as anger descended over the king. It was disrespectful for anyone to wear a helmet in the house of God. The young man's headgear covered most of his face except for his eyes. King Charles could see the striking blueness of them; they shimmered in the shadows of his helmet like a great cloudless sky. His eyes raked the young man again. He is very small indeed, the king thought. I cannot believe the great Baron De Bouriez squired this runt. Perhaps De Bouriez is absent because he is embarrassed by his son's size.

Under his scrutiny, the king saw Ryen's deep blue eyes fill with pride, and something else. Before he could discern what that strange spark was, Ryen fell to one knee, bowing his head in reverence.

Somewhat pacified, King Charles commanded quietly, "Remove your helmet, Ryen," and turned to retrieve a ceremonial sword cushioned upon a pillow of velvet. As he reverently removed the sword, the king heard rustling and the clang of armor behind him and knew Ryen was removing his helmet.

Suddenly a collective gasp spread through the crowd like the wind whistling through a field of wheat.

King Charles whirled at the sound. His eyes grew wide and he gaped as the reason for the young man's diminutive stature became quite apparent. The "man" was not a man at all!

He was a *she!*

Why, she could be no more than fifteen! Amazement rocked him like a blow to his stomach, leaving him breathless and stunned. The girl's soft dark hair cascaded in waves over the metal shoulder plates. Her nose was a delicate sculpture of perfection, her lips full. Her chin was strong, with a slight cleft etched into it. Beauty shimmered beneath her childlike features. She had the innocent face of a cherub . . . an angel. King Charles stared for a long moment.

The king knew now what that look in her sapphire eyes had been: defiance. It accented her features with determination.

The king turned to glance at her brothers. Andre had suddenly found interest in a piece of imaginary lint on his spotless white velvet tunic, and Lucien was studying the painted angels on the stained glass windows. King Charles's lips thinned and his gaze returned to Ryen.

A girl! How had she been able to keep this secret? he wondered.

King Charles stared in shock. No wonder Baron De Bouriez is not here, he thought. He gripped the sword tightly until his knuckles hurt with the effort. He knew he should not knight her, that she should be punished for her audacity, but her deeds surpassed the defiance that her stubborn raised little chin represented. He wanted her in his army, needed her strategic skills. These were desperate times.

He lifted the sword in a sweeping gesture and saw her body stiffen, as if expecting a blow. He brought the sword down, lightly touching the tip of the blade to each of her shoulders in the customary colée, finishing with, "Rise, Sir Ryen De Bouriez."

The young girl slowly and unsteadily rose to her feet. Her large eyes were wide, ringed with happiness; her rosy lips were parted in disbelief.

King Charles bent close to her and lay his hand on her shoulder. "Ryen, the road before you will be laced with hardship. Be a true knight, and courageous in the face of your enemies. Be brave and upright. And remember that you spring from a bloodline that has always been strong."

"I shall," Ryen said earnestly, her expression solemn.

The king held out the sword to her. Ryen carefully took the gleaming blade in her bare palms and pressed her lips to it before accepting it from King Charles's hands. She studied the sword for a quick moment, a flash of pride lighting up her soft features, then slid it into the scabbard at her waist.

King Charles leaned in close to whisper, "However, if you or your brothers ever pull a trick like this again, I will have your heads." He straightened to his full height and proclaimed, "Now. Be thou a knight."

Ryen bowed, giving King Charles her loyalty and her gratitude. The king repeated the knighting seven more times, after which he stood back and watched as the men—and the woman—turned as one to face the congregation. Ryen led the way down the aisle. As she passed her awestruck brothers, the king watched Ryen shoot them a smug look of triumph. Throwing her shoulders back, holding her chin high, Sir Ryen De Bouriez strolled confidently past the mass of whispering people.

One

England, 1414

The cheers from the gathered crowd sounded like a thunderous rain as the horses charged at each other, their hooves kicking up dirt from the grassy field. The two knights, fully armored for this joust, bent low over the heads of their equally well-protected mounts, their brightly striped lances gripped firmly. The white plume on the helmet of the challenger knight appeared defeated and submissive as it flattened under the rush of wind created by his speeding stallion. The champion shifted his shield to the front of his body, where the challenger could see it—a snarling red wolf strikingly painted against a black background. Through the slit in the challenger's visor, the champion saw his opponent's eyes widen in fear. Seconds later, the champion's lance struck the challenger's chest, the wooden tip crunching as it hit the man's breastplate, and lifted him cleanly from his horse, depositing him roughly on the ground.

The crowd sprang to its feet, wild with applause and shouts of joy. The champion slowed his horse and turned, raising the visor of his helmet to reveal dark, impenetrable eyes. These orbs watched patiently as his staggering opponent was helped to his feet by his squire. Bryce Princeton waited for the defeated knight to stumble from the arena before he urged his horse around the field for his victory lap.

The peasants who lined the jousting field's fence shouted his success. "Prince! Prince!"

The rush of power that surged through his veins at every joust, at every triumph, gave Bryce the feeling of invincibility. He savored the taste like a favored wine, relished the shouts. He had never known defeat, either in battle or in Tournament.

As he rode past the nobles' stand, all the women batted their eyelashes at him and some bent over the wooden railing to dangle their favors before him. He gladly accepted them— all of them. But he returned most of their heated, lusty gazes with a cool disdain. These pampered and powdered women brought only an occasional twinge of curiosity to his mind. They were all too much alike to be of any real interest. Some men cast him envious glances, while others seethed quietly. Finally, Bryce came to a halt before King Henry's chair. He dismounted and bowed before his sovereign.

Henry grinned at him and stood. The king was a tall and muscular man, his brown hair trimmed in a bowl cut.

The crowd quieted as Bryce approached the stand. He slid his helmet from his head to reveal a thick mane of long black hair that fell to the middle of his shoulder blades. It gleamed in the sunlight, wet with moisture. His face was bronzed by the sun. There was an inherent power in the set of his jaw, the sensual curve of his lips, his dark eyes.

"You have done well today, as always," King Henry said loudly, so all could hear. "You are truly England's champion."

Huzzahs and gleeful shouts erupted into a deafening roar.

Henry bent toward Bryce. "Come, walk with me, Bryce," he commanded.

Bryce led his mount across the field and handed the reins to his waiting squire as a small boy ducked under the wooden fence that surrounded the field and dashed up to him. Bryce smiled and ruffled his dark hair as the boy exclaimed, "You were great!" His eyes shone with excitement and admiration. "I knew he wouldn't defeat you."

"You had doubts, Runt?" Bryce wondered, a mock frown drawing his lips into a pout.

"Never!" Runt exploded.

Bryce couldn't help but smile at the pride and boundless love that emanated from those large, inquisitive blue eyes. Then he noticed the dirt that dusted Runt's small hands as the boy reached for his helmet. Bryce quickly surveyed the boy's brown cotton tunic, noticing with mild annoyance that it was spotted with mud. He ran a finger along one of Runt's cheeks, leaving a trail of clean skin through the dirt. "You should bathe," Bryce offered, showing him the smudge that stained his fingertip.

The boy groaned and shuffled his feet. "I hate bathing," he mumbled.

Bryce sympathized with him. As a youth he had hated to bathe. It took up too much of his time and there were more important matters to attend to . . . such as imitating the knights. "A knight cannot meet the king with dirt on his face," Bryce told him.

Runt nodded grudgingly. "All right."

Bryce's dark eyes searched the dais for his king. He found the platform empty and followed the path of rich blues and satiny golds of the court until he spotted the king heading for the streets that led into the town. As Bryce turned to leave, he heard Runt say, "I hope to be as great a knight as you."

Bryce paused, turning back to the boy. Runt gazed up at him in wonder, his big blue eyes round with admiration. "You will," Bryce promised, before moving toward the dais. A procession of fashionably dressed lords and ladies followed the king, as always, and Bryce was hard pressed to catch up with him with the weight of his plate armor impeding his movement. In his hurry, he almost stepped on a duke's long green cloak. The duchess accompanying the duke turned a shy smile to Bryce, a wisp of her pleated coiffure at the very top of her head flapping with each step. Bryce bowed slightly and rushed by her. At a fast walk, he managed to reach King Henry as he stopped to speak with a man selling apple cider.

"The cider is wonderful in the village. No matter how hard they try, my servants can never duplicate it," King Henry told Bryce, lifting a goblet of it to his lips.

Bryce nodded absently. He glanced at the nobles trailing the king like well-trained falcons, vying for his attention. Bryce did not miss the contemptuous stares many of the nobles cast his way. He despised them and their pretentious ways. If they sought attention, they should *act*—take a castle, contribute finances to the impending war. Instead, they hoped to win the king's favor with their beautiful clothing, and their pretty faces and witty words. It was to Bryce's credit that Henry chose to speak with him and not one of the fanciful dressers. The king was not a fool.

"I have been told it is a secret of the Roza family," the Earl of March said. He wore a golden houppelande that flowed to the ground and was embroidered with flowers. The edges of his long sleeves were cut in the shape of leaves and trimmed with jewels. He was the most prettily dressed of all the nobles.

"Yes, well . . ." The king waved a hand, dismissing the matter and the earl, and turned to continue down the dusty street. The sun was hot, the ground parched. The dust rose in little whirlwinds on the road before them.

Bryce walked at King Henry's side, towering above most of the lords; even the king was dwarfed by his size. In plate mail, Bryce Princeton was an enviable vision.

"There are far too many ears in the streets, don't you agree, Bryce?" King Henry wondered.

"Aye," Bryce answered, and followed as the king cut through the village to the countryside.

The Earl of March tried vainly to keep up. He was panting

hard when he produced a lace handkerchief and patted his forehead with it. "It is a hot day, isn't it, my liege?" he called.

King Henry cast him a sour glance. "March, go see to the countess. I believe she is having as hard a time keeping up as you."

Bryce's gaze shifted to the countess. She had swooned into a man's arms and was being eased to the ground. Most of the court had lagged behind by now, and it was quite apparent to Bryce that the king wished to speak with him in private. He wondered if the earl was truly so oblivious.

But the earl simply bowed, saying, "As you wish."

King Henry continued into the grasslands of the countryside. Bryce followed, thinking it was becoming much too hot to be wandering through the countryside in sixty-six pounds of plate mail.

"How are things for you, Bryce?" King Henry asked, taking a sip of cider.

Bryce shrugged his large shoulders slightly. "Dark Castle is in capable hands. The peasants are producing enough to support the lands. I believe it will be a good year."

Henry nodded. "Good." He stopped walking and looked out over the fields that stretched before them. The wild grass seemed to sigh as a breeze drifted through the long blades that reached to Bryce's mid-calf. "Then you are prepared to leave England at a moment's notice?"

"Aye," Bryce said anxiously. He had been waiting months for the fleet of English ships to cast off for France. "We leave soon, then?"

Henry gazed hard at Bryce. "There is rumor of a plot against my life. I fear that I may not get to France as soon as I would like."

Bryce frowned, his body stiffening with suppressed anger. "My lord, I offer my services to find out if these rumors are true."

Henry smiled a weary grin. "I have others who will be my ears and eyes."

Bryce scowled, ready to object.

Henry continued, "No, Bryce, you are a fighter. I need you in France. I cannot leave England until this is resolved." He lifted the goblet to his lips again and continued walking. Bryce followed.

"Have you heard anything of this French knight called the Angel of Death?" the king wondered.

Anxiety rippled through Bryce like a flag in a soft breeze. Bryce had heard of his deeds, but he knew little of the man. Still, the way the king had asked . . . it was as though he were being tested. "I have heard the name."

Henry turned to Bryce, his inquisitive eyes asking for details, his raised eyebrows encouraging more.

"He has taken and held land for the Armagnacs," Bryce continued, and watched as a smile tugged the king's lips before he averted his gaze. Bryce's brows drew together in confusion. "He does well for his country," he added, shifting uneasily. He had somehow failed the test, and it annoyed him.

"Yes, he does, doesn't he?" Henry chuckled.

"Is there more to know?"

"Much." Gradually, Henry's smile faded and he slowed his pace. His words were thoughtful and full of woe as he spoke. "The Angel of Death has caused more enemy deaths than any other French lord. This knight is unlike any we have ever come across."

"He is mortal. Blood runs through his veins. And that blood can be spilled."

"According to rumor, this Angel of Death has ice for blood."

"Pah. Rumor is the gossip of cowards."

"Yes. I suppose it is—Prince of Darkness."

Surprise rocked Bryce. He knew he shouldn't have been amazed that the king had heard the name, but he could not suppress the shock that flooded his body. The rumors had traveled so fast . . . and so far! The court. It thrived on any kind of gossip. "The peasants labeled me that," he explained.

"Not without reason, I hear."

"I am merciless only to our enemies, my lord."

"And that is why you must be the one to go to France and find the Angel of Death. There are ships waiting to take you and your army across the channel."

"Do you wish to keep him for ransom?"

"I would prefer a ransom. We can use the finances for the war. But if you cannot take him captive, then take his life. I will join you in France as soon as I can."

"As you wish, sire." Bryce bowed slightly.

"Many men have fallen beneath the knight's sword," King Henry added. "Be cautious."

Bryce nodded and took a step away.

The king stayed him once again with his hand. "I warn you, Bryce: do not underestimate the Angel of Death."

King Henry watched Bryce Princeton stride away. Perhaps he should have told him. But if he knew the truth, Henry was sure he would underestimate their enemy by far too much. Besides, the man needed a jolt to disturb that confident gait of his. He only hoped Bryce would be able to kill this Angel of Death . . . when he found out she was a woman.

Two

East of Yprès, France, 1415

The clang of metal against metal rang out in the large clearing as the two swords met, the echoing melody of their clash spreading throughout the surrounding forest.

"Watch out for her parry!" a voice called, joining the reverberating tune as it reflected off the nearby trees. Andre De Bouriez lounged on his side in the thick grass, his objective gaze scrutinizing the combatants as they swung their heavy broadswords. He nodded with satisfaction as his sister, tiny compared with Lucien's height and broad shoulders, easily deflected a thrust of her brother's. Andre chuckled low in his throat, his brown eyes twinkling merrily. She was good. She knew the limitations of her sword and her strength well; she was patient and observant. This made her a very dangerous opponent despite her size.

Ryen finished an arc, the impact of the weapons jarring her arm. She stepped back, panting. A trickle of perspiration ran from her hairline down her cheek, sparkling in the sun like a diamond. She brushed a strand of brown hair from her forehead with her free arm.

A perfect smile lit Lucien's boyish face. "Come, come. You cannot tell me that you tire after so few exchanges!"

A cold grin stretched across her shapely lips. "I tell you no such thing, Brother. Only to guard your blind side." Ryen lunged and then feinted right.

Lucien caught the blow with some effort and countered with an arc overhead.

Ryen sidestepped the swing and Lucien's blade crashed into the ground. As he pulled it up, a clump of dirt came with it, impaled on the tip of his blade.

"You know she's too quick for you, Lucien," Andre called.

Ryen laughed at the dirt on Lucien's sword. "Don't take your anger out on the ground, Lucien. Your opponent stands before you, not below you."

Lucien came after Ryen with two quick lunges. She easily parried the blows and drove forward with an arc of her own, then retreated and stood staring at Lucien.

"Little sister, you're growing up," Lucien commented.

"Don't goad her, Lucien," Andre advised, too late.

Ryen suddenly charged her brother, hitting him in the stomach with her shoulder. The impact knocked him onto his back. Breathless, Lucien lay stunned for a moment. Before he could recover, Ryen stepped on the wrist of his sword arm and placed the tip of her weapon to Lucien's neck. "Yield or die," she stated.

"I yield to the Angel of Death!" Lucien hollered good-naturedly.

Ryen lifted her foot from his wrist and withdrew her sword. She gently kicked his arm with her booted foot. "I hate it when you call me 'little sister.' "

Lucien sat up, rubbing his wrist. "I won't make that mistake again."

Ryen stepped back, offering her brother a hand. Lucien clasped it and she helped him to his feet.

"That was a good move," Lucien commented. "But a little reckless."

"It beat you," Ryen replied, bending to pick up a cloth from the lush grass.

"If I had raised my sword, you would have run right into it."

"But you didn't," Ryen said, wiping the cloth smoothly over her blade. "Don't criticize my move just because it landed you on your buttocks. You yielded. I won. There are no 'ifs.' "

"She has a point," Andre agreed, stepping up beside Ryen. "She beat you and I'm afraid it grates on your nerves."

"Nonsense!" Lucien exclaimed, brushing the grass from his yellow tunic. "I simply—"

"Angel!" a tiny voice called from the forest, interrupting Lucien.

Ryen's head shot up and she saw her page, Gavin, crashing through the bushes in his hurry to reach her. His brown cotton smock caught on a branch, but he quickly yanked it free and continued toward her, gasping, "Angel!"

Ryen placed her hand on his shoulder. "Take a breath, Gavin, and tell me what's happened."

"We . . ." he started, breathlessly.

"A deep breath," Ryen urged.

Gavin drew in a long breath and blurted out, "We've caught an Englishman, m'lady!"

Ryen raised an anxious gaze to Andre before moving to re-trace Gavin's path. She heard the heavy footfalls of her brothers as they followed her into their camp. The scent of venison wafted to her on a light breeze and her stomach rumbled despite her anxiety. She maneuvered through the sporadically placed tents like an expert, dodging a barking dog, stepping around two men who were absorbed in a game of chess.

She slowed upon seeing Jacques Vignon, her advance scout, approaching. "You found him?" she asked.

"Aye, m'lady," Jacques replied.

It always unnerved Ryen to speak with Jacques, for while he was the best scout she had, looking into his face was like gazing into an emotionless abyss. His eyes were black, so black that she could not discern the pupil from the iris. Jacques had never done anything to earn her suspicion; on the contrary, he was a loyal fighter, as good at swordplay as he was at disappearing into shadows, but there was something cold about him that set off every warning within Ryen. He avoided the sun, so his skin remained white, almost as white as the porcelain doll her father had once given her sister. His skill at infiltrating the English was what had earned him Ryen's respect; his command of the English language surpassed even her own. "Where?" she demanded.

"Northwest of here," he answered. "He said he was separated from his army. Lost."

Ryen moved past him, eager to see her enemy. As she neared the prisoner tents, she noticed that, suspiciously, more than a few of her men were seated near one tent. Each head was bent over the work, the men diligently sharpening weapons or polishing armor until it sparkled like a gem. Ryen knew they were eagerly awaiting the outcome of the interrogation. It had been almost two weeks since they had seen any battle, and they were eager to confront the English.

"What can I do, Angel?" Gavin wondered.

Ryen stopped and the boy ran up before her. He was panting vigorously and Ryen knew he had run the entire way to keep up with them. She smiled at him and patted his unruly hair before carefully handing her sword to him. "Take this to my tent. Then find Mel to look after it."

Gavin's brown eyes widened as he stared at the blade. "Aye, m'lady," he whispered reverently. He gazed at it a moment longer before heading toward her tent at a slow, careful walk.

Ryen exchanged a grim look with Lucien before continuing.

Two guards stood outside the tent, looking more like stone gargoyles poised on the pillars of a church than like men. They were clothed in chain mail, white tunics washing over the metal links that protected their bodies.

Ryen shoved the tent flap aside and entered the tent.

The prisoner was tied to a large, planted stake, bound hand and foot. Small in build, and dressed in a leather jerkin, the Englishman reminded Ryen more of a squire than a foot soldier. His jaw was set with determination, his dark eyes cautious and distrustful. He assessed Lucien and Andre with a swift glance and his lip curled. When his head turned to Ryen, his eyes widened in surprise.

He was not dirty. His cheeks were not sunken from lack of food, nor were his lips parched from lack of water. "He is not lost," she muttered. She didn't think the prisoner would understand her French words but murmured just in case.

"I agree," Andre stated.

Ryen stepped toward the prisoner.

Lucien followed protectively and stood beside her.

"What lord do you serve?" Ryen asked the man in perfect English.

His brow furrowed in confusion and his gaze slowly traveled over her body appreciatively. She straightened slightly as his insolent, laughing gaze locked with her eyes.

Lucien slapped the man's impudent face and the blow twisted the man's head to the side.

A silver chain around the prisoner's neck glinted in the candlelight. Ryen stepped forward and the man gazed down at her with defiant eyes as she peeled his jerkin aside. There, hanging from the chain, was a medallion of a silver wolf enclosed in a circle. Ryen stared at the pendant for a long moment. Her teeth clenched slightly and her hand trembled with anger as she reached out, encircling the pendant with her fingers. Its cold metal bit into her palm as if it were alive.

"He's closer than we thought." Lucien sneered at seeing the crest.

Ryen nodded. "Much closer." She dropped the medallion to the man's chest. Her blue eyes lifted slowly to meet his gaze. "Bring me the truth powder, Lucien," Ryen said. She watched recognition wash over the prisoner's face, followed closely by fear and disbelief.

"The Angel of Death," he gasped.

"He will tell us where the English army is camped. I will have the Prince of Darkness before tomorrow's dawn."

Three

Bryce jolted awake, every nerve in his body tingling. Something was dreadfully wrong. He sat up, trying to pierce the darkness with his eyes, his ears ringing with the effort to hear more than just silence. After a long moment, his eyes adjusted, but still he heard nothing.

He tried to relax, raking his hands through his ebony hair, but with every passing moment a feeling of impending disaster grew inside him, eating away at his nerves. It had been one day since his advance guard had missed their scheduled rendezvous. It had also been one day since Bryce had noticed the tightness knotting his stomach.

Bryce swung his legs from his bed of straw and stood. He began to pace, hoping to end the unease that was settling over him. But his mind dwelled on the war . . . and the cause of his troubles. The Angel of Death had proved to be a tricky opponent. The French Army had repeatedly tracked his steps and retaken French towns that Bryce had won in the name of King Henry.

This Angel was a worthy adversary, and Bryce had learned to respect him. Then, yesterday, amid his growing anxiety, word had reached him of a new rumor about the knight, the most disturbing yet. The Angel of Death was said to be a woman.

Quickly, Bryce grabbed a pair of black hose and pulled them on. He donned his black leather boots before flinging aside the flap of his tent to gaze upon the starry night.

What if the Angel of Death *was* a woman? That would explain the irrational, unpredictable, and, to Bryce, totally maddening way in which the French Army moved.

But no woman was that brutal. No woman was intelligent enough to command an army. And certainly, no woman could wield a sword with enough strength to disarm a man, much less unhorse him at Tournament—as legend told of the Angel of Death.

A movement caught his eye and Bryce turned his head to see a small, familiar shadow walking through his camp. "Runt," Bryce called.

The shadow stopped and turned toward him. The moon paused for a moment to reflect in the boy's eyes before it disappeared behind a cloud. Again, Bryce had a momentary pang of guilt. Runt was so small, so young, to be here. He should have left him back in England. But as quickly as it had surfaced, the doubt was gone. Runt belonged here, with him.

As the boy approached, Bryce asked, "What are you doing up at this time of night?"

Runt gazed up at him through a lock of rebellious black hair that refused to be swept aside. "I can't sleep," he replied.

"You either?" Bryce mused, his gaze shifting to the horizon, a row of hills just beyond the camp. He narrowed his eyes, trying to see something that wasn't there. It bothered him that Runt couldn't sleep, more than he was willing to admit. He and Runt were of the same blood. They had a sense of self-preservation that transcended any rational thought. Survival was instinct to them.

Memories washed over him as he stared at the hills. Bad memories. His father was sick, very sick. He could barely stand when the heavy plate mail was positioned over his shoulders. Once they had to have two knights ride next to him so that he would not fall from his saddle. He could barely stay atop his horse during a melee. He was the first to fall in every tournament, in every joust. The people began to call him "Lord Yield," and the phrase was quickly picked up by the nobility.

The sickness lasted most of Bryce's youth. He was five years old when his father began to lose jousts, six when the other children began to tease him. He had received a black eye more than once, fighting to protect his father's name . . . his name.

Knights in his father's service began to leave and his father had to replace them with mercenaries. He hired a group called the Wolf Pack, who wore thick animal skins and never bathed. Their hair, beards, and mustaches were matted and unkempt. At dinner, they paced the floor, waiting anxiously for their turn at the roasting boar. After his father had taken his meat and returned to his seat, they attacked the spit with the savageness of wild animals. After they had snatched handfuls of meat, they retreated to corners around the room to eat in darkness, away from those they thought would try to take their food. Often times, Bryce wondered why his father kept them on, why he actually paid to have them in his house. Then, one day, Bryce was wandering the fields, watching the few remaining knights practice their skills. He was nine years old and he had an urge to fight that was very strong. His father had never asked if he wanted to learn. So instead, Bryce would watch the knights practice and try to emulate their movements in the privacy of his room. On that day, three knights were out on the practicing field, two arcing their swords at each other, the third watching, shouting advice from the wooden fence surrounding the field. The Wolf Pack approached from the forest. They almost always traveled in groups, and this time was no exception. There were five men coming toward the practice yard. As they entered the field, Bryce wondered if the knights would put these savages in their place.

The knights told them they were not allowed on the field.

The Wolf Pack had looked among themselves, one to the other, until one man stepped forward. His hair was black, his face scarred from his cheek down to his neck and farther, the rest of the scar hidden beneath the wolf skin he wore over a torn tunic. His boots were ripped near the heel with what looked like a knife cut. He was shorter than the knight, but built like a stone wall. "We go where we please," he said in a gruff voice.

"Is that a challenge?" one of the knights wondered, laughter in his voice.

"We do not challenge," the man stated. "People let us be."

"Not this time, barbarian," the knight replied, and approached with his sword drawn. "I told you that you were not welcome here."

The man slowly brushed aside the wolf skin he was wearing and pulled his sword from his belt. The knight attacked immediately and the man defended himself for a short time. Then, with a howl, he pushed forward. Bryce watched with large eyes as the knight was disarmed in two moves.

"I believe it is you who are not welcome here," the man said, the tip of the sword to the knight's neck.

The three knights had fled the yard with as much dignity as they could muster. Two days later, they resigned from his father's service. The following day, Bryce began to follow the Wolf Pack, and more important, the man with the scar, whom he learned was called Night. He started to copy them, their behavior. Especially Night's. At mealtime, he waited until his father was seated before running to the feast and grabbing food with his bare hands. He slept in the Great Hall with the Wolf Pack. He followed Night on his watches. But they never paid him any heed.

Until the day he was attacked by two squires as he was walking alone one night through the town. They shoved him and called him "son of Lord Yield," and "Puppy." When Bryce threw the first punch, they jumped on him. He tried to defend himself, but he was clumsy and young, and the squires were two years older. They left him with a bloody nose, a swollen lip, and more aches than he could count. He got to his knees shakily, wiping a sleeve across his bleeding nose . . . and saw them. Not far down the street, three men of the Wolf Pack stood watching him. Slowly, they turned their backs and walked away. Bryce was too embarrassed to follow them that night. And it wasn't until the next morning that he realized *they* were watching *him*.

He had awakened with sore muscles and a grumbling stomach. He stumbled to his feet and was making his way down the hallway of his father's castle when a voice called, "Child!"

Bryce came to a halt and turned to find Night standing half in the shadows of a stairway.

"You have been following me."

Bryce did not move. He wanted to flee, but his legs would not obey.

"I will help you, child."

Bryce's eyes lit up. "You'll teach me to fight?"

"Oh, I will teach you much more than that."

During the next months, Night taught him to track and to hunt, but most important, he taught him how to fight. Day and night, Bryce had to stay alert, waiting for Night's attack, anticipating his next strike. His innate sense of survival was honed to razor sharpness.

One evening, when Bryce was twelve, he was sitting near Night before the fire in the Great Hall when Night seized his arm and cut it. More from shock than from the pain of it, Bryce pulled away, and watched with heart pounding as Night ran the blade across his own arm. He grabbed Bryce's arm and pressed his open wound to Bryce's, their blood merging as their cuts touched.

"Always remember, you are one of us," said Night, and withdrew his hand.

The next day, Bryce had raced down the stone stairway and into the Great Hall . . . only to find that the Wolf Pack had gone. He was bitter and angry. He did not understand why they had left, but even more important, why they hadn't taken him. When his father tried to comfort him, Bryce rejected him. It was later that day that Bryce had his last confrontation with the boys of the castle.

It was damp and cloudy, and Bryce could still recall the strong scent of leather from the blacksmith's shop. He had been carrying his father's sword back from the yard, thinking about a conversation he had just heard between his father and their steward, who was afraid the mercenaries would turn against them and try to take over the castle. Lost in these bitter thoughts, Bryce turned a corner and collided with three squires. He attempted to move past them, but they blocked his way, taunting him. The anger that surged inside him was swift and consuming. He threw down his father's sword and attacked the closest boy. They rolled across the ground, through the dirt and mud, furiously throwing punches. Then the other two joined in. Bryce didn't remember much, except for the fact that when it was over, he stood with his fists clenched at his side while the three squires ran away from him.

Bryce had not lost a battle since then. Night and his Wolf Pack had taught him well. Yet now, that old feeling of anxiety snaked through him. He looked down at Runt, who was quietly standing at his side, gazing off into the distance, as he had seen Bryce do. He knelt beside the boy and put his hand on his shoulder, turning him until those blue eyes gazed at him. "In case of attack, remember what I told you."

Runt nodded enthusiastically. "Fight with honor."

"No." Bryce scowled. "You must go to the rear of the army and await the outcome."

"I want to fight," Runt said, his lips drawing down into a disapproving frown. "I want to cut down one of those Frenchmen."

Bryce's lips twitched with a proud smile, but the thought of Runt hurt was sobering. "This is not a game, Runt. This is war. Those men will kill you. You're too small yet to battle an armored man."

"But I've been practicing," Runt objected wholeheartedly.

"I know. And you've improved. But not enough to stand against a man twice your size," Bryce patiently explained. "Promise me, Runt. You must go to the rear of the army."

Runt sighed in disappointment and kicked at the dirt.

Bryce squeezed his shoulder gently. "Promise me, boy," he persisted.

Runt nodded grudgingly. "I promise."

Bryce stared at the crestfallen look on his face. It broke his heart to have to refuse the child, but he was not willing to risk the boy's life in a battle. He reached up and brushed aside the lock of black hair that fell over his eyes. "Try to rest, Runt," Bryce advised. "If we are right, it will not be long until we see battle."

Runt scurried away.

Bryce stepped back into the tent, allowing the flap to swoosh back into place as he turned to the basin of water on a stand near his bed. He braced himself over the table, hands on either side of the basin, and stared blankly into the dark water. What had happened to his advance guard?

"Hell," Bryce growled, and plunged both hands into the water, cupping them to collect a pool to shower over his face. The water was cool against his hot skin.

He splashed another palm of water onto his face, the water trickling from his chin down into the basin. Sighing, he rubbed the water from his eyes. There's only an hour before dawn, he thought. There's no point in trying to get any sleep.

A single candle rested next to the basin, its shimmering image reflecting in the still water. As Bryce watched, the image shifted, moving slightly. Slowly, the water began to ripple, distorting the figure of the candle. The ripples became stronger and more pronounced. And then he heard it, a thundering rumble in the distance, growing louder with each passing second. Bryce bolted upright. Horses! Coming in fast!

He pulled his sword from its scabbard, the silver metal hissing as the night air kissed its surface. Scowling deeply, he urgently wrenched the flap of his tent aside and charged out into the night.

Sharp black hooves thundered down upon him! He leapt back instantly, dropping and rolling. The riderless horse spat flecks of foam from its mouth as it whinnied and sped by.

Battle cries resounded throughout the camp. God's blood, he thought. We're under attack! Someone screamed, the man's cry piercing the air with sharp gasps of pain. Bryce moved toward the voice, crouching low, his hand clutching the hilt of his sword tightly. He turned right, moving around a tent, and saw an invader slumped over a barrel. Bryce smiled grimly as he saw Brian Talbot wipe his sword on the dead man's tunic. Talbot was his second in command, the closest thing to a friend he had found during the last few years spent waging King Henry's war.

Talbot looked up to see Bryce approaching.

"What the hell happened to our sentries?" Bryce yelled out to him, the din surrounding them threatening to drown out his words.

"I don't know!" Talbot shouted back.

"Who are they?"

Talbot reached down to the invader's corpse and ripped off a piece of cloth from his tunic. He held it out to his lord.

Bryce took the cloth and glanced down at it. His lips curled into a tight sneer, his eyes growing cold, as he clenched his fingers, crushing the fabric tightly in his closed fist. He recognized the symbol immediately, the silhouette of a black angel against a white background.

The mark of the Angel of Death.

Ryen finished her battle with an Englishman, cleanly slicing his sword arm, and raised her eyes to assess the situation. Her fully armored knights exchanged blows with men who were partially clothed. Many of the English had already fallen, and her men were closing in on the rest. The battle was almost over. The gritty taste of smoke filled her mouth and the crackle of fire could be heard as one of the tents burned brightly.

She scanned the battlefield. Only a few tents remained standing and only a few Englishmen held their ground and refused to turn and run. Amid the armored men and flashing swords that remained, she saw a man who stood out from the rest by his height. His black hair defiantly reflected the firelight as easily as his quick sword deflected the blows of her men. He downed one, then another of her knights as she watched. Angry, Ryen moved to spur her white war horse forward, but a thick cloud of smoke suddenly obstructed her vision. She furiously swatted aside the shield of smoke, but when it blew past and was gone, so was he. Ryen quickly looked left and right for the man, but he was nowhere to be seen.

She dismounted and surveyed the grim scene before her. The sun hesitantly peeked over the horizon, as if afraid to illuminate the death and destruction covering the battlefield. Most of the tents had been trampled and men lay sprawled, dead or dying, everywhere. She shifted her gaze to watch the last of the English flee.

Lucien jerked his horse forward, eager to pursue them, but Ryen seized his reins and shook her head. Let them go. They would serve her purpose, she knew, to spread the word of her victory. And of the Prince of Darkness's defeat.

"Find the Prince of Darkness!" Ryen ordered. She was sure he was here somewhere. He would never run. He was either dead or unconscious. And she hoped he was not dead. She wanted to see him. He was said to have evil black eyes, and dark hair that hid the horns of a demon; he had been raised by wolves, and his arm had the strength to cut down five men with one good swing of his sword. Ryen chuckled. He was probably a skinny man, nothing like his legend. But Ryen preferred to paint her hated enemy in the first, darker light. It added to his mystery, his legend, which claimed that he could steal a woman's heart with one glance, a look heated from the very depths of hell.

Again her eyes surveyed the carnage around her. I have truly earned my reputation this day, Ryen thought grimly. She walked out into what was left of the English camp, around smoldering tents, past impaled men. She stepped over a fallen knight, blood oozing from the fatal wound in his chest, his plate armor having fallen away to reveal the chain metal beneath. She paused, hating herself as she did it, knowing that the longer she stared at the man, the more human he would become to her.

Ryen gazed into his open eyes and wondered, as she had done a thousand times before, if he had a family. Who would mourn him, now that he was gone? A wife? Children? Oh, she hated herself. Why did she torment herself? This would not be the last man she would order killed, nor the last time she would wander among the dead and gaze at their faces, wondering. What was it like to be loved? To be sent to battle with a kiss?

His hand twitched and Ryen stepped closer. His lids closed and a groan escaped his lips. Ryen knelt beside her enemy, concern etched in her brow. Perhaps he would, after all, return to those who loved him. She pushed back her chain mail hood and looked for something to staunch the flow of blood. Her eyes fastened on a tunic, trampled in the dust. Ryen seized it and immediately pressed it to his wound through the chain mail.

His eyes flashed open, eyes filled with fevered pain. They locked on her and for a moment there was blankness.

"Rest," Ryen said in English. "The battle is over."

His gaze focused on her and confusion washed over his dust-covered features. Then Ryen watched in dismay as his lip curled in contempt.

"Are you the Angel of Death?" he sneered.

Ryen ignored him, pressing the shirt against his open wound, trying to move his armor aside. "You will need a leech, or you will not survive." She lifted her eyes to his and saw such hate and loathing there that she was taken aback.

"I would rather die than have your foul hands touch me," he said, and spat in her face.

Stunned, Ryen sat back on her heels. She had tried to help him! To save his life so he could return to his loved ones. But he'd spurned her efforts. Anger swiftly replaced her amazement. Her mouth closed and her eyes narrowed. Slowly she stood, towering over him. The wind picked up, whipping her cape out behind her, dust swirling about her feet. It was her turn to loathe him. Her eyes dulled with bitter hatred and she lifted her arm to wipe the spittle from her cheek.

The lashing of the wind's fury suddenly died, and for a moment everything was still as Ryen gazed down at the man. "Then you shall die," she said, and whirled away.

"Ryen!"

She turned, outrage boiling in her veins. "What?" she snapped.

Lucien tore off his helmet in excitement, his blue eyes glittering.

Ryen knew the look. She had seen that confidence many times before. It meant only one thing. Success. Her anger washed away and she felt excitement fill her veins. They had him! He was in her camp . . . her prisoner! The Prince of Darkness was hers.

Lucien said, "I will bring him to the tent for the truth powder."

Ryen nodded. Then, as Lucien turned to leave, her hand shot out to capture his arm. When he glanced at her, she jerked her head at the fallen knight. "And order a leech for that cur."

Four

The cloud of white parted slowly before Ryen as she stepped through the soft, whirling smoke created by the smoldering candles placed around the tent. Quivers of anticipation rippled through her as she saw the whisps swirl around the shadowy shape. She stopped, not wanting the thrill to dissipate from her veins. So often in the past did a man not live up to her expectations that she was afraid she would be sorely disappointed by him, the mightiest of legends. But his shadow beckoned to her and she pushed any doubts aside. She had to know his secrets.

Ryen continued to move through the frosty smoke, the dark blur of his body forming into a solid shape. He had fought to the end, she thought, just as I would have. Lucien said it had taken twenty men to bring him to his knees. Twenty men? She wanted to believe this, but surely Lucien must have been exaggerating. Yet it wasn't like him to inflate the truth. She moved toward the figure chained to a post in the tent, stepping out of the mists.

His head was hanging down, his long black mane draping over his chest. So he did have black hair! Was it truly hiding horns?

Ryen moved closer, slowly, her gaze appraising him, his body. He was no disappointment there. The urge to touch him was overwhelming. She stretched her fingers toward him and touched the hair on his naked chest, running her hands along his torso, marveling at the size of his muscles. They were hard, sculptured curves of warm flesh. Magnificent, she thought. The smell of him, the heady musky scent of him, enveloped her.

Her prisoner stirred, his head moving slightly from side to side, as if he were struggling to clear his mind. His head slowly lifted. A thrill of anticipation touched Ryen's spine as his dark eyes, the eyes of midnight, rose like the moon to gleam at her.

"Enjoying yourself?" he asked, his voice low, suggestive.

Through the darkness he wore like a veil, she saw the flash of his white teeth. Ryen pulled her hands away and watched the shadows slide off his features as his face slowly came into the flame's light. A shiver snaked its way up her spine. The candlelight revealed a sensual mouth with a cynical twist to it, a Spartan chin hewn from an ancient line of warriors.

Ryen realized that she had been holding her breath and released it slowly in admiration. She could not believe the sight that greeted her. This is the man who was born without a heart? The man who is in league with the devil? The most feared barbarian in all of England?

Then how can he be so handsome?

She ignored his comment and stepped back, the mist swirling around her body like a cape. She quickly regained her composure and her blue eyes swept him without a hint of emotion. "So," she murmured, *"you* are the Prince of Darkness."

He stared hard into her eyes as if he were reading her mind.

Ryen watched the emotions play over his face: recognition, disbelief, and then furious anger.

His eyes widened with incredulity. "The Angel of Death? A woman?"

"You have heard the legends—?"

"Unchain me this instant!"

Ryen could not help but laugh as he rattled his chains and ordered her around like a serving wench. "I welcome you to my camp."

His eyes grew cold, narrowing to razor-thin slits. When he spoke, his voice was a thick growl of acrimony. "I don't feel much warmth in your greeting, woman. Perhaps you are truly made of ice, as the stories say."

Ryen felt the heat of his hateful gaze sweep her body. It chilled her blood. "And should I welcome a most deadly enemy with open arms?" she asked softly. Her slim hand flew to her belt in a sudden, swift motion, drawing forth a sharp dagger. "Or with the edge of a blade?" She paused, waiting to see the fear flash over his handsome features.

But it never came.

Instead, her prisoner laughed.

Fury, immediate and hot, coursed through her body in a churning black cloud of rage. Like a lightning bolt, erupting from a dark haze of anger, her hand shot out and she slapped him. The edge of the dagger caught his cheek, cutting the surface of his skin, and the open cut spewed forth red, glistening blood. She watched the crimson liquid drip down his face and a feeling of horror cooled her flaring temper. She had not meant to hurt him.

The smile never left the Prince of Darkness's face as he cocked his head. "You are indeed brave, my lady. It takes the stoutest of hearts to strike a defenseless man."

She recovered with a nervous laugh. "Do you take me for a fool? Shall I release your bonds so you can snap my neck with your bare hands?"

He turned his unscathed cheek toward her. "Perhaps you'd like to cut this side."

Ryen stood, appalled. However, his goading made the idea attractive, and she raised the sharp blade to press it against his skin. Her knuckles brushed his cheek and a tremor ran down her spine. She stared for a long moment at his profile, realizing how close she was to him, and that the shiver was not coldness nor repulsion. She enjoyed touching his skin. Angry with the knowledge and with herself, she narrowed her eyes and gritted her teeth. Her hand trembled as she pulled the blade away. "You'd like it too much."

"Bitch," he snarled.

Ryen ignored his outburst. "Tell me how many men your Henry has in his army."

As she expected, the Prince of Darkness's witty mouth remained closed to her question. She returned the dagger to its sheath.

"Is he going to attack France?" she asked, lifting her eyes to meet his, slipping the tips of her fingers into the pouch tied to her belt. The powder felt soft and velvety to her touch. It was a mixture of herbs, roots, and wildflowers all ground together into a fine powder. Lucien had gotten the ingredients from an old Gypsy woman he used to frequent when he wanted his fortune told. Ryen had used it well, its strange power adding potent fuel to the spreading fear her legend had ignited in the weak minds of France's enemies.

"If you really expect me to answer your questions truthfully, then you must be more of a halfwit than legend has it," he replied.

Ryen dismissed his insult and leaned close to him so their lips were almost touching. "You will tell me all your deepest thoughts. Nothing will remain a secret from me."

"I think not," he spat.

Ryen, seeing the confusion in his eyes despite his brave words, grinned. She lifted her powdered fingers and ran them seductively over his lips before he could turn his face away. She stepped back as he jerked his head from side to side, spitting out the powder.

Suddenly, his teeth started chattering. Then his entire body twitched! Ryen knew spears of ice, thin and sharp, were speeding through his blood, solidifying, threatening to burst his veins. He struggled to speak, the powder speckling his lips like pixie dust. "I . . . I . . . ." He stopped as another onslaught of chills racked his body. "I . . . will . . ."

"Yes, you will," Ryen said. She frowned, feeling cheated.

It had been so easy to subdue the legendary Prince of Darkness. He was no prince, she thought. He was just a man like all the others.

She saw him force his teeth to be still and raise his head to glare at her, his eyes ablaze with ebon fire. "I . . . will . . . kill you for this," he gritted through clenched teeth.

Ryen's eyes glittered with the challenge. No man had ever needed two doses. But this *was* the great Prince of Darkness. A second dosage ought to bend his will, she thought, as she again touched the powder. The white flecks adhered immediately to her fingers. She raised her hand, but as she neared, he turned away and her fingers brushed his cheek, his wound. Ryen pulled back quickly, staring down at his blood on her fingers. When she looked up she saw the Prince of Darkness force back a cry of pain. She knew he was cold. So very cold. His shoulders were hunched against the chill of the powder. Her gaze traveled over his naked chest. She was awed by the size of the corded muscles in his neck and shoulders, the firmness of his chest, the ridges in his flat stomach. His body shuddered, and then he was still.

She stepped closer to him. His eyes were blank, as if his mind had suddenly been emptied. "What is your name?" she asked him, absently rubbing her fingers together.

"People call me the Prince of Darkness." His voice was flat as he answered.

"Your birth name."

"Bryce Princeton."

"Tell me the number of men in King Henry's army."

"Enough to destroy you completely and mercilessly," he muttered without a hint of emotion, toneless.

"I didn't ask for your opinion," Ryen snapped. "I asked for the numbers."

"Two thousand archers and five thousand men at arms."

Ryen smiled. This was valuable information. "Tell me of these archers; are they as good as everyone says?"

"Yes, they are good, but . . ." Bryce said, then his voice faltered.

"Go on. You must tell me all you know," she said.

"The archers . . ." he muttered, "the archers are ineffectual now. Many bowmen have died. It will take half a year to train more men to replace them."

Ryen could barely control the laughter that bubbled in her throat. "Is Henry planning to attack France?" she wondered.

"He's only planning on taking back the lands that rightfully belong to England," Bryce stated blandly.

"So he *is* going to attack! When? Tell me when!"

"I don't know," he replied.

For an instant, Ryen thought she saw a flicker of light behind his dark eyes. She frowned. A moment of doubt attacked her reasoning. Is the powder strong enough? Is it working? She wiped her thoughts free of uncertainty. The powder had never failed before. She had no reason to distrust it now. But she was sure that it would not last much longer.

Ryen studied her prisoner. His eyes were dark and unfathomable, mysterious. Strangely, they reminded her of a wolf's. But she knew it must be his legend throwing shadows over her thoughts. His unruly hair gleamed in the light of the candles, giving him the aura of a wild animal. A pang of guilt touched Ryen's heart as she saw that a lock of his black mane was caught in the moist blood on his cheek. How could I have cut his face? It was so flawless, so perfect . . .

She reached up to brush the hair from his wound, but her hand froze in mid-air. What am I doing? He's the enemy! He deserves far worse than a simple cut! She whirled away, sickened by the feelings he stirred within her, incensed at her weakness. Anger stabbed at her. How could he make her want to touch him? How could he soften her heart when his words were full of hate? The devil! The rogue! She stood with her back to him for a moment, clenching and unclenching her hands. When she turned back, she was ready to explode, to strike out at him, for making her soft, for making her feel like a helpless woman!

A wind whipped up from outside, blowing the tent flap aside and swirling in around Ryen, flinging her hair wildly about her shoulders and face. The fire in her soul reddened her cheeks, caused her blue eyes to sparkle.

His eyes widened and he gasped.

Ryen stopped, confused at seeing a wondrous expression on his face. She brushed an annoying lock of hair away from her eyes. "What?" she demanded.

"You're beautiful," he whispered.

Shock immediately replaced her anger as she stood dumbfounded, gaping at Bryce. "What did you say?"

Bryce looked away from her.

Ryen had clearly heard his words, but her mind was refusing to acknowledge them. "Beautiful" was not a word men used to describe her. The Angel of Death. Ice Queen. Black-hearted Bitch. These were the phrases men used to portray her.

She was so astonished by his declaration that she was unsure how to proceed. Ryen became flustered by her hesitancy. She was losing valuable seconds. She had to think of a question. A question . . .

Beautiful. He said I was beautiful. She felt herself softening, looking at him not as an enemy, but as . . .

No!

She burst out of the tent into the night air, racing past a group of men rolling dice. In her mind, Bryce's voice softly repeated the words of praise. She ran around a spit of smoking duck as the bird was being basted by the cook, almost knocking the man down. Beautiful. The word was like a plague, spreading through her body, infesting her thoughts. She reached her tent and barely paused long enough to tell the guard who stood like a statue before the flap, "I am not to be disturbed," before disappearing inside.

Ryen stopped just inside her quarters, her eyes sweeping

the tent until they came to rest on a wooden chest bound by great bands of silver metal. She remembered what she had been given by her aunt about five years ago, in hopes that she would become more ladylike. Ryen had never used it. She kept it hidden in the chest with her dresses and fancy undergarments, elaborate combs and jewelry, embarrassed by the femaleness of it all.

Ryen flung open the chest. After years of disuse, it squeaked with objection. She fell to her knees and thrust her hands into the mounds of clothes, digging through lacy night clothes, bolts of silk fabric, a necklace of pearls, ruby earrings, jeweled rings . . . all the items that she had accumulated through the years, rummaging for the one object that she wanted, until finally she found it.

It was a hand mirror made of gold with diamonds set into its intricately sculptured metal. She clasped it with both hands and stared at the person she found looking back at her. She was not the child she remembered from five years ago.

Her face was slender and soft, her cheekbones high. Her eyes were the blue of the deepest ocean.

Ryen tilted the mirror, trying to see her profile. She could see nothing that made her attractive, nothing that made her different. Yet he had said she was beautiful. She had never thought of herself like that. No one had ever told her she was. Not ever.

She was inspecting herself when she saw, in the glass, the flap of the tent open and Lucien ducking inside.

"What did you find out?" Lucien asked, excitement barely hidden under his words.

Ryen ignored him, staring hard at herself in the mirror, twisting her head to try to see what Bryce had seen.

"Ryen?" Lucien's brow wrinkled with momentary confusion, then darkened with rage. "Did he hurt you? What did he do? I told you I should have been there with you!"

"Lucien," Ryen said, and turned to face him with a trusting look, "do you think I'm beautiful?"

Surprise was written all over his boyish face, and for a moment he could not move. Suddenly, he threw his head back, laughter bubbling from his throat like a spring.

Ryen's face turned a deep red, her eyes going from a light blue innocence to the deep blue of an angry sea. Slowly, she replaced the hand mirror and closed the lid on the heavy wooden chest, her jaw clenched.

Lucien ceased his laughter when he caught Ryen's murderous glare. He chuckled a bit and looked away from her. "Oh, Ryen. I'm sorry. I didn't mean to laugh at you. It's just that . . . well, if I had even suggested the possibility, you would have cut out my tongue."

Her jaw was still set like stone. No one laughed at her.

"Please, Ryen," Lucien said sincerely. "Forgive me."

Ryen whirled away from Lucien. "Get out."

"What?" He stared at her with surprised eyes.

"Get out before I say something I will regret," Ryen clarified.

Lucien studied her for a moment, then whirled and departed from her tent. After her brother's footsteps faded away, Ryen chastised herself. You are not beautiful. You are a warrior, a knight. Knights are not beautiful. They are strong, rugged, relentless. I have never been pretty.

Still . . . in the eyes of the mightiest of legends, the fiercest of English knights, she *was* beautiful.

The truth powder never lied.

Five

The sun was hot on Bryce's bare shoulders. His arms were bound before him and his feet were tied from ankle to ankle, the rope running beneath the horse he rode. None of this bothered him, even though they had been riding all morning. His mind was absorbed with his captor. He could not stop staring at her riding so primly at the head of the army. Rage consumed him. He could feel the ropes around his wrists digging into his flesh as he clenched and unclenched his hands. The disgrace of being captured by a woman! Even as he thought this, his mind raced, trying to figure out a way to escape. Still, he could not tear his eyes from her.

If the Wolf Pack ever saw him now, how they would laugh! The great Prince of Darkness, captured by a woman! The thought of those men mocking him made Bryce clench his teeth. Damn, he thought. What was I thinking? Every sense in my body was shouting a warning! But I ignored my instinct. She was so quiet, so deceitful. How did she ever overpower my sentries? He gritted his teeth in frustration. Enough of this, Bryce thought. It is over and done. I must not dwell on it. There is nothing to do but wait until an opportunity presents itself. And it will. I will be ready for it.

She brought the army to a halt and dismounted. His eyes followed her every movement as she stopped and spoke with one of her men, a man who towered well over her. How can they allow themselves to be led by a woman, Bryce wondered. He saw her pause and he swore that she glanced at him before disappearing into a small glade.

Suddenly there was a tugging at the rope around his feet. He glanced down to see two of her men undoing the rope. His gaze assessed them quickly. They were fully armored, except for their helmets. He could outrun them, but he could never outfight them, especially with his hands bound.

He allowed them to pull him from his horse and he fell to the ground with a thud. They hauled him to his feet and shoved him forward. His legs ached from being immobile for so long, and he almost stumbled. He quickly righted himself when he heard a chuckle from one of her men behind him. He briefly wondered where they were taking him, but another shove answered his silent question. They were heading toward the glade. As he walked past the army, he noticed that many heads turned to regard him. There was resentment and anger in their eyes, and Bryce had a moment of satisfaction. They should hate me, he thought. As I hate them.

He was led through a small glade until he saw her standing near a tall tree. He stopped, frozen by the thought that she had summoned him. What does she want of me, he wondered. More torture?

The knights shoved Bryce to the ground at her feet. Dirt and dust filled his mouth, making him gag. He spat it out, easing himself to his knees, rubbing the dirt from his eyes with his bound hands.

The knights behind him placed a rope around his neck and handed the other end to her. For a moment he wondered if he was going to be hanged, but then he saw her tie the end of the rope around the base of a tree. Did she intend to keep him leashed like some sort of pet? When she finished, she ordered the knights away.

Bryce turned to watch them depart, then swung his head back toward her, his eyes scanning the clearing curiously.

They were alone.

She was either very brave, or very, very foolish. She had

cursed his thoughts from the moment he had seen her stepping from the mists like an angel coming down out of the clouds.

She turned away from him and Bryce felt a surge of frustration—how could he tell what she intended if he could not see her face?

He stood. Taking a large step, he came up behind her, chuckling softly. "You think tying me to this tree will save you, Angel?"

He felt her stiffen; her soft hair brushed his knuckles before he touched her cold plate mail.

"Save me from what?" she said with a tremor. "You are my prisoner. Or have you forgotten so soon?"

"It is true my wrists are bound," Bryce murmured, bringing his hands up as fast and unexpectedly as lightning to place them about her neck. "But my hands are far from helpless."

Squeeze, he told himself.

She whirled and Bryce could not move. Those eyes, the color of the deepest sea, froze him where he stood. Was this more of her poison? Those lips, full and red as the softest petal of a rose, entranced him.

She moved easily out of his hold. Bryce stood, facing the tree, absolutely stunned. Was this the woman who had captured him? It cannot be! he told himself. God's blood, she was a delectable little morsel. Even now, his passion pounded through him like a roaring flood.

He shook his head. What had come over him? He had his fingers around her neck! He could have ended her life! She must have used more of that poison on him to cloud his judgment. Instead of torturing prisoners like a true knight, she fought with powders and womanly wiles! Coward.

Angry, he turned. She was there. Watching him with those eyes—inviting, yet fearful. She was such a small thing. The fact that she led an army was inconceivable to Bryce.

She *did* capture you, a voice inside him mocked.

She turned away from him and her luxurious hair cascaded

over her cheek, well past her shoulder. It shone in the sun like the wing of a sleek black bird.

A woman! Bryce thought. It could not be. A man had to help her. "Your lovers command your army for you." It was part statement, part question.

Furious eyes snapped up to lock with his. "I need no help to command *my* army."

His brows furrowed. She lies, he told himself. No woman could have captured him without the help of a man. He straightened his shoulders against the feeling deep inside him that she spoke the truth. His eyes narrowed, trying to see the real woman, not the loveliness of her. But even as he squinted, her anger blazed across her brow, tightened her lips, and only enhanced her radiance. He cursed.

Quickly, she bent down to pick up a flask from the ground. "You must be thirsty," she murmured, her voice tight with hidden anger.

Bryce did not reply. Was the flask filled with more poison?

She approached him and he couldn't help but notice the slight sway of her hips. She stopped just before him, holding the flask out. He stared at it for a long moment. Then, his eyes shifted up to hers. He saw the grin she wore. She knew. She knew he didn't trust her.

She took the flask, uncorked it, and brought it to her lips. Bryce watched her slender throat work as she drank the liquid. Then she stopped and handed it to him. The thought of his lips touching what had just moments before been pressed so intimately against hers kindled his anger and desire. He could have pulled her to him and kissed her with all the passion and frustration that was pummeling his body. Instead, he grabbed the flask and raised it to his lips, angrily drinking down the wine. The liquid flowed smoothly down his throat, some overflowing from his lips to wash down his neck. Somehow, as he drank, his anger receded. He had been thirsty. Very thirsty. When he lowered the flask to look at the Angel of Death, he realized that his thirst was quenched, but his hunger was still very much alive. He handed the flask back to her.

She turned her back to him and bent down. Bryce's gaze was fastened on her every move, the way the plate mail fit her tiny figure, the way her delicate hands picked up a loaf of bread. She straightened and turned to him.

He eyed the bread warily. She broke the loaf in half and presented him with one part. Bryce frowned as he took the offered bread. "Have you no one else to attend me?"

A smile touched her face, curving her lips, easing the tension and solemnity there. Bryce found his spirit lifting against his will.

"Would you not do the same if I were *your* prisoner?" she wondered.

Aye, he thought. I would attend you. But in an entirely different manner. He took a bite of bread.

She looked troubled for an instant and shifted her gaze away from him.

He could not clear his mind. All he thought of was the way her white throat worked when she drank the wine. It was ridiculous. He could not believe that she, this small woman, led an entire French army, one that conquered his troops and captured him. Why, most women cowered before him. But not this one. "You are not frightened by me?" Bryce asked.

She straightened and locked eyes with him. "A knight is never frightened."

He stepped closer to her and watched with amusement as that little chin rose in challenge. When he was towering over her, looking down into her deep blue eyes, he whispered, "But you are a woman, too."

Her eyes crackled with insolence. "I have never known fear."

"Perhaps you should learn," he murmured, and ripped a piece of bread from the loaf with his teeth. A mocking grin curved his lips.

"I suppose you have known enough fear that you could teach me," she answered.

"I have instilled enough fear that I can teach you."

"Teach away," she replied with a slight shrug of her shoulders that sent a lock of her hair tumbling about her breastplate. "You will find that I am a most uncooperative subject."

Bryce caught the lock of hair with his fingertips and raised it, turning it this way and that, inspecting it. He was fascinated that it was so soft. Not at all what he'd expected of a warrior.

"Is that your way?" she asked suddenly. "To intimidate?"

Startled, Bryce raised his eyes to hers. "I did not know I was intimidating you."

She pushed his hand away from her hair. "You looked as though you were going to eat me up."

His grin was wolfish. "The idea is not unappealing." She appeared startled and then furious, her cheeks turning a deep red. It only enhanced her already flushed cheeks and Bryce was somewhat dismayed to find that his passion flared again. Angry with himself, he reminded both the Angel and himself, "Even though you are French."

Her cheeks turned redder. He watched her full lips thin, her blue eyes spark.

"And you find French women so unappealing," she demanded.

He shrugged, stating the truth. "Usually."

"I've heard to the contrary. You are said to take females in every town, be they French or English . . . or horse or sheep."

He gritted his teeth. Her words were truly barbed. If his hands were not tied, she would not speak so to him, the Prince of Darkness. "Untie me," he ordered.

"You treat all women like servants. Well, Lord Princeton, you have much to learn. And I will gladly teach you. For now you are *my* slave."

Bryce's fury was boundless. If only he had another chance. If only he could escape. If only he hadn't underestimated her!

Suddenly, she was before him, grabbing his face with one hand, his chin in her palm, her fingers squeezing into his cheeks, pulling his chin down. Startled, he bent his head and she pressed her lips angrily, roughly, against his open mouth, stealing a kiss. Just as quickly, she shoved his chin away from her.

Surprise washed over him like a warm rain. Every nerve in his body was tingling, demanding response.

Her chest was rising and falling with her heavy breathing, her eyes large with surprise. He stepped toward her.

The Angel of Death retreated a step and he watched the cold wall close over her face before she turned her back to him.

Fury crashed down around him. He silently cursed himself for his instant response to the feel of her lips on his, that uncontrollable rush of sheer pleasure that warmed his entire body. Again he cursed. What was this game she was playing? Was that kiss the start of his lessons? He tightened his jaw. If it was, he had a few surprises in store for her.

"Guard!" she cried out.

Bryce stiffened as an armored man came running into the clearing, his eyes fastened accusingly on Bryce.

"We ride. Return him to his horse."

Bryce opened his mouth to speak, but she was leaving the clearing. He slowly closed his lips and found that he was clenching his teeth. He looked down at his bound hands.

The loaf of bread was crumbled into pieces, flaking and falling through his fingers to the ground.

Six

"We should stop for the night," Lucien said from behind Ryen.

Ryen's mind refused to focus on his words. She watched the sun set beneath the horizon, smearing a trail of blood red across the sky. Somewhere inside of her, she knew Lucien was right, but she was worried, afraid of the dreams the night would bring . . . the dreams of hot lips and a dark face with eyes the color of shadows. He would be there in her fantasies, beckoning to her.

Ryen urged her horse forward with a slight kick. Why did I do it? she wondered, staring down at her hands as they clutched the reins so tightly that her knuckles turned white. Why did I kiss him? Was it truly to show him his proper place as my prisoner? Even as she thought this, Ryen knew it was not true. She had wanted to feel his lips against hers from the very first moment she had seen him in the tent.

Even now, she could not concentrate. He filled her mind, dominated her thoughts. She wanted to see him, to touch him. Ryen imagined being held in his strong arms, pictured how tenderly he would gaze at her, and then lower his lips to hers—

She shook her head harshly, driving the thoughts from her mind. He is the enemy! she told herself. Even as she did so, she reined in her horse, allowing Lucien to pass her, a scowl clearly creasing his brow. Andre was next, his eyes boring into hers with concern. Then, the rest of her knights filed by. They were weary from the long ride that was bringing them ever closer to De Bouriez Castle, and some grumbled as they rode by. Ryen paid them no attention. Her eyes were searching the middle of the column of men where the prisoners were guarded.

She spotted him immediately. His tall form sat straight in the saddle. With the sun behind him, his bare shoulders glowed red. His hands were bound and his ankles were tied beneath the horse, but the guards still gave him a respectful distance.

"You certainly don't look like the Prince of Darkness I pictured," Ryen heard one of the guards say as they drew closer to her.

"They must give out titles to any beggar off the streets in England," another mocked.

"Where are your horns?"

"Where is your legendary strength?"

"If this is the best England has to offer, then we have nothing to worry about—isn't that true, dog?"

"Come on. Show us how strong England is," one of the men goaded.

Bryce's head remained bent, his eyes lidded as if he were resting, but Ryen saw his shoulder muscles bunch and release, noticed the stiff set of his jaw. She knew if he were not bound he would have her men's hearts in his hands.

"He has no strength. Why, my woman could bring him to his knees."

"And she'd like it, too," the second guard guffawed.

The first guard clubbed the second with a clenched fist.

"Do you think he understands us?" the third man wondered. "Maybe he speaks no French."

"He understands," Ryen said, guiding her horse up beside Bryce's. "Look at his eyes, see how they burn with hate. All the fires of hell are locked within his body."

"And they burn only for you, Angel," Bryce said in English, his dark eyes swiveling toward her.

Ryen felt herself being swept away by the heat of his gaze.

Her heart began to pound, and flames of excitement burned up and down her spine, leaving her weak. She could not tear her eyes from his. As the horses moved, their thighs bumped, and even through the chain mail she wore, she could feel the strength in his legs. Ryen felt a tremor race through her body.

"Have you come to torture me with kisses?" he wondered in a husky voice.

Ryen could not take her gaze from his lips as they caressed each word. Remembering their kiss, she felt her own begin to tingle. Finally, Ryen looked away, licking her lips as she did so. Bryce's soft chuckle reached her ears and she straightened her shoulders.

"Apparently, your legend precedes you," Ryen stated, quickly changing the subject. Bryce did not answer, and Ryen raised her eyes to his. She saw the frown of confusion that darkened his brow. "Many would meet you. And make you suffer for the sins of your king."

Bryce's jaw tightened. "Sins I would gladly suffer for."

Ryen watched him, amazed at the regret she felt constricting her chest. They would throw him in the dungeon or have his head on the executioner's block. Either way, Ryen wished . . .

She had no right to wish anything where he was concerned! He'd murdered her people. He'd pillaged French towns. He had the most mysterious eyes . . .

Ryen dropped her gaze again.

"Perhaps the Angel of Death's heart is not made of ice, as the stories say," Bryce ventured.

Ryen steeled herself against the emotions she felt stirring in her heart. "You are mistaken."

"Am I?" He chuckled softly.

Ryen glanced at him. It was a mistake; she knew it immediately. He was staring at her, the corners of his lips curved up in a smile. Warm tingles shot up her spine; fire ignited in her lower stomach, warming her. She wanted to touch him. She felt an overwhelming urge to run her fingers through his mane of wild black hair and was shocked to find herself leaning in to do just that. She quickly straightened. She was shaking with the emotions he aroused in her. She had to escape the trembling that raced through her body. It wasn't right! She spurred her horse and returned to where she belonged . . . the front of her army, wishing she could flee her emotions as easily as she had the Prince of Darkness.

"You're beautiful," Bryce whispered in her ear, and nuzzled the soft nape of her neck. His strong hands stroked her back with a feathery touch before pulling her into a tight embrace. His warm lips traveled lightly up her neck, across her delicate jawline, up to her mouth. His kiss was . . .

Pretend. Ryen opened her eyes to lonely darkness. Her mattress felt cold beneath her. The sounds of the night drifted into her tent—chirping crickets, faint clanging as men saw to their weapons and armor, murmured words. She paid the familiar noises no attention.

Her mind burned with the memory of the kiss. Guilt was but a shadow in her heart. In the darkness of her own tent she let her mind run free. It ran to Bryce. The Bryce of her fantasies, the man with the gentle touch, the soft words, and the tender smile.

Ryen did not understand what it was about this man that dominated her, why she could not dismiss his body from her mind. She didn't want to think of him, but the thoughts, the images, were so . . . pleasant.

Suddenly, the tent flap swooshed open and she was pulled out of her reverie. Immediately, Ryen rolled to the side of her sleeping mat, her hand instinctively going for her sword.

"Ryen," a familiar voice called.

"Andre," she replied, and removed her hand from the hilt of her blade. She sat up as he moved to her bedside.

"I sent two men ahead to announce our arrival at De Bouriez Castle," Andre informed her.

"Yes. Good," Ryen responded, distracted. Her white linen nightdress rustled softly as she pulled her knees up to her chest and hugged them. "Father will be pleased to hear of your return."

He stood for a moment beside her mat. Even though she could see a sparkle of light from the chain mail he wore, she could not see his expression. She knew that he was trying to study her and was thankful for the cover of darkness, not wanting to reveal her traitorous thoughts about the prisoner, thoughts that only moments before had been dangerously blissful.

"That's not fair," he said.

Ryen lifted confused eyes to him.

"Father will be pleased to see you also."

Ryen nodded dubiously. "Perhaps. After all, I have brought him the Prince of Darkness."

"Father has always been pleased to see you."

"He humors me. It is the two of you he sees as real knights."

"Ryen," Andre's voice was gentle. "All father ever wanted was for you to be happy."

"Father wanted me to be like Jeanne. Every time I return home with this grand army behind me, he asks if I have been to court, or what the current fashions are. As if I know, or care."

"Father wants what's best for you."

"Father wants me to be a proper lady. He has never seen me as a soldier. I thought that once I became a knight he would regard me the way he does you and Lucien. But he hasn't. Not once."

"This is why it was so important for you to capture the Prince of Darkness, wasn't it? Just like when you had to take Burgh Castle."

"This time will be different," she continued, ignoring Andre. "Father has to see that I, too, am a knight. I have captured the Prince of Darkness." Her voice trailed off as the pride in her accomplishment warred with her disturbing feelings for her prisoner.

Andre knelt before her. "Ryen?" His voice was concerned.

Ryen did not respond. She could not. There should have been joy at the prospect of bringing the Prince of Darkness to kneel before her father. But suddenly all she felt was apprehension and a sense of impending disaster. She folded her hands nervously in her lap.

Andre was so still that she couldn't hear his armor rustle as he breathed.

Ryen did not like the feel of his constant, intense gaze. She stood, brushing past him. She put her hands in her hair, running her fingers through her locks, a tormented tigress. "Do you want the truth? Oh, Lord. Sometimes I fear I'm losing my mind! I can't seem to stop thinking about him. I don't know what it is that holds me captive so, but I feel like I'm the prisoner, not him!"

"You needn't worry about your feelings. When we reach De Bouriez Castle, Father will imprison him," Andre stated.

"No one shall lay a hand on him except for me," Ryen said, determination furrowing her brow. Just as quickly as the words were out, surprise raced through her. It had been second nature to protect Bryce!

"Then do it," Andre said.

Ryen turned to him, scowling in confusion. She paused for a moment, trying to see his face through the darkness, but could not. *"I-I* don't understand. Do what?"

"Take him as your lover."

"What?" Ryen exploded. "He is our enemy!"

"He is a man."

"I would not think of betraying our country by lying with the Prince of Darkness!"

"One night of passion does not constitute betrayal."

"I will not do that!"

Andre stood, his form towering over her like that of some

ancient god giving judgment. "Get him out of your mind. He is fogging your ability to judge."

To lie with the Prince of Darkness . . . the thought horrified her. Yet there was a tightening of her stomach, a tingle of excitement, as she thought of his lips on hers, his hands touching her bare skin. Andre's words sent ripples of turmoil rolling through her body like a rock shattering the tranquillity of a still pond.

"I only give you the same advice I would any other warrior," Andre said. "If we come up against the English, I am afraid in your present state of mind you would be a poor leader as well as an easy target." Andre turned and started for the exit.

"Andre," Ryen called softly. "The men take women prisoners so easily?"

Andre smiled. "Not under your command, but in other armies, yes. Your men take willing townswomen. It usually serves the same purpose."

"And you think Bryce will be willing?" she wondered, trying to suppress the shiver of excitement that raked her body.

"I have never known a man to turn away a woman."

"You give this advice to all the men?"

"Yes."

"What advice would you give your sister?" she asked.

He gave a short chuckle that surprised Ryen. "I advised her to stay home five years ago," he said, and turned. "I will bring him to you."

"No, wait!" Ryen called, but he was gone. She whirled away from the tent opening and paced nervously. *He won't bring Bryce. How dare he tease me? I should take Bryce as my lover just to spite him.*

She continued to pace, waiting. Her stomach knotted, her knees shook. Ryen hugged her elbows, trying to shield herself from the cold. When the long minutes crawled past and Andre didn't return, she moved to her sleeping mat and sat down. Andre wasn't going to bring him, she realized with an odd twinge of disappointment. He would not have his sister violated. But to a warrior it was not violation. It would be used to ease a need.

Why was it so much easier for a man?

Ryen waited a few minutes more, and when no one approached her tent, she lay down. An inexplicable feeling of emptiness filled her as she closed her eyes.

He was not coming.

Seven

The sound of light footsteps woke Ryen. She sat up to face the intruder and knew instantly who the shadow in the dark was. She leaned over a small table to light a candle, then turned her gaze again to him. The flickering candlelight ran over his muscles like liquid gold. He was so powerful, so roguishly handsome. Ropes bound his wrists together tightly behind his back, but he barely seemed to notice as his dark eyes locked on her.

"You requested my presence?" Bryce asked coldly.

Ryen swung her legs out from under the covers and stood. She knew it was wrong that she had these feelings for him. Still, she could not help taking a step toward him.

His gaze boldly traveled the length of her body. The light from the candle made her nightdress virtually transparent, allowing him to absorb every curve. She watched as his breath became shallow.

She took another step, and another, until she was directly in front of him. How she wanted him to touch her! The ghost of a smile crossed her lips at the irony. She had finally found a man she wanted to touch her—and he was the enemy. As she looked up into his black eyes, she saw his frown of confusion and irritation. She wanted to comfort and reassure him. Ryen reached out a hand, meaning to stroke the wound on his cheek, but Bryce flinched at her touch and drew back. "I won't hurt you," she whispered, realizing the absurdity of the statement as soon as it had left her lips. The scar that would form on his cheek would be permanent proof of her harm. She withdrew her hand and took a step away from him.

"What do you want from me? Why did you summon me here?" Bryce inquired.

She looked away from him and stepped back toward her sleeping mat. "You are a handsome man."

He eyed her suspiciously. "Am I here to discuss my looks?"

Perhaps it was ridiculous, Ryen thought. Men never seemed to have a problem with taking what, or who, they wanted. Maybe I'm making this more complicated than it should be. She raised herself up, straightening her shoulders. She boldly took a step toward him. "In a way, yes," she answered. She watched the frown etch its way into his brow. I am not afraid, she told herself, and approached until she stood before him. He is my prisoner.

"I will tell you nothing," he snarled. "Even if you give me more of your poison."

"I do not want to know anything else," she replied. Ryen raised a hand to his arm, marveling at the strength and elegance of his muscle. He clenched his fist and the muscles bunched as she touched them. The explosive power that moved beneath her fingertips amazed her. With her heart pounding, Ryen traced her fingers across his upper arm to his chest.

"What do you think you're doing, woman?" he demanded.

"Your presence has been a . . . *distraction* to me. I sought to cure it." She looked up and saw those dark eyes hovering over her. His black hair washed over his mighty shoulders. She raised a hand to touch his thick mane.

Bryce pulled back instantly, gazing at her fingertips out of the corner of his eye, searching for the white powder.

Ryen wrapped her fingers tightly in his hair, leaning into his strong chest. "Do you fear my touch?" she wondered in a soft whisper.

Bryce's black eyes scanned her face, but Ryen could not read his thoughts. His dark look lowered over her neck and down to where her chest pressed tightly against his. She shuddered slightly as if he had touched her there.

Then his eyes rose back to hers. "Loathe is more like it," he said.

She could feel the lie through his leggings and smiled. "Your body betrays you."

"Step away from me, witch," he snarled.

Ryen never took commands well. Especially from one of her prisoners. She stood on the tips of her toes and pressed her lips against his. At first, they were unmovable, like a rock wall, but suddenly they parted and the hot passion he was trying to hide was released. His tongue slipped into her mouth, warring with hers. His face pressed hard and demanding against her own.

Then, with a groan, he ripped his head to the side, away from her lips.

"Do not forget who is the prisoner here," she purred. She couldn't resist the urge to run her hands over his broad chest. He was like a sculpture carved from pure marble. There was not a flaw. As if molding the marble with her own hands, they followed the curve of his torso down to his leggings. She ran her hands along his clothing. Is the part covered by his leggings as perfect as the part that is bare? she thought. She wanted to see the rest of him, to touch it and marvel at the exquisite details of his rippling muscles. But she couldn't. She drew her hands away.

"Afraid?" he taunted.

The dare was enough. Her hands moved to his leggings and untied them. Suddenly she stopped, stepping away from him. She was trembling all over and she knew it wasn't from anger. She raised her eyes to his, searching for something— guidance, anything!

Bryce took a step and he was touching her again. His black eyes burned into hers. "Untie me," he whispered.

As if under his spell, she obeyed, pressing herself against his chest, reaching around him to undo the ropes that bound his hands. They fell away, landing in a pile on the floor.

Ryen saw the change instantly. His shoulders straightened in confidence; his eyes sparkled with lust. One hand snaked to the back of her neck, the other to her waist, and he pulled her close to him, slamming her hips into his. Ryen's breath caught in her throat as his hot breath feathered her cheek. "Is this the cure you were looking for?" he asked in a deep voice.

Ryen felt herself respond to the feel of his hard, muscular body pressed so intimately against her own. Yet the pure animal rage she saw in his eyes paralyzed her. She swore she could see fire in them as his gaze lowered to her chest. Ryen drew in a sharp breath and her breasts pressed against the fabric. She lifted a shaking hand to place it on his broad, naked chest. A fire seared through her lower stomach as he pressed his hips closer to hers and she trembled. She lifted her head to his, parting her full lips, inviting a deep, languorous kiss.

Bryce stared at her moist lips and moved toward them, then stopped sharply and pulled back, his lips curling into a feral snarl. He placed his hand against her throat again and Ryen felt it tremble. His thumb caressed the side of her neck. She saw his hard look soften, saw a warmth so heartfelt wash over his face that she wanted to throw her arms around his neck. Then, without warning, his jaw clenched and the angry look returned to his eyes. He grabbed the neckline of her nightdress and yanked down sharply. The fabric split easily with a loud rip and he tore it away from her, tossing it to the floor.

Shocked, Ryen tried to pull away from him, but his grip was firm and unrelenting. She saw some kind of satisfaction on his face and knew that she had mistaken the vengeance in his eyes for desire.

Bryce's gaze swept her body and he cupped one of her

breasts in his hand and squeezed it. The flesh was firm, the nipple erect and rigid. He pulled her closer to him, his other hand still at the small of her back, and put his lips to her breast. He sucked on her flesh with an urgent hunger, pulling on her nipple with his teeth.

Ryen arched toward him, sharp stabs of pleasure shooting down to her stomach, adding fuel to the already blazing fire. She felt sensations that she had never felt before, and she wanted to feel more. She wanted him to stop the aching she felt. She knew that he would gently whisper her name before the night was through. She wrapped her arms around his head, pulling him closer, burying her face into his dark hair. "Bryce," she murmured.

Bryce let his one hand roam lower, cupping the cheek of her buttocks. She groaned and he dipped his fingers even lower and touched the folds of her womanhood. Gently, he bit down on her nipple as he thrust a finger inside her.

Spirals of ecstasy swirled through her mind and she moved her hips to the tempo of his hand. Never had she dreamt of such pleasure!

Bryce grabbed her hair and pulled her head back, exposing her bare neck. How easy it would be to sink his teeth into the white, creamy flesh and shake her until she was still. He pressed his lips firmly onto her skin, nibbling at her throat.

Ryen was lost in a world that focused on Bryce. His fingers expertly sent waves of ecstasy crashing through her.

He eased her down to the carpeted ground and knelt between her legs.

Ryen couldn't help thinking of him as a stalking wolf as he crawled over her. She felt something brush her thigh and looked down. The mere size of his manhood shocked her— surely he would split her in two!—and suddenly she felt her nerve failing her. She tried to back away from his advance.

"This will cure any of your ills, Angel," Bryce said bitterly. He put his full weight on top of her, pinning her down.

His manhood throbbed with an aching lust. He reached down to his groin and gripped his member, guiding it toward her.

Ryen squeezed her eyes shut, preparing for the worst, and steeled her body against the blow.

"Open your eyes," he said.

They remained closed.

"Look at me!"

Hesitant, Ryen opened her eyes and saw only the infinite blackness of his loathing.

He thrust his stiffness into her.

Only years of self-discipline prevented her from crying out in agony. She gripped his shoulders tightly, hoping that this was all there was to "taking" someone, hoping he would not move.

Bryce began to thrust, his body rocking back and forth, back and forth, back and forth.

She held her body rigid against his assault. With each impalement, more of her fantasy crumbled to dust. The pain brought tears to her eyes, but she would never shed them. She put the knuckles of one hand into her mouth to keep from crying out. The other hand pushed weakly against his chest. It could not be like this.

Ryen felt his body stiffen and heard him groan. Finally, he lay still on top of her. She felt relief course through her body and relaxed for the first time since he'd entered her. She stroked his shoulder gently, kindly, wanting the same from him. It had been so brutal! If only he would whisper a tender word . . . if only he would say her name, then she could overlook his roughness.

He shrugged off her hand and put his face close to her ear.

She knew he would say it now, knew he would whisper her name softly to her.

"Slut," he said scornfully.

The last remnant of her fantasy shattered into nothingness and she was left barren, shocked, and hurt. She turned to face him, totally vulnerable for the first time in her life. She looked into his eyes hoping to find some sympathy or explanation.

Disdain filled his expression as he saw her expectations so clearly written on her face. He pushed himself up, tying his hose as he rose.

She grabbed the fur from the bed to cover her nakedness and watched him leave. Quickly, so she would not see any more of him, she blew out the candle to hide alone in the darkness.

Eight

"Damn," Bryce muttered as he shoved aside the tent flap with all the anger that coursed through his body. *I could not kill her!* he thought. *Even as she used me to service her lust like a common dog, I could not bring myself to strangle the life from her body!*

The aroma of freshly roasting venison wafted to him on a soft breeze that stirred his hair. He lifted his head slightly and suddenly realized that he was outside—with no guards.

Escape!

The thought barely entered his mind when hands slammed down upon his shoulders and arms like heavy weights, dragging him to his knees. He struggled, but his arms were wrenched in front of him and chains slapped upon his wrists and ankles before he could even take another breath.

He silently cursed. The harlot had distracted him again, this time costing him an escape. He was pulled to his feet and shoved forward. Four men led him back to his tent, where he was chained to a stake and left alone.

Sitting on the hard ground, buried deep in the night's blackness, Bryce closed his eyes and struggled to will his anger into submission. There would be a time for revenge, but this would not be it. He exhaled a slow, controlled breath as the thought of what had transpired a few minutes before came churning back to the surface of his mind. He had been nothing but a means with which to service the wench's desire. Fierce anger burned in his chest, tightening his lips. God's blood! he thought. How could she be so cold? He could have planted his seed within her! Did she not care about that?

Perhaps she does not know.

The thought was like a blow, stunning him. No, he thought. It could not be. She was a harlot; the seductive way she stood before the candle in that sheer nightdress was engraved upon his memory, scorched there like a brand. It could not be that she was inexperienced in such things. But as he thought this, his mind replayed the sequence of events that led to their lovemaking. She had seemed tentative about touching him. She had been shy about her nakedness. But perhaps this was just a game she played. The way she kissed him, the groans and arches of her soft body, the careless abandon, argued she was experienced at lovemaking.

Still, he had seen fear cross her face at the moment of their coupling. The memory of her body pressed against his caused a stirring in his loins. I could not kill her, he thought again. Not with those brilliant blue eyes staring into my very soul, wearing the look of hot need so naturally. Perhaps I should not have been so rough . . .

She is French! She used me and I am feeling sorry for her. His lip curled in a grimace and he shifted his position. Slowly, his brow furrowed as he thought of the moment he had taken her. His brows met as he concentrated—had there been a barrier?

He put his hand inside his leggings, feeling the wetness there, the only physical evidence that they had actually been together. He removed his hand and raised it up before his face, studying the stain on his fingertips. His scowl deepened as he wondered what kind of wanton devil his captor was. Why would she have done such a thing? He could think of nothing of value she could have gained from their encounter. Unless this was not the proof he was looking for, but her monthly flux.

The doubt festered in his mind like an annoying gnat. He replayed their encounter in his mind again, as he knew he would do a hundred times in the future. He had to know. Had she been a virgin?

The next day went slowly, and no matter how hard he tried, there simply was not enough to occupy his mind. Images and sensations that he wanted to forget kept returning. The rebellious chestnut curls that hid the soft, delicate curve of her neck. Her moist, parted lips that hinted of honey, a sweetness that he now wished he had tasted.

Bryce pounded the ground for the fifth time, deepening the indentation that was already there.

He had to know if she was a virgin. If she was . . . he had acted like a rutting dog. Had he known, he would never have taken her. No, he thought fiercely. She must be accustomed to taking men. She had many prisoners. Surely, he was not her first. He could not be her first! Why would she have picked her enemy to take her maidenhead?

He had many women, that went without saying. Some married to great lords, some common harlots. But never had he taken a virgin. They were trouble. He had learned that from a friend a long time ago. Years ago, when he had been a squire about to be knighted, his friend Charles Burke had slept with a farmer's virgin daughter. Later, she accused Burke of raping her. Burke had to pay a rich sum . . . even though the wench had lied.

Bryce avoided virgins like the plague. Even at Dark Castle, where it would have been customary for the lord to sleep with peasant women on their wedding night, he had never exercised his right.

If a married noblewoman stopped at Dark Castle and was interested, he would take her without guilt. Many of the noblewomen wore a night with the Prince of Darkness like a valued jewel for their peers to envy. He gave them what they wanted and then dismissed them from his thoughts.

But he could not do this with his enemy. She had seduced

him. She had invited him to her quarters, not knowing whether he would strangle her or not. She stood before him like some daring temptress. She could not be a virgin!

No decent woman had ever matched his lovemaking. Not even Angel. You did not give her the chance, a voice inside him chastised. He pushed the thought aside. They all lay beneath him, pretending to be fearful of the great Prince of Darkness, acting the defenseless maiden. He despised them when he was finished, as he despised his French captor.

Whores sometimes matched his wild lovemaking. He kept two of the best at his castle near Sussex. There was Elli, the blond. He had made her cut her hair short to remind him of the women of the Wolf Pack. She loved to please him. And she did. She also pleased most of his men. But it did not bother him.

And there was Lotte. He loved to wrap his hands in her long black hair and yank on it when he took her from behind like a dog. She had big breasts, the biggest he had ever seen. But she had to eat like a cow to keep them that way. Bryce knew that she never slept with the other men. She thought of herself as his, and when he took Elli, it enraged her. He lost track of how many fights he had witnessed between the two whores.

But the whores had not been virgins when he had taken them. None of his women had ever been. If the Angel . . .

No, he thought. Why would she choose me? Why not choose one of her men? Surely she could have found a Frenchman to satisfy her. Had she no suitors? Or was it the legend that surrounded him what intrigued her?

Then the thought returned to him from the night before, nearly paralyzing him with apprehension. Have I planted English seed into the belly of a French woman? What have I done? He had been careful with all his women, careful to remove himself so as not to get them with child. But he had been angry with Angel. He had not been thinking. He only wanted to punish her, to show her the strength of England.

This was one way to incapacitate the Angel of Death, he thought with sarcasm.

The thought of a French bastard made him cringe. He had never shirked his duty; if she had a child, he would care for it properly. But how could he protect a French child from English ridicule?

These questions were driving him mad! He had to have the answers. He had to see her.

"Guard!" Bryce shouted.

Ryen had gotten little sleep the night before, her dreams echoing Bryce's condemnation. She sauntered distractedly through the camp as her mind replayed her actions of the night before.

The way she had summoned him to her tent, the way she let him touch her. She had been no better than one of the camp whores. A slut.

The word still stung. It was like putting salt in a wound every time she thought of it. And the wound was deep. He had not been gentle. How could she have mistaken his glances for caring when all they were were stares of hate? He was her enemy, and while she had forgotten, or chosen to overlook it, he had not.

"You're avoiding me."

Ryen looked up to see that Andre had joined her. His forehead and dark red tunic were wet with perspiration. His sword hung in its scabbard at his side. "No, I'm not. I've been very busy this morning."

"Preparing to meet Father?"

"Yes," she lied. Ryen had not considered her father once. All her thoughts had been of Bryce.

Andre stared hard at her. The seconds grew to minutes, and even though she did not meet his gaze, he still watched her.

She bridled under the silent pressure. "Well, not exactly," she finally admitted, her eyes wandering to the ground.

"How did it go last night?" he wondered.

"He came to my tent, as you know."

"And . . . did you take my advice?"

"Yes."

A long moment of silence passed and Ryen raised her head to stare off at the horizon and the blue sky. She shifted her shoulders so the chain mail rested comfortably.

"Have you gotten him out of your system?" Andre asked softly.

"Yes. Absolutely. I never want to see him again," Ryen stated emphatically.

Andre sighed with relief "Then it worked," he said. "Good. Because he's asking to see you."

Ryen's lips tightened into a grimace. What did Bryce want? To take her in his arms and gently kiss her? Ryen chuckled bitterly to herself. Not likely.

Ryen raised her chin, her eyes narrowing, and gave Andre her answer.

Nine

"What do you mean, she doesn't want to see me?" Bryce demanded, outraged. He had been waiting hours for a response he was sure would be positive. He had half expected Ryen to come herself. "I *must* see her!"

The guard stood mutely during Bryce's outburst, his dirty chain mail reflecting the lackluster expression on his face. When he finished, the guard spoke evenly. "*She* doesn't want to see *you*."

Bryce seethed with anger and paced back and forth, his manacled feet allowing him only to shuffle along the ground. He turned back to the guard, repeating, "I must see her!"

The guard remained silent, an amused grin on his face.

"Wipe off that smirk, damn you!" Bryce growled.

The guard smiled wider, showing his teeth.

Heathen bastard!

Bryce shot forward, diving, and rammed his head into the guard's chest. The man's chain mail bent beneath the impact as he doubled over. Bryce was dazed for a moment, but as the guard grunted heavily and went down, he hurriedly shuffled for the tent flap and lurched—

—into the arms of three guards standing outside. They slammed him to the ground, one of them pinning him firmly with a knee to his back.

"*Angel!*" Bryce cried out, before a guard clubbed him into unconsciousness.

* * *

Bryce's head pounded. He wished he could rub it, but the manacles that bound his wrists to a stake in the ground would not allow him to reach his head. Did they think he would chew through the metal links? He wanted to laugh, but his head hurt too badly.

She doesn't want to see me, he thought. His lips twisted in a grimace. She was no virgin. How could she be, with an army of men following her? The sight of her smooth buttocks and those spread thighs as she rode her horse would drive any man mad with lust. At least half a dozen men had probably had her by now.

He shook his head in disgust. I should have killed her, he thought.

He sighed, lying down in the dirt. The tent flap was closed, but through the slit of the opening Bryce could see the glimmer of a small campfire from somewhere outside in the dark.

When he had regained consciousness, he'd discovered a tray of bread and cold duck beside him. Even though he had no hunger, he had eaten it to keep up his strength. He had to stay strong for his escape.

Suddenly, his senses came alert. There was movement outside the tent and the soft crunching of footsteps on the dirt . . . someone who was not armored; the footsteps were too light. Through the slit between the flaps, a shadow moved to block the campfire. The person was short, too short to be a guard, too small to be a knight.

Bryce boosted himself up on his elbow, his brows furrowing. The flap opened and the figure entered the tent, clothed in a ragged brown cotton tunic and black hose ripped at the knee.

Anger and fear fought for control of him, tightening his stomach, thinning his lips. "Runt," he gasped.

The smile slid over the boy's face easily. "I'm here to free you," Runt said, brushing a lock of black hair from his eyes. "I haven't figured out how, but I will."

Bryce reached out to him, but his manacles jangled and yanked his arms short of grabbing the boy. "I want you out of here. Now."

Runt's lips turned down and his small head tilted slightly to the side. "I can't leave you here."

"I told you to go to the rear of the army. Weren't you listening?" Bryce demanded, his anger rising to drown out his fear.

"I did. And then they ran," Runt replied in disgust. There was a stubbornness in his large eyes, a determined set to his small jaw.

He won't run. I taught him that, a voice inside Bryce reminded. But he was becoming panicked at the thought of this small boy in the enemy's camp, risking his life to try to free him. "You must leave now," he commanded, angry with himself for not being able to throw him out of the camp.

Runt scowled at Bryce. "I won't leave without you."

Orders never worked with me, Bryce knew, and it would never work with the child. Bryce fought to bring his emotions under control. "Listen to me, Runt," he stated, his jaw tense, "you are just a boy. You cannot battle an entire French army alone."

"I have you by my side," Runt said simply.

Bryce raised his hands and the manacles clanked and sparkled in the light from the campfire outside. "I am bound. I am of no help to you."

"I'll free you," Runt insisted.

"Runt!" The anger surged inside Bryce again; he could feel his hands clenching into fists. The boy stepped back fearfully. Bryce forced his rage down, his teeth clenching, and sat back on his heels. "It is dangerous, Runt. Everywhere you turn there will be enemies. And I will be heavily guarded. You cannot free me. You must escape."

"I am not a prisoner," Runt said. "They think I am one of

the town boys coming to aid in the battle. The guards let me in here so I can get your tray." He grinned, proud of his accomplishment.

But all Bryce saw was the danger the boy was in. What if the Angel of Death discovered him? What if she used the boy to get more information from him? Could he endure Runt's cries from torture, or would he turn traitor to his country to save the child? If she knew his one weakness was standing defenseless in her camp . . . He looked at Runt, a scowl creasing his brow. "Runt, you don't know what could happen here. You must trust me when I say you cannot stay."

Runt frowned. "I am not in any danger."

"You are. Far more than you realize. And by your being here, you put me in more danger than I have ever been in before."

Runt's brow furrowed, an imitation of Bryce, and he looked at the ground. "I just didn't want them to hurt you."

Bryce's heart softened immediately. He wanted to help the boy, to tell him that what he was doing would have been right had he been a man. He wanted to tell him that he would make a fine knight someday and that he was proud that he had attempted to rescue him. But he knew if he did that, Runt would see it as a signal to stay and try to impress him further by freeing him. He had to be stern. "Come here, boy," Bryce commanded.

Runt walked up to him, his eyes full of disappointment.

Bryce gently placed his hands upon the boy's shoulders and looked into his blue eyes. "I can take care of myself. I need you to leave this camp and find King Henry. You must not stay here."

"But I know I can rescue you. I can free you, Prince," Runt said sincerely.

Bryce's frown deepened. Persistent. He was so damned persistent. Why wouldn't he listen? "No. You can't stay. You won't be able to free me. I want you out of this camp. *Now.*" He had never raised his voice to the boy before, but he had to make him leave. "Go on. Leave me here. I will see you at King Henry's camp." He released Runt and watched him back up to the tent flap, where he paused. "Go on," Bryce insisted.

Runt swiped at the lock of hair that fell before his eyes and Bryce saw the sparkle of tears before the boy ducked beneath the tent flap and was gone.

"Afraid of the Prince of Darkness?"

Bryce sat up straight in the tent, listening to the ridicule in the voices.

"Hey, you didn't get the tray!"

The guards. A protective anger surged inside Bryce. He wanted to rip out their throats for talking to Runt with disrespect.

"Coward!" They broke into laughter and Bryce exploded, lunging forward. The boy had more courage than the guards could ever dream of having. His bonds caught him and pulled his arms back. Still, he fought to move forward, out of the tent. The guffaws continued to echo in the night air, enraging him. The chains dug into his flesh, pulled at his arms. He fought against the manacles' biting hold, pulling with every last ounce of strength. The chains held fast. Slowly the sounds of the French mockery faded. Bryce tried one last time to lunge forward, pulling with his chest and digging his feet into the ground. The manacles refused to move, holding strong against his every effort. Finally he gave up his fight, letting his arms drop. I am chained and useless, he thought. I cannot even defend Runt. He would never forget this feeling of helplessness. Nor forgive those who had caused it.

The next morning, one of Ryen's men came for him, ordering him to his feet and out of the tent. The sun was low in the sky, and Bryce knew it was very early. The camp was quiet and still; only an occasional man strolled between the tents.

The guard led him past the camp borders and through a thick row of shrubbery, deep into the forest. Large trees shot up all around him. The early morning sun peeked through the leaves far above their heads, and bushes and weeds peppered their path. Escape raced through Bryce's mind, but the shackles that bound his wrists and ankles, and the sword the man held to his back, prevented any action. The guard urged him through a small line of bushes and they emerged in a large clearing. Bryce stopped.

She was there.

Ryen's forehead was dotted with perspiration, a broadsword not far from her driven into the ground. She wore an oversized green tunic, cuffed at the sleeves and bound around the waist with a large leather belt. White leggings conformed to her shapely legs, and her black leather boots accented her curvy calves. Desire coursed through Bryce and he silently cursed himself for his lack of control. The sunlight glinted off the helmet on the ground near her feet. Her hair was loose and hung wildly over her shoulders.

"Were you a virgin?" he blurted as he drew closer, the question spilling forth from his lips as if his obsessive attention to it had given it a life of its own. He half expected a slap for his blunt question, especially in front of her man, but when none was forthcoming, he presumed that the guard didn't understand English.

But Ryen did. Her eyes narrowed. "You didn't care when you took me."

"I want to know," he said, as calmly as possible.

"It doesn't matter." She turned away from him, looking toward the trees at the other end of the clearing. "I am not one now."

"Angel," he said softly, an overwhelming desire to take her in his arms sweeping over him as he heard the anguish in her voice. "You brought me to your tent in the middle of the night half clothed. What did you want me to do?"

"You did everything I expected you would," she said bitterly.

"Then you were not a virgin."

"Why is it so important that you know?"

Bryce watched her closely, listened for the change in her voice. "You could tell me this, at least. After all, I did service you quite adequately."

She whirled, fury burning in those sapphire eyes. "Quite adequately? I bled that night! I owe you nothing!"

"All virgins bleed."

Ryen averted her gaze, a slight blush spreading over her cheeks. Bryce had his answer. "God's blood! Why would you pick your enemy to teach you the ways of love? Why not a Frenchman? Why not one of your own?"

She clenched her fists into tiny balls, her jaw tightening. "Unshackle him," she snapped at the guard in French.

The guard took Bryce's arms and slid the chains off his wrists. As he bent to remove the shackles around Bryce's ankles, Bryce rubbed his chafed wrists, trying to force circulation back into them. His dark gaze never wavered from Ryen's. What is she up to? he wondered.

Again, Ryen spoke to the guard. "Give him your sword."

"My lady?" the guard replied, straightening and turning to Ryen.

"Give him your sword!" Ryen shouted.

The guard hesitated only a second before pulling the sword from his sheath and extending it hilt first to Bryce. Bryce glanced down at the sword in the guard's hands, then up at Ryen. He saw that her breath was coming hard.

She yanked her broadsword out of the ground and stepped closer to him.

Bryce's eyebrows shot up in amusement. She wanted to fight him! "I did nothing you didn't want me to." Bryce's gaze swiveled to the guard. He was older and probably experienced in battle, but shorter and heavier than Bryce. He could defeat the guard. And Angel was no challenge.

Ryen's words were sweet. "This is lesson number two."

Bryce ached to feel the hilt of the sword in his palm. He knew he could defeat both of them, but he needed to get

Angel alone if he hoped to escape. "I'm no fool. Your man would cut me down in an instant if he saw your life was threatened, despite any orders you gave him," Bryce said flippantly.

Ryen again spoke to the guard. "Get Andre."

"And leave you alone?" he answered.

A grin twitched the corners of Bryce's lips.

"I gave you an order!"

The guard stiffened and turned to leave, the sword in his hand, the shackles slung over his shoulder.

Bryce's hopes faded. His chance was gone. She had already changed her mind about fighting him. Then what did she want with him alone in the forest? To kill him?

"Leave the weapon," Ryen ordered.

The guard turned back to her. He paused to glance down at his sword, then threw it to the ground before running into the forest, disappearing through trees and shrubbery.

Ryen grinned at Bryce, her eyes flashing with challenge. "You have only minutes to overcome me before my army descends on you. Think you can do it?"

"Undoubtedly." Now was his chance. This Angel was very foolish. But Bryce had to admire her courage. He bent and picked up the sword, a smile on his face. *If she chooses to fight me, then so be it.* He stared at the blade for a moment, deep in thought about—

—striking at her, which he did without warning, driving his sword forward!

She easily knocked it aside. "If that is the best you can do, this will be a sadly easy defeat."

"I've already put my sword into you once; don't make me do it again."

Ryen's face softened with hurt and Bryce took advantage of her vulnerable moment to attack, bringing his sword in low and up in a dip, the point heading straight toward her stomach.

Suddenly, Ryen's sword came to life and caught his swing.

With a twist of her wrist, Bryce's sword spun into the air and then landed on the ground two feet from him. She stood for a moment with her sword tip to his neck.

Shock paralyzed Bryce before he masked it with a forced grin. No one had ever done that before! I have been toying with her, he reassured himself. But he had not anticipated such a lightning-fast defense. She was good. For a woman.

She smirked. "Is that the best you can do?"

"You should be thankful your swordplay is better than your seduction," he retorted.

"Pick it up," she said.

It is time to teach her her place, he thought, and moved for his sword. He picked up the blade and turned to face her again.

She smiled full out. She thrust quite unexpectedly, and when he parried, she brought the blade high and down. They locked swords and she grabbed his wrist.

The feeling of her small hand on his skin sent tingles up his arm. Angry, Bryce tore his wrist free and pushed off.

Ryen swung her blade around to the side.

He expertly blocked it and came back with a blow of his own. "Why so bitter, Angel? I gave you what you asked for."

Ryen deflected the attack. "Do all men finish so quickly?"

"If you hadn't acted like a bitch in heat, then I might have acted more politely."

"To an enemy? You wanted to hurt me. Just like you want to kill me now."

"Killing you now would be too easy," he said.

"Don't flatter yourself. You're not as good as you think," Ryen answered, and swung the large blade again.

Bryce blocked her strike and counter-thrust. She raised her sword and sparks flew as the metal blades collided. His face was inches from hers, and he stared into her blue eyes. "You are good, Angel, I will admit that." Her full lips were so close, so inviting. He put his weight against the sword, moving his face closer and closer. She fought valiantly, but vainly. He was stronger than she was and his lips drew nearer to hers. "I get what I want, Angel. Surrender to me."

"Never," she whispered, her hot breath fanning his lips.

"Ryen!" a voice shouted from the distance.

Bryce pushed himself away from Ryen and turned toward the trees where the voice had come from.

"Put down your weapon," Ryen advised in a hushed tone.

Bryce glanced at her. Was that concern in her voice?

"Ryen!" the call came again, this time closer.

Bryce looked toward the voice, then quickly turned to look the other way. The branches of the trees on the opposite side of the clearing swayed in the breeze as if beckoning to him, but he knew he would never make it. Not with the stiffness in his legs from being confined for so long. An arrow in the back would bring him down before he could hide himself in the woods. He turned to look at Ryen. She watched him with those clear blue eyes, her sword arm relaxed at her side, as if she were waiting for him to make a move. His first impulse was to put his blade to her throat and hold off her men by threatening her life. He took a step toward her and grabbed her wrist. Much to his surprise, she didn't resist. He knew he could take her and she would let him. For an instant, the realization confused him, and he hesitated. Voices echoed in the clearing. By the time he had made up his mind to take her, the trees seemed to magically part and a large group of men burst forth, shouting angry words and brandishing weapons.

Bryce released her arm and quickly dropped the sword. He held up his hands and backed away, but a tall blond man tackled him to the ground. The other men surrounded him and began pounding on him with their fists, lashing out with their feet. Bryce kicked and heard a satisfying thud as his foot struck French flesh. But there were too many of them. He tried to bury his face protectively in his arms, but a boot caught him in the back of the head and his vision blurred for a moment as pain hammered his skull. Hot agony flared in his stomach as another foot struck him.

Bryce's vision cleared and he looked out through a haze of pain to see the glint of a polished sword poised above his abdomen.

Bryce. When she came out the other end of the battle she expected to see men writhing in pain, blood soaking the leaves on the ground.

Ten

"Lucien!" Ryen screamed, reaching for his raised sword arm.

Andre reached him first, catching the downward swing of his forearm with an open palm.

Ryen felt her heart hammering in her chest. Her stark terror at seeing her brother about to butcher Bryce dissipated, immediately replaced by a scorching fury. She had to get Bryce back to camp, away from Lucien and her men. Trembling with anger and frustration, Ryen looked down at Bryce. "On your feet," she commanded.

Bryce moved his arms away from his face and looked at her. For only a moment, she read disbelief in those dark eyes. Then, with a groan, he rolled to his stomach and pushed himself up to his hands and knees, swaying unsteadily.

Ryen moved toward him, protectiveness surging inside her.

"She said on your feet," Lucien snarled and lashed out with his foot, catching Bryce in the ribs, sending him back to the ground.

Ryen whirled on Lucien, her fists twined into knots at her side. "Touch him again and I will personally see to it that you are clapped in irons." She turned away from him and knelt beside Bryce.

He was lying on his back, clutching his stomach. Ryen saw the pain in the thinning of his lips and the tension in his neck. Otherwise, his face was void of any kind of emotion. His eyes were closed for a long moment as if he were trying to bring the pain under control. When he opened them, they were dark and unreadable.

Ryen whirled, again seeking out Lucien among the men, and shot to her feet to face him. "Are you mad?" she demanded. "You could have killed him!"

Lucien's brows crashed together, his jaw clenching. "And he could have killed you."

"I was not in danger," Ryen snapped.

"No danger?" Lucien roared, the words firing from his lips like arrows from a bow. "You gave the man a sword! He's a notorious murderer! He's killed thousands of our people! And you gave him a weapon!"

"That was my decision to make. He is my prisoner and I will do with him as I like!"

"Ryen. Lucien." Andre stepped between them, his body forming a barrier between their rage. "This is not the place, nor the time," he said softly but harshly.

Lucien shouldered his way past Andre to confront his sister. "I will not allow you to give him a weapon. You endanger yourself as well as every man here."

"*You* will not allow me?" Ryen roared, her eyes flashing with rage. Lucien opened his mouth to speak, but Ryen continued, "I will not allow you to beat him."

"What do you care? He is English! He deserves everything he got."

Her fury knew no bounds. She wanted to grab Lucien and shake him until he saw the foolishness of his words. She stood for a long moment absolutely still, knowing that if she moved, or if Lucien said a word, she would explode. She looked away from Lucien, trying to control her anger. But her eyes came to rest on Bryce as he sat huddled on the ground, an arm about his middle. He was watching her with curiosity and a bit of amusement. "Get him out of here," she murmured.

"You heard her!" Lucien shouted. "Move the dog back to his tent."

Her burning eyes snapped to him. "Not him. *You.*"

Lucien stared at her incredulously, but when she glared back at him, he whirled and pushed his way through the gaping men.

Ryen's gaze returned to Bryce.

"I'll have him taken to his tent," Andre whispered to her. "You'd best go rest. I'll come by later."

"I want him in my tent until his wounds are mended," Ryen said.

"Ryen—" Andre began.

"I feel responsible. If I hadn't given him a sword, none of this would have happened. I just want to make sure he recovers. No prisoner should be treated like this."

Andre waved his hand, signaling men to take Bryce. Four men stepped forward and gathered around Bryce. One man reached down, offering Bryce a hand. Bryce shoved the hand away and climbed slowly to his feet, scorning any help.

Ryen felt his gaze on her the entire time. His look burned through her skin into her soul until she turned to lock gazes with her enemy. His eyes were dark and mysterious with a glow that sent tingles up her spine.

Andre shoved him forward and they moved toward the camp.

After a moment, Ryen followed them through the bushes. She hugged her elbows, suddenly chilly in the breeze that wound its way through the trees. Why had she allowed this to happen? Why couldn't she stop her men? Had they acted out of concern for her, or was it their hatred for Bryce?

Bryce. She caught a glimpse of his powerful strides through the wall of men that had surrounded him. Her gaze scanned his naked torso, his strong neck, his sturdy back, until she saw the ugly red welt forming on his side, near his ribs. Ryen's brow creased. She was so intent on studying the bruise that she stumbled over a root and almost fell.

Andre glanced back at her for a moment as she quickly regained her composure. They had to hurry, she thought, an urgency filling her. They had to get him back to the camp so she could bind his wounds. The tanned, slightly sunburnt, skin of his torso caught her attention again. It was my fault, she thought, a stab of guilt slicing at her heart. I should never have allowed him out of his tent. I should never have seen him.

Then, she straightened her shoulders. No. I refuse to take responsibility for this. It was Bryce who demanded to see me. I should hate him, she thought, her eyes narrowing.

Even as she told herself this, even as she forced her eyes to narrow, the memory of his searing gaze sent waves of heat splashing over her hate.

Finally, they emerged from the trees of the forest and entered into her camp. A breeze blew softly, stirring her hair around her shoulders. As they moved around the tents and smoldering campfires, Ryen's eyes continued to study her prisoner. There were scrapes on his arms, and small red welts covered his stomach. But the bruise forming rapidly near his ribs was what concerned her the most.

As they neared her tent, she quickened her steps to hold aside the tent flap. She watched anxiously as they escorted him inside. As the four guards exited, Ryen saw Andre standing in the doorway, holding chains in his hands.

"At least let me chain him, Ryen," he pleaded.

Ryen glanced at Bryce once before nodding, and Andre moved to Bryce. She watched him take his wrists, and saw Bryce's arms tense before Andre slapped the manacles on. Then, he did the same for his ankles. Andre surveyed his work for a moment, his chain mail sparkling dully in the morning light, before turning to Ryen.

He moved closer to her and whispered, "You're in danger here, Ryen."

"Lucien asked for it," she defended. "He has no right to tell me what I can and cannot do."

"I'm talking about your feelings for him." Andre jerked his head at Bryce. "I was wrong suggesting that you take him. It has only enhanced your attraction."

"How can you say that?" Ryen demanded. "I despise the man."

"It cannot be that you despise him when you gaze at him with such tenderness."

Ryen glanced at Bryce, her feelings in battle. She should hate this man, this enemy of France, for the way he treated her. She should have known that there is no kindness in England. Still, as she gazed at him, her heart warmed. He was so strong willed, unrelenting in his determination not to give up. Even in the face of immeasurable odds he would not surrender. She saw his resistance every time she looked into his black eyes.

A shower of sunlight splashed through the flap of the tent, bathing Bryce in a pool of light. It ran over his muscled arm like rain, reflecting off of the chains around his wrists. If only he had been born French, she thought. If only they could have been allies, instead of enemies.

"You have never fought openly with Lucien before," Andre said. "You defended the prisoner over your own brother—in front of the men!"

"Lucien acted like a barbarian! Even the men acted like common animals. What happened to honor, and pride? Bryce had put down his sword. He was defenseless!"

"They were protecting you, Ryen. Lucien and the men believed he would harm you."

"I don't need protection. Not from Bryce."

"Are you so sure?"

Ryen's gaze again found Bryce and her brow furrowed. What was he doing to her? To her life? Under her gaze, he stiffened. The metal manacles tinkled like a bell.

"You need more protection from him than even you realize," Andre murmured before departing the tent.

Ryen walked over to Bryce's side. A strand of black hair fell over his forehead, a rich black against his tanned skin. Her eyes dropped to his. She was surprised to find them pensive. Ryen's gaze sank to his ribs, to the red welt. She reached out to touch it, but Bryce pulled away. Ryen glanced at him, startled. Then, resignation washed over her face and she looked quickly away.

He raised his wrists, displaying the manacles. "Is there a need for these?"

"Many think so," she replied softly.

"Do you not command this army? Isn't your word law?"

"They will not touch you again."

"You can't promise me I won't be attacked."

In her mind's eye, Ryen saw the armored shoes kicking him, heard her ineffectual commands to stop.

"They want to kill me," Bryce stated.

"You are the enemy," Ryen replied stoically.

Suddenly, his fingers were on her chin, gently turning her face toward his. "Ryen." Her name was a sigh against his lips. "Your men will try to hurt me again."

Ryen felt the warmth of his hand seep into her chin. He was so close that his breath kissed her lips. For a moment she could barely move, barely breathe.

His fingers gently stroked the fine line of her jaw, sending the heat of his touch blazing throughout the rest of her body.

"Unchain me," he whispered.

Ryen couldn't help but watch his lips caress the words as he spoke. Bound by some irresistible force, she lifted her lips to his, parting them in anticipation of his kiss.

"Let me go."

Her eyes shot open wide in shock and horror. She shook her head fiercely against the idea; her knees were shaking as she stepped back. "I can't do that."

His eyes narrowed slightly and he looked away, disappointment etched in the tight line of his lips.

"How can you ask me to betray my country?" she demanded. "To abandon my oath? For you." He looked up at her sharply, anger in his eyes. "You would not do the same for me."

"You are a woman," he rationalized.

She straightened her shoulders. "Do you truly believe that a woman would give up everything she has worked so hard for . . . even for the love of a man?"

"Yes," he replied.

Ryen sadly shook her head. "I would not do that. Not even for you, a man who has no love in him."

They stared at each other for a long moment, and strangely, Ryen felt a sense of regret and sadness fill her. His face was hard and cold, unbending beneath her emotions. She turned and retrieved the basin of water off her nightstand near her mattress. "I will tend your wounds."

He turned his back on her as she approached. "No French man, or French woman, could inflict a wound against me that I would not recover from," he stated.

She paused in the middle of the floor, halfway between Bryce and the nightstand. How he must hate her, she thought . . . as much as I should hate him. She turned and replaced the basin of water. "At De Bouriez Castle, you will be safe from harm. My father is waiting there to greet us," she explained.

"Your father will be no different from your men," Bryce sneered.

Ryen straightened. "He is my flesh and blood. There is a part of him in me. He will be different."

"He's a man. There will be no kindness, no show of mercy from a Frenchman."

She whirled, angry. "You are so quick to judge us. Do you know us so well?" Ryen wondered, bitterness accompanying every word.

Bryce slowly raised his black eyes to her. Like fire, they burned through her until her heart melted. She felt his fire flaming through her until she could no longer look at him without wanting him to touch her. What was this control he had over her? Was he truly a devil? she wondered.

"I think I know you very well," he whispered, his voice mocking and seductive in the same breath. "If you take me to your father, it is as good as sending me to my death," he stated.

A sudden chill doused the flames his look had ignited. She could not shake the finality of his words. She stepped back from him before turning and leaving her tent. She ordered four of her soldiers to escort Bryce back to the prisoner tent.

Through the remainder of the day and well into the night, she could not forget Bryce's words. "Sending me to my death . . ." She fought the image of Bryce lying dead in a pool of blood and would not believe that her father could do such a thing. All she wanted was for her father to see the Prince of Darkness and know that it was she who had captured him.

Ryen recalled the day she'd decided she would take the oath and become a knight. She was telling her father about her lessons. Ryen was so excited that day that she'd run all the way to the jousting field. Her father had nodded and grinned at her stories. But all the while his eyes had been locked on the jousting field where Andre was sharpening his skill. When she told her father that her teacher had said she was far ahead of many of his male pupils, her father had cheered and raised his hands to the air. A grin lit her face as she saw pride in his eyes. Pride and fondness . . .

Until she realized that he was staring out onto the field. Ryen's eyes followed his gaze and her heart cracked. Andre's opponent lay sprawled in the dirt. Her father's delight had been not for her, but for Andre and the talent he'd displayed as a warrior.

Ever since that day, Ryen had wanted her father to look at her the way he had looked at Andre, the way she had seen him look at Lucien. Instead, when he looked at her, all she saw was patient amusement and tolerance.

She crossed her arms behind her head, staring at the top of the tent.

She imagined her father's warm eyes gazing at her, his

lips slightly turned up in a smile when he saw she had
brought the Prince of Darkness to him. He would be so proud
of her. He would say . . .

A loud cry shattered the night's silence. *"Fire!"*

Eleven

"*Fire!*"

The urgent cry of alarm roused Bryce from his slumber and he hurried to his feet, his battle-honed senses instantly alert. He had heard the cry a few times at the castle while growing up and he had been trained to respond quickly. His fellow knights fought off the threat of flames with as much energy as they put forth to dispel any attacker.

Fire was an enemy hated by all men.

The back wall of Bryce's prison tent glowed faintly with the orange-red light of flames. The fire was close! Smoke curled in through a gap between the tent wall and the ground and slowly drifted upward.

Outside the tent he could hear men screaming for more water. A horse whinnied in fear, then galloped off into the distance.

Suddenly, a hot burst of light bloomed on the tent wall in a fiery red glow as the blaze moved closer. Bryce felt the temperature in his prison rise dramatically. Droplets of sweat rose on his forehead and then dripped to the dirt, while a sheen of moisture appeared on his arms and legs. The manacle on his left foot slipped lower over his ankle. Bryce dropped back to the ground and started working on the manacle, turning, pulling, pushing.

Behind him the wall crackled. He stopped what he was doing only long enough to see a tendril of fire snake into the tent through the gap and start to crawl up the wall.

He turned his attention back to his ankle. When the guards had failed to chain him to the post in the ground, he knew this was his best chance. He had managed to remove one of his boots and had made some progress with his shackles earlier. Now, with his sweat lubricating the manacle, he was certain he could remove it. He had to; it didn't appear as if anyone was in a hurry to get him out of there.

Outside, the cries grew louder as they competed with the roar of the blaze. More shouts for water. More horses making sounds of terror. Men running in all directions.

Bryce worked intently at the manacle on his ankle, talking to himself under his breath. I'm going to escape. All I need is to get this off and I can escape. The night will be my ally, my cloak. She will hide me well, as she has so many times in the past.

The tent grew hotter. The sweat flowed more freely from his body. The manacle moved even lower. The metal cut into his skin as he forced it lower and the salty sweat stung the tear in his heel. Blood seeped out of the wound. Bryce pulled on his shackles, ignoring the pain his effort was causing. This is nothing compared to what those searing flames will do to me, he told himself.

Then, to his amazement, his foot came free. He jumped to his feet and limped for the tent flap, the chains still attached to his right foot clanking as he ran.

Behind him, the tent wall disappeared into the belly of the inferno, eaten by the ravenous fire that was quickly surrounding him. The sound of the blaze swelled to a deafening roar as he raced outside.

His guards were gone from their posts, obviously busy fighting the fire. He saw at least fifteen tents burning, and several others were already piles of smoldering black ashes. He ran to a nearby tent and cautiously peered around the corner. He looked left and saw a clear path to the woods in the distance. He started to move toward the trees, but a small shadow at the corner of his eye caused him to turn and look back in the direction of his former prison.

The haze of smoke partially hid the figure of the small boy as he hurried inside the burning tent. No! It can't be! Bryce dashed toward the burning tent.

He reared back as he entered. Fire was everywhere, the heat almost unbearable. Bryce squinted as the dark smoke bit at his eyes. His keen ears heard a snap in the roaring flames and he instinctively dived to his left as a burning tent support suddenly crashed to the ground! He felt the searing flames whip around his legs and he pushed himself to his feet, driving forward to escape the heat.

He saw the boy lying on his side in a corner of the tent with his legs pulled tightly to his chest, his face buried in his arms. "Here!" Bryce shouted, but the fire howled around him, drowning out his voice, demanding human flesh to feed its insatiable appetite.

The boy lay unmoving behind the shroud of flames.

Bryce felt his insides tighten with fear and, shielding his face with his manacled hands, he jumped through the curtain of fire. Pain seared his back, but he willed it away. He bent and scooped the boy into his arms, pressing him against his chest, trying to protect him from the heat of the fire.

Bryce exploded through the side wall of the tent, bursting past the charred canvas, moving out onto open ground. He hurried farther away from the flames, away from the intense heat, and then dropped to his knees, cradling the boy to his chest. He could not let him go. He was afraid, afraid of what he might find if he looked into the boy's face. Runt was so still in his arms, so limp. Tears rose in Bryce's eyes as he squeezed the boy close, willing his life into the child, wishing it were him instead of Runt. Slowly, he moved the boy away from his chest, feeling as if he were tearing a piece of skin from his body. I told him to go, he thought desperately. Why is he still here?

Finally Bryce lay the boy gently on the ground and looked

down into his wide eyes. There was no life there, only the reflection of the full moon. He reached toward the boy's shoulder, but stopped as he saw his own hand was shaking.

He clenched his fist for a moment afraid that when he touched him, Runt would not move. "Get up, Runt," he called hoarsely.

Nothing.

He cautiously prodded Runt's shoulder. When the child didn't stir, Bryce felt a desperation surge inside of him. He seized the boy's shoulder and shook it, almost savagely. No, he thought, tears threatening to choke him. "Come on, boy," Bryce commanded. "On your feet."

But the child didn't move; his eyes didn't blink.

"I said on your feet!" he shouted. A moment passed, then another. When Runt did not move, Bryce sat on his heels, staring dumbly at the child. It can't be, he thought. I won't believe it. This cannot be Runt. I told him to leave. I commanded him. He would not disobey me.

Then, he saw it. That lock of dark hair that was forever in the boy's eyes was lying limply at the side of his head, brushed aside for all eternity.

Bryce began to shake. He scooped Runt up into his arms, holding him tightly against his heart, and buried his face into the child's neck. "Oh, God, Runt," he whispered, barely able to get the words past his closing throat. "Why didn't you listen to me? Why couldn't you go . . ."

He stroked Runt's dark head, his chest constricting tightly, tears blurring his vision. Finally, his sorrow and agony and pain overwhelmed him. He threw back his head. *"Nooooo!"* he roared, and his anguish echoed through the night.

In the nearby woods, wolves began to howl.

Twelve

As Ryen approached, Bryce whirled on her, crouching wolf-like, his upper lip curling, almost snarling. Ryen stopped cold, her gaze captured by the still figure Bryce held close to his chest. Her brow furrowed as she saw the ashen complexion of the small face through the soot that fell on them like black rain, then her eyes moved from the boy up to Bryce's bleak face. The orange light of the fires burning around them caused long shadows to pool beneath Bryce's eyes. He looked so lost, Ryen instinctively stepped toward him, meaning to comfort him.

Bryce pulled back from her approach, and again, a long, anguish-filled groan surged from deep within his throat. Startled, Ryen retreated. Who was this boy that he could evoke such feelings from the Prince of Darkness? And what was he doing here in her camp?

Three of her men rushed up beside Ryen and stopped in their tracks as they saw the Prince of Darkness. One of the knights glanced at her, then at Bryce and stepped cautiously forward.

Bryce shifted the boy to his left arm, his face contorting with hate. "Don't touch him," he growled, clutching the boy to his chest.

The knight glanced helplessly at Ryen. She stepped forward tentatively, holding her hands out placatingly. "Bryce," she said softly, trying to soothe him.

His dark, loathful eyes turned on her. "Stay away from me," he snarled.

Ryen's arms dropped. "The fire was an accident," she told Bryce, trying to keep patience in her voice as she looked up at him once again. "No one meant to harm the boy."

His eyes narrowed with disbelief. "Harm? You and your bloody French killed him!" Bryce shouted, his voice full of pain and rancor.

Ryen's men had spread out around him, surrounding him. She began to shake her head to stop their maneuver but her command came too late.

Bryce saw one man coming and flattened him with a fist to his jaw. The other two jumped Bryce from behind, knocking him to the ground, pinning the boy beneath him. Ryen watched in awe of his strength as he held the two men on top of him off the boy with the power of his muscular arms.

Lightning flashed in the sky, illuminating Bryce's tormented face. The two knights managed to grab his arms and yanked him to his feet. Ryen opened her mouth to command them to halt, when Bryce kneed one man in his stomach and pulled him to the ground. He turned on the last man, seizing him and picking him up over his head as easily as a rag doll, throwing him to the ground.

Breathing heavily, he turned to the boy as another spear of lightning cut the darkening sky. Tenderly, he bent and lifted him up from the dirt, then whirled and advanced on Ryen.

"I can't let you go," she said, her pulse racing. But how could she stop him? She had no weapon and he was so powerful.

"I'm not asking you," Bryce stated flatly, halting just a step before her.

Ryen stood her ground, unmoving.

"Don't make me hurt you," Bryce warned, his face shadowed in darkness, his shoulders outlined by the dying fire behind him. "I have never hurt a woman before."

The first splash of rain touched her cheek. Ryen swallowed hard. She watched his jaw clench and finally raised her chin to him. "You'll have to kill me to escape."

His lip curled. "And you think I would not? After what you did to him?"

"I did not harm him, Bryce."

"If you had not captured me, Runt would still be alive!" he exploded.

Ryen stared at him. The anger, the hate, but mostly the pain etched themselves deep in the lines near his black eyes. Her eyebrows rose slightly in sympathy; her eyes went soft with understanding. "I wish I could bring him back."

His brows crashed together and he looked down at the boy in his arms.

The rain began in earnest then, quickly drenching them through to their skin. "I will not allow him to be buried in French soil," he said in a hushed voice. "And I will not let your efforts be for naught," he whispered to Runt.

Suddenly, Bryce jerked forward, slamming Ryen's shoulder with his, jarring her enough so that he could race by her and into the forest! Ryen recovered quickly. A quick glance into camp revealed that the fire was confined to two tents burning in the distance. She turned and immediately followed him into the trees and brush. She pushed through one row of bushes, just able to see his back as he disappeared into another set of thick foliage. The child in his arms and the chain around his ankle were slowing him down, enabling her to keep up with him. The rain pelted her face, the branches slapping her arms and tearing at her clothing. Ryen would not let anything stop her. He will not escape, she thought, an inconceivable fear rising inside her. He can't escape! I have to feel his touch again. No. Where had that thought come from? I have to get him to Father's castle.

She pushed forward, willing her legs to go faster. As the forest thickened, the darkness closed in around her, making it difficult to see. She reached out blindly, trying to avoid the trees that reared up to stop her. She could hear him ahead of her, hear the crunch of leaves beneath his booted feet, hear the bushes giving way as he crashed through them. Her heart pounded in her ears, her breathing hard and loud. She pushed her way through the foliage, desperately following his sounds. He must not get away, she thought. He can't escape.

Suddenly, his surprised cry echoed in the night!

The shock she heard in his voice rent her very being and she hurried forward, driving on, panic and horror rising within her. Was he hurt? Had one of her men found him defenseless in the forest and put a sword through him? The next thing she knew, the forest was gone and she was in the middle of the air, suspended far above a glistening pool of water! Then, she was falling, falling down into the blackness that waited to swallow her. Her scream was cut short as she crashed into water, plummeting beneath its surface. She pushed toward the surface with her arms and legs, but a strong current seized her and whirled her around beneath the dark water.

Suddenly, she was spit out from the water, erupting into the night air, sputtering and gasping for breath. Ryen was tossed about in the raging current, barely missing the rocks that stuck out of the rapids, their dangerous shapes lit only by an occasional bolt of lightning. Her hands flailed, trying to grab onto anything that rode the current with her. But the water was too fast, forcing her on. She fought for breath after breath as if the river were trying to devour her, wave after wave sucking her beneath the water.

The black rock rose without warning out of the murky depths and Ryen slammed into it, her back hitting the hard stone full force, sending a spear of pain shooting through her left arm. She opened her mouth to cry out, but the water assaulted her again, filling her mouth and making her choke. She tried to press her right hand against the pulsating ache, but the turbulent strength of the water kept her too busy fighting to keep her head above the waves. The water pushed her on and on until finally, after what seemed like hours, the waves of rapids stopped. For a moment, she floundered in the water, catching her breath. She was dazed and weak, her left arm burning where the rock had bitten into her tender flesh. The current, now slowed, pushed her on through the dark night and the darker waters. She was so tired, so very tired. How easy it would be to give up the fight, to let the river cover her head.

Then she spotted Bryce, far ahead of her, his dark shape shadowed by the lighter sky. He was atop a large rock, hanging onto the boy with two hands. The boy's legs dangled in the rushing water. There was a last surge of power through her limbs. With a kick and a quick arm movement, she tried to maneuver over to Bryce.

Then she heard it. The large roar of a waterfall! As she approached Bryce, the thunder filled her head. The water suddenly became stronger again as it dragged her on. She tried to fight against the new current, but as she drew closer and closer, she found she was moving forward faster than she was moving closer to Bryce.

Bryce maneuvered to the side of the rock, holding the boy's shirt with one hand as he held his other palm out to her. She saw his lips move but couldn't hear his words above the roar that filled her head. She reached her hand out, kicking with her feet as hard as she could. She was going to miss his hand. He was too far away!

Then he lunged forward and caught her hand. The water pushed her forward until her feet were dangling over the side of the falls! Below her, the mouth of darkness swallowed up the cascading water.

"Grab my hand!" he hollered, his words finally discernible above the thunderous sound of the plummeting water as it crashed and churned below her.

Ryen raised her left hand and grabbed his wrist, but the water made it slick and her hand slid away.

Her desperate eyes sought his again.

"Grab it!" he commanded.

Ryen raised her hand to his, but as she touched his skin, their hands slipped. She cried out as she was dragged toward the falls.

Bryce caught her fingertips, his face straining with the effort to keep their hold. Bryce was stretched out over the rock in his attempt to rescue Ryen and keep hold of the boy. One hand held the tips of Ryen's fingertips, the other gripped the boy's shirt as the water swept at his limp feet with a hungry pull. Bryce couldn't hold on to both of them.

Ryen saw Bryce glance toward the body of the boy. Anguish rent his face as he turned back to her. He cursed once—and released the boy to grab her wrist. She watched the small body tumble over the waterfall, gracefully, silently, as if it were jumping into the water below.

Bryce pulled her out of the water and onto the rock into his hold.

For a moment Ryen lay in Bryce's arms, holding him tightly, trying to catch her breath; she couldn't even open her eyes. The constant rain pelted her already wet face. Finally, she looked up toward his eyes only to find them gazing first to one side, then the other, scrutinizing the riverbank. Without looking at her, he asked, "Can you swim to shore?"

Ryen didn't reply. She knew she couldn't, now. Not without getting some rest. She began to shake her head.

A flash of lightning filled the sky as he turned his unwavering gaze to her. The eerie light cast his face in long shadows, making him look like a dark prince, as he was called. Under his probing gaze, she became distinctly aware of his strong arm around her waist, his legs resting beside her thighs, the intimate way he held her nestled between his spread legs. She looked away from him.

His soft, angry chuckle reached her ears. "Try to keep your desires under control, Angel."

Her gaze snapped up to his, fury burning in her eyes, but it was rage at herself that fueled the fire. Was she so transparent? "You misread me," she stated imperiously.

As he bent his head closer to her, she raised her chin. His eyes burned with disdain. "Then you do not need me to service you . . . now?" he wondered bitterly.

"Or ever again," she snapped. "I would just as soon throw myself over the falls."

"That can be arranged." His tone was serious, but he had not removed his arms from her torso. "Now, can you swim or not?"

She could hear the sound of the water sliding over the falls and crashing somewhere far below. The shore was so far. She knew she would not make it. Still, she wished with all her heart that she could, just so she could get away from this overbearing, conceited cur.

"Answer me before I throw you in," he commanded.

She straightened her shoulders. "I do not take orders from prisoners."

His chuckle sounded again in her ears, closer this time. "I believe it is *you* who are now *my* prisoner."

Ryen reared back, breaking free of his hold and turning on him. She lost her balance and began to tumble from the rock. Bryce's arm shot out and he caught her wrist, steadying her. She angrily pulled free of him, being sure to lean forward this time instead of backward, but a shooting pain flared up her left arm and her vision blurred for a moment. She fell into Bryce.

He caught her by the arms, leaning back to catch her full weight without going into the water. He felt her body go limp for a moment before she struggled to sit up. She put a hand to her forehead. "You're hurt," he said.

"No," she insisted weakly. "I'm all right."

"Stay here," he commanded, and slid out from beneath her.

As he stood, Ryen found that her eyes were drawn to him like moths to a flame. When lightning speared the dark sky, his body seemed to glow with a radiant fire.

He dived into the water, cleanly cutting it with his body,

and she watched as he disappeared beneath the surface of the black liquid only to emerge seconds later near the shore. Still, she saw the effort it took for him to battle the current. His powerful arms speared the water, his booted feet slamming down with each kick. Even with the power in his limbs, he was nearing the side of the falls. Ryen leaned forward, silently urging him on. What would she do if he didn't make it? Ryen watched, holding her breath, as he reached out to a bush and just barely missed it. He gave another kick, and she a silent prayer. Then his hand closed around a tree branch and he pulled himself closer and closer to the land until he was able to stand up and walk. He sat down heavily on the soggy earth.

Ryen sat back and closed her eyes, letting out a sigh of relief. He had made it. The thunder rumbled as if in warning, and Ryen glanced up again. The shore was empty.

She almost stood in her panic. Had he left her alone? Left her on this rock to die? Of course! What better way to escape? She berated herself. What was she thinking? How could she have let him go?

Her eyes scanned the shore. It was dark amid the bushes and trees that lined the bank, making it next to impossible to discern any movement. Damn! She stood up on the rock, judging the distance between the rock and the shore.

Something wet and sinewy brushed her cheek and she cried out, her hand brushing at it frantically. She heard a splash and looked into the river to see something slither away. A snake! she thought. It disappeared and she nervously searched the water for any movement. She had heard of snakes capable of eating a whole man. A shiver raced through her.

As she searched the waters, something fell over her head and dangled in her eyes like a piece of wet rope. Another snake! Ryen reached up and grabbed at it only to find that it was some sort of vine. She pulled it tight and followed it with her eyes until she saw Bryce standing on the shore, holding the other end. He signaled for her to tie it around her waist.

She closed her eyes in silent thanks.

Ryen did as he indicated, tying the vine tightly around her waist. Without warning, he yanked the vine hard and she flew into the river, sputtering and floundering as she hit the water! The current immediately seized her, casting her toward the falls. But there was another force tugging at her waist, pulling her toward the shore. It was the vine. Bryce.

She tried to swim, but her left arm throbbed every time she moved it. Finally, she felt the muddy earth of the shore beneath her feet. She staggered a few steps on tired, aching legs and fell to her knees on land.

Bryce began untying the rope at her waist.

Ryen whirled on him, pushing his hands away. "You could have told me to jump!"

He pulled back, stepping away from her. "You wouldn't have heard me."

She stood up, scowling at him. She tried to untie the vine, but every time she moved her arm, pain flared into her shoulder. She tried again, but the agony was too much. She turned her back on Bryce. "That doesn't give you the right to drown me."

"Drown you? I saved your life."

Ryen braced her left arm against the vine, holding it still, and managed to unknot it. She threw it down and turned to him.

"Your arm!"

"I'm all right," she said, even though she knew she was not.

A fork of lightning ripped the night sky, highlighting Bryce's wet body. With only leggings and one boot on, he might as well have been naked. Then, the light was gone and she could only see him as a shadow. She looked up into the sky, but could only see the leaves of trees, feel the splash of the rain.

"Do you know where we are?"

His voice came to her through the darkness and she turned to him. "I can't tell without the stars." She brushed back a strand of wet hair that fell into her face as she surveyed their surroundings.

"We need to find shelter," he said.

"We can build something with leaves and branches," Ryen said, her gaze sweeping the forest floor.

"We go down," he said. "There may be a cave beneath the falls."

Ryen's gaze snapped to him.

"Move," he commanded, and reached out to her.

Ryen stepped back, outrage on her face. "Don't command me like a common servant."

"I command you like a prisoner," he stated indifferently, and again reached for her.

She moved out of his reach. "I am not your prisoner. I fully intend to return to my camp . . . with you."

"Then your intent is wrong." His hand shot out and he grabbed her wrist, pulling her after him.

She fought him, struggling against his hold, her booted feet slipping in the mud. His grip was like a manacle. She could not break it. Then he bent, grabbing her around the legs, and hoisted her over his shoulder. Outrage consumed her and she pounded his back with a clenched fist. It was like hitting stone. He moved through the forest, headed downstream. The hill sloped, but his footsteps were sure and confident. She squirmed, and for a moment he lost his balance.

"Don't make me bind you," he threatened.

Even though his voice was low, she heard him over the pounding, thrashing sound of the water. Rage filled her body and she clenched her teeth, vowing to escape him. He came to a halt at the bottom of the hill and slid her to her feet. The falls shimmered before them.

Thunder rumbled high over their heads as Bryce began to enter the water. Ryen took a step into the dark water before she brought up her foot, hitting Bryce square in the middle of the back. He fell forward, into the water, losing his grip on her arm.

Ryen turned and bolted into the forest, racing past trees, the thought of escape fueling her tired muscles with renewed energy. Her feet slipped in the mud as she dashed through the darkness, skirting more trees, leaping over fallen branches. Then her anger faded and she faltered, slowing her pace. I need him, she thought. I must return him to camp. I must bring him back.

Her slowed pace was enough. She knew without even looking that he had already closed the gap between them. She heard his steps coming up behind her. That alone was enough to rouse her defiant spirit. Ryen surged forward, but it was too late. He had her, grabbing her around the stomach and picking her up off her feet. As she fought against his hold, twisting in his arms to hit his head, he turned her and roughly thrust her back into a tree.

Pain shot up her left arm and she whimpered, cradling her elbow as he slid her back to her feet. When he raised his head, his eyes were glowing with the reflection of the lightning. "You cannot escape me," he whispered, his voice deep and dangerous. "Not now. Not ever."

She could feel his body pressed up against hers to keep her in place, to keep her still, to keep her captive. Ryen could not tear her eyes from his. How he must hate me, she thought.

Then his lips were on hers, searing across them, demanding entrance. She was startled for a moment, raising her hands to his chest in a weak protest. Then, slowly, his lips fanned the flames within her until she relaxed and parted her own. He drove his tongue into her mouth, pressing his body against her, demanding that she yield. Ryen felt every stone-cut muscle of his strong, powerful physique against her own. The heat of his lips drained her will. She closed her eyes, letting the feel of his kiss wash over her, like the rain.

Then he pulled back. She couldn't move, didn't want the kiss to end, didn't want the tenderness to be over. When she finally opened her eyes, she found a mocking grin curving his lips, laughter in his eyes.

"Maybe I have been using the wrong method to control you," he whispered.

Humiliation, hurt, and hate raged within her. "No man can control me," she retorted, struggling to break free of him.

He pressed himself closer to her, stilling her vain efforts at escape. "Shall we put that to the test?"

"You cur," she snarled. "You have no honor. How could your king ever have knighted you?"

"I was wondering the same of you."

Angry eyes clashed as lightning ripped the sky and thunder rumbled in the forest around them. Bryce grabbed her arm and shoved her past him, toward the river. "Now, move," he commanded. "Lest I try to control you again."

Ryen stumbled, sliding to her knee in the mud. She quickly stood, and marched through the downpour to the river. There she came up short. The river was still, except for the crashing of water onto the rocks. Tiny drops of rain stung the pool. She heard his steps through the mud as he approached her from behind. She braced for a shove.

"Your arm is bleeding," he said. Ryen was surprised by the concern she heard.

She clutched the back of her left arm. There was a tear in her tunic and as she touched the skin, hot pain flared up her arm. She pulled her fingers back to find blood on them.

Bryce stepped up to her. She could feel his presence close to her. "It needs binding," he murmured.

Ryen did not reply. The blood on her fingers was a deep red, even though the rain diluted the color. She had to get him to take her back to the camp. Lucien would see to her wound.

Ignoring the throbbing in her fingers, she stepped into the river, heading for the falls. As she drew closer to the tumbling water, she could see that Bryce was right. There was a cave behind the falls. She climbed over the boulders, heading for the shelter. Behind the cascading waterfall was a small ledge, and she crept along it until she reached the entrance to the dark hole in the cliff wall. The cave was small, with room enough for only about five people lying down. Large enough for her and Bryce.

But it was dark and wet. The floors were damp, and water dripped from the ceiling. There was a chill to the place, and as she entered the cave, she shivered.

"Take your clothes off," he stated.

Ryen whirled on him. Was he going to rape her? Here? He was silhouetted against the water, a dark shadow standing in the entrance to the cave. She could feel his eyes on her.

He stepped forward and Ryen retreated until her back hit the stone wall. "I will not yield to you. I will fight you with my last breath."

He chuckled quietly, his laughter echoing through the cave. "I would not have it any other way." He reached out a hand to her shoulder.

Ryen found herself trembling as he lifted her wet hair and brushed it behind her shoulder. "Remove your clothes or I will do it for you," he said.

"I—I only have a chemise on," Ryen replied breathlessly.

"I've seen many before," Bryce answered. "Yours will be no different."

Angry, Ryen shoved him away. He stepped back, his eyes never wavering from her. She stared hard at him, trying to decide what it was he wanted. Unable to read those dark eyes, she raised her chin, narrowed her eyes, and lifted her tunic over her head. She stood holding the wet tunic, her furious eyes locked on him.

"Your leggings and boots, too," he commanded in a somewhat husky voice.

Ryen tossed the wet tunic on the ground and sat on a rock. She raised her left foot and pulled the boot off. Then she repeated the movement with her right foot. She stood and shimmied out of the leggings. These followed the tunic to the floor.

Bryce approached her slowly and Ryen dropped her hands from her hips. The gauzy material of her chemise was wet

and clung to her body as she moved. The sleeves of her chemise were mere straps and the waist was gathered. The skirt
was shorter than average, falling only to mid-thigh. She usually gathered the material and tucked it into her leggings, then
secured her tunic with a belt. The chemise was the one feminine item she could never seem to rid herself of. It protected
her skin from the rough wool tunics she sometimes wore.

Bryce stared at her for a long moment and she returned
his heated gaze with fury. Finally, he bent and picked up her
tunic, leggings, and boots and turned away from her.

Ryen watched as he spread out her clothing on the floor
of the cave. Then he sat on a rock. A spear of lightning lit
the cave and she saw his shoulder muscles bunch and release
with the effort of pulling his boot off. His dark, wet hair
hung over his shoulder. He paused for a moment, staring at
the chain around his other foot. Then he rose, staring at her.

Ryen looked back at him. His intense gaze burned into
her, sending shivers down to the core of her being. She was
suddenly very aware of how transparent her chemise was.
She crossed her arms over her chest in a futile attempt to
cover herself from his gaze.

A grin lit his lips. He stood and came back toward her.
Ryen felt her heart pound; tingles shot up her spine.

Bryce was much taller than she was, and more powerful.
Heat radiated from his body like the sun; she could feel its
scorching intensity burning from his eyes. She refused to
back away from the danger, refused to yield to him, even
though she might be burned, even when he raised his hand.
She would fight him, she vowed.

"Believe me, Angel," he said, in a strangely husky voice
that was filled with hidden anger. "My mind is on other
things."

Then he touched her left arm. Waves of desire crashed
over her and she floundered in a sea of passion, battling
against the waves that assaulted her, yet relishing the warmth

of his touch. Then his hand was gone and she was slapped back onto the shore of reality.

He raised his hand up between them and she saw the blood that stained his fingertips.

"Let me help you," Bryce said.

Ryen was shaken by his effect on her body and knew she had to separate herself from him before he infested her mind, as he had before. She pulled away from his touch. With the movement, pain shot through her arm. She tenderly clutched at it, feeling the wetness of the blood. "I don't want your help," she answered.

Bryce pulled back. He towered over her for a long moment, refusing to take his eyes from her. Finally, he withdrew to the other side of the cave.

Ryen sat down on a rock. She wasn't sure whether she was exhausted from the wound, the water, or her constant war with Bryce. All she knew was that she had to get back to camp . . . and she had to bring Bryce with her. Somehow.

Thirteen

Bryce turned to Ryen for the thousandth time. He watched the morning light wash slowly over her with the rising sun. Her makeshift chemise was almost dry now, the fabric conforming around the smooth, rounded curves of her body. She was still nestled between two rocks near the back of the cave, and he had not been able to get a look at her wound. He knew the cut was deep from the pool of blood that had collected near her hip. Why was she being so stubborn? he wondered. Would she truly allow herself to die?

He absently rubbed his chafed wrist. He had removed the rest of his chains during the night, working them off in the water only after he was sure she was asleep. He glanced out of the cave where the waterfall hid them, not really seeing what lay beyond. She was the cause of all his pain. It was true, he thought, thinking back on her words. She does look into my eyes and see hate, as she should. I should hate her. For daring to stand against me—the Prince of Darkness! For outwitting me. But most of all, for killing Runt. If she had not captured me, then he would never have been in her camp.

Again the boy's image rose in his mind's eye. That one lock of hair hanging before his blue eyes. Grief welled in his throat, closing it until he could barely breathe. He would have made a fine knight, Bryce thought sadly. A great knight. Now, I cannot even give him the burial he was entitled to. The waters claimed his body just as the fire and smoke stole his breath. Damn this French land.

He shook his head. I will build a memorial for him when I return to Dark Castle, he vowed silently. And I will bring his killer back to England, so she can suffer for killing him.

Again his eyes were drawn to her. She looked so pale and helpless, so small. How could she possibly command an army? he wondered angrily. Who would call himself sane and put a woman in charge of men?

Ryen shifted and her face contorted in pain, a soft groan issuing from her full lips. Bryce immediately stepped forward and knelt at her side. Her head was tilted to the right, a strand of dark hair falling over her cheek. Her left arm was turning a purplish color, and for a moment he wondered if it were broken, but he recalled her moving it and knew it was not. He had to see the wound, see how deep it was.

He moved closer. His knee brushed her thigh and Bryce glanced down. Her chemise had slid up her leg, revealing most of her silky white thigh. Intense desire flared inside him and he suddenly found that he could not move. Slowly he raised his eyes. The small strap at her shoulder had flopped down her arm to pool at her elbow. Who was this woman that she could evoke such powerful lust in him? His eyes slowly moved across her small waist, up to her breasts and to her full lips . . . a trail his hands longed to follow. Why did she trouble his thoughts now more than ever?

He reared back from her as if struck. Because he wanted to touch her. He wanted to see her arch beneath him, cry out in pleasure as their naked bodies entwined in the throes of passion. And yet he knew he could not. She was forbidden— an enemy. He could never show Runt's killer any pleasure. The thought should have been repulsive, yet it was all he could think of when she was close. I must not view her as a woman. I must see her forever as my prisoner, as my enemy.

He stood and moved quickly to the entrance of the cave. "Wake up," he called.

Her eyes snapped open, her hand instinctively reaching for the spot where her sword should have been, but all she grabbed was air. Her blue orbs focused on him with an alarmed expression.

"On your feet," he commanded.

She shot to her feet. "What is it? What's wrong?"

"It is time to move on," he said.

Ryen stood, dumbfounded. Then he watched as anger seeped over her face. She scowled at him for a long moment, then straightened with indignation and adjusted her sleeve, pulling it up over her shoulder.

Bryce steeled himself against his desire by concentrating on how much he wanted to kill her. To put his hands around her neck, and squeeze. These thoughts did nothing to lessen the lust in his loins. He knew he could never kill her. He narrowed his eyes. "Do not try to seduce me, or I will take what you offer."

Her mouth dropped open. "Would you rather my clothing fell from my body?" she wondered.

A dark smile curved his lips.

Her brows furrowed. She turned away from him only to have the pain consume her body. She clutched at her arm, keeping her back to him so he would not see her agony.

Bryce knew she was in pain, and some part of him wanted to go to her, but he did not move. She did not want his help; she had made that clear. He waited until she straightened, bringing the pain under control enough to face him. "You are a fool for not letting me see your wound. It could well become infected."

"Why would you care?"

Her question startled him. "I do not wish my prisoners to die," he stated. "As you did not."

"I am not your prisoner," she responded weakly, and sat on a rock.

Bryce's sharp eyes saw that she could barely move the arm. Perhaps it was not wise to argue with her when she was so pale . . . so weak. She sat in the dark cave, her head bent, her dark hair hanging in long curls over her shoulders. He watched that damn sleeve slowly slide down her arm again and wished that her clothes were dry. They had still been wet when he had scooped them up and carried them to a rock outside only minutes earlier. The damp cave had not allowed them to dry at all.

Finally, Ryen raised her eyes to him. "We need food," she said. "Or do you plan to starve yourself?"

Her words were as sharp as a sword's blade. "I have already eaten," he said, thinking back to the berries and roots he had gathered and eaten before sunrise. He watched disbelief flash in her large blue eyes and almost smiled. She had no way of knowing that he had picked enough for her, also. She shot to her feet and marched past him, but he caught her right arm. "Where are you going?" he demanded.

Her eyes narrowed, her back stiffened. "Take your hand off me."

"I have no intention of letting you out of my sight."

Her lip curled as her eyes swept him. "You think if I wanted to escape I could not?" She yanked her arm free of his hold. "You selfish English dog! I hold nothing but contempt for you."

"You would not talk to me thus if you were a man."

"Then you have known only cowards," she retorted.

What a fiery little wench. He thought back to the Wolf Pack for an instant, the way they stood up to the knights in the field. " 'Coward' is not a word I would use to describe the men I have known."

"No? How about pigs? Louts? Flea-ridden maggots?"

A chuckle churned from his throat. Ryen marched past him, but before she left the cave, he said, "There are berries and roots in the corner."

Ryen stopped and turned. He watched her hide her embarrassment under a coat of pride. Most women would have broken down in tears long ago, but not Angel. She traded insult for insult. She could easily fend for herself; but what was most impressive to Bryce was that she did not cower before him.

She straightened her shoulders, adjusted her sleeve, and moved to the corner of the cave where he had placed the food. She knelt, her small hands scooping up the red berries. As she brought a berry to her mouth, that accursed sleeve slid to her elbow again where a chestnut curl caught it. Her hair had dried in rebellious spirals along her back. Bryce found his eyes roaming over the path of her dark tendrils until they ended at the curve in her back near her waist where another curve began. Without her armor, she was a very pleasing morsel.

As if reading his thoughts, she straightened and looked over her shoulder at him.

Those blue eyes glistened in the light that shimmered through the waterfall, those full lips slightly parted. Bryce turned away from her. The little vixen! How could she have been a virgin with sultry looks like those, especially surrounded by all those men? He stepped quickly out of the cave. I cannot think of her like that, he reminded himself. She is a French prisoner. I must treat her as one.

Still, the image of that demure sultry look was engraved on his memory. Those lips . . . so tempting. So ripe for kissing. He wanted to feel them against his own again.

No wonder those weak Frenchmen had put the little wench in charge of their army! With fiery looks like those, it took all his will not to drop to his knees and pledge his eternal devotion to her. He reached out with both hands to the waterfall and scooped up some water. He doused his face and shook his head, trying to free himself of her spell.

"Bryce."

She was right behind him. Prisoner, he thought. Just a prisoner.

"I think my arm is broken," she said quietly.

"Can you move it?" he asked tersely.

"A little. Lucien can set it. I've seen him do it before."

Bryce's back grew rigid. Escape. Was her mind always working? He turned to her. Her eyes were large and alluring. "I can set it," he said. She withdrew until her back was against the stones at the entrance to the cave. He suspected by the way she moved it that her arm wasn't really broken.

Bryce stepped forward. He stared at her for a long moment. Her eyes were a dark blue that reminded him of the sky on a very clear day, her lips full and kissable. He lowered his eyes. Her chemise was almost translucent and he could see her dark nipples through the thin material, see the shape of her breasts. He swallowed in a suddenly dry throat and reached out to take her wounded arm gently into his hands. He felt her trembling and raised questioning dark eyes to her. Was she cold?

Wide, innocent blue eyes returned his gaze before falling to his lips. Carefully, without taking his eyes from hers, he slid the sleeve down her arm. The roar of the waterfall was nothing compared to the roar of passion that raged through his body. He stepped closer to her, his hot body touching the linen chemise, his hard muscles caressing the softness of her skin. He felt her inhale, pressing her breasts against his chest. A curl from her hair floated down the side of her face, and he reached up to brush it aside. Her arm was all but forgotten; his fingertips traced the outline of her cheek as he brushed the strand back. Her hair was as soft as her chemise. He ran his fingers through her mane of curls.

Crushing the waves of her hair in an iron grip, he suddenly pulled her face close to his.

She opened her mouth slightly and her sweet breath fanned his lips. Her body pressed close to his, hot and soft.

Then he was kissing her. His hot kiss moved across her mouth, demanding entrance, forcing her to yield to his expertise. When she parted her lips, he drove his tongue deep into the recesses of her mouth. It was like tasting a sweet berry. And he wanted more . . . so much more.

"Ryen!"

It was his passion crying out to her. God, how he wanted her.

"Ryen!"

Bryce broke away, glancing over his shoulder. Voices!

"Ryen! Where are you?" A search party! Had they been seen?

He turned back to her. She was opening her mouth to call out. He quickly clamped his hand over her lips. "Not a word," he hissed. His passion had suddenly cooled. Had she somehow seen them coming? Tried to distract him by saying her arm was broken? He glanced down at her arm. He had seen many limbs that had been broken in battle, but hers looked nothing like those. It had been a ploy, he was sure. He glanced back through the falls, trying to make out how many there were, but he could not see even one. He swiveled his head to the cause of all his problems. She was staring at him with those large eyes, eyes that only moments before had seduced him into wanting her. He would deal with her seduction later. He moved her back into the darkness of the cave.

"I won't be taken again," he promised her. "Not by the French."

Something flashed in those large eyes . . . something soft and tender.

"Ryen!"

Bryce braced himself for her attempt at escape, but she was motionless against him. He pulled her back into a dark corner of the cave. Again his eyes sought the entrance. He could see no movement through the waterfall, but they were out there. He glanced down at Ryen. She was staring at him, quietly, not moving. He frowned. If it were him, he would be fighting to free himself. Perhaps she realized a fight was useless against his strength. Perhaps she was smarter than he realized. Or perhaps, just perhaps, she had enjoyed the kiss as much as he had . . .

Cursing, he whirled her around so her back was pressed full against him, his hand tight over her mouth. God's blood!

he thought. I cannot enjoy the thought of such things. She is my enemy. I must see her delivered to England.

"Ryen!"

Even though the voice was growing closer, he didn't fear discovery. The falls would hide them well enough. The French knights didn't know they were here. But then Bryce tensed as a new thought struck him. The clothes! Good Lord, if they discovered the clothing, they would scour the area and there would be no chance for escape.

He pulled Ryen to the waterfall, holding her close against him, and stepped out onto the ledge. He peered cautiously around the falling water to the spot where he had placed the clothing between two boulders to dry in the sun. His sharp eyes searched the surrounding wood. No one was near the clothes. They were safe.

Then the branches on a nearby bush shook and parted as a French knight stepped forward, moving closer to the muddy shore of the river. He was looking down, searching the ground, flicking aside stones with his drawn sword. All he had to do was glance up over the boulder to his right and all hope for escape would be gone. Bryce held his breath. He had never prayed to God before, but he did now. The knight stepped closer to the rocks.

Ryen shifted her stance just then and her foot hit a small stone, sending it over the ledge and into the roaring water.

Bryce angrily pulled her back against the wall. His eyes fastened on the man. Had he heard? The knight was using his toe to brush aside a small plant growing in between the rocks. Bryce glanced down into the falls, following the path of the small stone. That's when he saw them, more small rocks littering the side of the ledge. He raised his eyes to the knight. Without releasing his hold on Ryen's mouth, Bryce bent and scooped a good-sized stone into his hand. He arced his arm over his head, sending the stone flying through the air. It landed behind the knight in the forest, cracking loudly against the trunk of a tree.

At the sound, the knight whirled, raising his sword before him. He hesitated for only a moment before moving off into the forest.

That had been close. Too close. Anger quickly replaced Bryce's relief. He pulled Ryen back into the cave and released her. His eyes narrowed as his gaze swept over her. "I will not be so easily distracted next time."

She turned her back on him. She could not be trusted, he decided. She would have to be watched. But could he watch her and keep his distance from her at the same time?

It was growing more and more difficult to convince himself that it was she who had killed Runt. She had not set the blaze. *But I would not have been in her camp if she hadn't captured me, and if I was not in her camp, then Runt would not have been there. So it was her fault! Still, if I had not allowed myself to be caught . . .* he did not like the way his argument was turning. Angry, he spun away from her to step onto the ledge.

Bryce's eyes scanned the forest. The knight was gone. There was no sign of any other men, either, although he knew they were still out there. He returned to Ryen and clasped her shoulder.

She pulled it free, wincing as her abrupt movement jarred her wounded arm. "You don't have to lead me around like an animal," she snapped.

His dark eyes narrowed. "I have no chains to bind your wrists; therefore my hands will act as such."

Her sapphire eyes danced darkly in the twinkling light that reflected through the shimmering waterfall. "Have no fear, Prince. If I chose to escape I'm sure that you, of all men, could easily thwart me. Your touch is not warranted, even by a mere slut."

His words thrown back in his face were unsettling. Yet the rich sarcasm with which she delivered them roused his anger. She was mocking him. Still, beneath the sarcasm he heard a hidden pain and he wanted to recant the accusation. Con-

fused by the emotions she fueled in him, he turned toward
the entrance. "Then follow me."

They had stopped only long enough to don their boots and
for Ryen to replace her wet clothing. By midday, her tunic
was dry, but the muddy forest and occasional puddles soaked
her boots through to her leggings. Her feet were cold and
her legs ached. Bryce had led her on, resting only once all
day. Ryen's pride would not allow her to request a break
from his grueling pace, so she had trudged along after him.

Finally, well after the sun had set, Bryce halted. Ryen's
entire body was numb. She was grateful for the pause and
leaned her back against the cool bark of a tree. When she
looked up at Bryce, his back was to her and the white light
of the moon washed over his shoulder muscles. His head
was raised to the sky for a long moment, his dark black hair
falling over his strong shoulders. Then he turned to her. "We
rest here for the night."

She waited only long enough for him to brush by her before she sighed and slid down the tree to the forest floor. As
soon as she rested for a moment, all her pains came to life,
culminating with a throbbing ache in her head. She put her
head in her arms, wondering what he was trying to prove.

Ryen raised her head slowly to see that Bryce was standing
not far from her, staring out into the forest. He was like a
statue, dark, impenetrable, and absolutely still. She wondered
if she would ever be able to break through his defenses. Not
that she wanted to, she told herself. She only wondered if it
were possible. He is my enemy, she thought, as he has reminded me so many times. I only wanted my father to see
what a great warrior I am to have captured the Prince of
Darkness. I do not care for him.

Then his head dropped in weariness and there was something in the movement that made her see him as a man instead
of a soldier. The need to soothe his tired brow brought her to

her feet. For some reason, she wanted to speak with him as if they weren't enemies, as if they were merely a man and a woman. Perhaps it was his refusal to speak to her throughout the day that made Ryen want his conversation, perhaps it was because he looked so miserable that made her want to comfort him. Whatever it was, she found herself moving up behind him and placing her hand carefully on his shoulder. She felt every sinew tense, felt the conflict that clenched his fists. "What?" he asked, tersely. "No dagger in your fist?"

Ryen refused to be baited. But she dropped her hand at his open rejection. "If I were an English warrior would you hate me so?"

He did not turn. "You are not English. And you never will be."

"Then why didn't you just slit my throat when we were alone in my tent?" she asked.

He turned then, his white smile glowing in the moonlight, his eyes dark and shadowed with anger. "I had no dagger."

She raised her chin. "Then kill me now."

His smile disappeared. "There is no need now. You are my prisoner." He stepped toward her. She retreated until he stopped mere inches from her. "Although I have every right, after what you did."

Fierce anger swept her. "I would never kill a child."

"And yet the fact remains that he is dead," Bryce snarled.

Ryen stared up into his black, hate-filled eyes. The boy was someone special to him, someone who had won his love. Suddenly she felt a flash of jealousy. "Who was he?"

The question seemed to startle him. Then his face tightened and his jaw clenched. A rage so powerful that it threatened to shake the very ground beneath his feet trembled through his body. "My son," he ground out.

Ryen's mouth dropped. Son, her mind repeated. How had the boy gotten into her camp? What in heaven was he doing in France? Why wasn't he home with his mother? Mother.

Even through her sorrow at Bryce's loss, a nagging question rose in her mind: did he have a wife?

She saw the bright agony that burned in his eyes, even through the fury. "Bryce, I—"

"Don't," he growled, and whirled away from her.

Only now did she begin to understand how deeply Bryce hated her. After a long moment, Ryen retreated to the tree she had sought shelter beneath. She sat at the base, pulling her knees to her chest and wrapping her arms around them. She watched him for a long time, standing only a few yards away, staring at the sky. She could not have felt farther from him had they been separated by a continent.

She knew nothing of this man. And yet his kisses rendered her helpless as no weapon had ever done.

A son, she thought again. The Prince of Darkness had a son. It had not been part of his legend. And somehow the thought made him more human. More touchable. Why would he bring his son, his most precious possession, into an enemy country? If she had children, she would see them safely tucked away in her father's castle.

Bryce came and sat at the bottom of the tree next to her. He did not look at her, did not face her.

After a moment of silence, Ryen couldn't help asking, "What was he doing in France?"

Bryce turned his head to her, angered by her obtrusive questioning. His eyes burned into her and she felt his anger as if it were a slap in her face. He rose swiftly and marched again to his post before the stars.

Ryen pursued him. "He was so young. Surely it was not your idea—"

Bryce whirled on her, his face a vicious snarl. "What better place for a son than at his father's side?"

Ryen was horrified. "In the midst of war?"

He stepped toward her, his look dark and dangerous. "And you know so much about my life. Tell me, Angel, would my son be happier enduring the ridicule and scorn of being a bastard, or fighting at his father's side? Was I to forsake my son, my only joy, when I believed the best place for him was with me?"

His voice softened suddenly and Ryen swore in the light of the moon she could see the shimmer of tears in his eyes. "He wanted to be an honorable knight, to fight a dragon, to lead an army for his king."

Ryen opened her mouth to answer, but Bryce smashed his fist into a tree beside him, making her jump.

"What honor is there in being dead?" he demanded.

She shook her head slightly now, at a loss for words. The only honor in death was the honor one received in dying. And he had died in the fire. "What was he doing in my camp?" she wondered softly.

"Trying to save me," Bryce answered bitterly.

Ryen stared hard at Bryce. The boy had returned for his father. Ryen knew grown men who wouldn't do as much. She turned to gaze at the stars, as Bryce had before her. There was honor in what the boy had done. And Ryen suddenly wished she had known him. "What was his name?" she asked.

"Runt," he replied hesitantly.

"He was a brave boy," she said. "You taught him well."

There was a long silence that stretched on. Finally, Bryce muttered, "I will miss him."

Ryen wished with all her heart that she could take his pain into herself so that he would not have to feel it. She wished that she could make the boy live. Suddenly, an image rose before her eyes. The figure of a very young boy with hair as dark as midnight brandishing a wooden sword at a make-believe dragon. Bryce's son. Ryen felt herself being swallowed up by his grief. She wanted to wipe away his torment with a caress, soothe his brow and his aching heart with her touch.

She turned to him to find his dark eyes looking at her, gazing at her so intently she could have sworn he saw through to her soul.

Ryen lifted a hand to place it on the arm at his side. His skin was hot beneath her palm.

Bryce reached out with his other hand and took her free hand into his own.

His palm covered her hand totally. She stared at his skin, marveling at the warm, secure feeling that spiraled up through her. When she raised her gaze to his eyes, her heart skipped a beat and she parted her lips as if to speak, but no words came out.

He leaned forward, and Ryen thought he was going to kiss her. Instead, he wrapped his arms around her back and put his forehead on her shoulder.

He needed her to comfort him, not to love him. She wrapped her arms around him and, sighing softly, rested her cheek against his soft hair. She closed her eyes, holding Bryce tightly.

"Isn't this a tender sight?" the French words intruded.

Ryen and Bryce separated instantly. Her hand went automatically to her waist, only to come up empty.

"A lover's rendezvous." The man stepped out of the shadows of the trees, dressed in a dirty woolen tunic, ripped brown leggings, and a torn black cape. He looked like a nobleman turned beggar, Ryen thought. She noted the confidence with which he squared his shoulders, the ease with which he had surprised them . . . as if he had done it before. He was a thief. She knew it instinctively. Her eyes searched the dark shadows of the forest for more men and for an avenue of escape.

There was movement to her right and she saw two more men rushing toward them. One was wearing only breeches with no shirt, and the other was very tall, with a thick black beard. She opened her mouth to shout a warning, but Bryce had seen them. In one movement, he had pulled her to his left and ducked as the shirtless attacker attempted to grab him; then he'd kicked the legs out from beneath the bearded man.

Ryen saw a shadow come alive. As he moved into the light

of the moon, she could see his pockmarked and scarred face sneering as he raised a fist and swung, catching Bryce in his already sore ribs. Bryce doubled over as Ryen moved forward to help him.

The thief grabbed her right wrist as she pulled it back to land a blow to the scarred man's face. With a tug he spun her around, crushing her against his chest.

"Aim for his ribs," a voice advised from the darkness, and Ryen looked to see a fifth man emerge from the cover of the forest behind Bryce. In the patchy moonlight that shone through the leaves of the trees, his small, beady eyes reminded her of a rat.

The bearded man drew back a fist and Ryen shoved against her captor's chest, but could not break free. She watched helplessly as the blow to Bryce's chin sent him sprawling.

Ryen twisted, trying to break free of the ex-nobleman's hold to get to Bryce. She gasped as the shirtless man, the bearded man, and the scarred man converged on him. He went down, buried beneath a sea of bodies and blows. Ryen held her breath for a long moment. Then the shirtless man flew off the group, landing with a thud in the darkness. A fist cracked the bearded man's jaw and he stumbled back.

Bryce rose before the scarred man like some sort of demon, his eyes glowing in the moonlight, his long hair a disheveled mass. The scarred man threw a punch. Bryce caught the blow in his open palm, closing his fist around it. His opponent quaked and gaped at the Prince of Darkness, his eyes going round with terror.

Suddenly from behind Bryce the man with the rat eyes charged, hammering down upon his ribs with his fist. Bryce stiffened as the blow hit him, then quickly recovered and whirled to face him. The man threw another blow to Bryce's wounded middle and Bryce staggered back, clutching at his sore ribs.

Ryen lifted her foot and brought it down hard on the ex-nobleman's toes. When her captor released her to grab at his foot, Ryen raced to Bryce's side. She pulled him back away from rat eyes.

A sixth man, trembling with fright, stepped from the cover of the trees to the ex-nobleman's side, offering any assistance. But the leader of the thieves pulled away sharply.

"Almost too late again, eh, Pigeon?" Rat eyes sneered at the cowardly new arrival.

Ryen cautiously eyed the group surrounding them as she held Bryce's arm. There were six of them, and even though she and Bryce were trained warriors, the numbers were not on their side.

"It's time we end this farce," the ex-nobleman stated.

The sound of metal sliding from metal rang through the night air as the scarred man and the shirtless man drew swords.

This doesn't help the numbers any, Ryen thought glumly, and moved closer to Bryce's side.

Fourteen

Bryce backed up a step, Ryen beside him, as the scarred man and the shirtless man approached, their blades gleaming in the light of the moon.

"You have fought well," the ex-nobleman said. "I only hope you know when to stop."

Bryce straightened, refusing to be goaded back any further. He knew that Pigeon had moved around behind them to join the bearded man. When Bryce stopped moving, they approached quickly, each seizing one of Bryce's arms to effectively hold him prisoner.

Ryen turned as if to move to his aid, but Bryce growled, "No." These men were not honorable. They were not knights, but a band of thieves.

Bryce's side ached from the constant blows and he bent slightly over, favoring it. He heard footsteps approaching behind him before one of the thieves kicked him in the back. Pain exploded through his side and with a grunt, Bryce fell to his hands and knees, arching his body to the side. The other thieves laughed. Bryce gritted his teeth.

"Stop!" Ryen yelled in French.

Bryce silently cursed as the ex-nobleman's eyes shifted to her. She would tell him now. Tell him that she was the Angel of Death and enlist their help to capture the Prince of Darkness. He would be taken prisoner once again. And the accursed thieves would do anything for a warm meal and a large sum of gold. Damn, he thought, and bowed his forehead to the ground.

But her next words brought his head up sharply. "What do you want? We have no gold. No jewels."

"That is too bad," the ex-nobleman replied, with a look that sent a fire of protectiveness roaring to life inside Bryce. Heat smoldered in the thief's eyes as he studied Ryen, and a hungry look spread over his face. Rage overtook Bryce like a wave, smothering every other emotion. His entire body tensed.

"We cannot afford to waste our time in useless mélees. Perhaps if you had told us in the beginning . . ." He shrugged. "We get something from every single encounter we have."

"We have nothing to give you," Ryen insisted.

"Oh, but you underestimate yourself," he said in a husky voice, and took a step toward her. The moonlight spilled over him, casting him in a strange white glow. His eyes, shadowed in darkness, looked evil.

Ryen flashed Bryce a quick look. There was alarm in her moonlit eyes as well as determination.

Bryce clenched his teeth and threw the ex-nobleman a hateful glare. "Touch her and you will die," he snarled.

Stunned silence filled the forest at his seemingly outrageous statement. Then a roar of laughter echoed in the night as each thief bellowed his disbelief.

"You would have to be a sorcerer to do that," Rat Eyes snickered.

Bryce felt the prod of a blade against his shoulder, but did not take his eyes from the ex-nobleman.

"Or be able to come back from the dead!" the shirtless man hollered.

"You've made a friend tonight, Jonas!" Rat Eyes chuckled.

The ex-nobleman grinned. "I guess I can never have too many."

Instinct relaxed his muscles as Bryce prepared for action. He knew exactly where each man stood without having to look. Pigeon and the bearded man held confident poses at

either side of him, Rat Eyes lounged behind him, and the
scarred man and shirtless man stood just before him with
swords. Not one of these men was the object of Bryce's
heated gaze. His eyes were locked on Jonas.

Then Bryce heard the crunch of twigs behind him as Rat
Eyes moved away from him and approached Ryen. Bryce
shot to his feet, only to be restrained again by Pigeon and
the bearded man.

"Come, girl, give in and it will not be so rough on you,"
Jonas hooted.

As he neared, Ryen lashed out with her foot, catching him
in the groin. Bryce knew a moment of satisfaction as Jonas's
assured stance crumbled and he fell forward to the ground,
groaning. Ryen whirled—right into the arms of Rat Eyes! She
struggled for a moment as he leered down at her before bringing her foot down on his toes. He cried out, grabbing his limb
and hopping around. Ryen put both of her hands together and
hit him hard across the face, knocking him back into a large
bush.

Bryce jerked forward, but the shirtless man pressed the
tip of his sword to Bryce's neck, stilling his efforts.

Pigeon roared with laughter, his gaze on Rat Eyes as he
squirmed in the bush.

Quickly Jonas got to his feet. Ryen turned, lurching away
from him, but he reached out, seizing her long hair, and
pulled her back to him. "Bitch," he snarled, gritting his teeth
from the pain that still racked his body.

Every fiber in Bryce's body froze as Jonas raised his hand.
When the blow struck Ryen so hard it sent her to the ground,
Bryce exploded. He easily pulled Pigeon, who was holding
his right arm, into the shirtless man, knocking the blade from
his neck. He lifted the bearded man and pushed him onto
the tip of the scarred man's blade, impaling him. Bryce
whirled in time to dodge a thrust by the shirtless man, who
had shoved Pigeon to the ground, and grabbed the thief's
arm, quickly twisting it back and up. A loud crack filled the

night air, and the shirtless man screeched in agony. The sword slipped out of the thief's hand to the ground, where Bryce swooped it up and rushed to Ryen. He extended a hand, and when she took it, he pulled her to her feet.

Pigeon scrambled to his feet, a blade in his hand. The scarred man pulled his weapon free of the body lying in a lump on the ground. Rat Eyes freed himself from the hand-like thorns of the bush and reached for his belt to pull his weapon free.

Bryce pulled Ryen behind him as the three men approached, spreading out around them.

"We can take him," Jonas assured his men.

Bryce's gaze locked on him. Instinct guided his movements in the dark, his senses heightened beyond intuition. He knew that Pigeon and the scarred man were preparing to come at him from their positions on his far left and his far right. Fools, he thought. They do not know who they dare stand against.

The shirtless man groaned in pain just before they rushed Bryce.

Bryce quickly stepped into Pigeon's raised sword, parrying the thrust and countering with one of his own that struck flesh. Before the man had completely fallen, Bryce whirled just in time to sidestep the scarred man's arc. His blade hit the earth and Bryce brought his sword around, meaning to slice the man in two. But the scarred man was quick, ducking Bryce's swing and whirling away. Bryce heard the whoosh of a sword and turned—

—in time to see Rat Eyes thrusting his sword at his chest! Bryce braced for the impact, instinctively bringing his sword up, knowing there was no time to block the blow. Then he heard it, the clang of metal against metal. The blade never touched his skin. It had been knocked away!

Ryen stood beside Bryce, a sword in her hand. She stepped in front of him to take Rat Eyes' next swing. Outrage engulfed Bryce. I should be the one rescuing her! he thought.

But he didn't have time to berate Ryen, as he had to shift his stance to block another swing. He backed up slightly and bumped Ryen. Despite them being embroiled in a swordfight for their very lives, Bryce felt a strong tingling race through him as Ryen's back brushed his. Even in the midst of battle, she stirs my soul, he thought. He crossed swords with the scarred man and intercepted a second swing from him before knocking his blade aside and thrusting, catching the thief squarely in the chest. As the scarred man slid to the ground, Bryce's eyes searched the shadows for Jonas. He spotted the coward turning and disappearing into the forest, a glint of a polished sword in his hand.

Bryce turned to glance once at Ryen. She was more than holding her own. Rat Eyes was breathing hard and was tiring under her constant and expert barrage.

Bryce took off after the leader of the thieves. He moved like a great wolf, silently, stealthily through the forest, his eyes never wavering from the figure before him. He easily marked his victim's way with the help of the moon's light. Soon, Jonas began to tire and a slow smile slid over Bryce's face as he quickly overtook him, circling around the forest in front of him.

When the thief reached the spot where Bryce waited, Bryce stepped out of the shadows of the forest like a phantom. Jonas reared back, raising his sword.

An anger so intense it threatened to sweep Bryce away flooded through him as his mind replayed over and over, the image of the man striking Ryen.

"Who are you?" Jonas demanded.

Bryce stalked closer as the man continued to back away. The thief opened his mouth to speak, but before he could utter a sound Bryce's hand closed around his throat. Jonas raised his sword arm, but Bryce grabbed his wrist, easily holding it at bay.

"I am the Prince of Darkness," Bryce sneered into his pale

face. "By striking the Angel of Death, you have forfeited your life to me."

Ryen rubbed her left arm. It was bleeding again. But she ignored the throbbing, her mind on Bryce. She glanced into the dark forest. Damn, she thought. I have lost him. He ran when I was defending myself. The ignoble lout. Still, her eyes nervously swept the shadowy trees and foliage again. Where was he? Was he hurt?

She heard a crackle of twigs behind her and spun, raising her sword, to face Bryce! Relief surged through her body and she visibly sighed. Then her brows furrowed as an irrational anger washed over her, drowning her relief.

He looked startled at seeing the sword at his chest, and just as the thought that she could take him prisoner jumped into her head, he easily pushed the sword aside with his bare hand.

"Where have you been?" she demanded.

An amused look crossed his face. "I didn't know I had to answer to you," he replied. He glanced at the sword she held.

Ryen looked down at it. He was going to demand she give it up. Not likely! she thought, preparing for a battle.

"We make a good team. Too bad we are on opposite sides in this war." He stepped past her to survey the body of Rat Eyes, which was sprawled on the ground.

She was so surprised that for a moment she could not move.

"You should keep the sword," he said. "If we come up against more thieves, it would be best if you could defend yourself."

Ryen looked down at the sword in her hand, dumbfounded. Didn't he want to hold her prisoner anymore? Was this his way of paying her back for saving his life? Or was this some sort of test? Ryen glanced up at him. The moonlight washed over the strong sinews of his neck, down his rippling shoulder muscles. I can take him now, she thought. I could club him over the head and drag him back to camp. Who am I fooling? I cannot lift him.

And I cannot hurt him.

The last thought stunned her.

A shadow separated from the rest of the shadows that surrounded them and moved swiftly past her. Before she could react, there was a dull thud and then Bryce was falling to the ground. Ryen whirled, bringing up her sword, to see the silhouette of a man standing beside her, a sword in his hand. His face was dark and Ryen peered closer, clenching the hilt of her own weapon.

"Good eve, m'lady," he stated in French.

Ryen gasped as she recognized him—her soldier who had captured the English spy! His white skin was hidden beneath a layer of mud, his clothing was all black. Jacques Vignon grinned and his white teeth caught and reflected the moonlight. "How did you—?" she began.

"I have been tracking you," he stated simply.

His unwavering gaze unnerved her and she glanced at Bryce sprawled on the ground. She wanted to go to him but could not with Vignon standing there.

"I have two horses not far from here," he said.

Bryce was her prisoner once again. The thought should have brought relief, but instead it brought a feeling of anxiety . . . something bordering on panic.

"Your brothers will be happy to see you."

"Yes. Well done," she murmured emotionlessly.

Fifteen

A constant pounding greeted Bryce as he opened his eyes. It took him only a moment to realize that the incessant throbbing was coming from inside his head. He tried to lift a hand to his temple to ease the pain, but his arm wouldn't move; his wrists were chained tightly behind his back! Bryce struggled to a sitting position using his elbow to prop himself up.

"Welcome back," a voice hailed from the darkness.

Bryce turned toward the voice in time to see Lucien stepping into the light of a candle that burned hotly inside the tent he now realized he was trapped in. Bryce's eyes narrowed instantly. A prisoner again, he thought. God's blood, the woman had no morals. She hit me over the head the instant I wasn't looking! And I gave her the weapon! Will I ever learn not to underestimate her? He silently cursed himself.

"By now you must realize how futile any attempt at escape would be."

Bryce's eyes shifted to Lucien. What did this blabbering idiot want? To gloat? He clenched his jaw.

"You can't escape from the French. We're far more intelligent than you."

"I would describe you in many ways, but intelligent never came to mind," Bryce murmured. He watched the hate and anger rise in Lucien's scowling brows and tightening lips. Slowly the man's face was turning red. Bryce knew that he would be smart to keep his mouth shut, especially with his arms chained. This man was like a coiled snake, ready to bite at the slightest provocation. "Fool was the first description I thought of," Bryce couldn't help adding.

"It's a shame you won't be returning to England to give your somewhat twisted portrayal of a Frenchman," Lucien sneered, "since you'll be burned when we reach De Bouriez Castle."

Bryce felt his fists clenching. All he had to do was say the right thing and this fool would be at his throat. It would be just what I deserve for trusting the wench, Bryce thought. A good thrashing would set my head straight.

The image of Ryen's argument with Lucien in the field immediately came to mind. He knew he could use her to goad this dog into swinging. "I wouldn't bet on it. Ryen will get me out of it . . . any way she can."

"What do you mean?" Lucien ground out.

Bryce could see the flames in Lucien's blue eyes, feel the heat of his anger. "I think you know."

The first blow hit Bryce's jaw and knocked him back to the floor . . .

"He could have hurt you," Andre stated from his bent position over her arm. "You were a fool to chase after him."

Ryen was seated on a chair in the middle of her tent, a small table with a basin of water beside her. Andre was carefully stitching her wound closed. The light of a candle washed over her skin like blood as he worked in the dark tent.

"I wasn't going to let him escape," Ryen insisted. She winced as he pulled a stitch through. "Not after everything I've gone through to capture him. Do you know what Father would have said?"

Andre stared long and hard at her. "You didn't want him to go."

"Of course not. He's England's most beloved hero. I would have been labeled the woman who lost the Prince of Darkness."

"That's not what I meant."

Ryen watched him in confusion. A feeling of unease spread from her lower stomach up her back to settle at her shoulders. Finally she turned away from him. "I don't know what you mean."

Andre finished up the stitch and tied a knot. "Oh, I think you do. Ryen, good Lord! You don't use common sense anymore, not where he's concerned. Do you know what's happening to you?" He stepped away from her, dipping his hands in the basin of water to wash off the blood.

"I got him back, didn't I?"

The flap swooshed open and Lucien entered, his dark features etched with concern. "Are you all right, Ryen?"

She glowered at Andre a moment longer before turning to Lucien. "Yes, I'm fine."

Lucien stopped short of taking her in his arms, but held her at arm's length and looked her face over, searching it as if for any sign of abuse.

"I'm fine," Ryen insisted.

"You had us worried to death," Lucien stated.

Ryen grinned at him and dropped her eyes. "I—" She paused, noticing a spot of red on his white tunic and raised a finger to it. "What's this?" she asked.

Lucien looked down and quickly stepped away before she could touch it.

Ryen glanced up into his blue eyes, slowly dropping her hand. When he didn't answer, understanding slowly filtered through her ignorance, followed closely by outrage. "You didn't!"

She bolted from the tent, running through the camp. Her knights stopped their arguing and chess playing to glance up as she dashed past them. She flitted around tents and leapt over sleeping men until she reached the prisoner tents. She startled the two guards who stood before one of the tents in mid-snicker, bursting inside to see Bryce lying on his side, curled up on the ground. His hands were bound behind his back. Ryen could see that his lip was bleeding, as was his nose. Her heart ached and she felt despair as she had never felt it before. She dropped to her knees beside him. "What has he done to you?" she whispered.

Ryen heard the flap open and whirled. Lucien entered the tent. She shot to her feet, her fists clenched in rage. "Get out!" she raged.

"He deserves much worse than that," Lucien snarled.

"Get out!" Ryen screamed.

Lucien's dark blue eyes locked on her, his jaw clenching. Then he spun, pushing past Andre, who was just entering the tent.

Ryen turned back to Bryce. She knelt and reached over him to undo the manacles that bound his wrists.

"Ryen," Andre called. "You shouldn't—"

"He saved my life," she said emphatically. She flung the shackles at Andre's feet. "You would think that would be worth something." She turned her gaze to Bryce, carefully pushing him onto his back. He groaned softly, his eyes fluttering open. When he saw her, his lip curled into a grin.

"Couldn't stay away?" he murmured with a soft chuckle.

"Don't talk," she said. "Get me water and a cloth," Ryen called to Andre, not taking her concerned gaze from the wounded knight before her. Ryen's hands skimmed Bryce's stomach, his already bruised ribs. Then her hands fluttered over his strong arms, his legs. Nothing. Nothing was broken. She breathed a sigh of relief and sat back on her heels.

"I don't think your brother likes me," Bryce said, smiling.

The light from the flickering candle cast a halo of light around his body, making it appear as if the fire were raging within him. She stared at him for a long moment before dropping her gaze.

Andre returned with a basin of water and some cloth, which he set at her side.

"You may leave us," she commanded.

"He's your enemy," Andre whispered. "Never forget that." Then he turned and went out of the tent, leaving them alone.

Ryen soaked a cloth in the basin of water, then reached for Bryce's face . . . and froze. The impulse to ease his hurt had been so natural. She had tended her father's wounds when she was younger and her brothers as she grew. But this, this was Bryce, not her brethren, not her family. He was her prisoner. Slowly she touched his face, carefully wiping the blood from his lip, and found that her hand was trembling. She willed the shaking to cease, but her fingers shivered as she began to wipe away more blood. As she drew the wet cloth across his mouth and watched his lips emerge, she recalled the fierce fire those lips ignited inside of her. She ran the cloth gently across his forehead, all the while staring at his handsome face, a face marred by the wound that she had inflicted, a bruise on his cheek and a light bruise above one brow. Her gaze dropped to his naked chest. It gleamed with perspiration in the candlelight, his stomach flat and lined with muscles. She wanted to touch him, to run her fingers over his smooth skin, skin that housed fire beneath its burning surface. Embarrassed and frightened by these forbidden emotions, she lowered her gaze unwittingly to the part of him that had joined them in their lovemaking. Even covered by his leggings, it was huge. She turned quickly away only to meet his dark eyes. Ryen froze for a moment. Did he know what she was thinking? She could not meet his gaze and dropped her eyes immediately, turning away to dip the cloth into the cool water. As she wrung out the wet cloth, she couldn't erase the feeling of embarrassment that racked her body.

I am bringing him back to Father, she thought. That is why I wouldn't leave Bryce in the forest. That is the reason why I ran after him. The only reason.

When she turned back to him, she saw the narrowing of his eyes as he regarded her and the change in his flippant countenance to a more quiet and pensive mood. Ryen reached up to the bruise that was turning a purplish color on his cheek. As she brushed over it with the cloth, she saw his jaw clench before he reached up and grabbed her hand, pulling it away from his face.

Her eyes locked with his black, mysterious orbs.

"I will never forgive you for the life of my son," he stated quietly.

Ryen dropped her eyes. It had not been her fault. But she understood that it was necessary to blame someone. If it would ease his pain, then she would take the responsibility. "I know," she murmured.

The silence stretched on in the small tent. Ryen knew the sounds of the camp were around her, the distant chatter of conversation, the *ping-ping* of the blacksmith's hammer. But she heard nothing but the beating of her heart. Then she felt his fingers squeezing hers and realized that he was still holding her hand. The grip became painful, and she looked up. His eyes were like an abyss, drawing her closer and closer. She felt him leaning into her and closed her eyes in anticipation of the feel of his lips on hers.

Suddenly the tent flap whipped open and Lucien stepped in. "Ryen, I think . . ."

Ryen jumped away from Bryce quickly, shooting to her feet.

Lucien stood for a moment without moving.

Ryen could not look at him. She knew he would read the guilt on her face. "Yes?" she asked.

Slowly, Lucien pulled his sword from its sheath, the metal hissing like a snake as it emerged from its protective covering.

Ryen stepped toward him. "What do you think you're doing?"

Lucien's turbulent blue eyes slashed past Ryen to Bryce. "Stand aside, Ryen!" he roared.

She found herself trapped between the two of them. "He is unarmed!" she cried. "Would you run him through without a chance to defend himself? It would not be honorable!"

His burning gaze shifted to her and Ryen saw resentment there. "Then you deny he was trying to rape you?" His voice was thick with rage.

It took a moment for the meaning of his words to sink in. Lucien had convinced himself that she would not touch an enemy. He was protecting her reputation! He was trying to shield the family name from scandal while achieving his goal of killing Bryce. Panic seized her and she had to fight to control the alarm that sliced through her. "Yes!"

"You stand there and tell me that what I saw was you *willingly* embracing our enemy?"

Ryen raised her chin in defiance, her eyes flashing dangerously.

"And if I had been a moment later, would you have parted your thighs for him, too?" Lucien snarled and shoved her roughly aside.

Ryen fell to her hands and knees. She heard Bryce say, "It will not be as easy this time. Are you sure you do not want to bind my hands again so I won't scar that pretty face of yours?"

Ryen heard a thud as Bryce and Lucien's bodies hit the ground. Their arms were entwined like those of lovers, but their faces were grimacing with hate. Bryce held Lucien's sword arm away from him as they rolled across the floor.

Ryen stood slowly, her knees shaking. She saw Bryce bash Lucien's hand against the ground until the sword jarred free. Lucien threw a blow to the side of Bryce's head that sent him flying.

As Lucien stood, Ryen launched herself at him, jumping onto his back, locking her arms around his neck. Lucien had always been able to beat Ryen in play fights, and this was no exception, especially since he wasn't playing. He grabbed hold of her tunic and pulled her over his head, sending her whirling into the canvas wall. "I would rather kill you myself than see you in his arms," Lucien threatened hotly, and spun away from her.

Bryce climbed to his feet and was greeted by a fist to the chin. He staggered back.

Ryen shook her head, trying to clear her vision. As Lucien went after Bryce, Ryen desperately threw herself at Lucien in an attempt to separate them, but Lucien pushed her back again. She felt herself falling, but Bryce's arms wrapped around her, and he gently set her out of the way.

Ryen saw Lucien dive toward Bryce and barely had time to shout a warning before Lucien hit, pushing him back away from Ryen. Bryce absorbed two blows to his ribs and one to his cheek before he threw a fist into Lucien's neck. The man went down in a heap of gags and coughs and Bryce pursued him to the ground, raining blow upon blow on his adversary.

Andre rushed in, flanked by two knights. They pulled Bryce from Lucien who lay unconscious on the ground, his face a mask of blood. Bryce was shaking all over, his fists clenched at his sides. He fought to free himself, struggling with the knights who held his arms. Two more knights rushed in to help subdue the Prince of Darkness.

Ryen knelt at Lucien's side. She could see his chest rising and falling with his breath. Thank God, she thought, before turning her eyes to Bryce. He was wild, twisting and turning in their hold, his strong muscles straining beneath their grips.

"Get him to the other tent. Chain him well," Andre ordered.

Ryen watched in anguish as they dragged Bryce from the tent, then dropped her head into the crook of her arm. Fool! she berated herself. What was I thinking, wanting him to kiss me here in the prisoner's tent? Lucien knows now. And he will do everything in his power to hurt Bryce. Or to kill him.

Sixteen

Bryce rode beside Ryen as the French troops entered the town, his wrists and ankles bound tightly by metal chains. Cheers deafened him. It seemed every villager had come out to welcome the army home, the loud, excited voices filling the air with an unintelligible babble. Women raced up to the mounted knights and handed them bouquets of brightly colored flowers. Small children ran ahead of the horses, shouting the knights' arrival. Still more people crowded into the already packed street to watch the procession.

And to watch Ryen. She was the pride of every villager there, showered with rose petals and looks of adoration as if she were some sort of heavenly goddess, some sort of . . . angel.

Bryce studied their faces, the love in the peasants' eyes, and the loathing when their eyes turned to him. He was amazed at how neat and clean the people were. Why, in the village of Dark Castle, there were children who could barely walk because they wore shirts ten times too big for them. And there wasn't a man who did not have the knee or elbow ripped on his tunic or hose. Bryce straightened. His people just worked harder. His eyes scanned the shadows of the streets. Every village had its beggars or lepers who lurked in the shadows, hoping for a handout. He scowled slightly, trying to peer into each doorway they passed, behind each barrel, but try as he might, he could see no beggars! Not one. They must be here somewhere, he thought. As his eyes swept over the people, he noticed something else. They all looked healthy, well fed but not fat. His mind thought back to his own people, women who could barely keep their clothing from falling off their thin bodies, old men who looked like skeletons. He scowled.

Bryce received his share of curses and laughter. As a cold stare in the direction of the offender would silence him, more laughter would assault him from a different direction. I was caught by a woman, he told himself. Twice! They *should* laugh. But this is no ordinary woman, he thought. She betrays me with a club to my head. All I wanted was for her to be safe from thieves and the like. The thought of what those men could have done to her makes me sick. Then, she hit me from behind. I should have expected as much. I was a fool to have given my trust so easily.

Fury rose in his throat like bile. He wanted to vent his anger on someone, something. He needed to release his rage, but the cold chains around his wrists restrained any strong action.

Unseen by Bryce, a small boy, standing farther up the narrow street, bent down and scooped up a handful of mud.

Bryce wanted to wipe the smirk from Ryen's face. She didn't have to enjoy his misery so much. He glanced up at the castle ahead. The drawbridge was lowered, the portcullis raised. The entrance was black with shadow—the mouth of a hungry beast, he thought, waiting to devour me.

The boy packed the mudball tightly in his palm. He tossed the compacted dirt from one hand to the other, impatiently fidgeting from one foot to the other.

Bryce shifted uncomfortably in his saddle. His thoughts raced from one possible escape to the next. He should try and make some kind of break before he passed under the sharp teeth of the castle's mouth, before he rode through the jagged shadows thrown by the portcullis, before he was trapped.

The boy grinned, pleased with his plan. He was going to get the bad man. Hit him right in the face. He had heard many stories about the bad man. Stories that made him tremble in the middle of the night. Stories that made him feel very afraid. The boy did not like to feel afraid. This would be his chance to strike back at the bad man. He packed the mudball even tighter.

Bryce glanced into the side streets, waiting for the right moment. But all he saw were throngs of people. Malevolent faces stared, casting hate and loathing at him from every direction.

The boy saw the horses approaching down the street, saw the bad man sitting on one. The fear came upon him like a tornado, swirling around him, making his fingers tremble as he clutched the ball of mud. He couldn't do it. The bad man would come after him.

Bryce was surrounded by the enemy. He had never felt more trapped in his life. He had never felt more desperate.

The boy suddenly realized that he was surrounded by people, by guards with weapons. The bad man *couldn't* get him. The guards wouldn't let him. He raised his arm, pulled it back and threw, hurling the mudball at the bad man. The clump of moist dirt sailed through the air, moving fast toward its target.

The boy's aim was off the mark.

Ryen turned as her eyes caught a sudden movement, but she didn't have time to react. The mudball moved straight for her face.

Bryce saw it coming a moment before Ryen. He reacted quickly, raising his hand to catch it.

The crowd suddenly grew very silent, thinking the Prince of Darkness was about to strike their Angel. A guard instinctively turned his weapon toward Bryce.

The mudball struck Bryce's palm square in the middle, hitting it with a resounding *smack*. He closed his fingers around it and pulled his hand back from Ryen's face.

Ryen stared in wonderment as Bryce showed her the flattened pancake of mud in his hand.

"I'm sure it was meant for me," he whispered to her, then let the mudball slip from his fingers to the ground.

Bryce watched her struggle with her emotions. Her full lips parted as if to speak, but then closed again. Not even a smile, Bryce thought with bitterness. But what had he expected? "We can't have you looking all dirty, now, can we?" he added.

Ryen's jaw tightened and she spurred her horse on, leading her army toward the castle.

As they approached, Bryce watched his hope of escape dissolve as the guards from the castle rushed out to greet them. With the guards came women who eagerly ran to embrace husbands or sons. The well-armed men closed in around his horse, separating him from Ryen.

The moat, he noticed as they crossed the wooden plank, looked deep and slimy. He wondered briefly if he could swim it.

Bryce was led under the portcullis, its jagged spearlike frame pointing at his head as his mount led him beneath it, threatening to crush him beneath its spikes. His horse stopped in the middle of a large square and he glanced up. Her castle was smaller than his by far. Its towers were rounded where his were square. But it was immaculately well cared for. He remembered once returning home to see that one of the inner courtyard walls of his castle had crumbled. It wasn't that there was no gold to repair it, it was just that his steward was a practical man, more concerned with keeping the castle properly armed and stocked with food supplies in case of a siege than with its appearance.

Bryce did not fight as hands reached up to pull him from the horse. Guards surrounded him and pushed him toward the castle. He paused before the great double doors to look back at Ryen. She was patting the neck of her war horse. Bryce wondered where her greeting party was. Had she no one to welcome her home? Then bitterness replaced his confusion. She did not even notice he was gone.

***

Ryen nuzzled her horse affectionately, burying her face in his white mane. He whinnied in response, nudging her shoulder. Ryen relinquished the reins of her horse to her squire and turned, searching for Bryce. His mount was empty! Ryen knew instinctively where he had been taken. The dungeon. The thought of him locked in the gloomy, damp, rodent-infested prison made her cringe. She started to follow, thinking to stop them from throwing him into such a horrible place. Then she stopped dead in her tracks. Such an act would border on treason. He was a prisoner. He belonged in the dungeon. Her heart sank to the depths of the castle with him.

Suddenly, she almost fell over as a little whirlwind ran into her, throwing her arms around her. "Ryen!" the voice cried in jubilation. Ryen pried herself free from the embrace and stepped back to stare into wide brown eyes.

"My Lord," Ryen gasped.

The girl giggled, covering her mouth with a small hand. "Please! Don't greet me as though I am a stranger! I couldn't bear it!"

Ryen could not catch her breath. Could this be Jeanne? Could this be her little sister? Have five years changed her so much I would not recognize her walking down a street? Ryen wondered. Jeanne had grown up. Her hair had changed from straggly straw to golden blond. Her skin was flawless, almost luminescent. Was this little Jeanne, the girl who teased me about masquerading as a boy? "You've changed," Ryen muttered.

"I should hope so! It has been a long time! I never have forgiven you for missing my wedding," Jeanne pouted.

"I'm very sorry, Jeanne. But I could not leave the siege. I tried to finish it before then. I lost twenty men rushing the castle," Ryen stated.

"Pooh. Don't talk of war. You know how it bores me. But the silks you sent from Paris. That was really too much, Ryen. They are so lovely that I couldn't help but make you a dress."

Ryen groaned inwardly. Dresses were confining and even

burdensome. "They were for you, Jeanne. You didn't have to go to the trouble—"

"It was no trouble at all. I've become quite good, you know. Jules says that I am the best dressmaker in all France. I believe he is exaggerating."

"You're happy, then?" Ryen asked sincerely.

Jeanne nodded and a dreamy smile touched her lips. "I am very lucky that Father allowed me to choose. He will do the same for you someday."

"Where is Father?" Ryen raised her eyes to scan the crowd.

"Oh, you know Father. He had to see Andre and Lucien."

Ryen's bubble of hope burst. "Yes. I know Father," she replied dully.

"Don't look so sad. Not on a day as wonderful as this. You've come home to us." Jeanne seized Ryen's arm and began to tug her toward the castle. "Come. You must meet Jules. And you really have to tell me all about this Prince of Darkness."

As Jeanne led her into the castle, Ryen was struck by the odd feeling that she was a stranger here. Nothing had changed, the entranceway was exactly the same as it had been, but there were little things that were proof of how long she had been away. She stopped at a tapestry hanging on the wall that depicted a knight with the De Bouriez coat of arms on his shield. She inspected the picture. An Englishman was dead beneath the foot of the knight. A stream of blood ran from the fatal wound in the fallen knight's chest. "When was this hung?" Ryen wondered.

Jeanne flicked her wrist, dismissive. "It's been here forever." She continued down the hall, holding her sister's arm tightly.

They rounded the corner and walked through the open doors to the Great Hall. Jeanne finally released Ryen's arm and ran across the great room to throw herself at a tall, dark-haired man standing near the fireplace, drinking and speaking earnestly with another man.

Ryen allowed her eyes to wander. The large room was in order, clean rushes on the floor, ale on the tables. A huge arced opening gave the room character and decoration. There were five entrances, each lit by two torches. The two arced entryways near the lord's table led to the upper levels and the bedrooms. The two opposite her led to the kitchens. Servants dashed in and out of the entrances to the kitchen and Ryen could smell the roasting duck. Some of the peasants she recognized, some she did not. But Ryen noticed with a bit of annoyance that all were casting glances in her direction. She stood forlornly in the doorway of the Great Hall, searching the hallway for any sign of her father. Finally, Jeanne and Jules approached her.

Ryen took a quick moment to study them. They were both fashionably dressed, Jules in a red jupon with elaborate gold leaf embroidery on the breast. The jacket just covered his hips. It is shorter than my tunic, Ryen thought with shock. Could this truly be the latest style?

Jeanne wore a houppelande that fell in voluminous velvet to the floor. The green material was secured just under her breasts by a brown belt. For the first time, Ryen felt out of place in full plate armor.

Jules extended his hand in welcome. Ryen clasped his arm in the usual warrior greeting and she noticed the surprise that splashed over his features for the briefest of seconds. She withdrew her hand.

"I am pleased to finally meet you," he said uneasily. "I have heard much of your brave deeds."

Ryen forced a smile to her lips and cast a glance over her shoulder, anxiously looking for her father. But the hallway remained empty.

Jules glanced at Jeanne. She set her arm on his shoulder. "Jules, you mustn't flatter Ryen. She doesn't like to be complimented. I have told her numerous times that she has lovely hair and she should leave it down. After all, if one doesn't make oneself pretty, one will not be betrothed to the man of one's dreams."

"I do not wish to be betrothed to anyone," Ryen answered. She turned her gaze to Jeanne to find her sister staring at her husband. For a moment, Ryen wondered what it would be like to live with a man she loved. Would Bryce gaze at her with the obvious adoration that Jules showed Jeanne? Where had that thought come from? she wondered, abashed.

Jeanne's smile was instantaneous. "You've always said that. But one of these days, the right man will come to you and you will not be able to imagine life without him. Just as I have Jules."

Ryen quickly looked away, down the hall. An uneasy feeling stirred in her stomach. Had she already found the man she wanted to spend the rest of her life with? She could not forget how it felt when he kissed her. And yet when she thought of a life with Bryce, perhaps a castle of their own, she knew it was only fantasy. He hated her. Still . . .

"Where is Father?" she asked, attributing the anxious feeling to her father's absence.

"He will be here," Jeanne said. "Come, sit by the fire."

Ryen cast one last look down the hallway. She could still hear the sounds of laughter and shouts of delight as wives, husbands, sons, and daughters found each other. But she did not see her father. He would find her. If she left the hallway to sit by the fire, he would still come. Ryen removed her leather gloves and followed Jeanne and Jules. A young girl appeared at her side, offering a goblet of ale. As Ryen shook her head, she noticed the fear and awe in the girl's large brown eyes before she bowed her head and backed away.

The Great Hall was emptying and Ryen knew it was because most of the servants were headed outside. As she reached the warmth of the fire, she heard his voice boom across the hall.

"Could that be my little Ryen?"

She felt utter joy race through her body as she turned. Jean Claude De Bouriez was strolling across the room toward her, his arms outstretched. Ryen's heart filled with happiness and she threw herself into those arms. Even though she wore armor, she could feel her father's strength as he crushed her in a powerful hug. She returned it wholeheartedly, reveling in the feeling of his embrace. Ryen knew he would be proud of her. She would look into his eyes and see the respect he had neglected to show her. He pulled back and his eyes bore into hers, a smile lingering in the depths of those brown eyes. Although so many things had changed in the castle, he hadn't. Those warm eyes were the same ones that had smiled on her all those years ago; those lips the same ones that had whispered words of comfort when she had fallen.

"Oh, Father!" Ryen exclaimed. "We took their army completely by surprise! We routed the English and—"

Jean Claude patted his daughter on the head, nodding patiently. "Don't worry yourself with matters of war now. You are home."

"But Father, I captured the Prince of Darkness," Ryen said, the happiness slowly draining from her.

"Yes. I know, child. And I look forward to seeing him."

"I made him tell me of King Henry and his English army. They are coming to France!"

Jeanne gasped and buried her face in Jules's chest.

Jean Claude scowled at Ryen. "You are frightening your sister. That is enough. Go change into proper clothing for our meal."

Ryen felt a hot flush creep up her neck to her cheeks. Jean Claude stood a hand's width taller than most Frenchmen, and even taller in Ryen's eyes. She did not move, and finally, Jean Claude turned his eyes from her to Jeanne. A serene smile inched over his lips and he said, "Jeanne, show Ryen the new fashions. Perhaps she would like to wear one of your dresses to dinner."

Jeanne relaxed, pushing aside her fear. "Oh, yes. You can wear the dress I made for you."

Ryen sank into despair. She allowed Jeanne to lead her across the room to the stairs.

As she reached the cold stone steps, she paused to look back at her father. His elegant blue velvet tunic shone softly in the lighting from the fire as he approached the door. Lucien was entering, and Ryen felt a moment of fear that made her falter. Would Lucien tell her father about her and Bryce? Even from this distance, she could see the bruises on Lucien's brow and cheek, his swollen lip.

Lucien looked around the room and his gaze halted on her. She saw his back straighten and felt the anger in his stare.

Her father's voice boomed across the room. "Lucien! You must tell me the tale of the capture of the Prince of Darkness!"

Ryen turned her back on them. Lucien would say nothing. It would only cause Father heartache and bring scandal to the family name.

"I hear tell that the English are approaching France," Jean Claude continued. Ryen mounted the steps, her heart breaking.

Seventeen

Jeanne fluttered around the room like a bird, preparing Ryen's clothing as if she were making a nest. She dashed to the wardrobe closet and pulled out a scarf, then flitted to the hand mirror on the table. She held the scarf to her neck and gazed at herself in the mirror, silently shaking her head. She put the mirror down and rushed back to the closet to toss the scarf inside. She began to rummage through piles of jewelry, holding a piece up to her neck and then, frowning, putting it back.

Ryen sat on her canopied bed and stared at her folded hands that lay listlessly in her lap. Why was he the only one she had never been able to stand up to? Why couldn't she demand the respect she deserved? Why had she allowed herself to be swept aside like so much dirt? Ryen groaned and ran her fingers through her hair, burying her face in her hands. Because he was her father!

"Why, Ryen, you haven't even begun to remove your armor," Jeanne said, sitting beside her, holding a sapphire necklace.

Ryen turned her face away from Jeanne. She wished her sister would leave her in peace just this once.

"Tell me how you captured the Prince of Darkness," Jeanne asked with a touch of sympathy in her voice.

Ryen separated her fingers to peek out at her sister in disbelief. "Jeanne, you couldn't even bear to hear that the

English were coming. How could you listen to the tale of how I captured Bryce?"

"Bryce?"

Ryen dropped her hands with a sigh. "The Prince of Darkness."

Jeanne was silent for a long moment and Ryen felt her gaze upon her. Finally, Jeanne patted Ryen's wrist and jumped up. "I will show you the dress. It will make you feel better."

Ryen stood, her jaw clenched. "I don't care about the dress!" Jeanne turned to her, and Ryen saw the hurt in her expressive eyes. She immediately regretted her harsh words and continued, more softly, "Not now. I want to know why Father doesn't listen to what I have to say."

Jeanne smiled. "Because you're a woman."

Ryen sighed. It was the one thing in her life that she couldn't change.

"Don't be sad, Ryen. We'll have a grand time. Did you know that the Duke of Le Mans is here?"

"No."

"We're in very good company tonight. The Count of Sens is also here. They came to see the Prince of Darkness. It appears the fiend has a reputation."

Ryen's brows furrowed. "What do they want with him?"

Jeanne shrugged her dainty shoulders as she turned to sort through her wardrobe closet. "All I know is that Father is planning a . . . well, a sort of reception for him. I must tell you that I am very excited to see him. They say that a mere look from him will sentence a maiden's heart to burn—"

"A reception?" Ryen wondered quietly.

Jeanne placed her hands on her hips as she turned to Ryen. "Really, Ryen. You must learn to listen when others speak. Yes. A reception. Apparently, Father has some sort of surprise in store for our enemy."

Ryen felt a cold chill of dread creep up her spine.

* * *

Ryen was a vision of femininity as she stood at the bottom of the stairs that led from the bedchambers to the Great Hall. And she hated it! The full chemise and heavy velvets of the dress's skirt swirled about her legs and inhibited her steps. She felt constrained by the cotte Jeanne insisted she wear beneath her chemise, to accent her feminine attributes, as she put it. The cotte was so stiff, Ryen felt as though she could not bend. But she had worn it for Jeanne. Then, her sister had helped her don the long, dark blue gown. Ryen was appalled at how it was fitted to her body, not at all like her tunics. And the wide, open neckline was so . . . revealing! Over this, Ryen wore a sideless surcoat made of velvet that had armholes that reached to her hips. Jeanne had giggled when Ryen swore the thing was going to fall right off her body! Jeanne fastened the surcoat to the gown with buttons that were hidden beneath the fur that edged the neck and armholes, assuring Ryen the buttons would hold it on.

The final straw was the headdress. Jeanne had pulled out this monstrous-looking thing with horns! Ryen had reared back and absolutely refused to wear it. She insisted that her hair be left down.

With that small, single victory, Ryen stood at the bottom of the stairway, wanting desperately to run back up into her room and put on her tunic and leggings. A gentle shove from Jeanne behind her urged her into the Great Hall, where all the guests had gathered. As she stepped into the room, voices began to subside as eyes turned toward her.

The longer Ryen stood, the longer the silence stretched. She was sure it was this horrible dress that drew their stares. It made her look weak.

Finally, Andre approached. "There's a man I want you to meet, Ryen." He gently guided her by her elbow into the gaping mass of people and the talking resumed, although at a quieter pitch.

Ryen halted and leaned close to him, whispering, "Does this dress look foolish?"

Andre paused to glance at it, then up at her face. There was confusion in his eyes. "What else would you wear in Father's castle?" he asked.

Andre himself wore a houppelande of dark green velvet that fell in folds to the floor, gathered around his waist by a black belt. Ryen felt the cotte confining her and wished she had insisted on wearing a houppelande. Finally, she swiveled her head around the room. "Why are they staring at me?" she wondered.

"They are impressed that you captured the Prince of Darkness."

"They thought I couldn't do it."

"Well, you must admit that most women would shiver and faint before your Dark Lord."

Ryen glanced at him, noticing the stress he put on "your." She briefly wondered if Lucien had spoken with him. She chose to ignore it, casting a glance at Jeanne, who was leaning in to hear a whisper from an elderly woman dressed in an impeccable white sideless surcoat. Jeanne raised her eyes to Ryen for an instant and there was pain in them, then she quickly cast her head away and answered the woman, who blushed and straightened before quickly moving away.

They hated her, Ryen was sure of it. She wasn't what they thought a woman should be—quiet, married, and obeying every word her husband said.

Ryen glanced at the nobles. As her eyes scanned them, she caught an occasional curious glance before the watcher noticed her look and quickly turned away.

Disappointment raced through Ryen. This time was supposed to be different! She had captured the Prince of Darkness, a task no one else had managed to accomplish. A task to make anyone the envy of all France. Yet still they looked at her as though she were some sort of freak.

Andre propelled her through the room again. The tables were being set up for their meal and the guests were congregating in the middle of the Great Hall. Most of the lords and dukes were in the middle of the room. They were dressed in richer clothing and would not be seen speaking with the common man.

When Ryen neared the men gathered around the hearth she recognized many of them from her army. Captain Navarre was there in a yellow tunic and black leggings. He nodded to her. "M'lady."

She returned his greeting and moved past him. Finally, they came to a tall man whose back was to them.

"Excuse me," said Andre, and the man turned. He had a kind face and understanding eyes, yet lines of pain etched his forehead. He appeared almost as old as her father. "Lord Merle? I'd like you to meet my sister, Ryen."

"The Angel of Death! How nice to finally meet you," he said enthusiastically. He extended his hand, palm up, but then stopped cold. He appeared panicked for a moment.

Ryen immediately grasped his arm near the elbow, in the soldier's fashion. His face seemed to relax as he returned her shake. "It's very nice to meet you, too, Lord Merle. You have traveled far."

"Yes. I have been here for nigh on three days. I could not miss the opportunity to see the Prince of Darkness," he replied. Ryen frowned. Dismayed at having apparently insulted her, he hastened to add, "Of course, I am delighted to meet you also. You are one of France's greatest warriors. I am honored to be in your presence." He bowed slightly.

Ryen forced aside her fears for Bryce and smiled brightly.

Andre interrupted, "Lord Merle was just telling us about the rumors that Henry of England has reached France."

"Yes, indeed," he murmured, his voice dropping conspiratorially. His demeanor turned serious as he said, "I have it by good and reliable sources that the English king is laying siege to Harfleur as we speak."

"He's in France?" Ryen asked. That would mean battle soon. *I should gather my men and leave for Harfleur,* she thought. No. I must wait until we are summoned. Perhaps we are needed elsewhere.

Someone grabbed her arm and she pulled it away before turning. Her father stood behind her. He was dressed impeccably, as always, wearing a houppelande of red samite that swept to the floor. It had a high collar that rose to cover his neck and dagged sleeves lined with sapphires. "Sirs, my daughter is needed elsewhere. Please excuse us," he said, and led her away by her elbow.

"What is so important, Father?" Ryen wondered. "Is it an emissary from the king?"

"Oh, no, my dear," he chuckled. "I think it is important for you to speak with the right sort of people."

"Lord Merle seems like a nice man," Ryen replied as they approached the group of noblemen.

"If you prefer people with small lands." Her father stopped and turned to her. "You must be seen with more important men. You must think of your future, Ryen."

Yes. Her future! To advance her career she must associate with men of power and wealth. And these were the noblemen, the arrogant, pompous men who knew nothing of warfare, but reveled in the grandeur of it. It was the soldiers who won wars and sieges for them. But she also realized that to be an effective commander, she must have influence with both sides.

Her father led her to a small man with hair the color of the ground on a muddy day. His rich red velvet houppelande waved like a flag as he spoke with a great flourish of his hands. It wasn't until they were closer that she saw he had the leggings of his plate mail on beneath the gown. Ryen had to force a smile down. In her experience, the only ones who displayed their own armor in this fashion were the ones who never involved themselves in anything more strenuous than barking commands from a tent far from the heat of the battle.

He was speaking with another man who was taller but just as thin. His padded blue samite jupon came to his hips. Ryen looked down to see that his black shoes extended nearly two feet beyond the tips of his toes, ending in points. Ryen almost giggled. She must remember to be careful not to step on them.

When they saw Ryen and her father approaching, the first man broke off his conversation to hail them. "Jean Claude!" he called. "How wonderful it is to see you again. And how is that charming girl of yours?"

"Jeanne is fine. She is here, you know. You must remember to speak with her," Jean Claude responded. "She was always very fond of you."

"And I of her," he said, his eyes coming to rest on Ryen. She couldn't help but be repulsed at his small form. He appeared physically weak and very vulnerable, and there was something about his eyes that reminded her of a sick hound. She smiled anyway.

"Ryen," her father said, "This is our dear friend Count LeBurgh. Michel, this is my other daughter, Ryen."

He extended his hand and Ryen clasped it tightly around the lower arm.

Surprise and disgust washed over his face and he quickly withdrew his hand. "Yes, well . . ." he murmured, offended at her greeting.

Her father scowled heavily at her. Well, how did they expect her to act? By lowering her eyes and batting her lashes at him? When she had finally gathered her wits and was ready to put the situation to right, the count continued, "This is Duke Armand Caron."

The duke smiled warmly at Ryen. His pale visage seemed to color with life at the recognition. "Yes, of course. The Angel of Death. I must say, the pleasure is mine."

He did not offer a hand, but bowed slightly. Ryen was grateful.

Count LeBurgh nodded his head and raised his nose to the ceiling, peering at Ryen down its slender line. "Ah, yes. The female warrior."

Even through his air of haughtiness, Ryen saw something

akin to apprehension flash through his dark eyes. Her legend, she knew. Everything he had heard of her was crowding his small brain. She wanted to smile, but could not embarrass her father with such open mockery. Ryen glanced at her father. His heavy eyebrows were drawn down in a pout of disapproval.

"Not just a warrior," Duke Caron went on. "But the knight who brought us the Prince of Darkness!"

"Yes," the count sighed. "He must be a pitiful character, after all."

Ryen felt her blood beginning to boil at the insult. "I beg your pardon, sir. But I am sure you would not wish to come face to face with him on the field of honor. I have been told that in—"

"Ryen, please," Jean Claude murmured. "These men do not wish to hear of the Prince of Darkness now."

Ryen frowned. Wasn't she supposed to impress them with her stature as a knight? To ensure them that their gold would not be wasted if they chose to add men to her army?

"Count LeBurgh, are you not looking for a wife?" Jean Claude continued.

Ryen's mouth fell open. Surely her father did not bring her over here to auction her off to these stuffy nobles like a prize stallion!

"On the contrary," Duke Caron interrupted. "I would be most thrilled to hear of the Prince of Darkness. After all, this is why we are here. Please continue."

Ryen watched with dread as her father placed an arm around Count LeBurgh's shoulder and steered him away. She saw the count glance at her and then nod and shrug at something her father was saying.

She wanted to run to her room, or the stables, or the practice yard, strip off this horrible, confining dress, and don her tunic and hose, swing her battle sword like she were cutting off someone's head . . . or nose.

Instead, she turned back to Duke Caron with the most

charming smile and related the bloody events that had led
to the capture of the Prince of Darkness . . .

Bryce followed the guards up the stairs. The red glow of
the setting sun stung his eyes as the light attacked him
through the windows in the hallway. Two guards walked in
front of him, two behind. They had dragged him out of the
dark dungeon after what he guessed had been two days and
two nights, not saying a word as to where they were taking
him. His wounds were healing and his side did not hurt quite
as badly, but he was weak from lack of any substantial food.
The chains that bound him in the damp cell had not allowed
for much movement, either; his muscles felt stiff and tight.

Bryce thought he recognized the tapestry that hung on the
wall as they passed and believed he was back in the original
hallway they had ushered him through when they first
brought him inside the castle.

The guards stopped as they reached a massive set of oak
doors, and pushed them open to reveal a room crowded with
people. It appeared Bryce was a popular man in France. Expectant eyes fell on him and the room grew silent. Like the
pickets of a fence, numerous armored guards were stationed
on either side of a wide path that stretched from Bryce to
the other end of the hall. Bryce followed the walkway with
his eyes. The rich colors and textures of the people standing
along the path made it clear that these were nobles. At the
far end of the room, Bryce saw a man dressed in rich blue
velvets seated in a chair. Beside him, a woman stood dressed
in a deep maroon that reminded Bryce of blood. He found
himself fascinated by the dark, rebellious curls that hung
over her shoulders, held out of her face by a simple, if somewhat outdated, headband. Somehow, it seemed that her curls
were waiting to spring free. Her figure was flawless and
Bryce found himself imagining her warming his bed. Then
his gaze was captured by the blue of her sparkling eyes, like

two great gems shining across the room. His dark eyes widened in astonishment as he realized who the woman was.

Ryen had discarded her tunic and leggings—her men's clothing—for a gown of crimson velvet. The fabric clung to her breasts and hips, accenting them with a femininity he knew all too well. And yet, not well enough. His dark eyes moved hungrily over the curves of her body. Desire flamed through his body stronger than it had ever before. He knew that he must possess this woman. He must have her again. And this time, he would see the passion in her eyes and drink from her honeyed lips. He would hear her beg for more.

He was shoved forward by a guard behind him and tripped over his ankle bindings. As he fought to right himself, he heard contemptuous snickers from the gathering. He immediately straightened, throwing daggers of hatred at anyone who dared look him in the eye. Of course they laugh, he thought. I am bound and they are safe. These people have the same look in their eyes as the French villeins in the streets, Bryce thought. They'd be just as amused to see my head in a basket.

He stopped only a few steps from the man seated in the chair. Bryce's black eyes swept the man from head to toe. He was old. In the Wolf Pack, he would no longer lead. The younger men would have challenged his authority many years ago. This society was weak to allow a man such as this to continue to rule. His clothing suggested his life was soft and pampered. Gentle. But as Bryce's gaze traveled up, he noticed the man's eyes. There was an edge to them. A hardness. A challenge. And Bryce knew that the man's appearance was deceiving. Bryce saw the grin that twitched the old man's wrinkled lips.

"So," the man said, "you are the one the legends tell of. You do not disappoint."

Bryce did not reply, but cast a quick, wary glance at Ryen to see that her face was empty of emotion, before his gaze slid back to the man.

"I am Jean Claude De Bouriez. Lord of this castle—and Ryen's father," the old man said.

It was not Ryen's castle! Bryce kept his surprise hidden behind a mask of indifference. Her father. Bryce found himself intrigued. He would have liked to speak with the man privately, to know why he allowed his daughter to be a warrior, but he knew this would never happen. "King Henry sends you his greetings," he remarked.

"I rather doubt that what you say is true. Henry barely knows who I am."

"On the contrary. You are the Angel of Death's father. Her legend is almost as great as mine."

"Such arrogance! Why, if I were in your shoes, I would be most meek. All of France favors my daughter. And you *are* in France, my dear boy."

Bryce threw Ryen a harsh glance. How could she throw me to these vultures?

Ryen returned his gaze with her chin raised, without a glimpse of remorse. She came down the two steps of the dais to stand before him and Bryce found his anger subsiding as his desire flamed anew. The velvet clung to her hips like a second skin and he longed to run his hand over the smooth material, to feel the curves beneath it.

Bryce heard the silence in the hall. Even the nobles were quietly watching as the Angel of Death, clothed in her crimson gown, stood before the Prince of Darkness, bound hand and foot, naked from the waist up. Bryce could not deny the malevolence that flowed around them, that threatened to sweep him away. Yet with all the interested stares and the gaping from the mass of people behind him, Bryce felt something else. There was something that bound him and Ryen, something far more powerful than hate.

For just a moment Bryce thought he saw regret in her eyes before they hardened again, a wall of stone rising between them.

"Kneel," Jean Claude commanded. "Kneel to me so that

all of France knows how *loyal* you are to this country." His
words dripped with mockery.

A murmur rose through the hall before deadly silence engulfed the room again.

Bryce's face stiffened. His answer was directed at Ryen.
"Never."

He heard a rustle of clothing and glanced at the dais long
enough to see Jean Claude place a hand on Lucien's arm,
holding him back. Bryce noticed with some satisfaction that
Lucien's right eye was colored by a fading black and blue
ring.

Jean Claude's eyes shifted to Ryen. A scowl crashed down
over Bryce's face and he, too, looked at Ryen.

"Kneel to him," she whispered urgently. "Please." The
sound of her voice kissed his ears, but the words stung them.

Bryce would have done anything for her when she used
that seductive tone. Anything except pledge his fealty to a
lord other than Henry. "I cannot. Not even for you, Angel."
He saw disappointment flitter across her face, and beneath
that, hurt. It angered him. How could she ask that of him?
Would she kneel to another so quickly?

Lucien shook off his father's hand and stepped up to the
edge of the dais. What was he planning? Bryce wondered. To
kill me here? Lucien inclined his head toward a place behind
Bryce. Had he gotten someone to help him? Is he still afraid
of me even though I am chained? Bryce turned to see a man
step forward, his dark eyes glaring at Bryce. "M'lord?"

Jean Claude sighed. "Yes, Sir Pierre?"

"I request the right to challenge an enemy of France."

Jean Claude nodded.

Sir Pierre turned to Bryce. "I challenge you to a joust."

Bryce grinned, pleased that he would finally get to exercise
his sore muscles. "I gladly accept." He had never lost a joust
in his life and he knew this bumbler would be no match for
him.

"Such bravado," Jean Claude exclaimed.

The people parted as a second man on the opposite side of the floor stepped forward. "I do challenge you, also."

Bryce hesitated, but only for a moment. He turned to the second challenger. This one seemed more of a fool than the first. Bryce's laughter was dark. "Had I known I was such a popular fellow here I would have come of my own accord." He swept a deep, exaggerated bow. "I am flattered, good sir, and I do accept your kind offer."

The second man frowned, insulted, but returned the bow and sealed the duel.

Behind Bryce, Lucien's voice boomed over the crowd, quieting it. "And I. I challenge you, also. To a joust to the death."

Bryce wiped the grin from his face. He could feel the hatred emanating from Lucien's body like heat from a flaming hearth. But he expertly masked his flash of apprehension and bowed at Lucien. "You do look like a man tired of living."

The room grew quiet again and Bryce fought off the prickling of danger creeping up his back. He addressed Jean Claude with a mocking smile. "Out of all your *brave* knights there are only these three swine who would challenge the Prince of Darkness? You make it far too easy."

The silence, and tension, in the hall grew.

"Are there any others?" Jean Claude quietly asked the assemblage.

Bryce heard the sounds behind him and he had the feeling that he shouldn't look. But he had to. And when he did, he wished he hadn't.

Every sword in the hall was raised in challenge.

Eighteen

It was ridiculous, Ryen thought, as she paced before the stone window in her room, the shutters open wide to the night sky. She did not feel the chilly air as it tried to wrap its frigid fingers around her bare shoulders; her body blazed with a blanket of anger. Her nightdress swooshed with each furious step. This was not a joust! It was murder. Knights did not behave in such an unchivalrous manner. What had happened to her men? To her brother? Had the war turned them into barbarians?

Ryen paused to stare into the black night. She wondered how she had come to see things so differently than Lucien. There was a time when everything was black and white, right and wrong. Now that was not so. Or maybe it was. But Lucien's right was suddenly her wrong.

A forbidden thought came to her. It would be so easy to go to Bryce . . . to . . . She crossed her arms over her chest as a sudden chill swept over her, peppering her arms with tiny bumps. What had happened to right and wrong? Life was so clear before. England was the enemy of France. But she was not France. Just as Bryce was not England. He was a man.

A man who had made her feel beautiful.

He is *my* prisoner, she rationalized, and I will not let a bloodbath take place. She whirled and stormed to the door, determined to see her father and put a stop to this lunacy. She threw the door open and stopped instantly when she saw Lucien leaning casually against the stone wall opposite her room, like a lazy lion waiting for its prey. He was flipping a small pebble in his hand.

Ryen's hand fell to her side, clenching into a fist.

"I thought you might be up late," he said quietly, tossing the pebble aside.

Tingles shot up her spine, and she had the oddest feeling of being trapped. As she walked into the hallway, the dim orange-yellow light from two flickering torches washed over her. "What are you doing here?" she wondered.

"Giving you one last chance," Lucien replied, a shadow flickering across his face. "I knew you'd fail."

Her eyebrows drew together in uncertainty.

"You see," Lucien continued, "I knew that when the jousts were announced, you would react as you have."

"He is my prisoner and I will not tolerate—" Ryen began, but stopped as she saw Lucien take a threatening step toward her.

"That's not the reason you protest."

"No, I protest because this is not a joust. It's a massacre," Ryen said. "He cannot fight all of France!"

"Have you no worry for your knights? Or your brother?" His voice was oddly quiet, menacing in its softness. "After all, he is the strongest knight in England. Their *best* warrior."

"You are mad," Ryen snapped in disgust, too angry to make him see the insanity of the situation through words of calm. "I won't let you joust. I won't let you fight him."

"But we *want* to. You cannot deny our right, Ryen. You cannot deny the Code of Chivalry," Lucien said.

"A hundred knights against one is *not* chivalrous!" she roared.

"Why do you defend him? Let him die in battle."

"I would, if it wasn't a slaughter!" Her eyes were dark with rage, her brows knit, her teeth clenched.

Lucien's eyes narrowed. "I don't think you would. I don't think you *could* sit there and watch him die. You love him, don't you?"

"No!"

Lucien stepped closer. "You do. I've seen the way you watch him."

"No!"

Closer still. "The way you light up when you see him."

"No!"

"The pain in your eyes because you know it's wrong."

The truth in his words stunned her. Yes. She did love Bryce. Why hadn't she seen it? How had it happened? Her hands began to shake and she had to turn away from him. She could not let him see how true his accusations were. But Ryen knew that turning away was confirmation enough and she hated herself for not being able to look him in the eye.

"I'm not going to let you interfere with this joust. I *will* kill him, if only for your sake."

"Lucien, no. You mustn't—"

Before Ryen realized what was happening, Lucien had seized her wrist in a grip as hard as iron shackles. He had pulled her halfway across the hall, toward her room, before she came to her senses and dug her bare heels into the floor. But his strength was too much for her and he easily flung her into her bedchamber, then closed the door with a resounding thud.

Ryen caught herself before she lost her balance and stood absolutely still as images of her childhood came gushing into her mind: Lucien, a boy of twelve, hair the color of golden daffodils, dragging her to her room; she, a small child of eight, crying and screaming helplessly. She remembered his hard grasp bruising her wrist as he tossed her like a rag doll into her room. And finally she remembered the chilling sound of the bolt sliding home as the door was locked.

Then, Ryen realized that the soft clang that echoed through her mind was not a memory! She ran to the door, pulling at the cold metal handle. The door did not open. Disbelief, followed closely by a feeling of dread, consumed her as she yanked frantically on the handle. Again it did not budge. She slammed her fist into the wooden door, screaming, "Lucien! Let me out!" She shook the handle again but the thick wooden door did not budge. She pounded on it, her heart aching with desperation, her mind filling with despair. "Oh, God," she mumbled, a light sweat making her brow shimmer. She raced to the window. Through the moonlit shadows of the night, she could see no movement below her. The moat was calm, the forest beyond was still. She was at least fifty feet up and the walls were too slick for scaling. The ledge had a curving lip so even if a ladder were laid against the castle wall no one would be able to gain access to the room. It had been specifically chosen and designed by her father so no man could scale the walls and whisk her away.

She *had* to get out. Bryce's life was in danger! The joust was at noon and she had to stop it! They wouldn't even allow his wounds to completely heal before they slaughtered him.

Ryen whirled, her gaze darting about the room, stopping on the impenetrable stone walls, the useless arced windows and then back to the bolted door. I did not find a way out before. Why should now be any different? she wondered. Her breath came in rapid gulps, as if the room were being sucked dry of air. A feeling of strangulation grabbed her and she put her hands to her throat.

She had to get out! But how? There isn't a way. She had looked and looked! You fool, she chastised herself. You were a child! Now you are a warrior. But what am I to do? Splinter the door? How do you win battles? she asked herself. Through brawn? No. Through brains. *Think!*

Ryen paced the room, trying to come up with a plan while attempting to calm the anxiety that was racing through her veins. Her gaze scanned the room again. She ran to the window, again a child of eight, and looked down the sheer wall of the castle. Like an abyss, the descent to the brackish water gaped before her. To a child's mind, the curving banks of the moat seemed to frown up at her.

Ryen turned away to scan the room once more. Her eyes

came to rest on the fourposter bed. Even if she tied all the blankets together, they would not be enough to reach the ground. It was too far. If the fall to the ground did not kill her, and through some miracle she reached the moat, it was unswimmable. Of course, Ryen knew this. For she had thought of it before.

Again she ran to the door, retracing the steps she had taken as a child. She pounded on the wood, screaming to be let out.

But no one came.

The tears of a scared little girl welled in her eyes. They would leave her here . . . she would never get out. She would grow old and die in this room, and no one would know.

Slowly, Ryen's hands clenched. Stop it, she told herself. Stop it. There *is* a way out of here. And it's not setting fire to the room, as you thought those many years ago. And it's not jumping into the moat.

Ryen forced herself to calm her breathing and walked quietly to her bed. She sat down, her chin bowed to her chest. There is a way out, she told herself

The blind fear of a child was slowly replaced by a burning anger. How dare Lucien lock me in here, Ryen thought. I will get out. And I will get him back.

Calmly, Ryen considered the door. It was much too thick to break down. But it was not the door itself that was her barrier. It was the bolt. She knew how a bolt worked. Somehow, she had to breach the bolt.

Ryen shot to her feet, ran to her bureau, and dug through the silk dresses and gauzy chemises as if they were old rags. Finally, after parting rich bolts of material, she found it. After all these years, it was still there, buried deep beneath layers of Spanish satin and Venetian velvet. Carefully, she picked it up and held it before her eyes. The candlelight sparkled off its long, thin metallic surface. It was a hunting knife, Lucien's pride and joy. She had taken it from him many, many years ago, after he had hidden a dead fish under her pillow. She grinned. He had never found it. It served him right for his prank.

She raced to the door and carefully inserted the blade between the frame and the door. She bit her lip, squinting as she pushed the blade up. All she had to do was slide the bolt back and push the door open. Slide the bolt back, she told herself. Careful. She felt the weight of the bolt on the blade as she slowly tilted the weapon to the side. But it slipped and the bolt slid heavily back into place with a thud. Ryen clenched her teeth. Getting angry won't move that bolt, she told herself. Her jaw relaxed and she took a long, slow breath before making another attempt. Lift the bolt, move it back. Back. I have it, she thought. It's working! Then, scrape. The bolt shot back into place. Silently, Ryen cursed. Lift. She wiped the perspiration from her brow. She pictured the bolt in her mind. Slide it back as if opening the door. Ryen bit her lip gently as the bolt eased back. Further. Don't pull yet. Not yet. Her hands shook with the effort of holding the bolt open. Then, Ryen yanked on the door. It swung open and she nearly stumbled back into a bedpost. Elation coursed through her like the dawn bursting through the night sky.

Ryen kissed the blade and quickly glanced down the hallway, half expecting Lucien to still be standing guard before her room.

The hallway was empty.

Ryen returned her gaze to the knife, staring at it for a long moment, knowing that she should bring it with her. The picture of her brandishing a knife before her brother seemed ridiculous. She would never hurt him, no matter what, and he knew it. Finally, she tossed the dagger back into the room.

Ryen closed the door behind her and slid the bolt back into place, just in case Lucien happened to pass by while she was gone. Swiftly but quietly, she made her way down the hallway toward a stairwell, her bare feet making no sound. The stairwell should be empty at this time of night.

The cold stones stung her feet as she descended, but she

ignored the biting chill, watching and listening for any movements.

"Are you ready for the joust?"

Ryen came to an immediate halt, the momentum of her forward movement almost hurtling her down the rest of the stairs toward the source of the voice. She pulled back into the shadows of the staircase, pressing her back against the wall.

"I can't wait to slice him in two."

"You must leave some for me. Not all the fun can be yours."

Ryen was certain the second voice belonged to Lucien and she pushed herself further against the wall until she could feel the stones against her skin. A chill twisted up her spine. She must not be found. Least of all by Lucien.

A chuckle sounded from below. "If you wanted to put your lance through him, why didn't you challenge him first?"

There was a rustle of clothing before Lucien's words, whispered and furious, ascended to Ryen's ears. "If you kill him before I have a chance, I will have your head!"

Then, footsteps echoed in the Great Hall as one of them walked away. After a moment, the second, softer pair trod the same path. Slowly, she took one step and then another, until she could see the Great Hall stretching out before her. Lucien and the other knight were gone, and the hall was strangely empty. Long flickering shadows cast by the torches on the walls stretched across its length.

Ryen dashed around a corner and ran down the stairs. It was dank and foul-smelling below. But the quick pounding of her heart pushed her on, down another narrower set of steps, to enter the dungeon from the rear entrance.

A small, dark corridor stretched before her, ending at a barred door. She approached slowly, her bare feet slushing over cold, wet stones. Where was the guard who was stationed there?

When she reached the door, she was surprised to find it ajar. Ryen stood on tiptoe to peer through the bars. The room

beyond was black and she could make out no movement. Foreboding snaked through her body as she pressed the tips of her
fingers to the door's slimy wood and it opened slightly. She
pushed harder and the hinges groaned as it swung inward.

She stepped into the dark room and the hem of her nightdress snagged on something. Fearing a rat, she lashed out
with her foot only to hit cold metal. Chain mail. She took a
quick step back, startled by her discovery. The guard!

Suddenly, Ryen saw a shadowed movement. Before she could
react, a hand clamped over her mouth, stifling her gasp. Instantly, another hand seized her slim waist and pulled her back
to a wall of muscle. Ryen's heart raced as she cursed herself
for being so stupid. She felt the sharp edge of a dagger press
into her chin, stilling any struggles before they could start.

"Not a word," a husky voice whispered.

A shadowed form stepped before her and looked out into
the hallway. "It's clear," the second man said as he moved
aside.

Ryen felt herself being shoved forward through the dark
hallway, to the stairwell, the first man right behind her.

A familiar chuckle caressed her ear. "Come for the escape,
Angel?" The hand about her waist loosened to roam upward,
caressing her skin. "Or perhaps for another romp?"

Bryce. Embarrassment blazed through her body, fueling
her courage, and she began to struggle. When the dagger's
tip was again pressed into her chin, she stiffened.

"Oh, no, my little Angel," the voice stroked her ear with
rich sarcasm. "We cannot have you calling attention to our
venture."

Relief and anger surged through her as he half carried,
half dragged her up the narrow stairs. He turned and continued up the next flight. Her bare feet scraped against the
ragged stones because she couldn't keep up with his large
strides as he took two steps at a time.

At the Great Hall, Bryce paused. Ryen tried to catch her
breath, but it was difficult while his hand was over her

mouth. They began crossing the large room. Fools, Ryen thought. How can they hope to escape through the Great Hall—shadows sneaking across the vast expanse of hall, metal glinting in the torchlight?

"Someone's coming," the other man stated.

They pulled back into the shadows of the stairway that led to Ryen's room. She heard a soft whistling accompanying the echo of the footsteps as the person approached from the hallway, the way Lucien had disappeared.

At that moment, a soft clang of rustling chain mail came from the entrance that led to the castle doors. It was the guards from the tower! And they were coming straight for them.

Ryen jerked, trying desperately to move toward the stairs that led up to her room. But Bryce's hold was like a shackle, binding her movements. If only he would follow her!

Ryen yanked her head away sharply, hitting Bryce in the cheek. He mumbled a curse as Ryen gasped, "The stairs." After a second's hesitation, Ryen felt his hold on her loosen and she grabbed his arm, moving a step up the stairs. She tried to pull him, but he was like a wall to move. He had to come of his own will. It was the only way he would be safe. In the soft glow of the wavering torchlight she beseeched him with her eyes.

Bryce moved unexpectedly, almost running her over. He bounded up the stairs, her wrist in his tight grip. Bryce paused at the top of the stairs and gazed down the hall. It was empty. Ryen hurried down the hallway, leading them to her room. She opened the lock and then the door, and let them pass before closing it quickly behind her. She breathed a small sigh of relief. Bryce was safe for the moment. Together, they could collect their thoughts and formulate a plan of action.

"It's a trap."

Ryen whirled, facing her accuser. It was the first time she had seen the man. And she disliked him on sight. His eyes were filled with loathing, his lip curled in a sneer. His clothes, the ragged trappings of a common beggar, were mud splattered and stained. Ryen looked closer at his eyes and saw an alert sharpness behind the loathing; this man was no beggar.

"Where is the escape route?" he demanded. "The witch has led us into a trap."

"Yes," Ryen answered bitterly. "You see thousands of my men crawling from beneath my bed to apprehend you."

The man raised the dagger he held in his hand and stepped toward her menacingly.

Bryce's strong hand rose in a motion to halt.

Ryen's gaze shifted to him. The candlelight washed over his features, bathing him in a soft, golden light. The scar on his cheek was ghostly. "This is no trap, Talbot," Bryce murmured.

As Ryen watched, his eyes shifted and she followed his gaze to the bed that stood invitingly near. She blushed and could not help turning back to Bryce. His dark, smoldering eyes raked her from the tips of her hair to her feet. Ryen crossed her arms over her chest, suddenly aware of how transparent her nightgown was.

"She must die," Talbot said grimly, approaching Bryce.

Bryce tore his gaze away from Ryen to look at Talbot.

"Vengeance for all those she killed in camp."

Bryce turned away from him. "I know."

With shaking hands, Ryen grabbed at the handle of the door. She had to escape! But a hand beside her head held the door in place when she attempted to pull it open. She tried once again, but the door didn't move even a hair's breadth.

Ryen closed her eyes and leaned her forehead against the door, prepared to feel the dagger's death bite on her throat.

It never came.

Instead, a gentle hand upon her upper arm guided her away from the door. Numb, she could not lift her head to look at him, sick with the realization that she would betray her country to help him and in return he would kill her—the Prince of Darkness would slit her throat. She had given everything to him. And he would give her death.

Bryce turned her body and seated her upon her bed.

"Here," Talbot said.

As Bryce left her side, Ryen looked up. Talbot stood at the window, gazing down. Had they seen something she had missed? There was no escape there—just the dirty jaws of the moat fifty feet below.

Bryce nodded. "Good."

Both men's gazes then shifted to her. There was a moment of indecision, and silent tension poisoned the air. Without a word, Talbot raised his weapon and came toward her.

Ryen squared her shoulders and raised her chin. She was a soldier. She would not cower before death.

"I'll do it," Bryce said.

Talbot faltered. He did not take another step, but his dark eyes probed Ryen as she sat on the bed; her eyes dared him to finish his task.

"Go," Bryce commanded.

Talbot took two steps backward before turning to Bryce. He replaced his dagger in its sheath.

Bryce did not take his eyes from Ryen. "I will join you in a moment."

Ryen watched incredulously as Talbot mounted the inside ledge of the window. She rose, crying, "You'll be killed!" as Talbot casually stepped from the window. She ran to the vacated ledge and quickly peered over the side to the moat below. In the light just before sunrise, the gray waters of the moat appeared tinged with red. There was no sign of Talbot.

Ryen's gaze swept from shore to shore, but the banks remained empty. Panicky, she turned to look at Bryce. The muscles in his right arm were twitching and Ryen's gaze followed the corded sinews to his hand. He was turning his dagger over in his palm, again and again.

Her gaze shot up to lock with his, expecting to see hate. But strangely, his eyes were shadowed with sadness.

"You knew that I would not kneel to your father." His tone was resentful as he stepped toward her.

Ryen began to back away from him. She saw a dangerous look hidden beneath the sadness. Yet she could say nothing to defend herself. She felt naked before his probing eyes, as if he could reach into her soul and pull out her deepest secrets. He continued to dog her steps, until the backs of her knees hit the bed.

Bryce stopped short before her.

Ryen's chest rose and fell with her breathing, the tips of her breasts barely brushing his chest. Was he going to kill her now? Her blue eyes blazed defiantly, staring into his dark, unfathomable orbs.

Suddenly, he tossed aside the dagger and seized her, pulling her close. "I could never kill you," he whispered. "I could never mar this flawless skin." His fingers caressed her neck, creating a line that an assassin would draw.

Ryen gasped at the gentle touch that sent spears of flame shooting through her body.

"Why did you come to the dungeon?" Bryce demanded. "Tell me why you risked your life to see me."

His closeness was overwhelming, and she could not think logically. All she wanted to do was to throw her arms around his broad shoulders and kiss him.

"Damn you, tell me," he grunted, shaking her.

He pressed his thighs against hers and Ryen could feel his passion through his hose. Ryen groaned softly. He wanted her!

He pushed the proof of his desire even closer against her. "Is this why?" he asked in a gentler tone, the heat of his gaze soldering her to the spot.

"No," she choked out. She tried to pull away from him, but he would not let her go.

Bryce cupped her face gently. He stared hard at her, as if battling emotions deep within him. "Come with me," he finally said.

Surprise rocked through her. He wanted her with him! Did he love her, as she did him? Did he want her like she wanted him? Then her elation dissipated and was replaced with doubt. Yes, he wanted her. As his prisoner. She dropped her gaze and shook her head. She could feel his stare burning into her skull.

"I'll find you again." His voice was filled with confidence. With promise.

She wanted to believe him. With all her heart she wanted to fall victim to his promise. But she knew that the war was more powerful than either one of them, the hate between their countries too strong. Suddenly, a feeling of loss filled her and she looked into Bryce's black eyes. The impact of Bryce escaping hit her full force. She was afraid she would never see him again, afraid that the place he had warmed in her heart would now turn cold. Anguish filled her entire soul.

Bryce reached up with his hand, caressing the softness of her cheek. He slowly lowered his head, giving her plenty of time to pull away.

But she did not.

His lips moved over hers, coaxing her to open to his exploration. Ryen parted her lips, and his tongue plunged into the recesses of her mouth. His strong arms encircled her, giving her no room to retreat.

Fear jolted Ryen and she shook her head frantically, suddenly more afraid of him than she had ever been before. She yanked her head back, pressing her hands against his chest. She had dreamed of him touching her with the softness and gentleness of a man who loved her and now that he was doing just that her powerful response to his caress was overwhelming. The ecstasy he was giving her with each stroke of his hands and lips was so wonderful that it made the pain of his leaving too much to bear. "If only . . ." she whispered. The barrier that separated them was huge, impassable. It was not a man. It was not a country. It was honor. It was allegiance. These were things they could not fight with a sword. She lifted a sad gaze to him.

He stared at her with an intensity of promise and anguish

that she felt through to her heart. She shivered under the searing look, wanting to curl up to him, wanting to kiss him, wanting to go with him, but knowing she could not. Beneath her open palm, she felt the hammering of his heart, racing as her own did until they seemed to beat as one.

Suddenly, there was a pounding at the door!

Bryce pulled away from their embrace and looked toward the door, every muscle in his body coiled tightly.

"Bryce," Ryen whispered, turning her sight to the door. She absently reached for his hand. She would accept whatever judgment was levied against Bryce upon herself as well. They would face it together. But when the warmth of his hand failed to engulf hers, Ryen glanced back.

Bryce was poised on the ledge, his dark gaze locked on the moat below.

Panic flared wildly inside of Ryen. "No!" she screamed, launching herself toward him. He would kill himself!

Bryce glanced up at her. In his dark eyes, Ryen saw a softness and a longing that she had never seen before. He lurched for her wrist, but suddenly stopped cold. He looked at his hand as if it were a traitor before he slowly drew it back. A rueful smile barely tipped his lips. Then, before she could reach him, he was gone.

Desperately, she ran to the window. The waters below rippled slightly, but there was no sign of Bryce. Ryen waited, holding her breath until she had to gasp for air.

Still Bryce had not appeared.

"No!" she cried at the waters, slapping her fists against the cold stones. "No! Damn it!" She felt hot tears trickle over her cheeks, blurring her vision of the gray waters below.

He was gone. The Prince of Darkness was gone.

Ryen wept into her palms, her shoulders shaking uncontrollably.

Bryce was dead.

Nineteen

The knock sounded again at the wooden door, echoing through Ryen's mind like a distant roar. She lifted her head from the cool stones of the ledge and turned her tearful gaze to the door. It took a long moment before she was able to compose herself. She rose slowly from her reverent position at the window and, wiping tears from her hot cheeks and eyes with a shaking hand, she moved to the door.

The booming knock came again.

Ryen leaned against the door, barely able to whimper, "Who is it?"

"Ryen? It's Jeanne."

Jeanne? For a moment, Ryen's hazy mind refused to acknowledge the name. Then, slowly, she put a face with the name. Her sister.

"I've been up since dawn. I couldn't sleep," Jeanne said. "Then when I happened down the corridor, I heard noises from your room. Are you all right?"

Ryen couldn't answer. Tears rose again in her eyes.

"Ryen?" Jeanne's voice floated through the wooden door. "I thought I heard you screaming."

"It was just a nightmare," Ryen whispered.

"May I come in?"

Ryen paused. She couldn't let Jeanne see her like this. Her sluggish mind searched for an excuse. Finally, she said, "I—I wish to get more sleep."

"Will you be all right?"

"Yes, Jeanne," Ryen replied, and staggered away from the door, her gaze riveted on the window and the ledge where just moments before Bryce had stood.

"I'll come by later to—"

Jeanne's voice drifted off as Ryen crossed the expanse of her room to return to the window. She bent over the ledge, her eyes scanning the moat below, but the water was like a silver mirror, showing her nothing of what might lie below its surface. He was gone. The sun's light edged toward the dark grave of the waters. Numbness spread through Ryen's body. All she could do was stare into the moat, hoping that somehow he would appear.

He didn't.

Ryen followed listlessly as Jeanne tugged her along, blazing a path through the gentry to the platform that was reserved for her family and honored guests. The large, muddy flatland that served as the field of honor was overflowing with people. Over the simple wooden fence that surrounded the field, anxious spectators hung like eager children waiting for a treat. Peasants sat on the small hills just beyond the standing observers. A rope separated the rabble from the local gentry. The nobility sat on brightly colored blankets, eating fine breads and drinking ale.

Ryen could not get Bryce's image from her mind. He haunted her thoughts like a vengeful ghost. The memory of the swirling smoke fading to reveal his dark visage, his long black hair, tanned skin, and the way his midnight eyes opened and pinned her, breathless, to the spot, made her tremble with the loss of this man who was so much more than just a man. Every time she closed her eyes, she saw him reach for her from the darkness. And every time she opened her eyes to find that he wasn't there, the pain of his death gripped her tighter.

The trumpets sounded, jarring Ryen from her daze. A

deafening roar erupted from the crowd and Ryen lifted her eyes to see the De Bouriez banner leading the way before the brilliantly dressed knights as they rode onto the field. Armor glinted in hot flashes as whinnying beasts took their riders around the field. The thunder of hoofbeats pounded in Ryen's ears and her heart ached. Bryce would have looked splendid in his shining armor, riding a magnificent battle steed.

Jeanne touched her arm. Ryen whipped her agonized gaze up to her sister. Jeanne's joyful smile disintegrated. Ryen pulled her arm away and turned, racing back the way they came through the crowd. She couldn't bear to be with her countrymen with the memory of Bryce's death so vivid in her mind.

Ryen hoisted the silken skirts of her houppelande above her knees and ran up the grassy hill toward the forest that surrounded the castle. She vaguely heard her sister call out after her but she paid her words no heed. She crashed through the foliage, sharp thorns and branches tearing at her dress, scratching her skin. The cheers of the crowd followed her into the darkness of the forest, mocking her attempt to escape his memory. She finally collapsed beside an old oak tree, burying her face in her folded arms. How could the mighty Prince of Darkness be dead? she demanded silently. How can a legend die? The moat surrounding De Bouriez Castle has swallowed many, but never one so strong as the Prince of Darkness! It cannot be. He cannot be dead. Fool, she chastised herself. You saw him leap from the window with your own eyes. No man can survive a fall that far.

"You set him free."

Ryen jerked her head up and turned quickly. Lucien stood behind her, his golden plate armor gleaming in the shadows like a torch, threatening to burn her where she lay. He held his helmet in his arm and his blond hair wavered gently in a breeze. He took a step and knelt beside her, his armored knee making a deep impression in the dirt. His sharp blue eyes coldly assessed Ryen's face for a moment before his upper lip curled in contempt. "Regretting your action already, Sister?"

His words shocked her and she sat up, brushing the tears from her cheeks.

"How did you get him out of the castle?"

"What?" she gasped.

"Which way did you send him?" Lucien asked through clenched teeth.

She began to shake her head. "Lucien, you don't understand."

"I understand quite well, Sister. I understand that you're a fool. He used you. He used you to aid his escape."

"No," Ryen gasped.

"You will tell me where he went."

"He jumped out the window, Lucien. Into the moat," she replied miserably, baring her soul, her pain.

"Lies!" Lucien roared.

Ryen jerked back as if he had struck her.

"Why do you protect him?" he demanded.

Her mouth dropped in disbelief. "He's dead! I can protect him from nothing!" she shouted, feeling her throat tighten to choke off her voice.

Slowly, Lucien stood and stared down at her, his upper lip curling in a sneer. "I do not need your aid to find him. I simply thought you might want to offer it."

Ryen watched as he strode away, the beginnings of panic rising up inside her. He did not believe her! Her own kin thought she lied. What would her people think?

Ryen gazed wearily into the moat. Tiny drops of rain pelted the gray water. Even after three days, she still could not believe Bryce was dead. His passionate touch seemed like a dream, another lifetime. At least it was easier for Ryen to think of it that way.

But there was also a nagging doubt that festered in her

mind. Why had she led him to her room? At the time, her feet had taken the path to her room out of instinct. What had she planned to do with him once they got there?

Had she really meant to set him free?

No! her rational mind screamed. Never. She had meant to hide him in her room until the joust was stopped.

They would have found Bryce. And then the joust would have been scheduled for the following day, or the day after. The only way to truly be chivalrous was to set him free.

No! she argued in silence. I simply meant to . . . I never intended to free him.

And even though she told herself this over and over, she could never come to believe it with all her heart.

A knock on the door startled Ryen out of her reverie. "Come in," she invited.

Jeanne bounced in and paused just inside the doorway, frowning. "Every time I come into your room, you are staring out the window. You must tell me what you see that fascinates you so."

Jeanne took up a spot beside Ryen and carefully leaned over the ledge of the window, following her gaze.

"Gads!" Jeanne gasped. "Please tell me you do not stare at that dreary water!"

When Ryen did not reply, but simply moved away from the window to sit on the thick embroidered blanket on the bed, Jeanne sighed. "Really, Ryen. You are much too disheartening these last days. I wish what I'm going to tell you would make you feel better, but I'm afraid it won't."

Ryen raised weary, burning eyes to her sister.

Jeanne shook her head. She went to Ryen and knelt at her feet. "Ryen, what is wrong with you? I have never seen you this miserable. Is it Father?"

"No," Ryen mumbled. "It isn't Father."

"Then what? Please tell me."

A sad smile tugged at Ryen's lips and she shrugged helplessly.

"Very well. But you can't keep it a secret forever, Ryen." Jeanne nervously smoothed out the folds of her skirt. "Jules and I are going."

"Going where?" Ryen echoed with something close to panic in her voice.

"Home, of course, to our castle. Jules has villages to oversee and duties to perform." Jeanne smiled just as glumly as Ryen. "Besides, you have your army to lead. Wasn't it you who said the English were coming to France?"

"But you just got here."

"We've been here for seven months now. It's you who have not been here."

"I'm so sorry, Jeanne. I've been preoccupied."

"Yes, I know."

"When are you going?" Ryen asked.

"Tomorrow."

"So soon?"

"I'm afraid so," Jeanne replied.

Ryen bowed her head, staring at her hands that rested in her lap.

Jeanne reached up and traced the curve of Ryen's chin. "Poor Ryen. Don't be sad. I couldn't bear it. We must be happy. We have only a few hours left together. I will dine with you later tonight." Jeanne climbed to her feet, carefully pulling her green skirts away from her feet. Her brown eyes, usually so happy and carefree, looked uneasy. "But now, Father is waiting for you in his private room."

Twenty

Ryen remembered her father's private room as a small, warm room where he had held her in his lap by the fireplace and told her stories. Now, it was anything but warm. She saw her father leaning against the stone hearth, staring into the embers of the fading fire, his rigid back to her. She was surprised to see Andre seated in one of the plush red velvet chairs that surrounded a small wooden table. When her questioning eyes caught his, he turned away.

There was a tapestry on the wall farthest from the hearth depicting the slaughter of a small fox by two armored men. She instantly felt a kinship with the fox.

"Leave us, Andre," Jean Claude said in a quiet voice.

Andre rose stiffly, hesitated a moment, and finally strode past Ryen, his head bent. Ryen frowned as he passed her.

When the door closed silently behind him, the foreboding that had followed her down the stairs settled on her shoulders and made her skin crawl. Even though Andre was gone, she felt more trapped than before. One defenseless fox against one mighty man.

Jean Claude said, "Sit down, Ryen."

The feeling of dread grew, stabbing Ryen's stomach, and her knees crumpled, landing her in the seat Andre had vacated.

The tension stretched like a bow strung too tightly. Ryen dared not move, dreading its eventual release. She watched silently as her father stared deeply into the fire. His blue silk jerkin reflected the firelight and when he turned toward her, the white fur around his collar looked red, almost matching the red in his cheeks. His face was unreadable, but his usually bright eyes were hard.

"At first you had many suitors. All of which you conveniently ignored."

Ryen bowed her head. Her father should have just posted a banner offering her to the highest bidder.

"Now, I'm afraid there are very few. Most took back their offers." His voice was strong, but strangely sad.

Good, Ryen thought. How could she hope to lead an army as someone's wife? He would want her home to produce heirs.

"I want to hear it from your own lips," Jean Claude said. "Tell me you did not free the Prince of Darkness."

All her years of swordplay could not protect her from his accusation. She could not parry his anger or dodge the anguish in his voice. Agony sliced through her like the sharp edge of a battle sword. Where had he heard such a thing? How could he believe it? Lucien. She opened her mouth to answer, to tell him the Prince of Darkness was dead, but she promptly closed it. Lucien had not believed her, so why would her father?

Jean Claude stared coldly at his daughter.

Ryen stood, stepping toward him. Her eyes burned with the effort of keeping her tears in check. He had to believe her! She stretched out her hands. "Father, please. I only wanted to bring him to you. I wanted him to kneel before you so that—"

"How could you?" he groaned, not hearing her confession, turning away from her. "You released him so that he could kill more of our people. Don't you see what you've done?"

Slowly, Ryen dropped her arms. She knew Bryce could never raise a sword again, never kill again, for he was dead. I wanted to make you proud of me, she thought. That's all I ever wanted. And for Bryce to love me. To tell me I was beautiful. But I couldn't do either. He did not love me. And you aren't proud of me. I have failed. Ryen struggled to straighten her back and raise her quivering chin. "I have done nothing wrong."

"Nothing wrong?!" he bellowed. "You have betrayed your king and your country!"

He believed she had freed Bryce. He would never believe that the Prince of Darkness was dead. He would never believe that his daughter was innocent of this betrayal.

"I feel I have been more than fair with you, Ryen. I have nurtured your whims for a long time. And I am sorry for what I must do now, but—"

Ryen's mind raced; her heart pounded. Something terrible was about to happen and she could not just sit there and let it. "Father—"

"The only marriage offer that remains open, and the one which I'm afraid I must accept, is from Count Dumas."

"No," Ryen gasped, stumbling toward her father, "you can't." Everything she had ever heard about Count Dumas raced through her mind. He was a hermit who was more than five decades old and had yet to see an heir to his estates. He had had five wives, all of whom were rumored to have been locked in a tower and tortured because they had produced no son. He was a monster!

"I'm sorry, Ryen," Jean Claude said. "Truly I am. But it is already done."

"Why must you accept? I am the leader of a French army! You do not have to—"

"You think your men will follow a traitor? I am saving your life. If you return to the army, you will be stabbed in the back at the first opportunity." He spoke more coldly than he had ever done before.

Ryen lurched away from him, horrified. Her own men would never stab her in the back! They would not believe these lies that her family believed. Even Andre . . . "Father . . ."

He turned away from her, his shoulders slumped.

Ryen felt her legs going numb. She raised her chin, again fighting desperately to keep back her fear and her tears. "When is the wedding to take place?" she managed to ask, her voice growing weak.

"In two months," he said softly. "Adequate time for you to prepare yourself and your things."

Two months, she thought. That would be November. A perfect time for the ice to form around my heart.

She turned and slowly walked to the door. She paused, her hand on the door handle. She wanted to tell him the truth, tell him that she didn't free the Prince of Darkness. But he wouldn't believe her. Just as Lucien did not. If she did tell her father the truth of what happened, she was afraid the guilt hiding beneath the surface of her thoughts would rise into her voice and betray her. And even with her confession, there would be questions she had no reasonable answers for. At least, no answers her father would accept. He would surely wonder how Bryce had gotten into her bedroom, and wonder why she hadn't cried out in alarm when she'd had the chance.

Her hand clenched around the door handle. Ryen wanted to say she was sorry for hurting him, for putting him through this. She wanted to tell her father how much she loved him. But she couldn't. Her hand trembled with the effort it took to keep her emotions in check.

He has already turned his back on me, she thought. Ryen opened the door and stepped out into the hallway, closing it softly behind her.

"Come in," Ryen called at the insistent knocking. She sat on the floor in a corner of her room, the leggings and tunic she wore her only means of defiance.

Jeanne pushed the door open. "Ryen, have you forgotten that we were to dine together?"

"I'm sorry, Jeanne. I wasn't feeling well. I'm not very

hungry," Ryen replied, looking up from whittling a piece of wood.

Jeanne shook her head. "Another arrow? I think the castle's armory will be supplied by you alone."

Ryen grinned halfheartedly.

Jeanne closed the door behind her. She looked worriedly at Ryen, who sat cross-legged, with a knife in one hand and a piece of wood in the other. "Is it true?" Jeanne asked. "Did Father really betroth you to that horrible hermit?"

Ryen nodded and began to run the knife against the wood again.

"Oh, Ryen. Why on earth did he do it?"

"He believes I did something dishonorable," Ryen replied. Her brows creased slightly in concentration as she gazed intently at her whittling.

"You didn't free him, did you?"

Startled, Ryen glanced up at her sister, hurt at the doubt in Jeanne's voice. She studied Jeanne's childish yet sincere face until she saw the doubt replaced by embarrassment. Finally, Ryen looked at the window, which was now shadowed with darkness. Jeanne deserved to hear the truth. Perhaps her only sister would believe her. "He jumped out the window, into the moat." Ryen heard Jeanne's sharp intake of breath, then her soft footsteps as she approached. Jeanne sat beside her.

"So that's why you stare out that window."

Ryen waited for the reproach for having Bryce in her room.

"Did he love you?" she asked, leaning toward Ryen.

Ryen looked at her in surprise. There was no condemnation in Jeanne's eyes, only sympathy and understanding. "No," Ryen admitted quietly.

"What will you do?"

"I suppose I must marry Count Dumas."

"I want you to come with Jules and me."

"Defy Father?" Ryen asked, aghast. When Jeanne nodded, Ryen shook her head. "I couldn't."

"You can't go to Dumas Castle! They say his last wife fell from the tower window to her death. More likely she jumped to escape that horrible man, or worse yet, was pushed!"

"I can still fight for France. Whether they want me or not."

"Please reconsider, Ryen. Come with us."

Ryen glanced at Jeanne. "And Jules agrees?"

Jeanne dropped her eyes under Ryen's probing gaze. "I— well, I haven't spoken with him yet, but I shall."

Ryen could never go with her. She could never come between Jeanne and Jules. And that was certainly what would happen. Ryen couldn't ruin Jeanne's happiness. She shook her head. "I appreciate the offer, Jeanne. But no."

"If you change your mind, know that you will always be welcome in my home."

Ryen reached out and took Jeanne's small hand. Not all her family had abandoned her. Her sister still believed in her, and for that Ryen would be forever grateful. She nodded, feeling the first spark of hope ignite within her soul.

She did not know how badly it would be dashed.

Twenty-one

It had started with two maids whispering. When Ryen stared at them, they stopped and glared angrily at her. As a puzzled look came over her face, they separated and continued on their way. It happened again in the main hall, and then again in the stables. The gazes were scornful and furious. Former friends and strangers alike began to turn their backs as she approached them. Ryen suddenly found that where yesterday she had been a famed knight, today she was a leper. She avoided the Great Hall and the practice yard, terrified that her father had been right, that her men believed the savage rumors.

Ryen stared out at the road below the sitting room window. Traders and merchants moved toward the castle door in a long line of carts and wagons. The smell of the forest just beyond the town wafted to her senses on a light breeze and she lifted her eyes to the tall trees that towered over the thatched roofs.

She heard the door open behind her and turned. Andre's head was lowered as he entered the room. Ryen's heart brightened. She had not seen Andre for a week and she missed him. Perhaps she could talk him into sparring with her. "Andre," she said happily, pushing herself from the window.

Andre's gaze snapped sharply up to hers and Ryen saw the slight drop of his mouth and the surprise in his eyes. For just a moment, his brow furrowed and his lips thinned in misery, before he bowed his head once again and turned away from her.

Ryen felt as though he had physically shoved her away. Hurt flared in her body, constricting her chest. Finally, she shrank back to the window, agonizingly aware that he was ashamed of her, of what he believed she had done. The rumors had conquered even her faithful brother.

"Did Father summon you here?" Andre asked stiffly.

Ryen answered with similar formality. "Yes."

Silence settled between them like an unwanted guest. Ryen returned to gazing out the window. She did not see the traders or villeins; she only saw the far and distant trees as they swayed in an unseen wind, beckoning to her. She and Andre had always been close. He had always respected her, cherished her. But now, in his eyes, she was a fallen angel.

The door opened again. Ryen turned her head and her eyes locked on Lucien. She watched the anger and disgust settle over his features as he saw her. She raised her chin, narrowing her eyes to mirror his look before turning away from him.

When her father entered the room, Ryen did not turn around to see him softly close the door and clasp his hands behind his back. "We are all aware of the events that have taken place within the last week, bringing disgrace and dishonor to our name."

Ryen's fantasy returned: she would tell her father that Bryce was dead and the rumors were all lies, and her father would smile, embrace her, and whisper, "I knew it all along." As quickly as it materialized in her mind's eye, the fantasy vanished. In truth, he would never believe her. People wanted to believe that a woman was weaker than a man. It wasn't proper for a woman to be out swinging a sword, defending her country. Now, it made no difference if it was true or not. And Ryen could not prove that Bryce was dead. No bodies had been found around the moat's bank.

"However, thank the Lord, Count Dumas is willing to overlook these matters," Jean Claude continued.

Ryen looked out the window. The sun was bright and hot,

promising a warm day. Ryen planned to go to the glen and practice later. She needed to swing a heavy sword, to work out some of the tension she felt.

"Naturally, since you are to be married, it is not possible for you to lead an army."

Ryen froze. He won't do it. He can't.

"As of today, Lucien will lead the men."

Ryen did not move. Her body was numb. Everything she valued was taken from her.

"Ryen? Did you hear me?" Jean Claude asked after a moment.

His voice came to her as if from a great distance. Ryen could not understand what was happening. She could not find the strength that had once flowed so strongly through her heart. She could not find the words to voice her objection to all the wrongs that were happening to her. She could not find the confidence to stand up against her accusers. The Angel of Death was gone, and in her place guilt ruled.

"Ryen?" Jean Claude repeated.

In her mind's eye, she saw the door closing. The lock sliding into place boomed in her head. She clutched the ledge of the window as blackness invaded her vision. For a moment, her world spun and she thought she was going to faint. I am the Angel of Death, feared by all of France's enemies, she told herself, her knuckles turning white as she clung to her ledge of consciousness, struggling to find the rage she knew she should feel. Slowly, the blotchy darkness receded, but the flame of her soul remained a dying ember.

"Yes, Father," she replied meekly.

"Good," Jean Claude responded dubiously. "Then Lucien, the army is yours."

"Thank you, Father," Lucien said.

Ryen turned and left the room, her head bowed like a compliant servant being dismissed.

* * *

The barren wasteland of unending white mist spread out before her. Ryen walked forward, not knowing where she was heading or even where she had come from. Her steps were sluggish and unsure as she continued on. Something behind her, a noise, made her stop. She turned to see that the cloud of white had turned completely red, forming a curtain of crimson. Her shoulders drooped as she turned back and moved deeper into the fog. She stared at her feet, watching the red seep out from beneath each step she took. Feeling like a poison, she moved forward, infecting the purity of the white cloud.

Suddenly, she stopped dead in her tracks. A shadowed figure rose before her in a cloud of dark vapors. His shining suit of battle armor blended with the mist, as if it were the chain mail of a ghost. He floated, his hands on his hips, surveying the area before him as if it were new territory to conquer. Finally, his gaze came to rest on her, his black eyes sparkling like hot oil, hypnotizing her with the force of his presence. His lip curved in a grin and Ryen felt herself drawn to him like a warrior drawn to the sound of a battle cry. He lifted a hand and reached out to take her into his possession . . .

Ryen sat bolt upright, her breath coming in rapid gulps. He is alive, she thought. She felt it to the core of her being. He is alive! Her heart pounded wildly with renewed hope.

Ryen flew from her bed and was running out the door, racing down the hall in the blink of an eye. When she came to Andre's door, she threw it open and dashed inside.

He sat up, reaching for his weapon, but her voice stopped him. "Andre!"

"By all the saints, you startled me, Ryen. Do you wish to be headless?" he asked.

Ryen paid him no mind as she leapt onto his bed, her eyes wide with excitement and anxiety. "Andre, you must help me search the moat!"

"What?" he asked, baffled.

"Please. We must search the moat," Ryen repeated desperately.

"Good heavens, why?" Andre demanded, leaning back on his hands so he could regard her. "We've already searched the banks."

"Bryce is alive."

"He escaped. Of course he's alive."

Ryen sat back on her heels, her hands twisting in her lap. "He jumped out the window into the moat."

Andre leaned toward her and, through the moonlight, she could see the questions racing through his mind as clearly as if they were written on his face. His dark brows knit. "How do you know this?"

Ryen looked down at her hands, feeling the heat of his questioning as if she were being interrogated.

When she didn't answer, Andre persisted, "Ryen, you're not telling me everything."

Ryen paused again, but when she looked up, Andre's scowl was so fierce that she thought he was going to strangle her right there. "He jumped into the moat from my bedroom window."

Andre straightened, his features suddenly shadowed. "What was he doing in your room?"

"I went down to the dungeon," Ryen explained, "only to find that the door was open. Bryce had an accomplice. Someone helped him escape. They took me prisoner."

"Did they hurt you?" Andre demanded. When Ryen shook her head he continued, "How did they get into your room?"

"I—I led them up there," Ryen stated. Andre's brow darkened with indignation and Ryen hurried on. "I never thought he would jump out my window. Never."

"Why did you lead him to your room? Why didn't you call for guards?"

"Oh, Andre," Ryen looked down at her hands that were clasped in her lap. "I couldn't. I didn't intend him to escape, but . . . I just wanted to keep him safe until after the joust."

Andre paused for a long moment. Finally, he said, "The fall from your window would have killed him."

"But no bodies were ever found around the moat. We have to search the moat. I have to know for sure."

Andre sat quietly in the shadows cast by the moon's frosty rays. He leaned back even further and Ryen could not see his features at all. "I would do it myself," Ryen murmured, looking away from him. "But the men won't take orders from me any longer."

"Why didn't you tell me this before?" he asked.

Ryen wouldn't look at him for a moment, embarrassed, ashamed that Bryce had thought she had brought him to her room for one last tryst, afraid that Andre would think the same thing. "You couldn't even look at me in Father's sitting room."

"I was ashamed," he admitted quietly.

Ryen tried not to let the hurt show on her face, but she was unsuccessful. "You see? You believed I had freed him."

"Ryen," Andre said, his voice tender, "I was ashamed of myself."

Ryen raised startled eyes to him.

"I knew that Father was planning to marry you to the count. I tried to dissuade him, but he wouldn't listen. I felt as though I had failed you."

Relief washed through Ryen, engulfing her in its calming pool. "I'm sorry," she whispered.

"No," Andre insisted. "It is I who will apologize. I should not have let him do this to you. The marriage, your army . . ."

Ryen raised her hand and gently cupped his cheek. "Thank you."

"What will you do if he is alive?" Andre wondered.

Slowly, Ryen's hand dropped and she turned to stare out at the night sky. The moon was high in the star-speckled night sky, almost full except for a sliver carved out of the top. Ryen was silent for a long moment. Then she whispered, "I don't know."

* * *

The torches illuminated the murky black water, casting a red glow over the moat. Two men rose from the depths of the water and moved toward the shore, dragging a large object behind them. As they slowly approached, the dark object that they pulled became the figure of a man.

They dropped him, facedown, at Andre's feet.

Andre held the torch above the body. Dark hair, strong physique. With a gentle kick, he rolled the body onto its back. The face was a mass of mashed bone, broken beyond recognition. One dark eye was open, rolled back into what remained of the head.

He glanced over the murky water to the place where the body had been discovered. Then his eyes scaled the castle walls, up to the tower directly above the murky grave. It was Ryen's room.

Andre heard a sound from behind him and turned. From the darkness of the road that lined the moat, Lucien emerged. "What are you doing, Brother?"

Twenty-two

"It was him, Ryen." Andre's voice was firm.

Ryen sat heavily on her bed. Suddenly, she felt as though all her breath had been sucked from her. Deep down inside, she had been afraid they would find his body in the moat's dark waters. But she still could not believe that he could be dead. "I want to see the body."

Andre lowered his eyes.

When he failed to respond, Ryen raised her head sharply. "What?"

"Lucien is displaying it throughout the streets," Andre replied. "There was nothing I could do."

The horrifying image of Bryce's body, bloated with the moat's brackish waters, dragged through the dirt of the streets behind Lucien's horse for all to see, filled her mind. Ryen shot from the bed, her fists clenched into tight balls. She headed for the door, but Andre caught her arm.

"You can't, Ryen. You can't stop him."

"I can and I will!" she snapped. She tried to yank free, but Andre's grip was tight.

"And what are you going to tell him?" he demanded.

"I won't let him drag Bryce's body through the dirt."

"The people already think you freed him. Don't make them think worse."

"Worse? How could they possibly think worse?"

"They'll say you were in love with the Prince of Darkness! He jumped out your window, Ryen. Your bedroom window!

What else could they possibly think?" Andre shook her, trying to get her to see the treason in her actions. "You hid him in your room so he would be safe."

Ryen roared, pulling her arm free and facing Andre with fury. "He was *my* prisoner! My responsibility. Could I live with myself knowing that my countrymen had killed him on the field of honor!"

"Better in battle than wasting away in a dungeon."

Ryen fumed silently. She did not know if she would have been content letting him sit in the dungeon. All she knew was that she had to stop Lucien. I will not allow him to display Bryce like some prize, she thought. I have to stop him. But first, I have to get past Andre. Ryen dropped her head, forcing her shoulders into a slouch. "You're right," Ryen whispered, her voice sad and contrite. "He is the enemy. And he is dead."

Andre's brows came together in disbelief.

"I'm sorry, but with what happened between us . . . it is difficult sometimes to see him as my enemy."

Andre nodded. "You must let him go, Ryen. It will do you no good to dwell on it."

"I know," she murmured.

Andre turned and walked to the window. He gazed out over the rooftops and fields of the village. "Give it time, Ryen. Lucien will forget and all will be as it was." He took a deep breath of fresh air. "Will you tell Father the truth now?" The silence stretched. When Ryen didn't answer, Andre turned.

The door was open and Ryen was gone.

She rode her horse like a madwoman, barreling through the streets, a cloud of dust churning behind her racing mount. The streets were strangely empty, the shops closed early. She sent a group of chickens squawking, scattering them in all directions as she tore through the town, looking for Lucien.

Finally, she came upon a farmer in his field. She reined up
to ask him where Lucien was when she saw a cloud of smoke
rising in the distance, near the outskirts of the village.

Ryen spurred her horse, heading for the thick black cloud
that billowed up into the red sky of the setting sun. As she
neared the last house, the stench of fire and burning flesh
made her skin crawl, her heart pound with fear. When she
guided her horse around the corner, her heart stopped.

Most of the villagers, men, women, and children, were
gathered around a large bonfire. The flames licked the red
sky. In the middle of the fire, Ryen saw the blackened form
of a burning body. For a moment, she could not move, frozen
to the saddle under the heat of the flames. Oh, my God.
Bryce.

Anguish gripped her heart. She stared at the part of the
burning body that had once been the face—now nothing but
a black shell. Bryce's image rose in her mind, his strong chin,
his sensual lips, his mysterious eyes, even the cut on his
cheek that she had given him. Tears rose in her eyes. Look
what he has done to Bryce's face, Ryen thought despairingly.
That handsome face.

She dismounted, pushing and fighting her way through
the peasants, making a path to the front of the crowd. Finally,
she found herself standing in the intense heat of the blaze.
It was so hot that she had to put up her hand to prevent her
face from burning. Her hair shifted slightly under the waves
of hot air that assaulted her.

Ryen peered beneath her hand, through the ripples of heat
that the flames fanned into the air. The fire had eaten away
the man's skin, and no matter how hard she tried, she could
not absolutely identify the man as Bryce. I will never know
for sure, she thought with a desperation that ate away at her
sanity. Tears burned her eyes. Finally, the smell of charred
flesh made her gag and turn away.

Lucien approached her. Ryen didn't see her brother; she
saw her torturer, the man who had condemned her to an

infinity of uncertainty. She launched herself at him, her hands curved into claws. "You son of a bitch!" she screamed over the roar of the flames. "Do you know what you've done?"

Lucien grabbed her wrists before she could slash at him, but he was caught off guard and the impact of her body sent him onto his back. She fought wildly against his hold, shouting, "You torched him! You burned his body!"

Lucien flipped her onto her back, easily straddling her body, forcing her arms above her head. Ryen would not give up; she kicked and screamed like a cornered cat.

He shook her, shouting, "Stop it! Ryen!"

She twisted her arms in an attempt to free herself, bucking and flailing her legs. It wasn't until his hand struck her cheek, hard, that she stilled her fight. The tears came easily then, running from her eyes like little streams.

Lucien released her, sliding from her. Ryen sat up, burying her face in the crook of her arms.

Lucien leaned close to her to whisper, "For God's sake, show some dignity."

Ryen peered up at him with red, swollen eyes. *"You bastard,"* she murmured.

"He is the enemy," Lucien retorted hotly.

"I'll never know for sure," she said, tears welling again in her eyes. "I'll never know it was him."

"It *was* him," he said positively.

Ryen stared at him for a long moment. Perhaps he *was* sure. But she would never know for certain. There would always be that doubt. And it was all because Lucien had to destroy his enemy. Slowly she rose. "I hate you," she gritted, before moving into the crowd. They opened a path for her and she walked stoically to her horse, mounted, and turned toward the castle.

She did not look back.

* * *

The rage in her heart remained strong the next morning. Ryen sought solace in the stables with her war horse, vigorously brushing his coat and thick white mane. She had just managed to get all the tangles out of his hair and was reaching over his back to run the brush through it again when she heard hoofbeats enter the courtyard, followed by a shout of welcome.

She placed the brush on the floor and hurried to the doorway to see a man dismount from a black horse. Ryen noticed that the horse's muzzle was flecked with white foam; the animal had obviously been ridden hard. She watched Lucien greet the man with a clasp of arms. They exchanged words and Lucien nodded before turning toward the castle. The man glanced around the courtyard once. That was when Ryen saw the insignia etched upon his tunic. He was the constable Charles d'Albret's man! A tingle of excitement shot up her spine. The man was a messenger sent by the king's closest confidant.

She hurried after them and entered the Great Hall just in time to see her father appear. Ryen pressed back against the cold stone wall, blending into the shadows. She could hear their words perfectly as they echoed through the room.

"Greetings from the constable," the messenger said. "I have a message for the Angel of Death."

A message! For me! The constable must want me to fight with them! Ryen thought. After all these days of pain, loneliness, and scorn, someone finally wanted her. And this someone was, next to the king, the mightiest person in all of France! Ryen's feet moved instinctively. She began to step out of the shadows.

"My daughter is to be married," Jean Claude said. "She will fight in no more campaigns."

She froze instantly. For a brief moment she had completely forgotten that she no longer led an army. The melancholy that had plagued her these last days consumed her again. Never to fight again, never to brandish a sword. Instead, to bear an old hermit sons.

The messenger hesitated a moment before saying, "It is a great loss to France. I will inform the constable of this tragedy."

"Tragedy? She is of marrying age," Jean Claude answered defensively.

"Forgive me. I meant no insult. But it is a tragedy to lose such a great knight. France has need of all her warriors, what with England in her realm."

"I command the army now," Lucien spoke up loudly. "We are, of course, at the constable's disposal."

"The constable has ordered all lords and their armies to Rouen."

"We can be there in three days."

"I will tell the constable," the messenger replied.

"First you must rest," Jean Claude stated. "Come, I have food and ale."

Their voices faded as they moved from the room toward the kitchens. Ryen turned and slowly climbed several steps before her legs seemed to give out beneath her and she sat down heavily. Her army would leave without her, with a new leader. She was never to fight for France again. There had to be something she could do. She could not sit on this step and let the world go by without her. She was a woman of action. She was a De Bouriez! Then how come she could not find the will to rise to her feet and storm down the stairs to confront her father?

Ryen stood and moved up the stairs toward her bedroom.

Ryen sat in a small alcove near a window. She stared down at the sword she held in her lap. The mirrored metal reflected her image. Her long hair hung over her shoulders, dark tendrils reaching for the blade and curling lovingly around it.

I cannot imagine never holding you again, she thought.

Never wearing my armor. Never feeling that thrill of riding into a battle.

The cold metal sat in her hands, strangely calming in its hypnotic power. Suddenly, shouts from the courtyard below reached her ears and she lifted her head to gaze out the window. Below, she could see her army preparing to leave for Rouen. She scanned the rows of men until she came to the head, near the doors of the castle.

With the help of his squire, Lucien was mounting his war horse.

A movement near the doors of the castle caught her attention. Her father was descending the stairs, his chest puffed out proudly.

Why is he so proud of Lucien? she wondered. Why does he bid farewell to my brother with a smile when all he had for me was a scowl?

Slowly, as her father stopped at Lucien's side, she rose to her feet.

Why is there admiration when he stares at Lucien? Ryen demanded, when for me there is nothing but disapproval?

Jean Claude spoke to Lucien and Ryen could not hear his words, but she saw Lucien's return smile.

Her hand tightened into a fist around the handle of her sword.

I will have the answers, she vowed.

Lord Jean Claude De Bouriez gazed in admiration at his youngest son. Lucien was mounted on his mahogany war horse, his bright golden armor resplendent in the morning's misty grayness.

Jean Claude's eyes sparkled and his voice boomed with pride as he said, "Lucien, you do justice to the name De Bouriez."

Andre nudged his horse up beside Lucien. "Where is Ryen?"

At the mention of her name, the glow on Jean Claude's face dimmed and he turned to Andre, shrugging. "In her room."

Andre's dark eyes shifted to her window, and Jean Claude noticed the disappointment written on his face at finding the space empty. Andre addressed Lucien. "The men are ready."

Lucien nodded. "Then we depart." He rode forward, leading the way toward the town where peasants waited in the streets to cheer the knights on to victory.

With a sigh of contentment, Jean Claude turned and walked into his castle. Never in all his life had he felt so pleased. His son was leading the army to battle the English.

He walked jauntily through the hallway and was almost at the stairs when he heard soft footsteps and turned. She approached him in brown leggings and a cream-colored tunic. Her back was straight; her dark hair swirled around her slender shoulders as she moved, like coils of wispy smoke; her blue eyes flashed in the light of the torches on the wall. Her hand rested on the pommel of her sheathed sword. He did not know the woman who approached him, had never seen the likes of her smoldering fire before.

"Father," Ryen said. "I would have words with you."

Jean Claude nodded reluctantly. He led the way to a large room. Five precious books were on pedestals near the far wall. This was his library. He shut the door after Ryen entered. Sunlight streamed in through the large windows across from the door. A fire had been lit in the fireplace between the two windows.

"You're very proud of him, aren't you?" she asked softly, a tinge of remorse edging her voice.

Jean Claude did not turn. He kept his hands on the handle, almost as if he were keeping open an avenue of escape.

"Why, Father? I want to know why you never looked at me that way."

"I cannot be proud of you any longer," he replied softly.

"I am not speaking of now. I am speaking of when I was

knighted. When I won the battle at Picardy. When I brought the Prince of Darkness to you."

Jean Claude replayed the events she'd named. Fragmented images flashed before his mind's eye accompanied by sharp and vivid emotions.

Embarrassment. A slip of a girl in plate armor standing boldly before his neighbors, his friends. How could his daughter, a maiden, become a warrior? She should not be *rescuing;* she should be *being rescued!*

Sorrow. A castle in flames, thick smoke rolling from its innards. Armored men on horseback shouting victory. A young woman strolling toward him, carefully stepping over fallen knights and horses. No man would want a woman who could cause this much death.

Curiosity. A tall, dark man walking toward him through a room lined with people. This was the legend. The great Prince of Darkness. Somewhere in the shadows, his little girl stood.

Through all the flashes of pictures, the whispers floated. "Does she really have a heart of ice?" "Her kiss enslaves men to her will." "She is the Angel of Death."

"I am a De Bouriez, too, Father. I am a warrior. I deserve the respect you show Lucien, not a casual dismissal when I come home," Ryen said.

Jean Claude turned and answered, "Mayhap you can gain the respect of your future husband. But I have no respect for a member of my family who betrays me." There was a long silence and Jean Claude almost regretted the words he had spoken, but he believed them.

Ryen stared hard at her father, finally saying, "I worked my entire life to please you. When I was young, I saw the way you looked at Lucien and Andre when they were training, heard how you boasted of them. Just once I wanted you to look at me the way you did them. Everything I did, I did for you. I may have disappointed you, but you have disappointed me, too." Ryen added definitively. "I'm sorry, Father. I will not marry the count."

"What?"

Ryen raised her chin slightly. "I am the Angel of Death and—"

"You are my daughter!" Jean Claude roared.

Ryen continued implacably, "And I will finish my days in battle."

"I forbid it," Jean Claude said, his eyes dark with fury. "You will remain at the castle and marry Count Dumas. I have indulged your fantasy for far too long, Ryen. That's been my biggest mistake. I should have stopped this nonsense when I had the opportunity."

Ryen's eyes narrowed with bitter resolve as she stared hard at her father. Then, with determined steps, she brushed past him stiffly as she moved to the door.

"I forbid it, Ryen!" Jean Claude hollered after her. "Do you hear me? By all that's sacred, you *will* marry the count!"

Ryen slammed the door shut as she left the room.

Jean Claude's fingers curled tightly into a fist. With a loud roar of rage, he smashed his hand into the small wooden table beside the door.

The wood splintered beneath his fury and the table collapsed.

Twenty-three

Lucien's horse shied to the side, whinnying nervously. He steadied the beast with an easy swivel of the reins.

Lightning ripped the sky in two, striking the barren field far off to their left. A cloud of dust exploded upward from the impact of the sharp spear of energy. The formerly white clouds had darkened quickly to a row of dirty cotton churning toward them from the left. The wind started to pick up and as its whistling grew louder the troops quieted.

Suddenly, Andre brought his animal to a halt, straining to see across the empty wasteland.

Lucien followed his brother's gaze. The empty field extended into the dark gray horizon. The end of the barren earth was nowhere in sight. As thunder rumbled above their heads, a dark dot appeared on the horizon, clearly visible against the unblemished gray sky.

Lightning flashed again, this time high in the air, stretching its crooked fingers toward the army. The black dot in the field grew until they could see that it was a horse. A horse riding hard, its rider driving it forward.

A clap of thunder startled a horse near Lucien and the animal reared, its forelegs kicking wildly at empty air.

Still the rider came, outlined by streaks of lightning, hailed by booming thunder.

Lucien drew his sword, the metal hissing like a snake as it came out of the sheath. "We meet this demon with death."

"Hold!" Andre called, seizing the reins of Lucien's steed

so he could not move. When Lucien snapped his gaze to bore into him, Andre continued, "I know that horse."

Lucien returned his gaze to the rider. Recognition slowly dawned on his face. "My Lord," he gasped.

Thunder clashed in the dark sky as drops of rain began to pummel the earth.

The rider stopped not twenty feet from Lucien, the white war horse pawing the ground as if in challenge.

For a long moment, neither moved until Lucien sheathed his sword and, blinking the rain from his eyes, muttered, "Welcome, Angel."

Ryen removed her helmet. It felt slick in her wet hands, the metal cold and damp from the persistent rain. Reverently, she placed the helmet on the ground beside her sleeping mat. It had been Andre's suggestion that she share his tent, and she had agreed. After days of riding, even her bones felt sore.

The army had arrived in Rouen just before the sun had set. She remained with the men to make camp while her brothers went into town to find the Constable Charles d'Albret, the king's commander who was to lead the fight against the English.

Ryen reached up to untie the leather straps holding her shoulder plates in place.

Andre had not asked what she was doing there. Lucien had not spoken to her at all.

She pulled the second shoulder plate from her arm and unstrung the straps that held the arm plates on. It was difficult removing her armor without a squire, but she could not ask someone to help her. Her pride would not allow it. And she had left Mel and Gavin back at the castle, not knowing what fate had in store for her.

Finally, she removed the final layer of her armor—the chain mail.

Ryen had not been invited to the meeting with the constable, and in a way, she was glad. If he, too, suspected her of treason . . . It was hard enough riding all this way with men, some she had known for years, scorning her. She had seen the shifting of the ranks, the moving away, wherever she drew near. She saw the bitter glances from people who used to respect her.

Ryen bent and unsheathed her sword. As she turned it, she caught sight of her reflection in the flat edge of the cold steel. Her hair hung down to her waist, dull with perspiration and dust. Her eyes were ringed with weariness, her complexion flaxen. How could Bryce have *ever* thought she was beautiful? She remembered his strong arms as he held her close, his breath hot on her cheek. And his eyes. How bright with passion they were, glowing like candlelight as they swept up and down her body, enflaming it.

Suddenly, a chill swept up her spine. She felt eyes on her. Eyes burning with desire. She gasped and raised her head.

But the tent was empty.

For a moment, she had been sure that Bryce . . .

Ghosts.

Shaking her head sadly, she turned her gaze to her weapon. Its handle was cold, its blade sharp. It was no comfort. It could not love her. And she could not love it. Not anymore. Not when one man's image was engraved upon her heart. Her skin trembled for his caress, her heart ached for his presence.

What am I doing? she thought. He is dead! I will never see him again.

Ryen lay back on the mat that served as her bed. His face hovered in the dark just above her, as it had since he had leapt out the window. But tonight, a restless feeling in her lower stomach would make sleep evasive.

A muffled sound. Ryen rolled instinctively away from it. Through the gray darkness, she saw the shadowy outline of a man, then the flash of a blade as it sliced downward, missing her by mere inches, imbedding itself into the covers she had just rolled out of.

Ryen shot to her feet, eyeing the man as he pulled the blade from her blankets. He was poised like a cobra, ready to strike at any moment. Ryen's eyes shifted downward to her mat. It was not the mat she saw, but her sword that lay beneath the covers. She stepped back, hoping to draw him away from her weapon. Even in the dark, Ryen could see the hatred that flamed from his eyes. He straightened, stepping over the mat.

"Traitor." The snarl came from the darkness like an arrow, piercing Ryen's heart. As she staggered back, the man lunged, swinging his dagger out. She thought she was prepared, but the bite of the blade as it caught the front of her wrist sent sharp pain spearing through Ryen's arm. She tore her hand back, quickly clutching at the open wound and stepping back. She had misjudged his reflexes.

Block out the pain, she silently told herself. I must get to my sword. She wavered beneath his gaze and, as she'd expected, the man closed in for the kill. She knocked his dagger arm aside with her bloodied fist and brought her knee into his stomach. She turned and dived for her sword.

Her fingertips brushed the metal handle of her weapon. She had it! Then the man seized her hair, yanking her head back sharply. She uttered a small cry as she was drawn away from the sword, her hand empty.

Through the stinging pain, she heard the tent flap swooshing aside. Then, the scrap of metal against metal and suddenly the pain was gone. Ryen lurched forward as the man released her, closing her hand over the handle of her sword. She whirled, weapon raised.

The shadow of two figures stood outlined against the white tent. Lucien's sword arm was extended and his blade was lodged in the man's chest.

The man collapsed to the ground.

Relief flooded Ryen so completely that for a moment she was unaware of the throbbing in her arm. Only when the pain flared did she remember she was hurt. She dropped the sword to grasp her wrist and sat heavily on her mat.

Lucien pulled his sword out of the body and turned to face Ryen. "Why did you come here? To my army?" he demanded sharply.

Ryen looked up at him, baffled.

"You knew this would happen! The men don't trust you any longer."

She had been warned by her father, but she had not wanted to admit that one of her soldiers would try to kill her. The hurt was unbearable. "Then why did you allow me to join? Why didn't you send me home?"

Lucien lit a candle and the pale light illuminated the tent. "Why didn't you go somewhere safe? Why couldn't you join Jeanne?"

"You know I couldn't do that!" she shouted. "How could you ask me to come between Jeanne and Jules?" Pain flared from Ryen's wrist and she squeezed it, fighting back a grimace.

"Ryen?" Lucien stepped closer to her. "You're hurt."

She glanced at her wound and then withdrew. "It's nothing," she replied stubbornly.

Lucien looked at the dead man and shook his head, then turned back to his sister. "This is no place for you," he said quietly.

"Your point has already been made," Ryen said.

Lucien reached out to a nearby table and pulled a clean linen from its surface and handed it to his sister. "If I hadn't come along when I did, you would be dead."

Ryen took the linen and absently wiped at the blood on her wrist. "And if I marry Count Dumas, the outcome might be the same."

Lucien's blue eyes danced in the fluttering candlelight as

he regarded her. Finally, he said quietly, "I would rather you join my army than marry that old hermit."

Ryen raised her eyes from the scrape on her arm to stare at her brother with surprise. Then, her shock faded and she looked away from Lucien. "Even after the war, I will not return to De Bouriez Castle," she announced.

"And what will you do?" There was disbelief and outrage in his voice.

"I am not helpless. I will sell my skills."

"Mercenary?" he stated with disgust. "No one will hire you. Not a 'traitor.' "

"I can't go back!"

"We'll never see you again," he stated quietly.

Lucien was right. She would never see her family again. Unless by some chance Andre or Lucien went to serve for the same lord that hired her. She swallowed heavily. "You must tell Jeanne that I'll miss her. And that I'm not a traitor."

Lucien tried to see into her eyes, but she averted them. "You think you're going to die in the battle with the English."

Ryen smiled gloomily. "If I am not cut down by an Englishman, one of our own may well stab me in the back."

Lucien's brows knit with anger. "Then don't fight!"

She stared at him, strangely pensive. "I have to. I have to fight the best I've ever fought, cut more of them down. This is my only chance to regain my honor."

Lucien bowed his head. "You don't have to do this."

"I only wish that I could make you believe that I did not betray our country."

His jaw tightened. But when he raised his eyes to her, Ryen saw a strange thing. His blue eyes, so like hers, were full of tears. She was so startled that she could not say a word.

Lucien rose until he towered over her. He nodded once and turned away, striding to the entrance. It was only after he left that Ryen wondered if they were tears of remorse, or tears of guilt.

* * *

Three weeks later, Ryen stood with the French Army at her back. They were fifty thousand men strong, blocking the way to Calais. When the English approached, the French knights had donned their sparkling armor and displayed banners that quickly drooped in the constant onslaught of rain.

Ryen sat atop her white battle horse, mud staining its coat. The English spread out over the plain before her, equally drenched. She estimated they had about ten thousand men at arms. Briefly, she recalled Bryce sweating under the influence of the truth powder . . . he had said there were five thousand men at arms! Ryen frowned as an ill feeling settled like lead in the pit of her stomach. Had Henry received reinforcements? That must be the answer. Where else would the extra men have come from? But the French were still more than four times their number.

"We will squash them like bugs!" The Duke of Alençon called, his fist raised as he shook it at the English.

He was echoed by more threats of vengeance and torture. Ryen did not join in. She sat silently staring at their enemy. There was something about the situation that made her uneasy. Maybe it was the quiet way the English stared at the French. Or maybe it was the arrogant attitude of the soldiers around her, an overconfidence that could easily lead to defeat. Doom settled around her as strong as the stench of war and she fought to rid herself of the foreign feeling.

"They won't attack today," Ryen said to Andre.

Andre looked at the setting sun, hidden behind gray clouds. "I think you're right."

"I believe he will lodge at Maisoncelles."

"Have the men sleep where they are. We shall await first light," Lucien instructed.

"Aye," Andre replied and rode off through the camp, passing the word.

As banners were furled around lances and knights began

to remove their rain-drenched armor, Andre returned to Ryen's side, nudging his horse up beside hers. "You're shivering. You should get out of those wet clothes," he murmured.

Ryen barely heard him. She felt her horse slide and looked down. Thick mud sucked at the animal's feet, engulfing his hooves. She scanned the field to see that all around them the ground was wet, and as the men and horses trod through the camp they created even more mud. On either side of them, rows of trees stood tall and majestic, encroaching upon the field as if they were anxious to see the upcoming battle. "This field is not suitable to battle the English. We should retreat to more solid ground," Ryen said.

Andre was silent for a moment as his gaze swept the field.

"The ground is slick and with the weight of our armor, let alone our horses, I'm afraid that we will have trouble," she added.

He looked across the field to the English camp. "Henry's men have traveled a long way. They are tired and far from home. They will be easy to defeat," Andre replied.

"The field is too narrow, the men packed in too tightly. We will have trouble using the archers. I can't see what the constable is thinking, waging battle here," Ryen mused.

"I disagree with you. With all our men, how can we possibly lose?"

Ryen glanced at him, her brow creased.

"Do not worry, Ryen. The coming morn will bring our victory."

That arrogance will be the downfall of the French, Ryen thought.

Twenty-four

Ryen De Bouriez was already awake when morning came on that fateful day in October in the year 1415. She had stepped outside her brother's tent and her lips immediately arched down into a frown as she watched dawn break on the horizon. The muted red rays of the sun brought only a cold dampness with them, a wet chill that seeped into her bones.

She turned at the sound of hoofbeats and watched two French messengers ride through the muddy field as they returned from the English camp. She had had little hope that they would be successful in their negotiations; if the English commanders were anything like Bryce, they would never surrender, even if they were outnumbered a thousand to one. And from the grim looks on their faces, she knew she was right.

She looked away from the messengers to study the French positions. The constable had placed the army between Tramecourt on their left and Agincourt on their right, thus firmly blocking the English army's route to Calais. But the field before them was restricted to about three quarters of a mile by the woods that fringed the two villages.

She frowned as she noticed that most of the French nobility seemed to have pushed themselves to the front of the line in their eagerness to participate in the expected massacre of Henry and his army. The dukes, counts, and barons had displaced many of the lowborn archers and crossbow men who were so crucial to the successful execution of the battle plan; how could they be effective if they were too far back from the line of attack? She shook her head.

"Did you hear that the constable has promised to cut off three fingers of the right hand of every archer taken prisoner so that none of them will ever draw a bow against us again?"

Ryen turned to see Andre stepping out of the tent. She pretended she hadn't heard his query. The idea turned her stomach. "I have an ill feeling about this battle, Andre," Ryen said, staring into the distance, toward the enemy.

"I think your feeling is due more to an empty stomach." He gently grabbed Ryen's elbow and tried to pull her with him. "Come, Sister, let us eat before we wage war."

Ryen resisted and stayed where she was. She turned her head, glancing at Andre from the corner of her eye. "I am not hungry." She didn't tell him that she had tried to drink a cup of ale when she awoke, but, fearful that the queasiness in her stomach wouldn't let her keep it down, took only a small sip.

The men grew restless as an hour passed and the English did not attack. Banners fluttered in the wind, so many of them that the constable finally had to order half of them furled so that everyone could have a direct line of sight to the English. By this time, Ryen had finished putting on her full battle armor and was in the saddle of her white war horse.

She patted her brave steed, whispering words of encouragement to him, when a flurry of movement caused her to snap her head back to the muddy field before her.

The English were moving forward!

Her horse danced nervously beneath her as the air thickened with anticipation. She watched the army approach, felt the anxiety of the men behind her as they waited for the constable to give the order to engage the enemy.

Just as suddenly as they had started, the English stopped some two hundred yards away. Ryen watched as Englishmen ran forward with large wooden stakes. They placed them in the ground, pushing them into the mud so that the sharp spikes stuck out of the earth, angled skyward. More men charged up behind the wooden spikes and Ryen could see them preparing their bows.

Archers! And a lot of them! But under the truth powder, Bryce had told her that they would be few in number because there were not enough skilled men to be found. Perhaps this was a ploy. Perhaps these men were not archers at all, but placed behind the stakes to intimidate the French.

Ryen's horse pranced skittishly, feeling its rider's anxiety. It took a stern hand to steady the animal. It was not as easy to settle the uneasy feeling inside her.

To Ryen's left, Sir Clugnet exclaimed, "I will take some men and go around to the west to strike at the archers. Sir William, you take twelve hundred men and go east, toward Agincourt. We will cut down those English archers before they can do us much harm!" The two knights rode off with their men eagerly following, shouting defiant words for all to hear.

The English suddenly uttered a loud cry and started forward again. Simultaneously, Ryen saw a great cloud rise from the earth and come toward the French like a swarm of locusts. Arrows! She quickly lowered her head, knowing that the arrows could not pierce her armor, and spurred her armored horse on.

The animal rode forward to meet the English, but Ryen felt his hooves slip and slide in the mud. The mud was so deep he was having trouble lifting his legs. Slowly, the French trudged closer, the thick mud retarding their movement. Arrows continued to rain down upon them.

Ryen ducked again as the arrows landed around her. She could hear the screams of her countrymen, and when she raised her eyes she was amazed at how accurate the aim of the English archers was. Many men already lay dead around her, arrows protruding from exposed flesh.

Dread passed through her. Bryce had lied. He had lied under the powder of truth! The archers were not in bad form at all. On the contrary, Ryen had never seen better aim.

She did not have time to consider the disastrous consequences because her horse stumbled, jarring her. She slid her
leg over the beast and dropped to her feet. The horse fell to
his knees before sluggishly regaining his balance. Ryen swatted the white steed away so he would not be harmed by the
arrows.

Around her the battle raged. The French were so thickly
packed that many of them could barely lift their arms, let
alone control their animals. She was almost knocked over
by a horse that brushed her arm as it passed. Ryen clutched
her sword in two hands. To lose it now would be death. Another knight collided into her from behind. This is madness!
Ryen thought. I haven't even encountered the enemy yet and
we are at war—with each other!

Amid the confusion, she heard someone shout to retreat.
She tried to turn, echoing the command, but could not because of the momentum of the men surging forward behind
her. The mud clung to her feet, inhibiting her steps.

Suddenly, the English charged and Ryen was immersed in
battle. She was surrounded by whistling swords, clanging
blades, and death cries. The mud sucked at her feet, pulling
her down. Still she managed to strike at the charging men,
cutting down one only to be attacked by another.

Ryen disposed of her next opponent, then raised her head
to quickly evaluate her position. All about her swords clanged.
The field was littered with fallen men. Knights who tumbled
in the thick mud floundered helplessly like turtles, the weight
of their armor weighing them down. Ryen moved forward to
help a soldier to his feet. She grasped his arm and pulled.
Under the added weight, her foot slipped and she almost fell,
but caught herself on his shoulder. After pulling him up, her
eyes again scanned the field. She could not retreat because
the anxious French, now out of formation in their hurry to
reach the English and gain fame and glory, were shoving forward.

Her only option was to forge ahead into the enemy. She

locked gazes with the knight standing beside her, saw the fear clearly branded in his eyes. Ryen knew he was one of the nobles not accustomed to the rigors of war and he would surely die if she did not help him. "Stay close to me," she ordered him firmly, and he nodded.

Ryen took a deep breath, preparing to push into the fray when she noticed two foot soldiers glancing about in confusion and desperation. Somehow they had become separated from their lord. "Follow me!" Ryen commanded, and they quickly fell in behind her. With the three men at her back, she charged forward, clearing a path through the English with a swipe here and a thrust there, her warrior instincts leading her on. She could feel the men fighting beside her with renewed confidence, could hear their blades clashing with renewed vigor. She smiled grimly with tightly clenched teeth as the fighting around her intensified.

Then, Ryen caught a glimpse of Andre. He was sitting on his horse, his armor smeared with blood, when suddenly he clutched at his stomach where an arrow had magically appeared. He slumped forward, rolling off his horse into the mud.

"No!" Ryen shouted, and turned, her legs aching with the effort it took to lift her feet.

She ran as best she could toward her brother. Suddenly, an English knight blocked her path, causing her to rear back. A savage scream of frustration ripped from her anguished throat as she arced her sword toward the enemy's head. Their swords clanged, hot blue sparks exploding from the point of impact as he expertly blocked the swing with his own blade.

Ryen's angry glare turned fully on him. Suddenly, she froze, unable to move, or breathe. It was his eyes that gave him away. His black eyes. She recognized them through the visor he wore. "Bryce," she gasped.

Ryen saw his lips move and recognition wash over his face before pain exploded from the back of her head and blackness invaded her vision.

Twenty-five

Ryen!

Bryce lowered his sword and was about to reach out a hand toward her when she suddenly crumpled to her knees, then slumped to the ground.

Bryce stared with shock at the blood forming at the base of her helmet as she lay in a heap. She had fallen on top of two knights who had died before her.

Died. The hairs on Bryce's neck stood straight; his flesh became cold at the thought. He heard a movement behind him. With perfect instinct, he turned to deflect a blow from an attacking French knight. His adversary rained blow after blow on him, pushing him back, trying to cut him down, but Bryce deflected every swing. Training guided his movements, training that had ingrained his skills so deeply that they had become habit—and the only thing keeping him alive, because all he was conscious of was Ryen.

Then, suddenly, his adversary's sword bounced off his armor, jarring his thoughts. Anger soared through every vein in his body, and power returned to his limbs. With an angry cry, Bryce swung his blade, the strength of years of experience behind the blow. The blades clanged only once before Bryce's sword snapped the Frenchman's weapon in two. Then, still shouting, Bryce ran his adversary through.

He had to finish this battle. He had to go to Ryen. Bryce fought like a man possessed. His black eyes glowered through his helmet, and when he downed one man, he turned for another. His thirst for French blood was unquenchable.

He whirled to take on a new foe. But there were no more enemies. All he saw was his own men—some locked in the grips of their last battle, some looking about for another adversary.

The battle was over.

Bryce swung his gaze about, looking for Ryen amid the carnage, but the field was littered with piles of bodies upon piles of bodies.

After only a few minutes of his search, Bryce saw the grimy beggars, the human vultures that always seemed to appear at the end of a battle, descend onto the field to loot the corpses. As he watched a beggar slide a sharp blade across a French knight's neck, the blood that splattered painted Ryen's memory in crimson. The beggar thrust his dirty hands in the knight's pouches and stole whatever he could find of value.

Bryce could not stand the thought of one of these men defiling Ryen's body. He had to find her.

"C'mon, ya bloody cur," Rafe said to his companion. Dressed in a piece of soiled brown cloth that hung to his knees, torn at the elbows and shredded at the wrists, Rafe looked as if his whole life had been a battle. He stumbled up to the next knight, his bare feet sliding in the mud.

"I think I cut me bloody toe on one o' the blades," McDowell, his companion, said, limping, trying to peer down at his mud-covered foot. He was an older man with a head full of white hair. His entire body was caked with mud, his skin barely covered by a tunic and breeches that were so torn and ragged they hung from his thin limbs like an old cleaning cloth that had long outlived its usefulness.

"Oh, quit your complainin'. We ain't got time." Rafe bent down before the knight and lifted his helmet from his head.

The knight groaned and Rafe stood quickly, backing into his companion, yelling, " 'E's alive!"

"Oh, bloody hog," McDowell replied, and shoved passed Rafe. He bent on one knee in the mud and produced a dagger from his belt. He threw back the knight's chin, exposing white flesh, and drew the blade across it. "You're such a bloody *woman*," he commented, before cutting the knight's purse strings and handing the purse to Rafe.

Rafe took it. "Don't forget his hands!"

McDowell shifted his position and reached for the knight's gloved hand. He pulled the metal glove off and lifted up the bare hand. One ring glittered on the knight's first finger, and it was promptly removed. McDowell handed the ring to Rafe.

"Blimey! I believe it's solid gold," Rafe gasped, and stuck it in his mouth, biting down.

His companion hit him in the leg and Rafe gagged before spitting the ring out into his palm. "What ya tryin' ta do, choke me? I coulda swallowed that!"

"Lookie 'ere, mate," McDowell said, and crawled over to another fallen knight.

Rafe followed and bent over the knight, hoping to find riches beyond measure. His mouth gaped at what McDowell had found.

McDowell lifted his hands to the knight's helmet and gently tugged it off.

The soft feminine face was totally out of place amid the destruction and death.

"It's *her*. It's the Angel of Death!" Rafe gasped, staring raptly at her face.

McDowell shoved Rafe out of the way and climbed over her body to kneel at her head. He gathered her smooth hair in his bloody, mud-splattered hands and said, "I want this as proof. No one will bloody believe it." His sharp dagger was dull with blood.

Rafe gasped as the demon appeared, coming out of the

midst of fire, heading toward them. His eyes glowed red, like the devil himself, and Rafe knew immediately who it was.

"McDowell," Rafe croaked.

"Can't ya see I'm busy here?" McDowell insisted, putting the blade to her white forehead.

Suddenly, a weight so intense it threatened to crush his arm bore down upon McDowell's shoulder and he was lifted up until his feet were dangling in mid-air. The pain dulled his shoulder and his arm, and he dropped the dagger. Then, he was spun around until he was staring into eyes as black as coal.

"She is *mine*."

The words seemed to come from the depths of hell, for the demon's lips barely moved.

"Beggin' your pardon, sir," Rafe interrupted meekly. When the black eyes turned to scorch him to the ground, Rafe quivered and stuttered, "Your Princelyship . . . Your Darkness . . . I—I believe she's dead."

For the first time, the Prince of Darkness's shadowy eyes fastened on the woman and he released McDowell, who dropped to the ground like a heavy stone. "Pray you are wrong," the giant snarled, and bent beside the Angel of Death.

Rafe edged around the warrior woman and the giant, moving to his friend's side. The two exchanged glances and then turned back to the Prince of Darkness . . . to find that his black gaze was fixed on them. The demon stood slowly from his crouching position and Rafe's knees shook.

"Be gone from this place," the demon said, his eyes glowing as if the fires of hell had leapt to life in his body.

The two beggars turned and ran. McDowell slipped once in the mud and blood of the battlefield, but quickly stood and raced after Rafe.

* * *

Bryce watched until the two scavengers were out of sight, then turned back to her.

"Ryen," he said, kneeling again at her side. And then more tenderly, "Angel."

He slid his hand behind her neck and attempted to lift her head, trying to awaken her. He immediately felt moisture and pulled his hand away to see blood staining his fingers.

Anguish jarred his body and he scooped Ryen up into his arms, pushing another fallen knight from her legs. "Ah, God, Ryen," he whispered miserably, wishing for the hundredth time that she was not a knight. And especially not his enemy.

With long strides, he took her to his tent.

Bryce stared at Ryen's face. Gently, he ran the rag over her cheeks, wiping at the mud. He had removed her armor and cleaned and bandaged the cut on the back of her head. Through the whole process, she had not moved, not even groaned.

Bryce's stomach was twined so tight that he thought he would snap. He wasn't sure what the ache in his chest was, a heavy pressure that constricted, crushing his lungs until he could hardly breathe. Perhaps he was getting sick. He found that he could not take his eyes from Ryen's somber face. It was as if she were sleeping. Her entire face was relaxed, her soft lips parted.

Bryce felt a sudden need for her. He wanted to kiss her, thrust his tongue between those lips. The memory of her kiss had lingered like the delicate fragrance of a rose these past weeks, unwanted and distracting. The thought had returned during the long, lonely nights, and he thought upon the vow he had given to Ryen in the last moments he was with her: *I'll find you again.* For weeks he had wondered what had possessed him to promise that. No woman could be as he remembered her. So defiant and headstrong, yet so soft and innocent.

As he stared down at her, she was more than he remembered. Softer, more fragile.

"Damn," he murmured, standing and raking a hand through his hair. Where had the hatred gone? Only weeks before he had convinced himself that he had vowed to find her so that he could bring her to England to be humiliated for the death of Runt, so she could be punished, imprisoned in his dungeons. He had told himself that had been the plan all along. Nothing more. The hatred had sustained him through the long nights and through the pain of missing Runt.

Then, in King Henry's camp, word had reached them of her "betrayal." He remembered the day with heavy guilt. He had been eating with Henry, discussing the strategy for reaching Calais. The French had been cutting off the roads so that forward progress was impossible. The conversation had somehow turned to Ryen.

"What is she like?" King Henry had asked.

Bryce had pondered the question for a moment. He would not lie to his king. "She is . . . a warrior, my lord."

"No, no. What is the woman like? Is she ugly?"

"No," he had answered, more quickly than he had intended. "When she does not have her armor on, she is delicate and soft. But she likes to pretend she is not. She is also as cunning as a fox." He had looked Henry in the eye. "If she were born English, all of England would be at her feet."

"I have never heard you praise a woman so. She is pretty, then?"

"The little vixen has caused me more than one restless night."

Henry bit into a pear tart. "And a warrior, too? It is obvious you are intrigued by the girl. What does she think of you?"

Bryce thought upon the night he had been called to her tent, the way she had responded to his kiss, his touch. He did not answer, but attempted to change the subject. "I look forward to engaging the French Army."

Henry's eyes narrowed, and he pursued the topic with an

unwavering single-mindedness. "She may not be there," he replied.

Bryce paused in mid-bite to glance at his liege.

"Tell me, Bryce, did she aid in your escape?"

The hairs at the nape of Bryce's neck tingled. "No. Talbot got me out."

"Most of France believes she aided you." Henry dabbed at his mouth with a napkin. "She has brought dishonor to herself."

Bryce's brow darkened with each slanderous word. He dropped the meat onto the table and rose, walking to the tent flap. He stared out at the tents of English knights without really seeing them.

"This news disturbs you?" Henry wondered, his voice curious.

Bryce could not answer for the anger that closed his throat.

If Bryce had looked up, he would have seen his liege studying him with pensive eyes, obviously intrigued by his reaction. "Because if that disturbs you, I know something that may disturb you even more."

Bryce felt his shoulder muscles tense, his neck grow stiff.

After a long pause, Henry said, "She has been betrothed to another man."

Betrothed! Bryce felt his jaw clench, his hands tighten to fists. Rage burned through him like a roaring fire, enflaming his veins. The thought of another between her creamy thighs . . . His knuckles cracked, he was squeezing his fists so hard. He wiped the image aside. That was not the reason he was so angry, he told himself. She had to return to England with him to pay for Runt's death.

"Bryce?" Henry called.

He turned and saw the glimmer of curiosity in Henry's eyes. He could not get the picture of her vicious people ridiculing her out of his mind. His jaw ached from clenching his teeth, and his mind burned with feverish fury at the tor-

turned his shining sword to its sheath. Henry moved toward the tent flap once again.

"M'lord," Bryce called, his voice booming over the commotion.

All sound ceased and Henry turned to Bryce.

Bryce paused, trying to judge Henry's mood. If he was jubilant over the victory, he would be generous. If Henry was angry over the French raids, he would order Ryen's death. Indecision flitted through Bryce's mind, an uncomfortable feeling he did not enjoy.

"You have something to say?" Henry wondered.

Bryce was aware that every gaze was upon him. He straightened his shoulders. "I would speak with you in private, sire."

The ghost of a frown crossed Henry's face before he motioned everyone out of his tent.

As the tent flap swooshed shut, Henry turned to face Bryce. "This had better be important. I am in the midst of a war."

"Sire, I have found the Angel of Death," Bryce said.

Henry's brows drew together, his look thoughtful. "Is she alive?"

"Barely," he answered, the word constricting his throat.

Henry moved past Bryce, saying, "I would see her."

Bryce followed him into the camp. As they exited, the others gazed with curiosity as the king paused to ask, "Where is she?"

"This way, sire," Bryce murmured, and moved to lead the way.

With each step, hope began to pound through his body. The king deemed Ryen important enough for a glance; perhaps he would see the wisdom of sparing her life.

When they entered his tent, Bryce had to glare at the other men to keep them from following.

Talbot's face was grim, his mouth a hard line as he bowed to King Henry and stepped from Ryen's side to let the king look down upon her peaceful form.

Bryce watched Henry carefully.

Henry's brow furrowed as his blue eyes scanned every curve. "She is not what I expected," Henry finally stated. "You were right, Bryce. She does not look like France. She does not look like my enemy."

"But, she *is*," Talbot snarled. "She alone has killed thousands of our men."

"Talbot," Bryce warned.

Henry turned slowly from Ryen's soft features to face Bryce. "Talbot, leave us."

With a slight, stiff nod, Talbot departed.

"He is right, you know," Henry told Bryce. "You said it yourself. She is as cunning as a fox."

"She has also been spurned by her people."

"True." Henry cast a long look over his shoulder at Ryen before looking back at Bryce. "But who do you think she will blame for it?"

Bryce frowned. He had not considered the consequences of his actions. He would deal with them as they arose.

Henry ran his hands over his face in fatigue and sat in a nearby chair. "How do you think it would look were I to spare her life?"

Bryce sat heavily across from Henry, watching silently for a sign of judgment.

"You have served me well, Bryce," Henry told him, his back straightening with the weight of his decision. "Many battles have hinged on your strategic manèuvers, your skill on the battlefield. Perhaps a castle would be a better reward."

"I have a castle, my liege," Bryce replied evenly.

"A man can never have too many."

"I am a fighting man. I am rarely at Dark Castle now."

"Perhaps there is something else you need."

Bryce glanced at Ryen. Her soft lips parted, her skin pale in her deathlike slumber, her long lashes resting like a feather against her cheek. He watched the rise and fall of her breast for a moment. It was ironic how so many fought for her death, and he, her most hated enemy, was the only one who fought for her life. He pushed the image of this glorious woman from his mind and conjured images of Runt.

When he looked back at Henry, his eyes were hard. "I ask that you spare her life, my lord."

Henry stood. "Damn it, man! I cannot do that. While she does not look like my enemy, she *is*. Nothing can change that," Henry said, and headed for the tent flap. "My decision is made."

Bryce rose in a panic. "My liege, she killed my son!"

Henry froze in mid-step as if Bryce's words had penetrated his skin like a chill breeze. Slowly he turned. When he faced Bryce, his eyes were carefully blank.

"I ask that you spare her life so that I can inflict on her the pain she has put me through."

"I should not allow this, Bryce. Harm could befall you, your castle, or even me because of her treachery." Henry sighed heavily as if the conclusion was apparent. "But since you have been so faithful, I will allow it."

Bryce rose from his chair as his heart soared. "You shall not be sorry, sire."

Henry scowled. "The gleam in your eye does not befit a man who speaks of torture and pain."

Bryce looked away.

Henry stepped closer to Bryce, having to raise his face to speak to him. "Do not take my boon as kindness. If, through any action of hers, my subjects come to harm, I will hold you personally responsible. *You,* not she, will answer to my punishment."

Bryce bowed, acceptingly. "Yes, my lord."

Henry nodded and moved to the flap. Before he exited, he paused to glance back at Bryce. "You are a stubborn man, Bryce," he said. "Beware. You have death in your camp."

Twenty-six

The castle rose out of the flatland like an erupting mountain of stone, its man-made square towers and rectangular walls sharply contrasting with the natural roll of the earth. Bryce led his weary party over the drawbridge, trudging across the wooden planks that groaned beneath the passing weight of the returning warriors, and through the open gate. The outer ward was quiet, the peasants long since retired for the evening. The moon hid behind the clouds, afraid to shed its light on Dark Castle, and cast only a ghostly hint of illumination over the heavily shadowed fortress.

King Henry had given Bryce and his men a much-deserved rest from the endless war with the French. Bryce had surprised himself by accepting Henry's offer without much hesitation. As he neared the castle, Bryce was not surprised that he had not been greeted by banners and villagers waving to him in the streets. They had not known he was coming. He was grateful. He could not be the dark lord they expected him to be and stand stoically before them. Not now. Every bone in his body ached from the three days' march to Dark Castle. He had not allowed his knights to rest, stopping only when the horses needed water or tending. Bryce's gaze shifted to the wagon he rode beside as he rolled his shoulders in an effort to relieve the tension in them. Ryen lay bundled in blankets and furs, barely visible except for her tranquil face.

He had driven his army on relentlessly because he wanted

to get her to Dark Castle. The weather had remained fair and he was worried that if it changed to rain, she would become ill. She had not awakened from her long slumber during the entire trip back to England.

There was a commotion behind him and Bryce straightened, his hand flying to his sword's handle as he turned. One of his soldiers was stumbling to his feet from the ground, being helped up by two other men. A third knight had captured the reins of his rearing horse before it could bolt away. The exhausted knight was rubbing his eyes and yawning. He must have fallen asleep on his mount and tumbled to the ground, Bryce thought. He sighed, attempting to relax, but his shoulders remained stiff, his neck tight. There were rumors that some lords were angry at King Henry for sparing the Angel of Death and had vowed vengeance. Bryce was tense, jumping into battle-readiness at every noise, every movement.

He was grateful they had finally reached Dark Castle, and without incident, even if it was the middle of the night. He knew Ryen would be safe.

As they crossed the outer ward gatehouse, he found the yard empty of people. Only the stone wall of the inner ward was there to greet them. Bryce led his tired group toward the towering gate of the inner ward. He knew the guards of the outer gatehouse were spreading the word of his return. Bryce expected that there would be no one in the inner ward to greet them, either. But as the gates creaked open, he saw a small group of raggedy people lounging in the middle of the square.

At last, Bryce felt the tension fall from his shoulders like a loosened cape. As Bryce brought his horse to a halt and swung his leg over the side, the group of five men and two women approached him. A comfortable grin spread over his tired features. Behind him, he heard the sound of sighs, shifting of clothing, and clang of armor as his men dismounted from their horses.

"It must be too cold to go roaming through the fields," Bryce said.

The group formed a semicircle around Bryce. "We needed some ale," one of the men replied. He wore brown breeches and black boots, and a pelt of fur hung loosely around his oversized tunic. He ran a hand over his white beard as he regarded Bryce.

"I think you're becoming soft," Bryce answered warmly.

A younger man with brown hair and a scrawny beard held out his hand. "It's good to see you, too, brother," he greeted.

Bryce clasped his arm tightly, nodding. His eyes drifted back to the first man. He looked older than Bryce remembered. Last time he saw Night, his beard had no gray and the hair on top of his head was dark. He looked into his eyes and saw the signs of age withering the corners.

Night nodded as if in answer. "Yes, it has been a long time."

"We've been here three times since you left for court," the younger man said.

Bryce's gaze returned to him. Cub was ten Yules younger than Bryce, born here at Dark Castle. Bryce looked him over with a quick glance. Cub had filled out. Where before he had been scrawny and boyish, Cub was now muscular and . . . a man. Cub wore a tunic of fur and breeches which Bryce recognized instantly. His eyebrows shot up. "Raiding my chests while I am away?"

Cub shrugged. "I figured if you didn't take it with you, you didn't need it."

Bryce nodded. "You are welcome to anything in Dark Castle." His eyes swept the rest of the group. Grey stood beside Night. He was Bryce's age, but looked older, gray peppering his brown, unruly hair. The chain mail he wore over his tunic was rusting. He wore a fur cape for warmth. Grey nodded at Bryce, a crooked grin tugging one of the corners of his lips. Bryce returned the greeting.

Hunter wore leather armor beneath a tunic of gray. His

face was scarred across the cheek and on the chin; his black hair hung well past his shoulders, tied back with a piece of fur. His dark eyes narrowed at seeing Bryce's appraisal.

Breed stood near the back of the group. He had a fresh cut across his cheek and a black eye. His hot temper had landed him in trouble again, Bryce knew. He wore a pair of breeches and tunic that Bryce knew were his. His eyes glinted with defiance and Bryce was amused by the challenge he saw in his stance. He chuckled and was rewarded by Breed's scowl.

Bryce's gaze shifted to the two women. He knew only one. Patch was thin and shapely, but far from feminine. Her blond hair hung in dirty clumps filled with thick knots. She wore breeches and a fur tunic. In her brown eyes, Bryce saw fondness as she gazed at him. He grinned in return.

Beside her stood a new addition to the Wolf Pack. She had the look of a hunted animal, her eyes constantly shifting from side to side, her wiry body bent as if in preparation to flee. Her dark hair was hidden in the folds of a woolen hood draped over her head.

Night stated, "Her name's Trap."

Bryce nodded once.

"Where's Runt?" Patch wondered, glancing beyond Bryce at the supply wagons that were now entering the inner ward.

Bryce straightened his shoulders. He tried to push every painful emotion from his body, but could not manage to rid himself of even one. The boy's image rose before his eyes, his black hair, that stray lock that fell into his blue eyes. In his mind, he heard Runt's joyful cry upon returning home, saw Runt dash into Dark Castle, calling for his mother. But the vision was agonizing, the dying voice echoing in his head only. A memory. Bryce tightened his jaw against the heartache that once again filled his chest and burned his eyes. "He died in a fire," Bryce replied, his voice cold, detached.

Patch's brows furrowed deeply in sorrow.

Bryce turned to the wagon where Ryen was lying. He

vaulted over the side and stood over her. As he gazed down at her still, pale face, his love for Runt consumed his heart. She had to be punished. It was in her camp that his boy died. It was on French soil. Even as he thought these things, the desire to touch her soft cheek, her silken hair, to kiss her full lips and breathe life into her again, to see her large, piercing eyes open, filled him so completely that he had to clench his fists tightly at his side to keep from acting on the impulse.

Finally, he bent and scooped her up into his arms. He pulled her close to his chest, shielding her from the chill of the night as he stepped off the wagon.

"Who is she?" Grey asked, moving toward him.

Bryce tightened his arms around her as if his strength would give her the power to recover. He looked down at the fur-lined brown cloak that concealed her face. A stray strand of hair had torn free from the wrappings and gently blew in the soft breeze that suddenly surrounded them.

"She is my prisoner," Bryce replied possessively, and marched toward the castle.

Grey cast a baffled, curious look at Night before following Bryce into Dark Castle.

Bryce sat in the chair beside Ryen, his face in his hands. He had been by her side for most of the night, refusing visitors.

"You can't stay in here forever," Talbot said from behind him.

Bryce had heard Talbot enter the room some time ago. "No," Bryce replied wearily, rubbing his stubbled chin, "only until she awakens." His gaze came to rest on Ryen. In the morning sun that shone through the window, Bryce could see how pale she was. He longingly remembered the red that had colored her cheeks when he had last seen her.

"What if she doesn't awaken?" Talbot asked. "Will you follow her into hell?"

Bryce's shoulders stiffened and set with anger. Only his friend would dare speak thus to him. She would not die. She could not. Not like this. He longed to hold her hand, to touch her skin, but he was afraid if he did that she would be so cold . . . that the last strands of hope would leave his body.

Talbot shook his head sadly. "Why do you sit at her side, my friend? You should awaken Lotte, tour your castle, or at the very least, get some sleep."

"I can't," Bryce responded stoically.

"You sit here like some lovesick pup! Think of what your people will say. Think how it looks! God's blood, Prince, she was responsible for the slaughter of hundreds of knights under your command! How can you allow her to live?"

"She was responsible for my son's death," Bryce answered quietly. "She *must* live. If only to pay for that."

Talbot released his breath slowly. "If that is the reason, then why did you not throw her in the dungeon? Why did you bring her to your own room?" When Bryce did not answer, Talbot continued quietly, "Bryce, I vowed loyalty to you many many years ago. But I also took a vow to England and to King Henry. I hope you will not force me to choose one over the other."

Bryce heard Talbot's footsteps recede as he walked across the floor and departed. Why had he brought her to his room? To make sure she recovered, he answered silently. She could die from drafts and rat bites in the dungeon. At least here, in his room, he could see that she was able to rest and be well cared for. He looked at her again. She could not die. The thought rose in his mind over and over. I will not let her.

"She is very pretty for a prisoner," the voice murmured at his side.

Bryce started. He should have heard Grey coming, had always been able to. But now, his mind was occupied by the Angel.

"Is she a duke's wife?" Grey wondered.

"She is Ryen De Bouriez," Bryce answered.

"A Frenchwoman?" Grey chuckled. "And this is all your mighty army brought back from France?"

"She is the Angel of Death."

Grey was silent for a long moment. "A woman? Intriguing."

Bryce squeezed his tired eyes closed and dropped his head. Yes, a woman. During his days of captivity he had pondered the outrageousness of it for many a moment. He rose out of the chair, stretching his arms above his head.

"You look like death itself." A smile touched Grey's weathered features. "Perhaps some food and a drink with old friends will resurrect you."

Bryce longed to leave his worries behind. He almost accepted. Then, he looked back over his shoulder at the woman lying in his bed. True, she was safer at Dark Castle than on the road, but even here there were people who would wish her ill. He could not leave her.

Bryce turned to Grey to tell him, but before he opened his mouth, Grey smiled a knowing grin as if seeing his innermost thoughts. "Patch will guard her while you eat with us."

The Wolf Pack had the most uncanny ability to see into his soul. He'd forgotten how the gift could startle him. Finally, Bryce nodded. He needed to say no more.

When they reached the door, Patch was there as if by intuition. She exchanged a nod with them before slipping into Bryce's bedchamber. Grey shut the door behind them and together they walked the long hallway. Two sets of empty plate armor lined the corridor, silently guarding the passage. They were in bad need of a cleaning.

They turned right and took the first set of steps into the Great Hall.

The Wolf Pack was already seated around a long wooden table that stretched out just below the three stained glass windows, each painted with a snarling red wolf. The hearth fire was blazing, and Bryce felt the warmth cover his body, warming his cold soul. He was home. It had indeed been a long time. Too long. He noticed that the rushes were in dire need of changing. The room stank of soot and rotted meat, not of violets and ale, as had the De Bouriez Great Hall.

Three of his hounds rushed to greet him. He paused momentarily to pat their heads and scratch behind their ears before he followed Grey to the table.

Grey hurtled his fur cape over the table onto the back of a wooden chair, then leapt over the table to take the seat. Bryce noted a vacant chair between Night and Grey intended, he supposed, for him.

Bread and ale were before him, and Bryce noted how not one servant had met his eyes, how they'd trembled in his presence. He had grown accustomed to Ryen and her defiant looks and barbed tongue. Their sniveling repulsed him.

Finally, an older maid he remembered as Polly lifted her eyes to meet his before quickly dropping them. She curtsyed and muttered, "It's good ta have m'lord home," then raced off.

Bryce was surprised at her boldness. Usually, the servants didn't dare raise eyes or words to him. Only his steward brought him word of important happenings throughout the castle, and then only when necessary. The villeins of his lands feared him as the servants did. As a result, most squabbles were settled before he had to preside over them. Only occasionally did he have to make a judgment.

Bryce watched the maid scurry from the room as fast as her plump little form would allow. An amused smile slid over his lips . . . he would have Polly care for Ryen.

"It seems you were truly missed," Night said, hunched over his bread, his eyes on the door through which Polly had disappeared.

"Perhaps no one thought they would see you again," Hunter murmured, tipping back his chair.

"We had heard that you were captured," Night went on. "By some Angel of Death."

Bryce cast Grey a quick look in time to see a sly smile spread over his face. Bryce reached for the bread and tore off a large piece with his hands, filling his mouth with food.

"Not once," Hunter snorted, "but three times." He ripped off a piece of bread with his teeth.

"I thought I taught you better than that, Bryce," Night grimaced.

"It was only twice," Bryce argued softly.

Grey and Breed laughed.

"Prince!" The voice exploded through the room, echoing from wall to wall.

Bryce didn't have to raise his eyes to know the voice. He was dreading the confrontation with Lotte. He heard her foot-steps race across the hall and stood to greet her. As she rounded the table, approaching him, Bryce saw she had put on weight. Her breasts were large and bounced with each step. Her face had grown rounder, but her hair was just as dark and long as he remembered.

Lotte reached for him with open arms, but Bryce grabbed her wrists to stop her embrace. Confusion washed over her features. She smelled of sweat, ashes, and burnt bread, not the sweet fragrance of roses. Her hair looked unkempt, as if she had not bothered to comb it in days, so unlike Ryen's soft, silky tresses.

Bryce found himself instantly repelled. He lowered her arms. Had she changed so much, or was it he that had changed?

Yet there was something in her eyes, something familiar that caused his heart to contract with pain. He narrowed his eyes, trying to figure out what it was. Then she gently shook her head and a strand of dark hair fell into her eyes.

Runt. He had his mother's eyes!

Bryce turned away from her, his throat tightening. "Runt is dead," he announced.

Lotte gasped, "No." She clutched her neck and stepped back.

"He was killed in a fire in the French camp," Bryce explained. He half turned to her, expecting a wail or tears. All she did was lower her head, chewing on her lip. There were no tears, no regret, in her features. Bryce straightened. "He is gone, Lotte," Bryce repeated.

Lotte glanced up at Bryce. She tentatively reached out to put her hands on his shoulders. "That doesn't mean that I can't still be yours."

For a moment, he didn't move, didn't breathe. All Runt was to her was a claim to him, a place in Dark Castle. The fury was sudden and hot. It clenched his fists, hardened his will. He pushed her hands off his shoulders, his face twisting into a mask of disgust. "Get away from me," he snarled.

Tears welled in Lotte's chestnut eyes. He could see her sharp mind working, plotting her return to his side. She raised her hands to cover her mouth, weeping. "My son! My son!" She leaned into his chest, resting her forehead against it.

Bryce jerked away. "Your grief comes just a second too late, Lotte."

As he turned to retake his seat, Lotte reached out a hand. "We can have another boy," she said desperately.

Bryce tried to control the anger that raced through his veins. It was useless. When he turned to her, his posture was stiff, his fists clenched so tightly that his knuckles were white. "The boy would not be Runt."

Lotte backed slowly away from the explodable rage that brewed inside of him.

Finally, when she had taken a seat very far away from him, Bryce was able to turn and sit. His anger fueled his every movement as he ripped off a chunk of bread and stuffed it into his mouth. He stared at his hands and was surprised to find them shaking. He dropped the bread onto the table and clenched his fists in an effort to stop the trembling.

Curse her, he thought. She never loved the boy. He remembered the burning embarrassment because his father was weak and sickly. He resented his father, then. But, through it all, his father had loved him. Bryce could not imagine what it was like to be unloved by your own mother.

The image of Runt lying lifeless in his arms blazed into his mind's eye. He could not have wanted a more loyal son. And now he was gone. He would never hear him laugh again. He would never have to brush that damn fool lock of hair away from his eyes. He would never get the chance to see him fulfill his dream of becoming a knight.

Bryce's eyes darted angrily toward his room, where his prisoner lay. Ryen must be punished for Runt's death.

It was then that he felt others watching him. He looked around the room to find Grey leaning back in his chair, one leg resting over the arm, casually munching on a piece of bread and regarding Bryce through lazy eyes. As he slanted a cursory glance at his friends, he found they were all surveying him with mild, silent interest.

His gaze finally returned to Grey. He tossed the bread back onto the tray.

Grey grinned sadly and took a long drink of beer.

Finally, it was Night who broke the silence. "The prisoner," he said, "what will you do with her?"

"I haven't decided yet," Bryce replied. He noticed how Night looked at Grey, who arched an eyebrow and shrugged his shoulders.

"She would bring a good bag of gold if you decided to ransom her," Hunter announced around a mouthful of bread.

Breed chuckled. "She was quite a piece. Perhaps you could give her to us." He gestured around the table at the other members of the Wolf Pack.

Hunter snickered lustfully.

Bryce straightened, his eyes narrowing on Breed. "No one will touch her while she is in my castle." His voice was dangerous, his posture stiff, threatening.

At his menacing voice, all eyes again turned to him.

"Who is this woman that she merits such protection?" Hunter wondered, drawing the rage in Bryce's gaze.

"She is the Angel of Death," Bryce answered.

Stunned silence fell over the room, blanketing it with curiosity and shocked surprise.

As Bryce continued to eat, his mind occupied by thoughts of his captive, he did not notice Lotte when she slithered from her chair and headed for the stairs.

Twenty-seven

The scream sliced through Ryen's pain-clouded mind like a blade. She struggled to open her eyes. And when she did, she saw a woman with long, dark hair coming at her with a dagger, her hair disheveled, her eyes wild with hate. Ryen fought to raise her hands to protect herself, but they were too heavy. The pain receded, and relief stitched closed her mind, sealing off the rest of the world.

The dagger arced down toward Ryen's heart just as the small whirlwind slammed into Lotte's side, knocking her to the floor. Patch howled and grabbed the hand that held the dagger above their heads as they rolled across the floor. Lotte's scream replaced Patch's roar as Patch pinned Lotte beneath her by straddling her body. Lotte fought for a moment before she was slapped hard across her face. With the jolt, the dagger fell from her fist and clattered across the floor to land at Bryce's feet.

He stood in the doorway, staring at the dagger. Then his eyes shifted to Lotte.

Patch rose, hauling Lotte to her feet. Lotte yanked her arm free, screeching, "She killed him! She killed Runt!"

Bryce bent and picked up the dagger. At first, his mind refused to accept the fact that one of his own people had almost stabbed Ryen through the heart. Here he was worried about another lord, and Lotte was the one who'd tried to end Ryen's life.

He turned the dagger over slowly in his hand, watching the candlelight reflect off its shining surface. It wasn't because Ryen had killed Runt. The woman had no feelings for her son—that alone was enough to make Bryce hate her. He stopped flipping the dagger. It was because Ryen had smashed every security Runt represented for Lotte.

Slowly his eyes rose, the hate shining from them like beacons.

"It was in her camp!" Lotte hissed. "She is responsible!"

"Thank you, Patch," Bryce murmured.

Patch nodded and brushed by him as she exited the room.

Bryce moved forward and Lotte retreated. "And you would kill her as she lay sleeping . . . *defenseless?*"

Lotte's eyes glinted. "For our son—"

Bryce's voice was low and dangerous. "He meant nothing to you!"

"Of course he did. He was my son, too."

"He was nothing to you except an heir to my estates."

"That's not true!"

"And now you feel that Ryen poses some sort of danger to your security here at Dark Castle."

Her voice changed to the controlled, even tone that signified her anger. "Ryen, is it? Not prisoner, not enemy?"

Bryce turned to her. Lotte's brown eyes were focused on the bed where Ryen slept. "Raise a hand to her again and you shall be banned from Dark Castle." Bryce suddenly realized with an absolute certainty that he'd never loved Lotte. She was cruel and manipulative. Even in bed, her touch was calculated not for pleasure, but to control him. He used her for a need and the fact that she had had his child meant nothing to him. He turned his back on her.

"You would choose the killer of our son over me?"

His knuckles closed tightly around the hilt of the dagger.

"If you cannot kill her, I will."

He was before her in two steps. His large hand wrapped around her arm as he hauled her to the tips of her toes. "Hear you nothing that I say, woman?"

"I will take vengeance for our son."

"She did not kill Runt," Bryce snarled.

"The fire was in her camp! She lit it to kill your son!"

"She did not know he was my son." At Lotte's confusion, he continued, but more to himself, his voice full of agony. "Ryen did not kill Runt! She would not have torched half of her camp to kill a small, insignificant boy." It had been an accident. *An accident.* He released Lotte suddenly, almost dropping her. Bryce bowed his head, staring at the floor. "It was because of me Runt was in France at all. And it was me he came after."

He smashed his fist into the wall beside Lotte's head. She cringed, broke away and ran past him.

He heard different footsteps approach from behind him.

"She did not kill Runt," Bryce murmured, his voice thick with sick realization.

"I know," Grey answered quietly. "You need time away, brother. Go. She will be watched."

Bryce lifted heavy eyes to Grey.

"And protected, if need be."

Bryce nodded. He cast one last miserable look at Ryen, wishing desperately that she was awake, before departing the room.

Pain cut deep into Ryen's mind, bringing with it hazy glimpses of people . . . a dark-haired woman, her eyes angry . . . a small, thin girl with a scar across her cheek bending close . . . Bryce, his dark eyes underlined with rings of sleeplessness, his brow creased with lines of worry . . .

Voices floated to her, quiet, hushed. At first Ryen could

not understand what they were saying, but after a moment, the mumbling became words as she recognized that they were spoken in English.

"She's going to die. Ain't no hope for it," a woman's voice murmured.

"Do na say that," a second girl's voice responded. "The lord would be most dis—dis—dis—"

"Distraught."

"Ya! Distraught. He's tried so hard ta keep 'er alive."

"She hasn't been awake for days. And she's so thin."

Ryen's eyes fluttered as she struggled to open them, groaning with the effort.

"She's tossin' again," the girl stated.

Ryen opened her eyes. A young girl was staring at her, a scar etched into her cheek. Her peaceful brown eyes went round in fright. "Gaw!" the girl cried. "She's awake! She saw me! Me limbs are turnin' ta stone!"

The girl merged into shadow as she leapt away from the bed, out of the small circle of light cast by a single candle.

"Don't be ridiculous," the woman said, as she moved into Ryen's view. Brown eyes gazed at her with indifference. "She's just raving. I'm tellin' ya, the fever will take her soon and she'll be out of our lives."

Ryen tried to speak, but her lips were brittle and cracked, and her words caught in her parched throat. Finally, she managed to gag, *"Water."*

The girl with the brown eyes peeked over the woman's shoulder like a frightened child to whisper, "Wha' that she sayin'?"

The woman shrugged her beefy shoulders, nonchalantly pushing a strand of dark hair from her eyes. "French. She's ramblin'. We might as well bury her now."

"My ma told me dat ya canna kill the Angel of Death."

English, Ryen reminded herself: What was the word for water? Her mind ached as she forced herself to think.

"We ain't killin' nobody, Kit. She's already dead, I keep tellin' ya," the woman said.

"But she's seen our faces. What if she comes back for us?"

"Water," Ryen gasped in English.

"Gaw!" Kit cried again, stepping back.

The woman turned hard, assessing eyes to Ryen. "Ya best get Talbot," she said to Kit, keeping her gaze on Ryen.

"Ya mean she might live? Polly! Ya bloody told me I could have her helmet! I already told—"

"Quiet," Polly snapped. "Go get Talbot before I leave ya alone with her."

Kit fled from the room.

Polly bent close to Ryen. She placed a cool hand against Ryen's forehead before turning to retrieve a goblet from the side table.

Ryen's head swam as Polly gently placed a hand beneath her head and lifted. The goblet was cold against her lips and, as the water cascaded over her parched throat, Ryen heard Polly murmur, "Ya are a fighter, I must say that. I truly believed ya would not live." Polly pulled the goblet from Ryen's lips after she took a few sips. "Not too much, or ya'll be sick."

Ryen ached for more of the soothing liquid, but she saw Polly place it back on the wooden table and did not have the strength to object. She laboriously turned her head to see where she was. Most of the room was in darkness. Soft pillows cushioned her head, warm blankets covered her body. A light, gauzy black curtain separated the rest of the room from the bed, except on Polly's side. There, it was drawn back. On a table beside the bed was a single candle, the only light in the tomb of darkness.

"Where am I?" Ryen asked.

"You are a prisoner." The answer came from the darkness.

Ryen tensed. Tingles of dread shot up the back of her neck. I know that voice, Ryen thought.

Polly rose and turned. "Sir," she said, "I believe she will live."

Silence.

"My lord will be pleased," she continued.

Ryen watched as one of Polly's hands wrang the other, again and again.

"Yes," the voice finally said tightly.

Her heart stopped as she recalled the last thing she had seen before the darkness took her; dark eyes staring at her through a silver visor.

Bryce!

Ryen's stomach tensed and she pushed herself up until she was in a sitting position. Pain flared through her head, and she put a hand to the origin, the base of her skull. She found a mended wound. Slowly, she lifted her head and saw the woman backing away from her, the fear in her wide eyes. She heard metal hiss and recognized the familiar sound—a weapon being drawn.

The sword came toward her out of the darkness, pointing straight at her face. "Don't think to try anything, *Angel*."

The room swam before her eyes and she willfully shook away the darkness that threatened to overcome her. He stepped forward and Ryen's eyes widened with recognition. She knew him immediately. His hateful gaze locked on her now as it had in her chamber. His right arm was in a sling, but other than that, he looked unscathed! How could that be? They had fallen fifty feet! They should both be dead!

"Bryce," she gasped, the anguish of months of thinking him dead rising into her throat. "Where is he?" Her heart beat hopefully, fluttering at the mere thought of him.

"You stupid bitch!" Talbot snarled. "He left you and still you cry out his name! He told me how you spread your legs for him, you ugly whore. You are *nothing* to him!"

Her own doubts from the mouth of another hurt her worse than if he had run her heart through. She sat stunned, unable to look away from his vengeful gaze.

"Don't you think if he cared for you he would be here?" his voice mocked.

The darkness crept forward from the edge of the room.

"Instead, he is in the arms of another," he whispered through clenched teeth.

The thought of Bryce's loving face hovering above the dark-haired woman who had haunted her dreams, fluttering kisses over her naked body—kisses she had imagined Bryce giving to her—sent Ryen reeling into the blackness that opened its arms to welcome her.

The voice came to her through a haze.

"Come on, now. Ya cannot sleep yer life away. I got orders ta get ya up. Ya should be eatin'."

Light assaulted Ryen's closed eyes and she groaned, tentatively opening one eye to squint into the morning sun.

Polly came into her view, her body blocking the light, her hands on her ample hips. "Now, ya can't be abed forever. 'Taint good for . . ." Her voice trailed off.

Ryen raised her eyes to meet Polly's and saw sympathy in the woman's gaze before Polly turned away.

Ryen raised a hand to block out the light, but her palm brushed against wetness. Startled, she ran her fingers over her cheek to find her face was wet. Dumbfounded, she gazed at her moist fingers. After a moment, she brought them to her lips. The salty taste of tears tingled the tip of her tongue. Surprise washed over her, followed immediately by humiliation. She wiped at her cheeks with her hands and then with the sleeve of her nightdress.

Nightdress? She glanced at the silky garment. It was more beautiful than any she had ever seen. It laced up the front and was made of the softest, smoothest white cloth she had ever felt. Who had dressed her? Who had attended her while she was unconscious?

"This will help."

Ryen looked up to find a towel dangling from Polly's hands.

Angry with herself for her weakness, Ryen turned away, burying her face deep in the pillow. She felt the bed bend beneath the maid's weight as she sat beside her.

"Ya needn't fret over a few shed tears," Polly said. "Many a maid would have lost their senses by now."

But I am not a maiden, Ryen thought, her fists clenching the pillow until her fingers ached.

"Why, jus' the other day I was sayin' ta Melinda what a—"

Ryen whirled on Polly, half sitting up. "Stop your prattling and get out!"

Polly rose, her large brown eyes wide with surprise. Quickly her look darkened. "Well, now. Ifn that's how ya feel . . ." She turned on her heel.

Ryen watched her storm across the room. Stupid woman, she thought. The Angel of Death, fretting over a few tears? Why, she didn't even know why she shed them! Just because she was a prisoner in a foreign land, kept by a man she'd once loved who'd used her, and who must now hate her.

Ryen's shoulders slumped. She raised her head to cry to Polly to wait, but the door slammed behind the maid. Ryen sighed quietly. A hundred questions raced through her mind. Why was she here? And why was she in this room as if she were a guest? She should be in the dungeon, if this was Bryce's castle.

His image rose before her eyes. Dark, dark hair waving in a soft breeze. Black eyes staring at her, calling to her with a hypnotic power. The corners of his mouth turned up in a devilish grin, the scar on his cheek looking white against his bronzed skin. He was leaning against a wall, his right leg bent at the knee, crossed over his ankle.

She had dreamt of him. The image was so familiar Ryen could have sworn it had been real. But she could not remember how the dream had ended. All she could recall was that he had stood like a dark god.

Ryen swung her legs out of bed. She faltered as a wave of dizziness crashed over her, sending the room spinning around her. She closed her eyes, forcing the swirling to stop. It took a moment before the sickness dissolved.

From her seated position on the bed, Ryen surveyed the room. It was sparsely decorated, with one chair near the window next to a small table by the fourposter bed. A dark woven tapestry on the far wall depicted a horned man rising from a cave opening. Around the cave were wolves, their mouths dripping with saliva, their eyes glowing red. Two wolves faced the man, subservient, their heads hanging down to their chests. The two others were turned away, growling at the people who cowered and crawled over one another to reach the man, their hands outstretched toward him, some empty, some with offerings. Behind him, the large moon shone as a silver sliver.

Something was agonizingly familiar about the smug look on the horned man's face, but Ryen couldn't place it.

Suddenly the door creaked and Ryen snapped her head around to see it pause halfway open.

"C'mon. I paid ya a shillin'. Ya said I could see her," a man's voice echoed in the room.

"But she might be awake. I—I don't think—" Ryen recognized the voice as the girl she had seen with Polly. Kit. "I could get a beatin', ya know."

"I won't let that happin' ta ya," the man whispered.

There was a moment of silence before the girl giggled. "Awright! Don't do that. It tickles me ear." The door swung open.

Ryen knew she should be angry at being displayed like some animal, but somehow she admired the girl's ingenuity. Her lips twitched with humor. As she straightened her back, ready for the confrontation, her feet swung and knocked into something.

She quickly looked down to see a small stool near the side of the bed. Her eyes flashed to the open door where two shadows were entering. An idea popped into her head and a grin lit her face. Without taking her eyes from her victims, she positioned the stool beneath her feet.

The girl entered first, her shoulders hunched. The man followed her. The girl lifted her head only steps into the room to lock gazes with Ryen. "Gaw!" she cried, and froze. "She's awake!" She backed up as if to flee, but bumped into the man, stepping on his foot.

"Ahhh!" he cried, and shoved the girl forward to the floor. "What 'ya tryin' ta do, Kit?" He hobbled, holding his wounded foot. Then, seeing the girl gesturing wildly at Ryen, the man shifted his stare to her.

Ryen raised her eyebrows and pouted, hoping to look defenseless.

It worked.

The man put his foot down. "Is *this* the bloody Angel of Death? She looks scared!" He turned a dark look on Kit. "Is this a trick?" He raised a fist to strike her. "I ought ta—"

Fear gripped Ryen's heart as her eyes focused on his raised fist. "I am Ryen De Bouriez," she said suddenly.

He turned his full attention to her and stepped forward, lowering his hand.

Ryen stared at him, carefully keeping her face blank.

He moved forward, one tentative step at a time. "You're the one whose looks can turn a man ta stone?"

Closer.

"You're the one who can turn a man's blood ta ice?"

Closer.

"You're the Angel of Death who sacrifices our children to your dark lord?"

He was directly in front of Ryen when he looked back at Kit. "There must be another one."

But when he returned his gaze to Ryen, she towered above

him, arms outstretched, fingers clawing the air inches before his face. Her eyes were wild, her teeth bared.

"Give me your heart! I must feast!" she growled in an inhuman voice.

He screamed and clutched his heart as he raced for the door.

Kit's scream joined his as she bounded after him. But she was too late; the door slammed in her face. Her fingers were clawing desperately at the wood when the sound reached her. She stopped, listening.

Laughter!

Slowly Kit turned, wide eyes gazing over her shoulder to see Ryen rolling on the bed, her arms wrapped around her stomach, gales of laughter issuing from her lips.

Kit turned, pressing her back to the door. She was frozen with fear.

When Ryen saw her, she wiped the tears of mirth from her eyes and sat up. She pitied the girl for listening so trustfully to the legends. "It's what he wanted, wasn't it? It was what he paid for."

Kit gaped speechless as she stared at Ryen with terror.

Ryen grinned mischievously. "And you got your shilling."

Kit did not move from the door.

"Kit, is it?" Ryen asked, rising from the bed. She held out her hand. "Pleased to meet you. I am Ryen De Bouriez. I am the knight people call the Angel of Death." When Kit didn't move forward or take her hand, Ryen lowered it. "I'm the person you see before you now, Kit. Just a woman like you who has feelings and fears. I do not worship Satan, I am not an ice maiden, and I have never, in all my life, hurt a child."

Kit swallowed. "Ya mean, yer not gonna eat me heart?"

Ryen chuckled, but quickly stopped as she saw the horror and belief etched in the girl's face and recoiling body. "No," Ryen stated simply, curbing the impulse to add, "I only do that when the moon is full."

Kit frowned. Hesitantly, she edged a step closer.

"I suppose I should be furious with you," Ryen stated. "After all, you did sell me for a shilling."

A different kind of concern filled Kit and worry washed over her face. "You're not gonna tell his lordship, are ya?" Ryen opened her mouth to reply, but Kit continued, "I didna see any harm in it. 'E just wanted ta get a look at ya, is all."

Ryen smiled brightly. "No . . . I won't tell."

Kit sighed, but then, just as quickly, doubt furrowed her eyebrows. "I ain't signin' me soul away now."

The door opened quite suddenly, causing Kit to whirl around.

Ryen saw Polly waddle into the room with a tray in her chubby hands. The old maid cast a sour look at Ryen, her fat cheeks puckered, her eyes narrow. Then, she turned her anger on Kit. "An' what are ya doin' here?"

"I—I—" Kit stammered, under Polly's berating tone.

"Out. Now!" Polly ordered, slamming the tray down on the night table.

Kit scampered to the door. Ryen saw Kit pause in the doorway long enough to cast her a thoughtful gaze. Then, she turned and was gone.

Polly whirled and with a "harrumph" was off toward the door.

Ryen opened her mouth to object, but the door was already slamming shut. With a sigh, Ryen lay back on the bed.

Her eyes were again drawn by the tapestry. The horned man's eyes seemed to be focused on her. They were dark, like a midnight sky, reflecting the moon in their obsidian depths. They were so familiar . . . like . . .

Venison. The smell wafted to her senses and she sat up. Following the smell with her nose, she inched toward the tray.

It was not until she saw the bowl of soup and the hard, crusty bread on the tray that she realized her stomach was rumbling. It had been days since she had last eaten.

The day before the battle.

She descended on the food like a starved child, shoving

things into her mouth, slurping the tasty soup. When she had eaten almost half, she found she could not eat another bite, nor take another sip, or her stomach would explode. Ryen slowly sat on the edge of the bed. She rubbed her stomach, letting the wonderful taste of the food wash through her body, filling it. She lifted the towel and wiped her mouth, running her tongue over her lips to get the last taste.

Ryen groaned with pleasure and looked gratefully at the half-empty bowl. That's when she saw it; it had been hidden beneath the towel.

The blade glinted in the morning light, and as if in a dream, Ryen reached out. Her long, slim fingers wrapped around the wooden handle of the dagger. She picked it up, holding it before her eyes, trying to convince herself it was real.

A dagger! She quickly looked to the wooden door. It somehow did not seem so large or impeding as it had before.

Ryen pushed herself to her feet, only to find that the room tilted suddenly and she had to clutch the edge of the small table to steady herself. I should rest, she thought. But the lure of escape was much too strong.

As soon as the dizziness faded, Ryen crossed the room on shaky legs, her bare feet treading lightly on the cold stones. When she reached the door, Ryen lifted the blade, easily sliding it between door and stone wall. She paused for a moment, wishing she had seen the lock, hoping it was similar to the bolt on the door of her room, the one Lucien had locked her in with.

Lucien. She froze, all of her nerves becoming numb. Where were her brothers? If they were alive, they never would have let her be captured. The thought flitted through her mind before she could stop it. Waves of cold terror crashed over her body and she had to slide the blade out of the door frame, afraid her trembling hands would drop it.

No, she told herself. I mustn't think of this now. I have to escape. I have to get away before Bryce . . . before I see him. Before he sees me and those deep eyes of his turn my senses into a confused muddle, before he touches me and brands me with his raw heat, before those lips touch mine and wipe out any rational defenses I have left.

She forced calm through her body. Again she slid the blade into the small opening. She moved the blade up until it hit the bar preventing her escape on the outside of the door. Then she worked it back and forth, searching for the knob. The blade caught on nothing.

Frustrated, she stopped, switching hands. Back and forth. Again, nothing.

"Damn it," she muttered, flinging the blade up. It hit the bar with a thud—and the bar swung free! It twirled in a half circle and swayed uselessly. The door creaked open.

Ryen stared, shocked at the simplicity of the lock. Slowly, she pushed the door open just enough to peek out.

The long cold hall was dim except for muted rays of clouded sunlight from the windows high above that speckled the bricks with spots of brightness. There was not a soul in sight as Ryen stepped from her prison.

Twenty-eight

Ryen hunched her shoulders, her bare feet treading delicately with each step as she moved down the murky hallway. She clutched the dagger in her hand, ready to do battle to escape. Anything to get away from Bryce. Her escape would humiliate him, as he had humiliated her.

She turned the corner, her white nightdress swirling about her ankles. The halls were strangely quiet. At her father's castle, the sound of children's laughter, the whispering of two maidens, or her father's bellow could be heard at any given time. But here there was nothing except a strange silence, as if she were in the bowels of an abandoned hell.

Suddenly, her senses magnified. The hairs on the nape of her neck straightened and she froze, listening. No sound, no movement. Was it a trap? Every fiber in her body tingled with warning. Something was not right. Slowly, cautiously, she resumed her walk.

A grumble in her stomach, followed by a sudden onslaught of nausea, caused her to stumble. She grabbed the wall with her hand and bent over. The soup that had tasted so good rose violently in her throat and she vomited until dry heaves shook her body. Tears dripped from the corners of her eyes as she wiped a hand across her mouth. Gasping, she leaned her back against the cool stones of the wall.

She heard a noise from behind her and slowly turned her head. A girl no more than twelve stood staring at her.

Ryen watched recognition wash over her young face. The

girl gasped and ran away. Ryen knew she should move, that an alarm would be sounded soon, but her body suddenly felt heavy, like the floor was pulling her down. As she pushed herself from the wall, her muscles ached with protest. Every bone in her body objected as she continued down the hall and her mind reeled, causing her to stagger more than once. Finally, she paused and shook her head, trying to clear it.

"It's the Angel of Death!"

Ryen looked up to see two knights. The shorter knight wore a full suit of chain mail, where the taller knight with the bright red hair and thick crimson beard wore only a tunic and leggings. They both stared at her in fear and awe.

Ryen's senses cleared enough to recognize their hesitancy. She raised the dagger before her. "Back away, or I will cut out your hearts."

"She is only a woman," the red-haired man said after a moment. "We can take her."

"She is the Angel of Death, McFinley," the second hissed, already backing away, his hand protectively covering his heart.

McFinley growled and stepped toward Ryen. Through the haze that had surrounded her, Ryen saw the respectful distance he gave the dagger as he circled to her left.

"Come on, girl," he goaded.

The dizziness fell over her like a blanket and she stumbled, lowering the dagger.

He came at her, and Ryen reacted by instinctively lifting the weapon.

"Argh!"

Ryen pulled back and shook her head to clear it. When the haze retreated, she gasped at the sight before her. McFinley was slumped over, clutching his arm. Her dagger was on the floor, its tip marked with his blood.

Ryen inhaled sharply and stepped back. She turned to flee, only to run straight into Talbot! His fist came around fast. The impact numbed her cheek as the force of the blow spun her to the floor. Blackness invaded her vision, and Ryen clenched her fists, willing the darkness away.

"My arm!"

"How did she get out?" Talbot's voice sounded in her head like a gunpowder blast. "Where did she get a dagger?"

Ryen felt the cold stone beneath her fingertips as she clutched at them for an anchor. Suddenly, she was pulled to her feet by her hair and held dangling before Talbot. Ryen tried to stop the pain that shot from her scalp through her body by standing on her toes. She grabbed at her hair where Talbot held it to prevent another sharp burst of agony.

His voice rang in her ears. "Where did you get the dagger?"

Ryen fought the pounding that rocked her head. But when Talbot shook her, yanking her hair until it felt like it was going to rip out of her skull, the throbbing exploded into a million stars of pain. Ryen wanted to scream from the agony that seared across her head with each tug, but she held it in with all her willpower. She vowed she would never show such weakness to these English.

Talbot snarled. "Who gave you the dagger?"

Even under his abuse, she did not open her mouth. Her pride kept her lips tightly shut. Suddenly, the violent shakes ceased.

"Perhaps a flogging will loosen her tongue," McFinley commented, eyeing her.

Ryen had witnessed many floggings, and fear stiffened her innards.

McFinley shoved his arm at Talbot. Blood dripped from the open wound and he snapped, "It is my right."

Ryen saw Talbot nod before McFinley seized her arm and pulled her down the hall and down a flight of stairs. She could barely keep up with the knight's large steps. She stumbled, only to be hauled back to her feet by his hold on her arm.

When they paused before the outer door of the castle, Ryen

turned her head to see an immense group of people following. Some were knights, some servants. All looked angry. Some opened their mouths, but Ryen could barely make out what they were saying. Through her fear and sickness, her mind muffled and combined voices so that she could not understand the words.

The door opened before her and a small boy dashed out into the dim sunlight, running down the road. Directly before her in the dusty courtyard she saw a small platform on top of which were two wooden poles, each with a rope dangling from it.

McFinley yanked her forward, drawing her toward the platform.

Stormy gray clouds rolled in, blocking the sun from view. Ryen saw lightning flash in the sky. A roar began in her head, and at first, Ryen thought it was thunder from the storm, but then, after it continued relentlessly, she realized it was the crowd. She twisted her head around to see that the large crowd was following them, streaming from the castle like jelly oozing from a spilled jar.

McFinley yanked her up the two stairs of the platform. Her nightgown entangled her legs and she would have fallen except for the knight's viselike grip on her upper arm. As he pulled her between the two poles, the first drops of rain broke from the clouds, spattering the platform below her feet. The knight seized her arm and tied it tightly to the pole, wrapping the rope around and around her wrist, until the blood stopped flowing to her hand.

Ryen stood still, her chin raised, gazing off down the road. Villagers were coming, running up the dirt road, a horde of incensed English.

A pellet of rain struck Ryen's cheek.

As McFinley tied her other wrist, the first villager reached them.

So did the first rock. The stone missed her by a foot, bouncing harmlessly on the wooden platform.

McFinley whirled on the villagers, his lips curled in fury. He held up his arm to show his cut. "First blood. I claim it. There will be no stoning."

A moan of disappointment rippled the crowd. Ryen saw some of the villagers open their hands. Rocks fell out.

Suddenly, her hair was yanked back and she cringed as McFinley stuck his face into hers. "Fifty lashes, love," he whispered before his snakelike tongue flicked out and ran along the length of her cheek. He released her and disappeared somewhere behind her.

She felt the neck of her gown being seized, and with a savage yank the back of the nightdress tore free from the front.

The downpour began, heavy and punishing. What was left of Ryen's dress clung to her body, the material hugging her tighter with each drop.

The crowd became strangely quiet and Ryen saw the men's eyes rake her. No one moved for cover from the rain. They wanted her hurt. They wanted blood. What kind of people were these? Ryen hated them. She had never hated the English as much as she did now. Her mind cleared, all sickness washed away by the cleansing rain.

She felt someone press against her back, heard a voice. "No, m'lord! She is ill! She will na last under fifty lashes!"

"Out of the way, Polly," McFinley answered. "There is a traitor in our midst, and I am to find out who gave her the dagger."

"But she is sick!" the woman protested. "M'lord Princeton will be furious."

"Stand aside, old woman," the knight's voice was stern. "Or you will be next."

Slowly, Polly backed away, wringing her hands.

Ryen heard the crack of the whip behind her. Instinctively she stiffened, preparing herself for the pain.

The crowd swayed with anxiety.

"Whip her!" a faceless voice screamed.

Another crack of the whip sounded behind her. Someone laughed. The rain trickled down her forehead, over her eyes and cheeks and into her mouth. Ryen blinked it away.

The crowd gasped and she prepared to feel the bite of the whip, waited for the stinging lash to strike her, steeled her body for the pain . . .

The pain of the biting whip never came.

Instead, the rope that held Ryen was unbound from first one wrist, then the other. She stood shuddering, her fists clenched against the sudden chill that engulfed her body. A blanket was hung over her shoulders, and heavy hands kept it in place. She felt herself being turned around. Ryen raised her eyes to the giant who stood before her. She blinked the downpour of rain from her eyes to see—

Bryce!

A sudden surge of happiness swept her entire body. He was not dead! She had wanted to believe it, wanted so desperately to let herself believe it, but until now, there had still been doubt. She wanted to throw her arms around his shoulders and cry with relief, but she could not move or breathe. At his touch, warmth seeped from his fingertips through the length of her body. She shivered, but it had nothing to do with the rain.

He guided her back toward the castle, but McFinley stood to block their path. He presented Bryce with the damage done to his arm. The rain smeared the blood, making the cut look ugly and gaping. "It is my right," he charged.

"Inside," Bryce commanded.

His voice, carefully controlled, sent stirrings of anxiety racing like goosebumps along Ryen's skin.

McFinley whirled, storming into the castle.

Bryce pushed her inside and the great crowd that had gathered to see her punished followed, surging through the doors. Bryce's grip was much gentler than the knight's. He curbed his long strides so she could keep up with him. Then he took his hand off her, leaving her to walk under her own power, and Ryen found herself missing the warmth his touch had offered her.

Once inside, Bryce halted. His dark gaze sought out the knight. "What is your grief with my prisoner?"

At his cold words, her heart froze. Prisoner? But I thought . . . her mind screamed. Fool! You thought what? That your enemy, the man who lied to you, who thought you were worth no more than to use you, would steal you away from your people, your country to—to *love* you?! Fool!

"She has taken first blood," McFinley stated, again showing Bryce his wound. This time the blood flowed freely from the sore. "It is my right to do the same to her."

"Talbot!" The word ripped angrily from Bryce's throat.

Talbot pushed his way through the crowd to stand before Bryce.

"How did this happen?" Bryce demanded.

"She escaped. A traitor gave her a dagger," Talbot answered.

Bryce swung his gaze back to Ryen. Hard black eyes stared at her, but Ryen stood her ground. "Who gave you the dagger?"

Ryen raised her chin. "It was mine."

"It is English-made, Bryce," Talbot supplied, staring at her with hostile, slitted eyes.

Bryce's gaze did not waver from Ryen. She would have withered under the penetrating intensity of that stare had she not been so enraged.

"I demand my right!" McFinley shouted.

Bryce turned to him. "I am your lord. You serve me. Therefore, first blood is mine—and I have already collected."

Bryce gripped Ryen's shoulder and turned her toward the stairs.

Ryen pulled her shoulder free, flinging his hand from her.
"Where is the blood, m'lord?" McFinley shouted.
Without pausing, Bryce said, "I took her maidenhead."

Bryce strode into the room after Ryen. He immediately
saw the stubborn set of her jaw, her squared shoulders as
she whirled to face him. Her hair hung in wet curls over
her shoulders. A surge of relief swept through him. Ryen
had been grievously ill for two and a half weeks. He himself
had forced soup down her throat three times a day so she
would not starve.

He had ridden north the last two days. The riding had
done wonders for his tense body, helped his nerves, cleared
his mind. And he was finally able to make a decision about
what to do with Ryen. He knew he had promised King
Henry that he would punish her, but he realized that he
never had any intention of harming her. The only alternative
now was to ransom her to her king with the intent of giving
the gold to King Henry. Why did I bring her to England?
he wondered. Because I want to feel her body tremble with
desire. I want to touch her as no man has before. When
I've tired of her, then I will return her to France. And I
will tire of her . . . as I have every woman before her. But
by then my people will say that I have tamed the Angel of
Death.

Again Bryce thought of the ransom and grinned smugly.
He had asked for such an outrageous amount of gold that
he knew her king would never pay it, not even for the Angel
of Death. But at least King Henry would have to acknowledge his efforts to enrich the royal treasury.

Ryen would be his in time to do with as he saw fit.

Then, as he was wandering through the forest lost in
thought, a rider had found him, delivering an urgent message.
Ryen was recovering! The relief that had surged through his
body almost made him groan out loud. He rode like a man

possessed, curiously the happiest he had been in days, driving his horse to the brink of exhaustion only to find Ryen about to be flogged! And now, hearing she had attempted escape! Gads! He didn't know whether to wring her neck or laugh. "How are you feeling?" he asked.

"Why didn't you let me die?" she demanded.

Her cold words evaporated his joy at seeing her well and put him on the defensive. "You are more valuable as a prisoner than as a corpse," he remarked coolly.

Ryen's eyes narrowed. "I think you have sadly overestimated me. I am of no value to you."

He stared at her for a long moment. Her rebellious locks hung damply over the blanket that concealed her wet nightdress. Bryce grinned. "Surely the Angel of Death, the infamous French commander, has some value to her king." He watched the reply on her lips die. Bryce wondered if she would tell him of her disgrace. Then he knew her pride would not allow her to.

Ryen turned away. "Perhaps not as much value as *you* seem to place on my life," she snapped.

"It sounds as though you are in disfavor with your king, *Angel*," Bryce prompted. "Did he clip your wings?"

She raised her chin, glaring at him. "My king will pay whatever you ask," she declared.

She stood there, so haughty and mighty—in *his* castle. He wanted to take her in his arms and teach her the respect his knights and peasants gave him. Still, there was something challenging in her attitude that sparked his battle senses. The desire to touch her coursed through his body and he grabbed that raised chin, forcing it down so she was not looking down her nose at him. "You had better hope so. The longer you stay here, the more dangerous it will become."

Ryen yanked her chin free to glare at him. "I am not afraid of you. I will bring no ransom if I am dead."

"I was not speaking of myself, but them." Bryce jerked

his chin over his shoulder at Talbot and a dozen other soldiers standing in the doorway. "They do not have as soft a heart as I," he said quietly, so that only she heard.

She stared hard at the men looming in the doorway before sadness entered her sapphire eyes and she lowered them. Ryen sat on the bed, refusing to look at Bryce.

Bryce wanted to take her into his arms, to assure her that no harm would ever befall her at Dark Castle, but hesitated. His men had just had her strung up to be flogged! How empty his reassurances would be. There would be a time, he told himself, when Ryen would be able to walk the hallways and be as safe as he was. But that time was not now.

He strolled to the door and closed it before the prying eyes. Then he moved to the bed and sat beside her. "Ryen, who gave you the dagger?" he queried gently.

Ryen looked away. "It was mine," she murmured stubbornly.

Bryce sighed. "If you do not tell me, I will have to find some appropriate punishment."

Ryen whipped her gaze around to him, her eyes wide.

"You have never been punished before, have you?"

"On the contrary! My worst punishment has been living these past months!"

Bryce grinned. He lifted a hand to touch her soft cheek. "You missed me so?" he taunted, expecting a barbed reply. But when she did not answer, he couldn't help trailing his fingers across her cheekbone. The softness of her skin sent a smoldering warmth sweeping through him.

She pulled away from him and stood. "If you think I will remain in this castle as your whore, you are sadly mistaken."

In her tower room in her father's castle she seemed so filled with desire for me, he thought. She was actually worried for my life. Now, I see the coldness of ice in her frozen sapphire eyes.

Bryce closed on her. "I already have two whores and I have no intention of keeping another." He continued to approach and she backed into the wall. "And for your own protection, you will never again harm one of my men." He towered over her, his dark eyes glaring down. Her large sapphire eyes gazed up at him with fierce defiance. "Who gave you the dagger?" he repeated, leaning down so his lips were only inches from hers.

Ryen's response was a lifted chin, challenging him. It only succeeded in bringing their lips closer.

"Do not underestimate me. This is my castle, and I am lord here," he whispered huskily. "My whim is law, Angel." He was so close that their noses brushed lightly. He felt a sharp stab of desire course through every fiber in his body.

Ryen opened her mouth to respond, but no words came out. Her gaze brushed over his lips, setting them afire.

As he leaned closer, he felt her body soften against him, mold to his body. All thoughts of interrogation vanished beneath the passion that pounded through his veins. He could smell the clean rain on her wet skin, feel the moisture of her nightdress as she let the blanket slide from her shoulders. He clasped her shoulders and saw the blue of her eyes deepen as her lids half closed. He leaned forward to kiss her . . . every dream he had of her was loving her, kissing her deeply, giving her pleasures she had never known.

He wanted to take her right then, but his honor rose like a shield. He could not touch her until the ransom was denied. And even the Prince of Darkness was subject to the Code of Chivalry.

Bryce stiffened suddenly, drawing away from her with a deep groan of anger and regret.

He turned his back on her. The lust that had ignited at the sight of her burned more painfully than any cut he had ever received.

He stormed to the door with every intention of leaving but paused when his hand closed around the handle. "Be dressed and ready for dinner. I will come for you." He closed the door, leaving her alone.

* * *

Ryen stood stunned. It was just a game. He was trying to get information from her, and when she would not yield, he had stormed from the room like a spoiled child.

Then Talbot *had* told the truth, Ryen thought. Bryce had only pretended an attraction to her to manipulate her. He had been with his lover while she'd recovered. He hadn't even cared that she was ill.

She paced angrily through the room. I never loved him, she told herself. But even as she did, she knew it was a lie. An old wound that ran so deep it ripped at her heart reopened, constricting her chest painfully. Frustrated, she threw herself on the bed. She could not endure being so close to him. She must escape. But first, she vowed, I will get my strength back.

Ryen was indignant when a servant brought in a velvet blue dress for her to wear to dinner. She donned it in protest, mumbling and cursing the man who kept her prisoner. She was running a comb through her hair when three burly guards showed up to escort her to the Great Hall. He hadn't even come himself, she thought bitterly. The guards were all armed with sheathed swords, and were dressed in jerkins and hose. They led her through high-ceilinged halls of stone blocks and massive arched doorways that made her feel as insignificant as a fly. When they came to the Great Hall, the scene that assaulted Ryen made her pause. Her lips parted in disbelief.

The large room was filled with decadent laughter and loud guffaws. Maids fended off groping hands as they attempted to keep mugs full of wine. Soldiers, *barbarians,* sat at the long wooden tables. The tables themselves barely supported the pounding of fists as the demand for food resounded through the room. Four-legged beasts sat beside some of the tables, looking more like wolves than dogs. A belch sounded in the air somewhere.

Slowly the clamor stopped as all eyes turned to Ryen. She felt the hatred in their gazes like knives through her skin. She glared around the room at each dark look. Then something called her attention to the front of the room. Bryce was sitting straight ahead, his dark eyes locked on her, his face unreadable. He was leaning back in a large chair, one black-hosed leg lying casually over the arm. His white shirt was open to his navel, and Ryen suddenly recalled how hot his skin had felt against her naked flesh. Ryen tried to push the thought from her mind, but it lingered like the aroma of a freshly cut rose.

An empty chair was positioned to Bryce's right. Had he saved that chair for her? Ryen felt a tingle of hope touch her breast because even if she hated herself for it, she ached for his acceptance. Next to that chair, a dark-haired woman sat hurtling venomous glances at Ryen, her dark-rimmed eyes overflowing with loathing. Ryen was sure she'd seen her somewhere before, but she couldn't remember where. She raised an unconcerned eyebrow, successfully ignoring the woman's poisonous stare. To Bryce's left sat a blond woman whose hair appeared to have been hacked off at the nape. She sipped from her goblet, keeping her gaze locked on Ryen over its rim. Beside the dark-haired woman sat a group of people who looked like nomads with their fur and unkempt hair. From their gazes, Ryen felt humor and curiosity, but no animosity. She wondered briefly who they were to be seated at the head table.

Bryce swung his leg off the chair, returning her attention to him, and rose. He grinned at her. Ryen felt her knees weaken at his heart-melting smile. She walked slowly down the long room leaving her guards behind, her gaze never wavering from Bryce.

"Join us," Bryce said.

Was she a prisoner or a guest? Ryen wondered. Did she have the right to refuse? Ryen moved around the long table, ignoring the English soldiers and their women as they turned to follow her passage, to sit in the chair at Bryce's right. But Bryce quickly grabbed her elbow and lifted her back to her feet. The dark-haired woman exhaled a hiss between her clenched teeth.

"Over there," Bryce said, and motioned to an empty chair at a table near the hearth, in the middle of his men.

Ryen knew that to show defiance now might be death. Although she feigned nonchalance, she could not help but feel disappointment. She silently berated herself for falling victim to his smile.

She was a prisoner.

Bravely she walked to the spot he had designated for her and sat down.

She glanced at the men around her. To her right was a man who wore a gray tunic with ripped leggings. His brown hair was unruly and looked as though he had never combed it. When he noticed her staring at him, a lopsided grin spread across his face. He looked like he belonged in the woods.

"Pour her some wine," Talbot suggested from his seat opposite her. "It will help loosen her bowels. They must be all puckered up, judging by that unpleasant look on her face."

The men roared with laughter. Ryen swiveled her head toward Bryce just in time to see a smile twitch his lips. He motioned for a servant to fill her glass.

"The unpleasant look on my face is from the company. It has nothing to do with my bowels," she retorted evenly.

Talbot ignored her and raised his mug high, some of the wine splashing onto the table. "A toast. To the dreaded Prince of Darkness, the man who captured the cursed Angel of Death!"

The men cheered and slapped their mugs together.

Bryce raised his golden goblet, nodding in acceptance of the toast. He took a deep drink.

Ryen watched his throat work as he drank, saw the way his lips kissed the lip of the cup. A rebellious stirring formed in her lower stomach. She quickly looked away to her own mug on the table. She fought the heat that surged through her body the only way she knew how . . . with defiance. She pushed the mug away.

"Perhaps she does not like English wine," a soldier sitting at her left commented, glaring at her.

"She likes English swords," McFinley chuckled. He was seated beside Talbot. "She let Prince show her how one is properly handled!"

All around her, the table shook with laughter and lusty chortles.

Ryen felt her jaw stiffen with outrage. She glanced up at Bryce to find him speaking earnestly with the dark-haired woman. He wasn't even paying attention to her! At least when he was in her hall she knew what he was doing every second. Her straight shoulders slumped. A lot of good it had done him, she thought. Her countrymen had still challenged him.

"Your gaze does not seem to be turning any of our blood to ice," Talbot murmured.

Ryen's gaze turned back to him. His eyes were narrowed, his mouth thin. He hated her with all his soul; she could see it in his eyes. He would like nothing better than to run her through.

McFinley stood, leaning over the table toward her. "Come on. Turn my blood to ice. Let me see one of your looks."

Ryen slowly raised her eyes to his. She did not say a word, but challenged him with a slight narrowing of her eyes. If only she had her truth powder, she would show him where that legend had originated.

Ryen wished with all her heart that she had a weapon. She didn't like the gleam in this knight's eye. She glanced down and saw that his wrist, where she had cut him, was wrapped in a dirty cloth. At his side, she saw her salvation—a sheathed sword. Confidence filled her.

Ryen felt eyes on her and subtly shifted her gaze to see Bryce watching her. He was staring at her with such intensity that it made her body burn. She swung her gaze back to McFinley. She needed to get close to him to get his sword. If only, for once, she could use her body to be seductive. But how? She was not trained in such things.

But the whores with her army were. She had seen how they seduced her soldiers. A sweet smile, a show of flesh, a bold caress. She smiled coyly. "The legend is wrong," Ryen said quietly, leaning toward him. "It is not ice." She glanced up at him through lowered lashes and watched as his lecherous gaze swooped down to her breasts, then hungrily rose to her eyes. As an afterthought, despite the growing feeling of nausea in her stomach, she licked her lips.

"Then what is the truth?" McFinley demanded in a hoarse voice.

As a hush fell over the table, Ryen smiled, savoring the moment of control. "Ask your lord." She casually reached for the mug of wine she had previously pushed aside.

McFinley vaulted the table, grabbed her elbow, and pulled her to her feet in the blink of an eye. Her wine sloshed onto the table as the mug was knocked over. "I wasn't asking him, I was asking you," he snarled angrily. His breath, thick with wine, was hot on her lips; his teeth ground each word out; his blue eyes burned into hers. "What does men's blood turn to?" he sneered.

Ryen stared at McFinley, returning his hot gaze with one of her own. "Fire," she whispered. She leaned into his body, reaching for his sword.

Suddenly, she was pulled away from McFinley and landed on the floor in a mound of blue velvet. Her head was spinning, and when she shook it clear and glanced up, Ryen saw Bryce land a blow to McFinley's jaw.

She stood quickly as Talbot and Grey planted themselves between the two.

McFinley rubbed his jaw and stood slowly. His brows were furrowed with disbelief, his lips drawn down in a pout of perplexity. He gestured at Ryen. "She's just a prisoner!" he said vehemently.

"She is mine," Bryce growled, and surged forward only to be caught by Grey and another soldier.

"We have always had free use of prisoners," McFinley stated.

"Not ransomed prisoners. Not *this* prisoner," Bryce replied. He calmed in the men's hold, but his jaw was stiff and his back straight. "Take Lotte instead."

McFinley paused, looking at Ryen, then slowly withdrew.

Ryen felt herself tremble as Bryce turned to her. The two men had released him and he approached her. His furious gaze made her heart pound. He grabbed her wrist and pulled her to her chair. She could feel the heat of anger radiating from him, feel his strong grip on her wrist. He leaned close to her and Ryen trembled. He whispered, "Next time, I will not stop them."

Her spine straightened at the threat, her heart beating frantically from the encounter. Suddenly, darkness began to close around her and she struggled to fight it off, but it advanced like a swarm of arrows.

Bryce's supporting hand withdrew and he started to return to his seat. Suddenly, he turned back to her to add something. But she never heard what it was, for in the next moment, she was falling under the impact of those arrows . . .

Thirty

Bryce stared down at Ryen, as she lay in his bed, at her soft, soft skin, her peaceful expression, the way her eyelashes rested on her cheek, her full lips. She was the picture of a sleeping angel. A smile curved his lips. *What a deceitful creature she is. Even in sleep she seeks to seduce me.*

Bryce rose and began to pace. What was he doing? he wondered. He had defended her before his soldiers, before his friends, and before the Wolf Pack. He had called her his. The idea that he could want this infamous French killer was outrageous. And still, when McFinley had touched her, Bryce had exploded with rage, a fury that had never taken hold of him before. The anger had flooded his senses and his logic, totally obliterating his self-control.

She stirred and Bryce moved to her side, sinking to one knee by the bed. He gently wiped a stray strand of hair from her cheek as he leaned over to be closer to her. He smiled softly to himself, not quite believing that he had rose to her defense so swiftly. He studied her angelic face. There was a serene quality to her restful features, a calmness that belied the troubled soul beneath. Then, just as quickly, his smile vanished. *I may be her protector now, but there will come a time when I will have to protect my people from the Angel of Death,* he thought.

The door banged open and Lotte entered the room.

Bryce rose from the floor, turning his gaze to her. "What is it, woman?"

"You told McFinley to take me. In front of all those men. They will think I am for their amusement," Lotte said, her dark eyes flashing.

Bryce merely turned back to Ryen.

"Prince," she whimpered, stepping forward, "she killed our son. She tried to sit in his chair. I—"

Bryce whirled on her. "I told you," he snarled, "she had *nothing* to do with the fire."

Lotte withdrew as his tall form loomed over her, her eyes filled with a cold realization. "She has changed you," she whispered. "You are not the Prince of Darkness any longer. The Prince I knew would have ripped out her throat for killing his kin."

"Hear you nothing that I say, Lotte? She did not start the fire! She would not kill her own men and animals just to kill Runt."

"Listen to yourself defend her," Lotte hissed. "She has worked magic over you."

"Leave me. Go to McFinley," Bryce said, his voice strangely calm, even while his hatred for her burned like the flames that took his boy's life.

Lotte gasped and slowly backed to the door.

He waited until she was gone and the door had closed behind her before he clenched his fists and turned toward the window. His anger stretched his nerves taut like a bowstring. He would not tolerate her disobedience. He stared out at the village beyond the window, his fingers still curled tight.

Ryen watched Bryce. She could see his corded neck muscles, the stiff set of his jaw as he stood at the window. A vague memory flashed through her mind of Bryce standing, half-wild, before the window in her father's castle. Suddenly, she longed to throw her arms around him to prevent him from jumping. She sat up in bed—

Bryce turned, and for a moment their gazes locked. Ryen shivered under the intensity of his rage, the flame of a candle reflected in the inky depths of his eyes.

He moved forward; the power in each step, each movement, was intoxicating. She found herself dizzy and calm in the same moment. He was wreaking havoc on her senses.

"Ryen," he said. His voice held no hint of the anger that was aflame in his eyes, but the timbre of his voice sent shivers of ice down her spine. Her heart pounded under the heat of his dark gaze.

"We have unfinished business," Bryce commented.

Ryen could barely swallow. She could not help but glance at his lips before turning her eyes back to his.

"A punishment," Bryce said. "Not only for attempting escape, but I warned you to stay away from my men."

It was like a bucket of cold water had just been dumped over her head. She scowled at him. "Punishment? Sitting among those savages you call your soldiers was punishment enough."

"Silence!" Bryce roared. He moved to the side of the bed, towering over her. "You have defied me, Ryen De Bouriez. I will not tolerate such insolence from my prisoners."

Anger, fierce and sudden, jarred Ryen. Her eyes widened with rage and she knelt on the bed, her back as straight as a board. "You ordered me down there! Did you not expect some sort of clash? Your people despise me."

His glowering eyes darkened and he reached out to seize her wrist.

Ryen dodged his grasp easily, moving to the other side of the bed.

Slowly Bryce straightened. His hair brushed the black velvet material that hung from the bed. His black eyes shimmered. "You are making this harder on yourself, *Angel*." His lip curled and she saw a flash of white from his teeth.

She stood facing him, the large bed a barrier between them. He never thought I was beautiful. He used the words to manipulate me. I will never forgive him. I must never forgive him. But his glare made her warm all over. She tried to fight the feeling that was washing over her like droplets of hot rain, inflaming her body slowly but completely. Ryen straightened her shoulders, her breath coming in harsh gasps, her chest rising and falling.

Bryce's gaze slowly lowered from her eyes to her chest.

Ryen watched as his look of anger slowly began to fade and was replaced by something else. His intense gaze burned into her, searing her to the floor, burning through her veins. He approached her, and she did not back away. She wanted him to touch her. She needed to feel the caress of his lips, his hands. She stood facing him. Tingles covered her body, running up and down her arms. He stopped directly in front of her. Her whole being froze, anticipating the feel of his strong arms around her, the heat of his body, his hot breath on her cheek.

But he did not touch her. "Your punishment, Angel," his voice caressed the words as his eyes devoured her, "will be to accompany me to break the fast, and dine. You will be with my soldiers and people as much as possible throughout the day. And you *will* show them respect." He lifted a finger and ran it along her sensuous lips. "The same respect you show me."

Ryen parted her lips slightly at his touch, his words drifting somewhere at the front of her mind unheard. The gentleness of his caress startled her into silence as she gazed at his perfect grin, the glimpse of teeth as he spoke. Then he was turning away, heading for the door.

Ryen knew a disappointment she had never felt before. Her lips tingled where he had touched them and her skin felt cold. Suddenly and quickly, shame wrapped itself around her in a blanket of guilt. She hugged her elbows.

He paused at the door and turned to look at her.

Ryen felt his heated gaze rake over her body, smoldering like a burning ember.

"Be ready for the morn. The savages await your company," he said, and quit the room.

Outside the room, Bryce paused, his hand on the latch. The burning in his body flamed outward, searing his very skin. He wanted her. The ache in his loins was hard proof of that. For a moment, he stood, battling himself. Her curves hidden beneath her dress taunted him. The dark riotous curls of her hair dared him to return. He knew it would not be honorable to take her, no matter how much he wanted her. He had to wait until the ransom was denied. Then, instead of being the infamous French commander, she would be merely a woman disavowed by her country, a woman in danger of being locked away in the dungeon for the rest of her life. Not that Bryce could ever lock away his attraction to her that easily. When the ransom was denied, he would arouse that fire in her again. The fire that closed her eyelids dreamily, the fire that parted those luscious lips in wanting. He would hear her call out his name in passion. He would make her his woman in body as well as in soul.

He pulled his hand from the door. But for now, he would wait. He hoped the messenger would arrive soon. He didn't know how much more waiting he could possibly endure. Already his blood boiled at the mere mention of her name.

"Prince!"

Bryce lifted his eyes to find Talbot approaching. "There is someone I think you should see."

Bryce's dark brows drew together and he pushed himself from the door to follow Talbot.

"Please, m'lord," the man whimpered, as his round eyes locked on Bryce.

The rising moon's rays streamed in through the windows and the Great Hall was flooded with illumination from the roaring hearth, but the light just barely hit the three men where they stood at the far end beneath the stained glass windows.

Bryce stood with his arms akimbo, his confused gaze sweeping the man before him. The way he hunched his shoulders and bowed his head made him look like an abused dog cowering before its master.

"You have nothing to fear," Talbot told the man, then turned to Bryce. "I overheard him telling the story at the Inn." Talbot then addressed the man. "Go ahead."

It was the way Talbot's voice coaxed the man that grated Bryce's nerves. He was up to something, and Bryce didn't know whether to believe what the man was going to say or behead them both.

"Go on," Bryce said, his voice echoing softly in the large room.

When he spoke, his voice was tiny. Like a mouse, Bryce thought. If he had a tail, it would swoosh. "I went up to her room."

Bryce felt an unreasonable rush of anger, but he kept his body absolutely still. He knew instinctively that it was Ryen they were speaking of. "Did you touch her?"

For a moment, the man looked baffled. His gaze darted to Talbot before he said, "No."

"Then what were you doing there?"

"I—I wanted to see the Angel of Death."

"He paid one of the serving girls," Talbot supplied.

The man clutched his hands before him. "Please, m'lord. Don't punish me. I only wanted ta see—"

"Continue," Bryce's voice boomed in the room.

Visibly trembling, the man swallowed hard and lowered his fists to his side before Bryce's dark demeanor. "She is a demon, m'lord. She has fangs the size of a cow's calf, glowing red eyes, and claws!"

"And you actually saw these fangs and claws?" Bryce asked darkly.

The man nodded vigorously. "And she flew!"

Bryce turned away and bowed his head.

" 'N she came at me like a bloody bat from . . ." He made the sign of the cross. "Lord protect us." The man looked up at Bryce and finished with, ". . . hell."

"You are dismissed," Bryce whispered.

"I jus' come in and she be all docile and quiet like. But as soon as I got close ta her, she swooped down, shrieking and saying she wanted me bloody heart!" He placed his hand protectively over his chest, his words now directed at Talbot, who was watching Bryce.

Bryce's shoulders trembled and Talbot was positive it was with anger.

"Go!" Bryce barked.

The man promptly scurried from the room, bowing all the way out.

Talbot frowned. "Prince?"

Bryce threw back his head and gales of laughter burst from his lips, echoing throughout the large room. A servant paused as he crossed the hall to the kitchens to cast a curious glance at his lord. A dog foraging in the rushes for food raised its head, his straight, pointed ears listening to the strange sound. The thought of his Angel, with the pliant lips and soft skin, depicted as a demon, was ridiculous! The only glowing he had ever seen in her eyes was the fire of lust.

Talbot's mouth dropped. "I—I fail to see the humor."

"Don't you see what the little vixen is doing?" Bryce said, after catching his breath. He put his hands on his thighs and bent over from a slice of pain in his side.

"You mean, besides scare the man half to death? I'm surprised she didn't sprout wings!"

"What a mind! Even here, a prisoner within my own walls, she continues her legend!" Bryce threw up his hands in exasperation. "And I thought it was her brothers who had spread the lies!"

"You don't believe she's a demon?"

"Good heavens, no." Bryce turned to stare at him, his mood sobering as he saw the seriousness in Talbot's eyes. "You can't tell me you, a warrior, a knight of the realm, actually *believe* in demons."

Talbot looked away from his questioning lord, giving Bryce his answer.

"Demon or no, as soon as France's missive returns and she learns that her king has turned his back on her, she *will* be mine—on my terms."

Thirty-one

Polly came rushing into Ryen's chamber before the sun had even risen. "It's going ta be a beautiful morn," Polly exclaimed, fluttering about Ryen like a mother hen.

Ryen stretched and glanced at Polly, who was continuing her monologue. "I can tell because farmer Naughton is still sleeping. If it were going ta rain, the man would be out tendin' his animals already. He's got a bloody sense about such things."

Ryen groaned and buried her face in the pillow. She wanted to return to the comfort and warmth of her slumber. Then, through the haze of sleep, Ryen suddenly realized that Polly was no longer talking. She lifted her eyes to the maid to see her standing over her, hands folded in front of her stomach.

"I—I wanted to thank ye," Polly said contritely. Her eyes pierced Ryen with such guilt that it sent waves of sympathy coursing through Ryen. "Ya woulda been flogged," Polly continued, as Ryen sat up. "I—I put the knife on the tray because—well, because the bread here can be like a bloody stone. And ya were sick. I never thought—"

"It's all right, Polly. I won't tell anyone," Ryen said gently, a slight grin curving her lips.

"Thank you." Polly turned away to open the door to the room. Three young women entered, each carrying a beautiful gown.

Ryen watched the nervous, jerky movements of Polly's

hands as she straightened each dress, smoothing the wrinkles. She doesn't believe me, Ryen thought. She stood, a stab of hurt in her chest, and approached Polly.

A vivid image of Jeanne, smaller and better dressed, standing before her wardrobe closet at home flashed through Ryen's mind, the dresses that lined the walls inside glimmering in the sunlight, Jeanne's disappointed voice saying, "I have nothing to wear—"

But then, Polly was speaking, her hands wrapping over each other nervously. "M'lord will come for ya." Her voice quivered, betraying her anxiety.

Ryen stepped forward, gently placing her palm over Polly's hand, stilling her movements. When Polly looked up into her warm gaze, Ryen grinned kindly at her. "I know," Ryen said quietly.

Ryen shifted her gaze to the dresses. She chose the gown closest to her. It was a samite light blue dress with a very dark blue velvet surcoat over it. Ryen pretended not to notice how the girl shrank before her as she took the dress. She brought it back toward the bed and Polly dismissed the girls with an impatient flick of her wrist. Polly helped Ryen out of her nightdress and into her chemise. She broke the silence by saying earnestly, "Ya really should be nicer to him. He did save yer life."

But Ryen didn't hear her words. She sat on the bed beside the dress, her head bowed. "Polly, I have to ask you a question."

Polly's face turned white.

"It's important to me, or I wouldn't ask."

Polly stiffened and declared, "I won't do anything against me lord nor me country."

Ryen's brows drew together in confusion as she raised her sights to the heavy woman. Finally, she said, "The battle. I must know. Who won?"

"We did, of course."

Ryen and Polly both started at the voice and looked to see

Talbot entering the room. While Ryen scrambled, pulling a blanket from the bed to cover her silk chemise from his view, Polly stepped forward, hollering, "Out, ya rogue! M'lord gave strict orders—"

"To bathe her," Talbot finished. "Not answer her every damn question. So get a tub and some servants to fill it with water." He strode past Polly to the bed.

Ryen raised her chin and narrowed her eyes at him.

Polly shook her head. "I cannot leave 'er in here *alone* with the likes a you."

"Now," Talbot commanded.

Polly harrumphed and whirled, heading out the door.

Ryen saw the hate in Talbot's stare, the anger and loathing. She prepared for a verbal mélée.

"We slaughtered your precious French army," Talbot sneered.

Ryen raised her chin further, clutching the blanket to her chest. "I don't believe you."

Talbot shrugged. "Believe what you will."

Ryen had been about to ask Polly about her brothers, but she absolutely refused to question Talbot.

Talbot stepped forward and Ryen moved away from him. She did not trust him. He fingered the silk dress lying on the bed, and somehow Ryen felt violated. Her back straightened.

"Your treacherous people struck from the rear, killing our squires and burning our supply wagons."

Outrage soared through Ryen. While her mind realized there was earnest pain in his voice, her heart refused to acknowledge that her countrymen would commit such an atrocity.

"Henry had all the French prisoners executed as retribution."

"What?" she managed to gasp, as his words murdered the hope she held in her heart for her brothers. "It cannot be," she murmured. Her brothers! She knew Andre had to have been taken prisoner. She had seen him wounded, struck by an arrow! Furious and frightened, she shouted, "Liar!"

Talbot raised his head. To her surprise, his eyes were sad, ringed with doubt and confusion. For a moment, they stopped in time, his finger still on the dress, her fists desperately clutching to the blanket she held before her.

Finally, Talbot spoke. "No warrior should die thus."

"It can't be," Ryen repeated helplessly. "I, too, would be dead."

Talbot's eyes hardened and the hate returned. "You should be."

Ryen blinked and her heart twisted in anguish. All prisoners killed. The French defeated. Their arrogance was, finally, their downfall.

But . . . Andre *must* have been captured. He *couldn't* be dead. She would never believe it. But the scene of bodies falling to the ground and being trampled and smothered beneath the thick mud filled her mind's eye. Ryen turned her back on Talbot, hoping to hide her turmoil and fear. Worry gripped her heart, squeezing it until it threatened to stop beating.

She had been so angry with Lucien. She had never forgiven him. He could not die without giving her that chance!

Despair filled her and her shoulders slumped even though she fought to right them. In her mind, she couldn't judge who were the more barbaric, the English or the French, and it tore her apart. How could she be certain that the constable had given the order to slaughter the English squires, and not some vengeful knights?

She was no longer certain who was right.

The door opened and Polly entered with a group of servants carrying pails of water, trailed by two others carrying a wooden tub. She was out of breath, as if she had run the entire way.

With a last glare at Ryen, Talbot quit the room.

Ryen did not watch him leave. She raised her head to see

the servants lift the pails they had carried in and dump the water into the tub. Steam rose, its white vapors twisting and turning as they reached toward the ceiling.

Polly came toward her. She opened her mouth as if to speak, but when she locked gazes with Ryen, she closed it and frowned. "Did that bloody scoundrel touch ye?" Polly finally asked.

Ryen shook her head. "I'm not going, Polly."

"But m'lord . . ." Polly's words disintegrated as she saw the pain in Ryen's face, her agonized gaze. "Yes. Ya are pale. Perhaps ya have a bout of illness. I'll inform Lord Princeton that you are not well enough to dine."

When Ryen glanced away from Polly, the maid's brows drew together in concern.

Ryen sat on the edge of the bed, letting her hands fall to her lap. Her brothers . . . her countrymen. She had to know. She had seen the arrow in Andre's stomach; the bloody scene played over and over in her anguished mind.

Lucien *must* have gotten him and dragged him to safety. But no one had saved her.

She distantly heard Polly clap her hands and shout for the servants to leave. Then the door closed.

She was alone. The fear ate away at the corners of her mind, demanding acknowledgment. But Ryen stood, pushing her doubts aside. She walked to the window and gazed out over the gates of the castle and into the town. Ryen saw farmers in their fields far in the distance.

She remembered that once, when she was younger, she had gone to watch the men practice their swordplay. Andre had been there, young and handsome. He had stopped to speak to a maiden from the village, and Ryen remembered how jealous and angry she had been at his attentions to the girl. Why, he hadn't even noticed that she had arrived. Ryen had thrown herself between the two, her hands on her hips, her eyes blazing, demanding to see his swordplay. He had smiled at her, his eyes full of humor and understanding.

She knew he had given up having a wife and family to fight beside her. Now, he would never have a family of his own. No, she thought, and turned from the window. He is *not* dead.

But images of Andre's kind face flooded her eyes. What if he is? a tiny voice inside asked. And Lucien? She had been so angry with him for burning the body she had thought was Bryce's. He couldn't die before her rage dissolved! She had to forgive him. She had to speak with him again. It couldn't be true! Had her brothers really been murdered by the English?

She found herself staring at the tapestry, at the horned man. His mocking grin, his knowing eyes. It was Bryce. He would know. He had the answers.

Ryen ran to the door and threw it open, intending to go to the Great Hall for Bryce. She reared back as a wall of flesh blocked her path. She jerked her head up to find Bryce standing before her. Her fear-filled mind clouded her reality and she did not see the dark, stormy look on his face.

"Attempting another escape?" he wondered, stepping toward her.

"No. I . . . was going to find *you*." She retreated into the room as he approached.

Bryce paused to close the door behind him. When he turned to face her, his eyes glowed hotly. "In your chemise?"

Ryen looked down, startled to find that he was right. She wore only the transparent cloth. "I—I . . ." her voice died as she turned large eyes to him. Ryen self-consciously crossed her arms over her chest, only to find her hands trembling. She felt her resolve weakening under his presence and tears welled up in her eyes.

Concerned, Bryce stepped forward. "Are you ill?"

"Bryce," Ryen gasped and swallowed hard. "My brothers."

Bryce froze at her words.

"Where are they?"

Something close to fear crossed his face before anger lowered his brows. "They're dead."

His words, delivered in a cold, vindictive tone, made her stumble back from him, her face pale. She backed up and wilted onto the bed like a dying flower.

Bryce stepped toward her, but Ryen did not notice. Dead. Her brothers. She felt her insides begin to tremble.

"Tears, Angel? Is that how the French handle defeat?"

Stunned, Ryen glanced up at him as if he had slapped her. His vicious sarcasm stunned her.

"Or perhaps you learned it from your brothers," Bryce continued. "Why else would they allow their sister to command them? Perhaps they were not men at all."

Slowly her mouth closed and rage colored her cheeks. The vulnerability disappeared behind a mask of loathing.

Bryce seemed pleased with himself, a tiny grin curling up his lips. "Now, bathe and get dressed."

Ryen sat absolutely still for a long moment, staring hard at him. Her jaw was clenched tightly and her heated gaze threw daggers of blue flame at him. Finally, Ryen brushed imaginary lint from her lap and replied matter-of-factly, "I wouldn't eat with you if you were the King of France."

Bryce's lips turned up in a grin. "But I'm not. And you *will* eat with me."

She opened her mouth to reply, but he raised a hand, stopping her. "If I have to feed you every drop, you will eat."

Ryen's eyes narrowed.

"I will return for you in a half hour. Be ready," he commanded, and strode to the door.

Ryen watched him walk away. His step was so confident, so arrogant. Rage consumed her body, twisting the emotions of pain and sorrow, and even love, until they were concentrated on hate. She wanted to hurt him. To make him wish he had not shown her coldness when she'd needed warmth. She made her voice velvety soft. "To think I wanted you to hold me and tell me that everything would be all right."

Bryce stopped cold, realization dawning through him.

"To think that I wanted your arms around me."

Slowly, suddenly aroused by her soft, delicate words, he turned to regard her. She was sitting on the bed, *his* bed, watching him with eyes the color of the sea.

"To think that I wanted you to touch me."

He took one step forward.

"Makes me sick," Ryen finished, before his foot hit the ground.

His foot came down hard. He stood glaring at her in shock for a long moment.

A slow, calculating smile slid across her lips.

At seeing her delight, Bryce straightened, dark eyes smoldering. He spun and quit the room, bolting the door behind him.

Bryce stood outside the dungeon doors, staring through the celled window at the darkness within. The hallway was humid; his clothing stuck uncomfortably to his skin. He could hear a *drip, drip, drip* somewhere in the cavernous corridor. The smell of mold, decay, and urine surrounded him. But all of it faded away as his black eyes focused on the cell.

A shadow moved restlessly within.

Tension tightened his shoulders. He watched the thing pacing back and forth. He rolled his shoulders, trying to ease the cramping muscles. But the tension and guilt were engraved there. I should tell her, he thought.

He knew he could not tell her. Not now; not ever. The man, the thing, inside the cell was wild, mad. Dangerous. He did not want Ryen to see him like this. It would be better to let her remember him as he was.

The wild thing stopped its pacing, and Bryce saw him lift his head. The torchlight in the hallway glinted off the man's orbs. Bryce's eyes narrowed as the prisoner called, "Prince? Is that you?"

Bryce did not move, even when the prisoner launched himself at him, his hands outstretched for Bryce's throat, until they stopped just inches short of his neck when the wild man slammed into the door that separated them.

"I will kill you! If it's the last thing I ever do!" he shouted.

Bryce stood for a moment, eyeing him blankly. Then he turned his back on Lucien De Bouriez.

Thirty-two

The hurt that swirled inside Ryen left her listless. She had dressed in the samite blue dress and velvet blue surcoat she had picked and prepared to break her fast, absently combing the soft waves of hair that hung like a trellis around her face.

Ryen rose and moved to the window. The sky was blue, the sun warmed her cheeks. People were moving about, entering and leaving the castle. Ryen leaned forward, resting her palms on the ledge, and leaned over to look straight down. A group of children ran past the window far below; a man herded a flock of sheep toward the gates. Then all was still for a moment. Ryen was about to pull back into the room when a movement caught her eye. Something in the shadows of the wall around the castle. Ryen frowned, staring hard. But the seconds ticked by and there was no sign of anyone.

Ryen straightened, about to turn back, when a man stepped from the exact spot she was staring at, moving into the bright light of morning. Startled, she jerked back into the safety of the room. The alabaster skin was unmistakable. It was Jacques Vignon! Her advance scout, the man who had recaptured Bryce after the fire. What was he doing here?

Ryen leaned against the wall, placing a hand on her pounding heart. Vignon! After a moment, doubt pressed in on her mind, and she dropped her hand. Maybe it wasn't him. After all, what would he be doing in England? Had he come to rescue her? Ryen peered out the window once again. But the man was gone, the courtyard empty. She pressed her palms against the stones to support her weight as she leaned out the window.

The door to her room opened.

Ryen whirled, her eyes large with expectation. She half expected Vignon to walk in and greet her.

Bryce stepped into the room, and met her gaze with a frown.

Her pounding heart was replaced by a different rush as her body heated. She hated him. He was an English dog with no warmth in his entire body, she had repeated to herself, over and over, preparing herself for just this moment. But now, faced with his scorching gaze, her blood did indeed boil, but it was not with anger . . .

He wore, in total disregard to conventional fashion, a roomy white cotton tunic, open at the throat to reveal just a trace of his broad, tanned chest. It was enough to ignite Ryen's imagination. Her gaze traveled over the rest of his body. The muscles of his strong legs were clearly visible beneath the hose he wore. They clung to his legs, leaving nothing to the imagination. On his feet he wore calf-length black leather boots.

Ryen felt her knees trembling. She tried to recall the rage she had felt yesterday, tried to remember the sting of his words as he told her of her brothers' deaths. But he was staring at her with those black eyes, enflaming every nerve of her body.

Bryce lifted a hand to her, palm up. It was an open invitation to take what he was offering. Including his apologies.

For a moment, she stared at his hand. She began to reach out. What am I doing? she thought, and brought her hand down so hard that it slapped against her thigh. She raised her chin in defiance, eyes flashing like brilliant sapphire gems, and straightened her shoulders.

He crossed the room in three strides, until he stood before her, his stare piercingly hot.

Ryen had to tilt her head up slightly to meet his gaze. She could feel the heat from his body as they stood, barely touching. She watched his dark, angry eyes melt into pools of hot oil.

Then, his hand lifted. Ryen could sense the movement of his corded muscles. He was going to touch her, to put his warm hand on her body. She waited, never taking her eyes from his deep gaze, anticipating the gentle feel of his caress.

And waited.

Finally, she tore her stare from his and glanced at his hand. It was near her shoulder, palm up, patiently awaiting her hand.

Ryen stepped away from him, unable to bear his arrogance. No sooner had she turned her back on him, than his amused voice came to her. "Ryen."

She refused to acknowledge him, instead embracing her elbows.

Silence engulfed her for long seconds. When next his voice came to her, it was whispered on a bed of clouds. "Angel."

She turned hesitantly, the soft timbre of his voice casting a spell over her body that she was unable to break. She expected to see victory and laughter in his eyes. But his expression startled her. It was warm and soft and caring. Everything she had ever wanted of him. Everything she had ever needed from him . . . except, of course, love. Confused, Ryen moved toward what she wanted to see, needed to see, in those inky depths. She placed her hand in his.

The jolt that rocked her body as she felt the heat of his flesh against hers made her dizzy.

Bryce watched her lower her eyes to their clasped hands. The gesture was simple, demure, and innocent, and he found himself aroused beyond reason. He felt his hand, the hand that held her fragile one so carefully, begin to tremble. Ah, God. How he wanted her. His grip tightened around her small fingers as he willed the shaking to cease.

Alarmed, Ryen glanced up at him, her eyes wide and questioning.

Bryce turned toward the door, quickly tucking her wrist under his arm.

As they moved, her hand resting on the inside of his arm, Ryen could feel the subtle tightening of his muscles as he reached to open the door. His chest brushed her knuckles and she gasped.

Bryce paused slightly, to glance at her. But when she did not meet his gaze, he continued on.

The door opened and a draft of cool air engulfed Ryen. It was fresh and smelled vaguely of flowers. She paused in the doorway, inhaling the invigorating scent.

Bryce glanced back at her. He misread the look on her face as trepidation and reassured her, "You needn't worry. No one will touch you as long as you're at my side . . ."

Ryen frowned at him. Worry? She had not thought of that. Not since Bryce had entered her room. But now that he'd brought it up, she knew she should be concerned. Last time she had entered his hall, she had been assaulted and ridiculed.

Suddenly, Ryen had no desire to leave the safety her room offered.

"They won't harm you, Ryen. You have my word," Bryce told her softly.

At his tender earnestness, Ryen felt some of her doubt fade away, and she let him lead her down the hallway.

The doors to the Great Hall gaped wide, and a loud hubbub spilled out from within.

Ryen glanced sideways at Bryce and he squeezed her fingers in encouragement.

Together they entered the room, England and France, the Prince of Darkness and the Angel of Death. Immediately, talking ceased and all eyes focused on them. Bryce led Ryen down the center of the room to the seat she had occupied before, amid his men.

When Ryen glanced up, she saw that Talbot was in the

seat across from her, his intense gaze upon her. She knew he saw not her, but the enemy. She looked away from him and noticed that McFinley's seat was occupied by . . .

Her mouth dropped open as she stared into the black eyes of Jacques Vignon! She fell into her seat, quickly closing her mouth, and looked away, unable to stare her countryman in the eye.

She hadn't been imagining! Why was he here? Was he a spy? Or an Englishman?

As Bryce left her side, she followed his movement to his table at the front of the room. Ryen spotted his chair, and to either side sat the same two women who had been there before. Her heart sank. His whores still had the place of honor. Suddenly, unreasonably, she felt miserable. She looked away and her eyes locked with Talbot's. For a moment, her hurt showed clearly on her face before she could mask it with indifference.

Talbot frowned as Ryen met his gaze, chin slightly uplifted, shoulders thrown back with pride.

Ryen could feel the eyes upon her, watching expectantly. She felt the pressure of the silence, the weight of their hate. Ryen's gaze moved past Talbot to eye the people about her. Although she purposely ignored Vignon, her mind could not. What was he doing here? Was he a traitor? Had she placed her trust in a spy?

Then, near the door at the rear of the hall, she spotted Polly among a group of servants carrying trays and pitchers of beer. When she noticed Ryen's gaze, Polly's lips turned up and she smiled encouragement before disappearing out the double doors.

Ryen's heart sang with joy. She had made a friend among these people who hated and loathed her. Then, like a stone crashing heavily to the earth, guilt fell over her shoulders and she swiveled her eyes to Vignon, who was sipping beer from a mug. He was her reminder of France. Of her men, of her duty. Of honor. She should try harder to escape.

Suddenly, a tingling along her spine made her swivel her head to the front of the room.

Bryce's gaze was locked on her. He was watching her. Had he somehow seen her reaction to Vignon? Was Vignon indeed English? Had he been a spy in her own camp? Was this some sort of test of her loyalty? And if so, who was testing her—Bryce, or France? She knew that last question would go unanswered for now and turned her attention back to the scene before her.

Ryen scanned the table to find it strangely empty of trenchers. She lifted her eyes again to Bryce. He was still staring at her, but an amused look had settled over his features. She noticed movement at the rear of the hall and turned her head. The servants were beginning to come forward, carrying large platters of bread.

One girl bent over Ryen to place the plate in the center of the table. Ryen's stomach grumbled at the sight of the small bread loaves piled high on the tray. As soon as the girl moved back, Ryen reached her hand out for a piece of bread. She had not made it halfway when a low growl startled her. She looked toward the noise to see the wild-looking man sitting on her right leap toward the platter.

Ryen pulled her hand back quickly, seconds before the other men dived for the food. Chairs scraped and tumbled, wild cries filling the room as she pulled herself as far away from the food as her chair would allow. Then the men sat back, each with a portion of bread. Ryen's stomach grumbled and she reached for the platter.

It was empty!

She sat back, stunned. Just moments before, the tray had been full. If it wasn't for the crumbs on the platter, Ryen would have sworn her eyes were playing tricks on her. Barbarians, she thought. She pulled her hand to her chest, massaging her fingers as if in preparation for the next round. She lifted her eyes to Bryce. He was still watching her, casually bringing a piece of bread to his lips. Ryen frowned at him. Her hungry stomach grumbled as her eyes watched pieces of bread fall from his lips onto the table and roll to the floor, where two hounds lapped up the crumbs.

Her eyes shifted to Vignon. He was clutching a piece of bread in each hand, eating them with a tenacity that surprised her. Obviously he was not new to this.

Her head jerked to the side as a grunt sounded. Like a starved wild dog just thrown a bone, the soldier on her left gobbled the bread that was smashed in his clenched fists, his eyes darting savagely from side to side. Ryen could swear that he held two loaves in his large hands. Her eyes scanned the faces of the men around her, noticing that each had the same savage-eyed look, and each had at least two, if not three, loaves.

Her eyes shifted to Talbot. He had only one loaf, and his body curled protectively around it, his wounded arm shielding the bread as best it could.

Ryen's lips drew down in an alarmed pout. Were these people starving?

Her head swiveled around the room, watching with disgust the manners of these barbarians, or the lack of them. Until her gaze came to the back of the room. In the shadows she saw men and women milling, pacing. One small girl was sitting dejectedly, her thin legs crossed, her large eyes staring straight ahead. Ryen frowned in confusion. What was going on here?

She shifted her gaze to Talbot. He was just finishing up his bread. He might hate me, she thought, but he has never lied to me. "Why don't the peasants eat?" she wondered.

"They eat when we are done," Talbot answered, wiping a sleeve across his mouth.

Ryen's eyes shifted to the empty platter. Her stomach rumbled and she rubbed it absently. "There's no food left."

"They eat the kill," he replied.

A small girl reached over Ryen's shoulder to fill her cup. As she straightened, her stomach bumped Ryen's arm. Ryen glanced up and noticed her protruding abdomen. Good Lord, Ryen thought, the poor girl is with child! And from the looks of her size, ready to deliver now! She could barely stretch across the table for the mound of belly that jutted before her. As the girl went to replace Ryen's cup, Ryen took it from her hand so that she wouldn't have to reach across the table.

The girl froze, staring at Ryen. In her brown eyes, Ryen could see fear. Ryen set her cup back on the table and reached for the next cup. No sooner had her fingers encircled the goblet than a large hairy hand slammed down around her wrist.

Ryen's startled eyes quickly followed the hairy arm up to a snarling face. The man to her left still held bread in one hand as he glared at her. His eyes narrowed hotly and his grip tightened. For a moment no one moved.

Anger slammed through Ryen's body. He thought she was stealing his property! What in heaven's name would she want with a goblet? Other than to club him in the head with. Ryen tore her wrist away from him and turned to the girl, extending the goblet to her.

Shuddering, the girl lifted the pitcher and poured. As the beer filled the cup, Ryen could feel the man's form rising behind her. When the girl finished, Ryen turned and sloshed the cup into the man's hands, returning his accursed goblet. The man's furrowed eyebrows shot up in surprise and confusion as he stared at the goblet.

Out of the corner of her eye, Ryen saw that Bryce was also standing. She ignored both of them and reached for the next cup. The knight did not protest, and Ryen had the cup back to him in a second. She stood, moving down the row, filling each of their cups. She felt a gentle hand on her arm and looked up to see Polly at her side. The large woman reached out and took the cup from her hands, saying, "Ya return ta your seat. This is no job for a lady."

Ryen stared hard at her for a moment until Polly smiled and urged, "Go on, now." Ryen hesitantly returned to her seat. She felt every eye on her, suspicion and confusion in every look. Anger burned through her veins. These barbarians! Didn't they know how honored a pregnant woman should be? She had to be careful lest she lose the life inside her. But these *pigs* made her lean over them, stretching and bending. They refused even to lift a finger!

Ryen turned her gaze to Bryce. He was taking his seat, but she saw a glimmer in his eyes . . . was it pride? Or worry and doubt? She could not be sure, so she raised her chin and turned back to the soldiers. Most had finished eating and were watching her.

They didn't know what to make of her. She could see it in their eyes! They were surprised she had helped the servant. The woman was English, after all. But she was a commoner, treated no better than the dogs beneath Bryce's feet. Ryen shook her head sadly.

Suddenly, the swarm of servants surged forward again. They were carrying trays of fruit. Again a platter was placed before Ryen, in the center of the table. She didn't even reach for the luscious-looking apples. Not after last time. If starvation was Bryce's punishment, then so be it.

She cringed as the men descended over the mound of fruit, pushing and shoving each other in their desperation to reach the food.

Suddenly there was a growl. At first, Ryen thought it was the hounds, but as she turned her head she saw two men rising, one's hands outstretched toward the second man's throat. The table cleared instantly and Ryen was pulled out of her chair by the wild-looking man on her right as a fist barely missed her chin. It was appalling. She sucked in her breath as a fist connected with a jaw. The grunting and growling should have come from two animals, not two men.

Ryen glanced at Bryce. He was sitting in his chair, his gaze upon her. His soldiers, fighting each other for food? Why did he do nothing?

Ryen watched Elli bend to him, lay a hand on his shoulder,

and whisper in his ear. Together they turned to her again. Bryce nodded. Ryen wanted to rip out the woman's throat as well as cut off her hand for laying it on Bryce. She stared hard at the woman—at her fingers caressing his arm—until she removed her hand. When Ryen turned her gaze back to the fighting men, she saw they were rolling across the floor, through the rushes, away from the table. One by one, the soldiers who had been sitting around her began to take their seats, ignoring the struggle.

She turned her gaze again to Bryce. He was still watching her, taking a large bite from an apple. But he wore an amused look. He casually tossed a slice of fruit over the side of the table, where the hounds sat at attention, staring at him. The youngest and most agile of the dogs leapt up and caught the slice in his mouth, swallowing it whole.

Ryen became distinctly aware that she was the only one standing. Slowly she made her way to her seat. When she was seated, a large roasted pig was carried in, supported by a spit. Ryen watched as Bryce stood and moved around the table toward it. She watched his body as he walked, the slight swing of his muscular arms, the confident gait of his legs, the tightness of his leggings over the bulge—

She felt heat rise inside her and looked down, hoping to hide her discomfort, but found that she could not keep her eyes from him, and they lifted, centering on his wavy hair, and then slowly perusing his body.

He turned his back to her and her eyes were drawn to his firm buttocks. He was the most attractive man she had ever known. She felt her insides warming; the anger dissipated, replaced by a dreamy sensation as her eyes lazily examined his strong body.

An impish grin tugged the corners of her lips. He was so handsome, she could watch him all day . . . as long as he didn't know.

Then he turned and stared directly into her eyes.

Ryen's eyes widened with guilt, and her face paled. She

watched the knowing grin spread across his smug face. She wished she were dead. She wished she could disappear. She wished she could run a hand over those rounded muscles. She blanched. Where had that thought come from? She quickly dropped her eyes to the table.

When she cautiously raised her eyes again, Bryce was walking toward his chair. He was carrying a plate, on which was a slab of the swine. Ryen saw Lotte's back straighten with vanity as Bryce stopped before her and lobbed a hunk of meat into her dish. Ryen's shoulders slumped slightly, her lips drooping. Lotte's face glowed as she cast Ryen an arrogant look.

Bryce then moved to Elli, who smiled coyly at him. He dropped a large piece of the pig onto her plate. Ryen was dismayed to find hurt swirling inside her; she forced her face into a blank mask, hoping to convey disinterest.

Bryce turned to her then, his dark eyes pinning her to her chair. Ryen hoped that the ache she felt did not show. Her mind replayed Elli's hand running over the length of Bryce's arm. His lover, she thought with a jolt. He had been with her as Ryen recovered. She felt the pain rise in her throat and fought desperately to keep it from her face. I don't care, she told herself over and over. But she did.

Something flashed across his face as he stared at her, and then he was walking toward her, his powerful legs carrying him quickly over the space between them. When he stood before her, Ryen raised her chin and met his gaze with a haughty indifference.

A smile curved his lips and melted her heart. He picked up a large portion of the meat and held it out to her.

Murmurings spread like wildfire across the tables.

Ryen's mouth watered like a river; her stomach grumbled. Bryce waited patiently as she lifted trembling hands to take the pork. She could barely keep herself from ripping into it. She licked her lips and raised her eyes to him. "Thank you," she whispered, so softly that only he and the closest knights could hear.

Bryce's eyes smiled at her, glinting in the torchlight. He turned and went to his seat.

He had no sooner sat than the room exploded in motion. All the men dived for the center of the room, grabbing handfuls of meat, chopping with their daggers. They were like ants covering a fallen piece of bread.

Ryen stared, shocked at the sight: the men hovered around the spit, the strongest in front, gorging themselves. As one finished and moved away, the next strongest took his place. Fighting was common.

Ryen took one bite of her meat, and then a second. She felt out of place, eating daintily. When she took her third bite, she noticed the peasants. They were edging forward from the shadows at the rear of the hall, circling the men and the meat, waiting for their chance.

Surely there must be more kill for the peasants, Ryen thought. But as the commoners edged closer and closer, their eyes anxiously scanning for an opening, Ryen realized this was their only meal. Outrage rocked her body, and slowly she stood. She watched as one of the peasants reached a hand to the pig to rip off a piece of meat. The soldier closest to him snarled before he backhanded the man across the face.

Ryen's mouth dropped open in disbelief.

"They eat what's left. It is our way," the man on her right said around a piece of meat in his mouth.

"You mean the peasants are no better than your hounds?" she gasped. "At least you throw the dogs food!"

"The strongest survive," the man said, wiping his hand across his mouth.

Ryen pushed away from the table, unwilling to see more. She didn't understand why they acted this way. She moved toward the doors, feeling disgusted. No one should go hungry, she thought. Unless for some reason Bryce's lands were not prospering.

As she approached the giant wooden doors, she caught a movement out of the corner of her eye and swiveled her head. There, in the shadows, hiding behind a bench that lay on its side, was a boy. His hair was matted, his clothing too small. He was eyeing Ryen with hungry, hollow eyes. Ryen looked down to see what the boy was staring at. She was surprised to find that she still held the pork in her hand. Immediately, she held out the meat to him. He started forward, licking his lips.

Suddenly, Ryen's wrist was seized. She looked up and locked eyes with Bryce's dark gaze. The boy jumped back, taking cover behind the table.

"That is your food," Bryce told her. "Give it away and there will be no more."

Ryen yanked her arm free. "He's starving," she snapped, and again stretched out her hand.

The boy hesitated this time, his large eyes turning up to Bryce for permission.

"Come on," Ryen coaxed. "It's all right."

The boy took a tentative step forward, those haunted eyes returning to Ryen.

"You can have it." She bent at the waist and reached out to him. The boy ripped the meat out of her hand and retreated to the overturned bench to hide and eat.

Ryen straightened, a satisfied grin tugging at her lips. She watched the boy for a moment, certain that he was well on his way to finishing it. Then she turned to face Bryce, who was watching her, expressionless. "Are all the children thus starved?" she wondered softly.

Bryce's shoulders lifted slightly, his eyes never wavering from her face. "Not the strong ones."

"But why? Aren't your lands thriving?"

"We've had the best harvest thus far."

"You live like savages," she whispered harshly, so only he

could hear. "Fighting for your food. I have never seen such barbarism."

His body stiffened and his jaw clenched. His black eyes narrowed. "Then it is lucky you will be leaving."

Ryen felt her chest tighten. His words had stung her. She had not meant to insult him. Still . . . she had no right to feel hurt. She was nothing to him except a conquest. He had made that clear the first day she was here when he'd announced to all that he had taken her maidenhood.

She turned away from him and her eyes locked on the small boy who was licking his dirty fingers. Her heart twisted. Perhaps before she left she could make at least one change. The peasants and servants . . . the children . . . did not need to be hungry. There were ways and simple foods that would satisfy them. They shouldn't need to carry weapons or learn how to fight just to eat.

"Bryce." She turned back to him, stepping closer. "Allow me to enter your kitchens. There is a dish—"

His eyes narrowed, his look darkening. "So you can poison all of us? I think not, Angel."

Ryen's mouth dropped. She had not thought of poison. But as she stood staring into his suspicious, accusing eyes, the thought became very appealing. Her own eyes narrowed, mirroring his. "You are the most evil man I have ever known. I would *never* hurt a child. I even trusted that spy *you* sneaked into my camp—your son."

Bryce stepped toward her, his eyes burning into hers with anger.

Ryen retreated a step. She could not take her eyes from his; they demanded her attention, lest he strike.

His voice was so soft as he towered over her that she barely heard his words, "I did not sneak him into your camp. He came of his own free will. Like a true Princeton. Like a *wolf.*" He was walking away before she could breathe again.

Bryce must have loved the boy very much. She wondered what it took to get him to care that much.

She pushed herself from the wall, doubting she would ever know.

A pair of dark eyes watched the enemy cross the room. Lotte straightened her bodice, causing her large breasts to thrust out. She would not allow this French bitch to take her place as Prince's favorite. No matter what Prince said, she knew she would win him back.

"He likes her," a voice cooed.

Lotte whirled to find Elli smiling at her. Lotte snorted and turned back to picking at the pork before her. "I don't know what you're talking about."

"No? I think she's quite pretty. Nothin' like I woulda expected." Elli shifted her eyes from Ryen to Lotte. "Don't you think?"

"She's too thin. And her hair is unruly. Look how she looks down her nose at the men. She owes her life to Prince, and she doesn't even try to be nice to him."

"Would you rather she be nice to him?" Elli wondered.

"I'd rather she was out of the castle. For good." Lotte stopped as Elli's soft laughter reached her ears and tore her eyes from Ryen to glare at her.

"Sounds to me like the green-eyed monster has a hold on you." Elli put a finger to her chin, pondering. "Or perhaps ye're just scared. After all, Prince has already bedded her. How long do you think it will be before he does again? And you, with yer high morals. Never letting any of the other men touch you, saving yerself for Prince. And turnin' McFinley out, ta boot. It looks like you might be the one turned out, after all."

"Shut up," Lotte hissed. Her eyes darted back to Ryen. "It'll only be time before he tires of her. Then he'll come back ta me."

"Are you sure? Are you *so* sure?" Elli's tinkle of laughter reached Lotte and she cringed.

Lotte's dark eyes narrowed to slits as she stared at Ryen, her lips turned down. She was not going to let some French tart replace her. Lotte would do anything to prevent that. *Anything.*

"It's time to return."

Ryen turned from her seated position at the table to see Talbot standing beside her. She made no effort to object or to quarrel with him. On the contrary, she was anxious to return to Bryce's room. The savagery of these people disturbed her; the total disregard of the peasants upset her. To see children starving was more than she could tolerate.

As they turned to leave the Great Hall, another knight rushed up to them. "Sir Talbot! Cooper and Darcy are fighting in the barracks."

Talbot grimaced. "Wells! Pavia! See her to Prince's room," Talbot shouted, motioning to Ryen with his head.

Ryen turned to see a large, burly man approaching her. When she turned back to the departing Talbot, she was shocked to see Vignon standing right beside her. She swallowed a gasp, awaiting a comment of some kind, but he remained silent, his eyes averted from her gaze.

The burly man ushered her toward the doors with a firm hand at the small of her back.

Silently, Vignon followed her, the other man beside him. What was Vignon doing here? Was he truly English? Or was he some kind of spy for King Charles? If he is a spy, why hasn't he sought me out to confide in me? Ryen wondered. The realization came all too swiftly.

Because I am a traitor.

Ryen's feet suddenly felt like lead, and she almost stumbled. She righted herself as they turned a corner. What if he is English and he was a spy in my camp? she asked silently.

Ryen wanted to turn and question him directly. But she knew she couldn't.

Then a thought occurred to her. Wells and Pavia. Talbot had said that Wells and Pavia would escort her to Bryce's room. So Vignon must be using another name. Unless, of course, Wells or Pavia was his real name.

She halted before the door to Bryce's room. She had never truly trusted him. Had her instincts been right all along?

Vignon reached around her to open the door.

Stoically she stepped through the entryway. Has he been sent to rescue me? she wondered, before the door was closed and locked behind her. Or to kill me? Either possibility made her nervous. Very nervous indeed.

Thirty-three

The roaring fire warmed the vast room, casting large, dancing shadows on the stone walls. Bryce, sitting with his men near the hearth, watched Ryen speak with the fat maid. She was wearing maroon today; the velvet conformed to her curvy hips, hiding her long legs. Her hair spilled over her shoulders in waves, forming the rebellious curls Bryce longed to touch.

As he watched, Ryen's brow creased with concern and she glanced at Bryce before quickly looking away. He had seen her friendship with the maid bloom over the last few days. He hadn't been concerned, but that changed when he saw a different maid, a younger maid, laugh with the Angel of Death. Then, he even saw old Ben, the stableman, speaking earnestly with her. Suspicion charged Bryce's thoughts. What was she up to? he had asked himself time and again. And now he wondered anew.

It had been days since he had returned to find Ryen drenched, strung up to be whipped. And every time he saw her, the intensity of his desire shocked him. Now, staring at her, even with suspicion brewing, he felt the passion burning in him again. God, how he wanted her! Yearning flared in every fiber of his body, racing through him as if it were his very lifeblood.

He watched as the chubby maid waddled away and Ryen turned to him. A scowl creased her usually smooth forehead and her full lips curved down in a pout. Bryce watched her straighten her shoulders and approach. He noted, with appreciation and something close to pride, the swing of her hips. He kept her standing before him for some time before he raised his eyes from her lithe body to her face. That rebellious little chin was raised, her blue eyes ablaze with cold flames. Some of the men near him chuckled.

Ryen scorched one of them with a murderous glare before Bryce drew her anger back to its source. "Do you want something, *Angel?*"

When she spoke, her words were clipped with fury. "I would speak with you." She shot hot glances at the rest of his men. "Alone."

"What you have to say can be said before my men. I have no secrets," Bryce replied, raising his goblet to his lips.

Surprise, followed quickly by anger, flashed over her face. Then, a strange calm settled over her body and she raised a sly eyebrow. "Why, Bryce, then I must assume you've told them of all your conquests. How you skewered your helpless victims with your mighty sword."

Talbot almost choked on the ale he was in the process of downing.

Bryce's head came up slowly to meet her taunting eyes. "Some are not 'helpless,' Angel."

Some of the men elbowed each other as they snickered.

"Only the virgins!" Talbot called out.

As guffaws met his statement, Bryce watched Ryen's cheeks turn a deep red. He realized she had intended her comment to be degrading and insulting. When she realized how his men had twisted her statement, she lowered her eyes, her back straightening, her chest jutting slightly. She nervously ran her hands over her hips, smoothing the garment over her waist, brushing imaginary lint from her flat stomach.

One by one, the men ceased their laughter until all eyes were riveted on her.

Bryce found his body responding to her subtle seduction. Did she know what she was doing? He tore his eyes from

her hands to look at her face. She gently bit her lower lip.
He thought he would explode at the innocence of the gesture.
Blood pounded through his veins like a drumbeat, blocking
out all sound and all rational thought.

Suddenly, he was on his feet and approaching her. He saw
the fear in her eyes, saw how she turned to flee. But he
grabbed her wrist and pulled her to him.

"Do not flaunt yourself to me, Angel," he whispered in
her ear.

She struggled in his grasp. His chest pressed tightly
against her own as he drew her closer to him. "I don't know
what you're talking about," she gasped, breathlessly. She
looked up at him.

Suddenly, her fighting ceased and she stared at him with
liquid eyes. Her luscious lips were but inches from his. Bryce
could feel her soft breath against his mouth, the press of her
breasts against his chest.

I am going to kiss her, he realized, as he closed his eyes
in anticipation of the taste of her delicate lips.

"Bryce!"

Bryce spun to find Talbot standing behind him, a slight
frown revealing his concern. Slowly, reality crashed down
upon him. Not a sound echoed in the Great Hall. His men
sat where they had been, but their eyes were locked on him.
Bryce's eyes swept the room, noting that every gaze was
upon him as he held Ryen.

His glance finally returned to the source of his troubles.
She was limp against him, her eyes slightly closed. But what
he could see of them were dreamy and anticipating. He
stepped away and yanked her by the arm toward the doorway.
Ryen's skirt tangled about her ankles and Bryce felt her
weight in his arm as she stumbled and he pulled her upright.
She struggled to keep up with him, taking two steps to every
one of his while lifting her skirt with her free hand so she
wouldn't trip again. They rounded a corner and proceeded
toward Bryce's room.

"Bryce!" Talbot shouted from behind them. But Bryce did not slow his step. His grip was brutal and relentless as he tugged her up the stairs. He kicked open the wooden door and propelled her into the room. Ryen's back smacked against the frame of the fourposter bed and she dropped straight to the floor. She sat there, her dress splayed out on the stone ground, her wide eyes staring at him as he kicked the door shut.

He approached her. "Next time you choose to seduce me, *Angel*, pick your location carefully."

Her jaw dropped and her mouth hung open.

His hand fell to his belt and he unhooked it. There'd been days of yearning for her, fitful nights of wanting, seeing only those eyes, her body. Now he fully intended to have her. Any woman who *dared* to taunt him would feel the hardness of his lust. Especially if that woman was Ryen De Bouriez.

"Please . . ." she whispered.

Bryce froze. She had not moved. Yet the word rang like a bell through his mind, slowly working its way through his body. Had that been desire in her voice, or fear? He searched her face. What am I doing? he demanded of himself. The scene of their first intimate encounter in her tent rose before his mind's eye. Are you going to take her to satisfy your need? a voice inside him mocked, or will you wait until she is ready, until you can show her what it is like to make love? His hand froze on his belt.

Sitting at the bottom of the bed, her dress spread out around her like the petals of a delicate flower, she drove him to the brink of madness. His body and his mind battled for control.

She is a prisoner! he reasoned with his growing need. A prisoner I am waiting ransom for!

Curse etiquette, he thought. I want her. He took another step toward her, then stopped. Even the Wolf Pack honored the unspoken law—never take what belonged to another man. When her king refuses the ransom, then she will be mine. With a low growl, he rebuckled his belt and turned away from her. "You wanted to speak to me *alone*."

Silence.

Bryce walked to the window and stared out on the afternoon. At the sound of shouts he looked to his left. Beyond the wall, just before the trees, was the training yard. Some of his men were practicing their sword skills, others jousting.

What would they think if they knew my only weakness was their greatest enemy, if they knew a small glance from her sapphire eyes could bring their lord to his knees? Bryce wondered. He clenched his fist and gently pounded the ledge. Damn, I must have looked like a fool in the Great Hall. If it hadn't been for the warning in Talbot's voice, I might have succumbed to her spell and fell to my knees pledging my devotion.

"I—I want to know why your peasants are hungry," Ryen's soft voice came from behind him.

"They are weak," Bryce stated simply, not daring to turn to regard her.

"They work all day! Bryce, please, let me into the kitchens," Ryen stated.

Bryce paused for a long moment. Then, he asked, "Why?"

"I can supervise the making of corn meal."

"Why would you want to feed me, your enemy?" Bryce wondered, never taking his gaze from the field, trying hard to ignore the pounding of his passion.

"The children," Ryen replied, anguished.

Bryce turned to her. She was standing near the bed, her hands folded before her stomach. Children. Yes, like Runt. But he had been strong.

"They're starving," she added.

Could she be trying to help the children because she felt guilty about Runt? No. Bryce stepped away from the window, moving closer to her. "Do not fool yourself. They are my people. They would not hesitate to stab you in the back if they thought it would please me."

"Would it?"

No, Bryce's mind answered, as he looked into her deep

blue eyes. She was perfect. Oh, so perfect. He wanted to touch her so badly that he felt his hands shaking. He turned his back on her and clenched his fists. "You are needed for the ransom."

There was no sound, no movement.

After a moment, he glanced over his shoulder. Her head was bowed, long wavy hair draped over her shoulder like a curtain as her slender finger traced the outline of a wolf carved in the bedpost.

He moved toward her until they stood shoulder to shoulder, his long black hair brushing the velvet of her gown. He could smell lilacs in the air about her. As she looked up at him, he could see the slight scowl that creased her forehead. He had a sudden desire to kiss her frown away. And it angered him. He stiffened, every muscle in his body fighting the impulse. He looked away from her into the room. Yet his eyes did not see anything as he proclaimed, "You cannot enter the kitchens."

He took two steps toward the door before anger washed over her. "Don't take out your hate for me on those children."

But Bryce did not stop. He quit the room, shutting the door firmly behind him. He was relieved to be alone, away from those haunting eyes, away from that seductive body.

Bryce gritted his teeth. The ransom reply would come within a week. He could wait. After all, it was only seven days. He had spent more than seven days in the agonizing boredom of the court. He had spent more than seven days marching with his army in a torrential downpour. He had spent more than seven days in full armor laying siege to Castle Moore. Bryce sighed.

It would be the longest week of his life . . .

The firelight cast flickering shadows about the room. Polly sat in a chair before the small fire, her short, plump legs stretched out before her. She held her wool skirt up so her pudgy toes were bared to the warmth.

"Gaw!" Kit planted herself in the vacant chair beside Polly. "I'm colder than a rat's arse." She tugged up her skirt and placed her feet near the fire. "I'd love ta put a curse on that Lotte. She's the bloody one who keeps us poor folks out o' the main room and away from the fireplace. Why, the bloody dogs are warmer!"

"Keep your voice down. If we're discovered 'ere, we'd have a fit trying to explain why," Polly hushed.

Finally, Kit sat back in her chair, staring contentedly into the flames. "Now, I bet if the Angel were lady of the castle, things would be different."

"Aye," Polly nodded. "She has a good heart."

"Who'da thought we'd be talkin' this way? I s'pected ta hate 'er. Then she goes an' does nice things. Did ya hear? She gave Jimmy her meat."

Polly nodded, a sluggish smile spreading over her face.

"Things would be different," Kit continued. "Even his lordship would be sportin' a smile."

"We'd be fed well," Polly supplied.

"An' we'd have a warm place ta sleep. We would not have ta sneak ta the kitchen. Ah. That witch, Lotte."

"Yer right," Polly said. "But until Prince can see the good Lady Ryen would do, we're stuck with snotty Lotte."

Kit groaned. "Da ya ever think he'll come ta his bloody senses?"

Polly shrugged.

"And ta think we believed all them bad things about her." Kit shook her head, her dirty brown locks swaying with the movement. "I still can't believe Talbot was goin' ta have her whipped."

Polly's face whitened.

Kit continued, staring into the flames. "Why, ifn I ever find out who gave 'er that bloody dagger, I'll—"

"It was me," Polly mumbled. Her heavy form sat absolutely still, shoulders slumping.

Kit turned her head to Polly. "What'd ya say?"

"It was me. That's why I tried ta stop them." Polly's eyes became teary with the memory. "Why, that lass would have let them lash her before she revealed me name."

"Oh, Polly. Why'd ya do it?"

"I meant no harm. But, ya know, the bread is so hard. And she was so thin." Polly turned to her with haunted eyes. "Do you know what they'd do to me if they ever found out?"

Kit's eyes grew round. "The dungeon!"

Polly nodded. "Ya mustn't tell!"

"I won't," Kit replied earnestly.

"Swear," Polly said, leaning forward to study her face.

"I swear it on me mother's grave, God rest 'er soul."

Polly sat back heavily, putting a hand to her chest. "Oh, but telling someone is a weight off me chest. I thought fer sure I would burst with the secret. But now I have you ta talk to."

They watched the flames dance before their eyes, content and warm.

"Lord have mercy," Polly whispered into the silence. "But I owe the Angel o' Death me life."

A glimmer flashed in the shadows behind them, and a dark shape receded, taking with it the white of a smile.

Thirty-four

The distant clang of metal against metal caught Ryen's attention. Ryen threw the comb down on the bed and raced to the window. Was the castle under attack? She strained and tilted her head to find out which way the familiar noise was coming from. Then she spotted it. To the left, over the castle wall, she could see a clearing where men clothed only in breeches were practicing their knightly skills. Warm memories flooded over her. She could have been in France, watching her own soldiers.

Except for Bryce. When he strode onto the field, she noticed him immediately. His presence filled the clearing like the dark lord he was named for. She watched him bend down and pick up his sword. Then, unmercifully, he attacked the man closest to him. His movements were swift and deathlike, each thrust a precise jab. Not once did he relent until his opponent lay defeated beneath him. Ryen's face brightened as she leaned farther out the window in an attempt to watch him better. He was magnificent, there was no denying that. His tunic lay discarded in the grass; his shoulder muscles rippled like waves beneath a fine layer of perspiration. His dark hair reflected the sunlight in its obsidian depths, casting the fiery orange light back in defiance.

Ryen felt a stirring inside her. She wanted to touch him, to caress that skin and feel the softness of his hair, but there was something else, too. There was delight at watching him best the other knights in swordplay, thrill at seeing him over-power all who challenged him.

Then, Ryen saw Talbot walk over to Bryce, his arm out of the sling and hanging at an awkward angle at his side. They spoke together for a moment and Ryen watched Bryce's shoulders set and straighten. Then, together, the two men turned and looked right at her!

Ryen yanked her head back into the room, smacking it on the bricks. She rubbed her injured skull and quickly with-drew into the room. She sat on the bed for a long moment, rubbing her throbbing head. She half expected Bryce to come up to her room and demand to know what she had been looking at. But as the minutes stretched on and the door did not bang open, Ryen knew he would not come.

I'm glad, she told herself, knowing as she thought it that it was not the truth. She turned her thoughts back to the men and how they were training. How she longed to swing a sword again, to feel the weight of a weapon in her hands! Her body felt stiff and useless. She stood and imagined an opponent's swing, and dodged to the side, ducking under the imaginary blade. But her gown tangled around her feet and she tripped, stumbling to the ground.

For a long moment, she lay there on her back, dazed. She looked around the room from the floor. Have I lost all my senses? she wondered. I can't practice in a dress! Ryen sat up and removed the dress. Then she stared down at her che-mise. It would still get caught between her legs. If only she could hitch it up somehow. Then her gaze came to a towel lying beside the basin on the table next to the bed.

Ryen carefully rolled the towel into a tight belt and pulled the skirt of her chemise up so it hung to her mid-thigh. She tied the towel around the skirt, about her waist. When she was done, she looked down at her makeshift belt. Her long legs were exposed from the knee down. Finally, she could move freely!

Ryen ducked and sidestepped imaginary blows. Again and

again. Her body, not used to the labor, ached. But it felt good doing the movements she had been used to. Still, even though the dodges and parries were helpful in getting her body warmed up, Ryen knew she needed a weapon.

Slowly, Ryen scanned the room . . . until she saw the tapestry. She moved to the elaborate hanging and stared at the devil's face. His dark eyes seemed to be staring at her, his dark hair waving in the mysterious night breeze.

Bryce. His smug smirk. The muscles that gleamed under the moonlight. She followed the picture up to the sliver of a moon and then to the rod that held the tapestry.

A rod of gold!

A sword!

She stretched onto her toes and removed the rod from the thin strings holding it. Sitting on the floor, Ryen yanked the rod onto her lap and pulled it free of the tapestry. It was a bit long, but it would have to do. She got to her bare feet, throwing the rod from one hand to the other, weighing it. She tested it by arcing it over her head, then by thrusting. Ryen took tentative thrusts and parries until she became used to the weight and awkward height of the rod. Then, she gave it her all. Thrusts, dodges, parries, arcs. *Everything.*

Bryce stood in the open doorway.

Ryen froze, staring into his dark look. Her hair was wild about her shoulders, the skirt of her chemise hanging down on one side, having fallen loose from the towel. She held the rod out at him. The thought made her grin. It was ludicrous that a small, thin rod would stop him. She watched his dark eyes slowly lower, taking in every curve. Heat rose into her face and Ryen lowered the rod and snatched a blanket off the bed to cover herself with.

Bryce stepped into the room. His eyes shifted to the rod she held in her hand. Then, his gaze whipped to her right.

Ryen watched outrage filter across his face, saw the clenching of his hands. She turned to look at the object of his sudden rage. Only when her eyes found the crumpled tapestry did she recall it. Her head snapped back to Bryce, who was approaching her, his brows narrowed accusingly over his turbulent eyes, a muscle clenched in his jaw. Instinctively, she brought the rod up, halting him three feet from her.

Bryce stared hard at the rod, as if he couldn't understand its purpose. Then he raised his eyes to Ryen. The storm of anger threatened to sweep her into its whipping winds and furious lashing waves. Bryce swatted aside the rod so hard that the vibrations shook her arm. He seized her shoulders in an iron grip. "Angel," he said, from between clenched teeth.

The shock of his naked touch against her skin sent tremors up her arms to her shoulders. Ryen clutched the blanket tightly to her chest, her tiny fist knotted into the folds of the cloth.

His lips were drawn down into a frown of displeasure. Then, his rage exploded and he shook her. "Damn it, Ryen. Why do you have to be—?"

Suddenly she was against his body, his lips searing agonizingly across hers. Hungrily his tongue forced her lips open, and when she parted them, he thrust deep inside, tasting her sweetness. He crushed her to his body, his large hands pressing her back closer against him, drawing her nearer.

"Bryce," Ryen gasped, tilting her head back to receive more of his kisses. .

He pulled back to gaze into her eyes and frowned down at her. He stepped quickly back, away from her.

Ryen furrowed her brow in confusion, then raised her chin and swallowed the sudden pain of rejection that rose inside her.

"Ryen—" Bryce murmured.

She stared at him, large eyes sparkling like sapphires. Hope ignited in her heart. He was going to apologize, to tell her that she was beautiful.

"You may use the kitchens," he said.

Ryen's jaw slackened as disappointment stabbed her. Was that all? she wondered.

Bryce turned and headed for the door.

"Bryce!" Ryen called desperately.

He paused not two feet from the door, his shoulders rigid.

Ryen stared hard at his back, a thousand questions racing through her mind. "Why did you kiss me?" she asked softly.

He did not move for a long moment. "Talbot will escort you to and from the kitchens. He will oversee everything you do."

The kiss was a punishment for the tapestry, Ryen thought, her heart aching. No, not the kiss, but the feelings that flooded her senses when he deprived her of another touch of those sensuous lips. That was the true punishment. She watched as he pulled the door closed behind him. Slowly, her shoulders sagged and she sat on the bed.

That night, Ryen ate alone in her room.

Thirty-five

Polly, Kit, and Jimmy stood before Ryen in the rear of the Great Hall, staring at her with expectant eyes. Jimmy's mother stood at her son's side, her hollow brown eyes regarding Ryen with distrust. Her cotton dress was filthy; her feet were bare. She had no intention of masking the hostility that burned in her eyes.

Ryen surveyed the room. At the tables near the front of the Great Hall, the soldiers attacked the bread the servants had just placed before them. The peasants lounged against the wall not far from her, waiting for their chance at the food. They all watched her with blank faces. Ryen couldn't help but notice how Jimmy's mother turned her gaze toward the food with a concerned look. *She thinks she will go hungry today*, Ryen thought, before turning to Polly.

"Where do you usually sit to eat?" Ryen wondered.

"Sit?" Kit asked, looking to Polly in confusion. "Why, we sit anywheres we can find a space. Sometimes we just stand."

"Aye," Polly agreed. "It's quicker to the food that way."

"A dark corner is the best," Jimmy piped in. "Then ya might not get yer food taken."

A surge of sympathy swept Ryen. The poor child. There was no need to live like this. Everyone could have food—perhaps not as good as the nobles', but nourishing and warm.

Ryen led the group to an overturned table in the murky shadows in the rear of the hall. "Here," Ryen said, bending down and placing her hands on the table's edge. "Help me."

Polly and Kit moved to her side. But Jimmy's mother stood, her hands rooted to her hips, glaring at Ryen. "What are ya up ta? Why should we work for *you?*"

Ryen was about to reply, but Polly exploded, "Ya best not be talking to her that way!"

" 'N why not?" the woman demanded.

"It's all right, Polly," Ryen said, after righting the wooden table with Kit's help. She turned to Jimmy's mother, studying her. Her face was streaked with dirt, her hair uncombed; two of her teeth were missing. Their life could be so much better. "Because," Ryen stated, "if you help me, you will eat until you are full."

" 'N why should I believe ya? Who are ya ta me?"

"What do you have to lose?" Ryen wondered, bending to right a fallen bench. She was pleased to see Kit dragging another bench up to the opposite side of the table.

"What 'ave I got ta lose?" she replied, wiping a ripped sleeve across her dirty nose. "Ya'll probably poison us all!" She grabbed Jimmy's arm and pulled him away.

Ryen watched them go. Her heart twisted for the boy. Because his mother was so stubborn didn't mean the boy should have to go hungry. She heard snickers from the people around the room and turned to see the men and women at the tables watching her as they shoved bread into their mouths. Ryen raised her chin and turned her back on them. She didn't need their help nor their approval. "Polly, your job will be to make sure this table is clean before every meal. And at the looks of this," she ran a finger along the top of the table, then raised the dirt-coated tip before their eyes, "it may very well be a hard job."

"Aye," Polly replied, beginning to rub the wood with her apron.

"And yours, Kit, is to bring the meals. Polly will help, if need be."

Kit nodded.

"There will be enough food to fill both your stomachs,

as well as everyone else's. So don't be afraid to ask for more. And Kit, always set an empty bowl. Everyone is welcome at this table." She shot a look at Bryce, who was sitting in his usual chair at the other end of the room. "Everyone."

When they were done scrubbing clean a small area of the table so that they could eat, Kit carried in their meal, a bowl full of pease pudding for each of them. As Kit sat beside Ryen to eat, she gasped. "Gaw! It's still warm! I never had a warm meal before. Gaw."

Kit plunged her hand into the porridge and Ryen blanched.

"Kit," Polly chastised, and when Kit glanced up, a smear of pudding on her nose, Polly scowled at her and shook her head. Polly lifted a trencher and delicately sank the bread into the pudding.

Kit raised her own trencher and stared at it for a moment. "Gaw," she said, before immersing it in the food.

Ryen grinned in pride and was about to put her trencher into the pudding when she felt a tug at her sleeve. She looked down to see Jimmy standing beside her. He licked his lower lip as he stared at her food.

Ryen smiled and pointed to the bowl next to Polly. She watched as the boy ran to the seat and ate to his heart's, and stomach's, content.

And the people came. There were more peasants at the noon meal, and still more at dinner. The food was good. There was hot, fresh bread with each meal. As it turned out, it was Polly who was an expert in the kitchen, having been the eldest of twelve children.

Two days later, they needed another table.

Bryce sat slumped before the hearth, having failed to drown his lust in the mugs of wine and ale he had drunk through dinner and into the night. Now, as he stared into the fire, a mug of ale held loosely in his hands, he saw only her blue eyes in those dancing flames.

"You *can't* allow it to continue," McFinley cried. "She'll turn your people against you." The redheaded knight glowered at his lord. When Bryce did not reply, he added, "I hear murmurings from the servants of how she's not such a bad angel."

"You cuffed one of them yesterday for saying something like that," another knight called.

"And I'd cuff another if they said it again," McFinley snapped, pounding his thigh with his fist. "She *is* the Angel of Death! How much worse can she be? Poisoning the servants' minds, little as they may be."

Bryce downed the rest of his ale, tilting the mug until the bottom was raised. Then he lowered his cup and continued to gaze into the fire.

"Did you hear me, Prince?" When Bryce did not reply, McFinley dismissed him with a wave. "Aw, you sit there like a wart on the king's ass."

"I heard you," Bryce grumbled.

McFinley paled. The last man who had insulted Bryce was at the end of his sword the following day.

"I just think you're wrong," Bryce said quietly.

McFinley quickly departed and Bryce noticed that the seats around him had vacated. He bent his head to stare into his empty mug. She was wreaking havoc in his home, his castle . . . among his people. She was turning the peasants against him, or so McFinley claimed. But though he had seen her befriend many of the servants, had seen her treat them well, never had any of them shown any rebellion against him or England.

So, what was he to do? The only difference he'd seen was in his men. They were angry because they feared her influence on him and his people. They thought the Angel of Death would somehow overrun the castle.

That was impossible. What could she do with no weapons

against a stronghold? But . . . he had underestimated her before. Was she truly turning his peasants against him?

"You seem to have frightened off your men," a voice stated.

Without looking up, Bryce knew it was Grey. He heard the seat beside him creak as Grey fell into it. "May I offer some advice?"

"No," Bryce replied.

Grey chuckled. "Your mood is foul, my brother. But I will give it to you anyway."

Bryce grunted. He knew that Grey would speak his mind, regardless of what he said. Grey was one of the few men Bryce respected as an equal. He was the only man he could never seem to defeat in battle, and who had never defeated him.

"You are very stubborn," Grey said. "Your Angel is a rare woman. She is smart, educated, be that good or bad, and beautiful. She can win the hearts of her enemy with just a look. And on top of all this, she is a warrior."

"And?" Bryce demanded sharply.

Grey leaned forward so his arms were resting on his knees. His face was less than a hand's breadth away from Bryce's ear. "I see how she looks at you," Grey stated quietly. "The way her eyes follow you when you cross the room."

"She is my enemy," Bryce snapped.

"Oh, no, my brother. She is just the opposite."

Bryce turned to look into his wise eyes. There was confusion etched into the wrinkling of Bryce's brows, disbelief in the scowling of his eyes.

"Forget the ransom. Make her yours," Grey advised earnestly.

"I can't do that," Bryce retorted angrily, returning his gaze to the fire. "How honorable would it be were I to bed her before the messenger arrived from France?"

Grey studied him silently for a long moment. "Why do you make excuses? You are in love with her."

"No," Bryce answered firmly. "I want her, yes. But I do not love her."

Grey sadly shook his head. "You are a stubborn man, Bryce Princeton. Answer me this. What does honor dictate you do when the ransom is denied?"

"She will be mine. I will do with her as I wish."

"You will bed her and then perhaps throw her in the dungeon?"

The image of Ryen chained in the dark, cold dungeon with murderers and traitors roused his fury. "That is not your concern," Bryce ground out between clenched teeth.

"And have you considered if her king agrees to pay the ransom?"

"That is impossible."

Grey chuckled quietly. He was about to speak when he caught sight of Talbot entering the Great Hall and crossing the large room toward them. Talbot stared at Bryce for a long moment before he announced, "The French messenger has arrived."

The day had finally come. Ryen would be his.

Bryce Princeton stood on a battlement of his castle walk, looking out over the town, past the harvested fields to the horizon. He found his heart soaring. He wanted to give Ryen everything. To make her happy. And he would finally be free to do this.

He stared at the rising sun in satisfaction. For the first time in his life he knew the course of the future . . . and liked it.

He turned from the scene before him and descended the stairs. He opened a wooden door and entered the castle.

It was silent inside, quieter than the dawn before a battle. The receiving room was being prepared for greeting the French emissary. Four large pillars lined the empty room near the center aisle, looking more like four massive giants overseeing the justice that was rendered. A large red velvet chair was being positioned against one of the walls . . . his favorite chair. The judgment chair.

"Beggin' your pardon, sir."

Bryce turned to find Ryen's maid friend wringing her hands before him. Polly was her name, he remembered. His gaze finally came to rest on her hands, which were nervously twisting in her apron. None of the servants had ever spoken to him, nor he to them. He found that his presence intimidated them, and he could not abide their shivering and shaking. He looked back at the chair. "What is it?"

"I was wonderin', sir. What might ya be doing ta the Lady Ryen when no ransom comes for her?"

Bryce's gaze snapped to her, his brows furrowed. "That's none of your concern."

"Yes, sir. But she is only a slip of a girl, and ya just can't be throwin' her into the dungeons now."

Bryce's look clouded over like an approaching storm.

But Polly was not interested in his frowns. "Sir, it jus' wouldn't be Christian—"

Bryce grunted. He did not believe in God. He believed man made his own opportunities. But he had never voiced his opinion. The church wielded almost as much power as the king himself. He could not afford to be in disfavor with either of them.

"She's a good girl, sir. She don't deserve ta be locked up like a common thief."

"Your opinion is noted. Not that you should have one."

Polly bobbed a curtsy. "Thank you, m' lord."

Bryce watched her waddle away. What had Ryen done to his servants? Since when did Polly exchange two words with him, let alone have the courage to speak her mind? Bryce shrugged his large shoulders. It was inconsequential. His mind drifted back to Ryen. What would her face look like when she found out that her king would not meet his demands for a ransom? Would she throw herself to her knees and beg for his mercy?

His lips turned up into a grin. Not his Angel. She would raise that defiant little chin and demand to know what he intended to do with her.

"Will you break your fast?" Talbot wondered, entering the room.

Bryce sat in his chair, his eyes coming to rest on his friend. "Not until she is mine. Show the messenger in."

Minutes later, the room was overflowing with the curious. Servants hid outside the door, hoping to hear what the French king would do. Some of Bryce's men lined the room while his officers placed themselves behind their lord. The Wolf Pack, as usual, lounged in the shadows that the morning sun created behind the pillars.

The messenger stood alone in the middle of the room.

Bryce eyed him. The man was thin and short, certainly not an imposing figure to face the Prince of Darkness. Bryce's spirits soared. He glanced at Talbot, who stood beside him. Talbot appeared cautious, his brows drawn together. Before Bryce had time to dwell on this, the messenger produced a scroll from his tunic. He unfurled it and spoke in broken English. "The royal King of France, his mighty lord, bids the English lord, the Prince of Darkness, to release his most valued—"

"Get on with it," Bryce growled. "Will he pay the ransom, or no?"

The messenger straightened with indignation. Dark eyes focused on Bryce as shaking hands rerolled the scroll and returned it to his pocket. "The King of France will not pay your ransom."

Murmurs broke throughout the room as the word spread.

Bryce broke into a smile. He stood, slapping Talbot happily on the back. She was his. Ryen De Bouriez would yield to his terms now. He had never felt so relieved. Bryce turned to go to Ryen, to tell her of her king's judgment.

"Count Dumas will," the messenger said.

The words froze Bryce where he stood. Silence sliced the room like a blade as all eyes shifted to Bryce.

Slowly, he turned a deadly gaze to the messenger. "What did you say?"

There was a cocky glint in the messenger's eye as he answered, "Ryen De Bouriez's fiancé, Count Dumas, *will* pay your ransom demand."

Rage crept over Bryce's face slowly, erasing all traces of his previous joy. His jaw clenched and his eyes narrowed before he turned and stormed from the receiving room.

Thirty-six

The door slammed open and Ryen jumped away from the window. She whirled to find Bryce approaching like a storm cloud, dark and ominous. Before she could move to shelter, his hands slammed down around her arms, buffeting her with the force of a gale wind. His white teeth gnashed as he growled, "Do you love him?"

Ryen's mouth dropped open.

"You do, don't you? Why? Why him? Did he love you, Angel?" Bryce crushed her brutally against his chest; his mouth closed over hers, savagely bruising her lips.

Ryen turned her face away long enough to murmur, "Stop it. Please," before his lips silenced her pleas.

Bryce tore his lips away from her and cupped her chin, forcing her to look into his eyes. "Did he touch you, Angel? Like this?" His palm closed over her breast, twisting and teasing.

"Bryce!" Ryen cried. "Stop it! Stop it!" She tried to push his hand away, but it was like rock, unmovable.

"What's wrong? Is my touch not as gentle as your lover's?" He shoved her away, hard, and Ryen's back slammed into the wall.

Bryce's face was twisted with anger, and something else, as he glared at her.

"W-what are you saying?"

"Your ransom will be paid. Your lover, Count Dumas, is paying for you."

Count Dumas? Ryen's mind screamed. "No," she gasped.

Bryce's eyes hardened. "No? You think your pretty thighs are not worth the amount I have requested? You're wrong, Angel. I would pay the devil himself to have you again."

His admission stunned her and she stood still before him, dumbfounded. He *wants* me, she thought, and although she heard the words in her head, it was a moment before they sank in. He wanted her with a hunger that drove him to this madness. She had never seen such . . . rage in a man's eyes, except in battle.

Bryce watched the play of emotions on her face. "Tell me of him," he commanded.

She stared up at him unable to speak, unable to say anything, *everything,* that was racing through her mind. His cold words chilled her blood, froze her heart.

"Come, come, Angel. Tell me if he is old or young. Tell me what color hair he has, how his eyes look. Tell me how his kisses affect you. Does he make you wet with desire?"

"What would you have me say?" she wondered quietly, hurt and embarrassed.

"Tell me! Damn you to hell, Angel! Tell me he made love to you. Tell me so that I can strangle that flawless white neck of yours!"

Her face paled and her eyes looked huge, the blue of a hauntingly clear sky. He turned away and stalked to the night-stand, where he stood for an unending moment, his long fingers grasping the side of the table. His black hair hung over his face, obscuring his profile from her vision.

Ryen watched his shoulder muscles bunch and release beneath a coat of anger. Suddenly, Bryce exploded, swiping a basin off the table. It shattered as it struck the floor, a hundred fragments spinning away in every direction.

"Bryce," Ryen said, softly. "Count Dumas is my fiancé, but—"

"Your admission comes a little late," Bryce snarled, turning. "I should have left you for dead."

Ryen's eyes filled with tears of humiliation before she turned her back on him.

Her tears pierced the blanket of rage that coated Bryce like a knife slicing silk. For a brief moment, he almost reached out to her. But he could not stop the image of his Angel in the arms of another man from snaking its way into his mind. He steeled what remained of his heart.

His obligation to king and country was complete with the paid ransom. If losing her was the taste of duty, he wanted nothing to do with its bitter flavor. The little tart's ransom was paid. What could he do?

Bryce backed away from her. "Prepare yourself. You will be returned within the week."

Dark, dark hair waving in a soft breeze. Black eyes staring at her, calling to her with a hypnotic power. The corners of his sensual mouth turned up in a devilish grin. The scar on his cheek looking white against his bronzed skin. He was leaning against a wall, his right leg bent at the knee, crossed over his left ankle. The wind ruffled his glossy hair as his ebony eyes caressed her skin, their gaze sweeping slowly over her breasts, hips, legs. Then they shifted, rising to hers. She saw the whispered words reflected in those eyes. "You're beautiful."

Beautiful.

Ryen tossed on the great bed. Tears streamed from her closed eyes. Groans escaped her lips.

Beautiful.

"M'lady!" Polly cried, entering the room with a tray. She rushed to the bed, placing the platter on the table. Polly grabbed Ryen's shoulders, shouting, "M'lady! Wake up. You're dreamin'!"

Ryen's eyes snapped open. She looked frantically around the room for a moment, her eyes mirroring her fright and confusion.

"It's all right," Polly soothed, her worried expression relaxing as Ryen's look calmed. Polly shook her head, offering Ryen a towel. "Another dream."

Ryen turned from her, embarrassed by her weakness. She wiped her cheeks with the cloth. She could not remember the end of the dream. She knew there was more, that it was painful, but she couldn't recall it.

"It's all right, m'lady. My mother told me once that tears weren't nothin' to hide. They are the heart's soul."

"Don't call me that," Ryen mumbled into the towel.

"Beg yer pardon?"

"Don't call me 'm'lady.' "

Polly gazed hard at her. " 'N what should I call ya?"

"Ryen," she answered. When the quiet stretched, Ryen turned to Polly. The older woman was staring at her with a glimmer of sadness in her eyes.

"I can't call you that," Polly finally said, shaking her head and looking away.

"I'm not your lady, Polly," Ryen said quietly, a hint of remorse in her tone. "I'm leaving the castle in a few days."

Polly nodded, kneading her apron. "Can't say that I'm pleased meself."

"Some will be very happy. Talbot—"

"Aw, but Sir Talbot has a good heart." Polly turned to the tray and poured Ryen some ale. "He just don't know ya, is all."

"Lotte."

Polly frowned and shook her head as if the name itself was painful to her ears. "That one is bad blood." She handed Ryen the cup. "If there's anything ta be glad about, it's that yer gettin' away from *her*."

Ryen looked down into the dark liquid. "Bryce."

"Now, yer wrong about that," Polly insisted. "His lordship may be stubborn, but he is very fond of you."

"Fond," Ryen repeated dully.

"Aye. He wants ya to stay. Don't ya see how miserable 'e is?"

Ryen shook her head and waves of soft hair swayed over her shoulders. "I haven't seen him for days."

"He's left the castle."

Ryen raised her eyes to look at Polly.

"Some sheep raiders . . . or somethin'."

"Oh." Ryen's shoulders slumped. Life here was so much better than life would be if she married that old hermit. She had been harboring the hope that somehow Bryce would find a way for her to remain. So she could . . . could what? Be Bryce's whore.

"Ya do want ta stay, don't ya?" Polly wondered.

Ryen turned to gaze out the window at the rising sun. Bryce's image, powerful and dark, rose before her mind's eye. To be with Bryce: it was everything she wanted. Every time he came close to her, she melted. She wanted to touch him, to feel the power she knew was coursing just below his bronze skin. But every time he looked at her, every time he touched her, she felt anger . . . and something else. Beneath his anger she sensed something . . . something more powerful, yet something he hid very carefully, even from himself. She wanted time to find out just what it was he guarded so closely.

She wanted with all her heart to stay with him.

But honor would not allow it. Her accursed loyalty to France, to a country that had scorned and labeled her traitor, would not allow it.

And yet even if she put honor and loyalty aside, could she live in the same castle as Bryce, knowing he only felt—

"Fond," she whispered. "I couldn't, Polly. I just couldn't stand it."

Polly's face saddened and she stepped away from the bed, her hands at her sides. "Talbot is waitin' for ya outside. We'd best hurry."

Polly helped her into a simple black velvet gown and

combed her hair in silence. When she finally stepped back, Ryen clasped her hands together and rose. She led the way to the door, and when she opened it, she saw Talbot standing in the hallway. He turned when she stepped outside the room. He stared hard at her, until she had to drop her eyes to keep him from seeing the agony that tortured her.

Wordlessly, Talbot escorted them to the Great Hall.

The meal was served and Ryen watched blandly from her seat with the peasants as the soldiers attacked the food like barbarians.

Ryen's eyes were again drawn to Bryce's empty chair. Sadness creased her forehead and drooped her shoulders. When Ryen turned back to the trencher before her, she hardly noticed how strangely quiet her table was as the peasants cast pensive stares her way. She picked at the bread, tearing off small pieces and nibbling on them.

Suddenly Ryen heard a grunt and a hollow thud. She glanced up to see McFinley standing over an empty chair, reaching for a bowl. A woman was on the floor, scrambling away from him.

McFinley inspected her bowl, then tossed it aside and grabbed more bowls and cups and tossed them to the floor. Peasants cleared the table, running for cover, and Ryen leapt to her feet.

"Stop it!" Ryen screamed, grabbing his arm. His fist came around to smash into her cheek. The blow was strong enough to knock her to the ground. Stars of pain blinded her. When the white blotches faded enough for Ryen to see, the man was grabbing the edge of the table and lifting it, flinging it onto its side. Trenchers, food, and mugs all fell, clattering into a heap on the floor. Ryen watched helplessly, slowly pushing herself up onto one elbow, as all her work, all her effort, was destroyed.

Then, suddenly, McFinley whirled on her. His eyes were wild with rage.

Ryen lay sprawled on the floor, her cheek stinging. She

watched as he took a step forward, his face filled with loathing, his eyes burning with hate as they glared at her.

Bryce was gone and somehow Ryen could not muster the strength to defend herself. She lowered her head to the floor.

"Ya ain't gonna hurt 'er," a small voice proclaimed bravely.

Ryen forced herself to sit and saw Jimmy standing before her, his arms akimbo, as he faced the brute.

McFinley's gaze, as well as his anger, focused on the boy.

Ryen shot to her feet, pulling Jimmy against her to protect him.

McFinley snarled, his lip curling, and took a step toward them.

Ryen's heart raced. If it were just her . . . but Jimmy. She couldn't allow him to be hurt because he was brave enough to defend her. She pushed Jimmy behind her.

Talbot appeared between them. "That's enough, McFinley."

"Out of my way, Talbot," McFinley growled.

"You need a rest, man. Go down to the yards and work it off."

McFinley stepped forward.

The hiss of metal against metal sounded in the suddenly quiet room as Talbot drew his sword and pointed it at McFinley's chest. "I think you've been drinking much too early this morn. Go to the yards—*now.*"

McFinley's eyes shifted to Talbot, and for a moment, the anger receded. Then, his gaze snapped back to Ryen and hate slammed down like a hammer.

He stepped back and reached to his waist to draw his own sword.

"Don't do this, McFinley. My word is law while Prince is gone," Talbot warned.

"Stand aside," McFinley said, his red eyes trained on Ryen. "I only want to teach her a lesson."

The tip of Talbot's sword lowered a hand's breadth and

Ryen stared in disbelief. He was going to let McFinley "teach her a lesson!"

Then Talbot's jaw stiffened and he raised his weapon again. McFinley moved swiftly, pulling his sword and arcing it down in a sweeping motion. Talbot deflected the blow with a slicing movement and the sound of swords clanging echoed in the hall.

As the men exchanged blows, Ryen's expert eye caught flaws in McFinley's techniques: his eyes gave away the direction of his thrust and he hesitated a split second before acting. But Talbot was faltering under McFinley's relentless attacks. She knew Talbot would not last much longer. He was not left-handed and his right arm was useless, forever damaged by his dangerous leap from her window. Ryen moved Jimmy to the safety of his mother's arms, her eyes scanning the room.

McFinley attacked with unswerving steadiness. He rained blow upon blow down about Talbot, who was wilting under his barrage. McFinley arced his sword and then quickly thrust. Talbot blocked and jumped back, but his foot caught on a fallen bench and he went down. His sword flew from his grasp and skittered across the floor as he crashed to his back.

McFinley stared down at his prone victim for a moment, his face void of any emotion. Then, with a grimace, he howled, raised his sword, and drove the sharp tip down toward Talbot's chest.

Before the deadly aim struck flesh, McFinley's arms were jarred as a sword struck his and his blow missed its target entirely. His blade struck the stone floor. Talbot rolled away, and rising to his feet, turned to see who had saved his life.

Ryen stood tall before him, gripping his sword with two hands, its tip pointing directly at McFinley's chest.

McFinley slowly circled to her left, away from Talbot, his eyes narrowed in contempt, his lip curled with hatred. "I have a debt to settle with you," McFinley snarled.

Ryen felt unsure, but she tried to hide the feeling deep in

her chest. It was not easy. The sword felt awkward, and her dress inhibited her steps. She knew she would somehow have to get rid of the dress or die. Her heart pounded as she saw his eyes shift to the left.

Ryen raised the sword and blocked the blow. Then he swung again and again. The impact of each parry jarred her arms. But confidence and familiarity began to creep through her body with each crossing of the swords. The old feeling of power came back to her with each clang of metal. This was who she was, what she did best.

He swung again and thrust. Again Ryen diverted the blows. She grew comfortable with Talbot's sword, but in order to defeat McFinley, she knew she had to get her legs free.

She allowed him to drive her back to the fallen table with each blow. She was defending herself and not attacking. McFinley became cocky, playing with her as though she were a squire. Let him underestimate me, Ryen thought with a smirk. Ryen kicked an overturned stool at him and he stumbled, falling heavily to the floor.

Instead of attacking, Ryen fled her foe, running for cover. As she ran, she slashed the heavy sword at her black dress, cutting the velvet material just above her knees. She ripped it as she ran and, pausing behind a fallen chair, tore the rest of her gown from her legs. As she tugged the black velvet off, Ryen lifted her eyes to find McFinley climbing to his feet. She grinned as she stepped from the tatters of velvet.

Free at last, the Angel of Death straightened to greet McFinley as he charged at her. He skidded to a halt just before the chair and eyed the confident grin, the new glint in her eyes. This was not the woman he had faced a moment ago.

Ryen saw a frown of apprehension slide over his features and she leapt to the top of the chair. As it fell flat, she rode it to the floor, bringing the sword up. She attacked him, giving in to the longing in her heart for a sword fight.

Under her blows, McFinley was forced backward until they had moved across the room, near Bryce's chair.

Finally McFinley responded with his own set of thrusts and arcs. But Ryen read his moves in his eyes, anticipating his swing. Ryen allowed him to attack, saving her strength until McFinley was panting from the exertion of the on-slaught. She raised an eyebrow at him and a grin lit her face. "Is that the best you've got?" she wondered.

A growl of rage issued from deep in his throat and he assaulted her with a flurry of thrusts until he could barely hold the sword up.

"Dance until your feet burn, all night long," Ryen sang, bringing the sword around to her right, attacking his left flank.

McFinley blocked her blow.

"Seven and twenty maidens singing a song." She arced the sword to his left.

He parried.

"When the song was finished the maidens said . . ." Arc right.

McFinley blocked her sweep.

"Your sword will be a lovely gift to set before the prince." Ryen thrust, catching his sword, and twisted her wrist, jarring the weapon loose from McFinley's hold. It sailed through the air and landed with a clang against the far wall.

Ryen raised her sword to McFinley's neck. A smile of triumph lit her face.

"I yield," he said, his voice rising so that all could hear him.

"You cur," Ryen snapped, every bit of humor disappearing. "Don't *ever* attack helpless people again. Do you understand? If you do, you will answer to me." She pressed the point of the sword against his skin.

"I yield!" he shouted.

A moment stretched in the silent hall as Ryen relished the return of the Angel of Death. She felt her heart pounding and the battle lust coursing through her veins, the familiar feeling of victory as McFinley stood defenseless against the point of her weapon.

"Give me the sword."

She raised her eyes at the words and saw Talbot standing next to her. Suddenly, she heard the quiet that had settled around her. Her gaze swept the room. Nobody was moving. Nobody even seemed to be breathing. Every eye was locked upon her, fearful yet curious. On the faces of the knights Ryen saw unabashed disbelief—disbelief and caution. She straightened.

Wary distrust was thick around her and Ryen suddenly understood the anxiety. She had a weapon. Did they really believe she would try to fight her way out? Against immeasurable odds? The Angel of Death was not that stupid.

She had worked her legend well.

Ryen flipped the sword up and gently caught the blade in her open palm. "It's a little unbalanced," she commented, offering the weapon to Talbot.

He carefully took it from the Angel of Death's hands. "I know." His face was grim as his eyes met hers.

"M'lord!" A young boy ran up to Talbot. He was out of breath as he reached his lord's side. "M'lord," he repeated when Talbot glanced at him, "the Frenchman has arrived!"

Thirty-seven

Ryen sat staring down into her lap where her folded hands twisted. She had changed from her torn dress into the beautiful blue gown Polly had brought her—the one with the lowest neckline she could find—hoping that at the sight of her Bryce would proclaim his love and take her into his arms. Or at least, find some reason for her to stay with him. But he could not do that if he never returned to the castle.

Ryen had kept watch all day, staring at the gate from the window of her room, willing his return. But as the sun crept over the horizon and there was no sign of him, Ryen's hopes dwindled like a rose withering from a lack of sunshine.

Why would he care? His ransom was paid. He had his gold.

Slut. His words came back to haunt her. *I already have two whores and I have no intention of keeping another.* So, she was being turned out. Still, what of the rage she saw in his eyes, the *hurt,* when he had questioned her about Count Dumas? Ryen's shoulders slumped at the thought of her fiancé. Why would he pay her ransom? What did he want of her?

Suddenly, the door opened behind her and Ryen came half out of her seat in her anxiousness.

When Polly entered the room, Ryen's wishes and prayers were once again smashed. She plummeted back into her seat, turning her gaze back to her hands, which lay limply in her lap. Ryen listened to the rustling of Polly's cotton smock as she came closer.

"Lady Ryen," Polly said, her voice calm, "the messenger awaits to escort you to your Lord Dumas."

Ryen felt despair overwhelm her. *My* Lord Dumas, her mind repeated.

"Lady Ryen?"

Ryen did not raise her eyes as she asked, "Has he returned?"

"No, Lady," Polly replied quietly.

All hope disappeared with the setting sun. Tears glistened in Ryen's eyes like dew. Good life, Bryce, she bade him in her mind, and stood. Without lifting her gaze, she moved past Polly. Together they headed out the door. She fought the urge to look one last time at the room, for although she wanted to, she did not think she could bear the memories. So close to him, yet so far . . .

She followed Polly through the hallway and down the stairway. Ryen knew she should try to escape, to stop this. Perhaps if she told Talbot the rumors of Count Dumas's cruelty . . . why would he care? Why would *they* care? All she was to them was a bag or two of gold.

They stepped into the hallway before the great wooden doors that led to the outside of the castle. The anteroom was large, almost as big as her room at De Bouriez Castle.

Two men stood near the doorway. One she recognized as Talbot, the other she had never seen before and could only assume was Count Dumas's emissary. He was an older man, his dark hair graying at the temples. He was dressed in a black tunic and leggings and a black cape. A dingy bag lay at Talbot's feet, and Ryen was sure it was the ransom. One bag of gold.

They turned to her in unison and Ryen visibly shivered at the coldness in the stranger's eyes. The repulsion she felt rising inside her threatened to crash down over her like a tidal wave and send her screaming, fleeing for help. But she was a De Bouriez. She was the Angel of Death. She would not cower from this man, nor Count Dumas himself. She lifted her chin and approached the stranger.

Talbot stood between her and the man as she approached. Ryen read the confusion in his eyes, the indecision. His dark brows drew down before he lowered his head and stepped aside.

Ryen's eyes came to rest on the man. He was thin and as tall as a small oak. She raised her eyes to his and saw his gaze traveling slowly over her body. His thin lips turned up in a grin and it sent shivers down her spine. When he reached out and took her arm into his hold, his finger brazenly caressed her skin.

Ryen blanched at him, pulling her arm free. His chuckle sounded like the breaking of glass in the quiet hallway.

He reached out and seized her arm again.

Suddenly the door flew open and a gust of wind swirled about their feet, rustling Ryen's gown.

Bryce stood there in the open door, a shadow against the darker night. His dark eyes were bright with rage as he took in the scene before him. Clenching his fists, he stalked to Talbot's side in two strides, bending for the bag.

The gold, Ryen thought in agony.

Suddenly, Bryce whirled, hurtling the bag at the emissary. "Take your gold and get out."

The bag hit the man in the stomach and he stepped back. It fell to the floor, gold coins rolling out, glittering in the torchlight as they skittered across the stones. "But . . ." the man said.

Bryce stepped forward, his teeth clenched, his body rigid. "She is *mine!*" Bryce roared. He moved to Ryen in two strides, grabbed her waist, and hoisted her over his shoulder.

Ryen was breathless as Bryce took the stairs two at a time, jogging her with each step. His strong shoulder dug into her stomach as he raced down the hall. He kicked open the door and proceeded into his room.

"Bryce, stop," Ryen begged, feeling her stomach churn. No sooner had she said the words than she was unceremoniously dumped on the bed.

Ryen tried to right herself, fighting down the layers of velvet and silk of her dress to see Bryce moving toward her, across the bed. He grabbed her arms before she could move and snarled, "You have bewitched me, woman. Your image haunts me wherever I go. I cannot sleep without growing stiff from wanting you."

Ryen gazed at him for a long moment. His anguished eyes bore into her soul, searing his want and need there. "Oh, Bryce," Ryen gasped, and raised her hands, gently placing them on either side of his cheeks. She touched every spot on his face, his strong chin gruff with stubble, his cheeks, his nose, and brushed the dark hair from his forehead. Her heart pounded with passion as she stroked his face with soft caresses.

His hands moved down her arms to her waist and he pulled her closer to him until their bodies were barely touching. "Did he have you?" Bryce asked, torment edging his voice.

Ryen's eyes moved to his lips, strangely hypnotized by their movement. "No," she gasped, unable to lie, even to formulate coherent thoughts. "I—I never met him." The physical need to feel his lips on hers overwhelmed her. She swallowed hard, hoping he would kiss her. His hand came up and slowly brushed her cheeks. Her skin burned where he touched her, starting a trail of fire as he traced the outline of her bow lips, then her chin, and then moved down her smooth throat.

Ryen couldn't suppress a groan as she closed her eyes and tilted her head back, baring her throat to the wolf. What was happening to her, she wondered. A feeling of growing hunger claimed her.

Bryce bent his lips to her throat, tasting her creamy skin. He pulled her closer with one hand and gently stroked her hip through the velvety material with the other.

Ryen encircled his neck with her arms, pressing him closer as his passionate nibbling slid down her exposed skin to her low neckline. She felt his tongue brush over one sensitive mound before his hand was teasing her breast, cupping it and squeezing it until it was free of the garment. Ryen lost touch with reality. Her whole world was filled with Bryce and the way he touched her.

His hands lifted her skirt. He turned to stare at her long, long legs. "God," he whispered, as he raised a trembling hand to reverently touch her silken skin.

Bryce pulled her close, kissing her lips urgently, his hands expertly unfastening the buttons of her dress. He moved away from her only to slide the dress and chemise up over her head. Rising up on his arms, he gazed at the gleaming flesh. With the weight of his body, he leaned into her, pushing her down onto the bed. Like clouds, the velvet and silk of her dress surrounded them.

Bryce tasted her lips again, drinking from the honeyed pot of her mouth. Gently he brushed his fingers over her nipples. As Ryen began to respond, unconsciously moving her hips, Bryce grew bolder, kneading and squeezing the mounds, until he could stand it no more and he lowered his lips to the rosy peaks.

Ryen threw her arms about his head, holding him against her heart. She floated on his love, high above the world. His fingers worked magic over her body, heating it until she thought she would die if he did not enter her. But he continued his exploration, bringing her to heights she had never known.

His fingers slid down to the spot that needed, nay, demanded him. When they plunged inside her, Ryen gasped, closing her eyes. She arched her back to receive more of his feathery touch, his moist kisses.

Bryce pulled away. Instinctively Ryen reached out to him, wanting to pull him back to her. Bryce shed his clothing with shaking fingers, almost ripping the cloth from his body in his hurry to return to her. Cold assaulted his body; but the fire burning through his veins kept him hot as he looked down at Ryen, her hair spread over the pillows like a fan, her lips swollen with passion from his kisses, her cheeks heated with desire. He fell on her, his naked body covering hers. With his knees, he gently guided her thighs apart.

Ryen felt the pressure at her womanhood. She looked up into his dark eyes to see the moonlight reflected in his ebony depths, then placed her hands on his large shoulders, tugging him closer. "Please, Bryce," she whispered.

He plunged deep inside her.

Ryen froze, pain stilling her passion. But Bryce bent his head, his lips searing his own passion into her, warming her with his desire. When he started to move again, Ryen was surprised that there was no pain, only hot yearning. She moved with him, their bodies locked together as one.

Bryce's gentle caresses and kisses washed warmly over her until desire ran rampant through her. It was stronger than revenge, more powerful than bloodlust. Ryen felt it fill her until she exploded, her entire body tingling and shaking with the impact. When the feeling left her, she was breathless and weary. She looked up at Bryce to find him smiling at her. His gaze was filled with all the tenderness that she had ever dreamt of seeing in his eyes. Ryen reached up and embraced him tightly.

He began to move again. He had not thrust more than twice when his body stiffened and he groaned.

For long seconds they lay together, exhausted and sated. She loved him. Oh God, Ryen thought. This warmth, this happiness, was what it was like to love someone. She smiled into his neck, nuzzling his throat.

"Does that mean you liked it better this time?" he asked quietly.

"Aye," she whispered. "Much better."

Thirty-eight

Ryen lay in Bryce's arms, held tightly against his strong chest. She could feel the muscles beneath her cheek, hear his heartbeat. She had never felt so wonderful, so warm and safe.

His chest rose and fell slowly, and his arm draped loosely over her waist.

Ryen languidly ran her hand over the planes of his stomach, marveling at their hardness. She ran her fingers to the edge of the blanket that covered half of his glorious body. Slowly, carefully, she lifted it, desiring to see the part of his body that had given her so much pleasure. Then a rumble of throaty laughter caused her to drop the blanket as if it had suddenly burst into flame.

"Little vixen," he said, grabbing her wrist. "I yielded to your insatiable appetite last night, wasn't that enough?"

Ryen watched the blanket magically rise before he easily flipped her onto her back and straddled her body.

His black eyes caught the rising sun in their depths as he smiled down at her. He held her wrists in his hands.

Ryen smiled, her gaze hungrily devouring his handsome face. She was surprised to find the hot flames of desire flaring through her body again, even after a night of lovemaking.

Bryce bent his mouth to hers.

Later, as Bryce led Ryen to the stairs, her arm in his, she asked, "Who wove that tapestry hanging in your room?"

"You mean the one that *was* hanging until a little wench decided to use its pole for a sword?" Bryce said, his voice light.

Ryen grinned. "Yes. That one."

Bryce stopped and his eyes grew distant with memory. "My mother," he answered quietly. "It was the last thing she ever did."

"I'm sorry," Ryen whispered, at the longing in his eyes and the pain that tightened his jaw. When he did not acknowledge her, she attempted to change the subject. "Do you have any brothers or sisters?"

"Not blood, no."

Although Ryen waited, Bryce did not elaborate. She turned to look out a window. The day was beautiful. Sun shone on the village; children's laughter filled the air. Ryen inhaled deeply, savoring the fresh scent of the new day. "Bryce, I have asked you for nothing since I've been here," she stated quietly, thinking to ask him to take her out into the glorious day.

"Except to be allowed into the kitchens," Bryce murmured with a quiet laugh.

At his casual comment, the image of McFinley knocking over the table while the peasants scattered beneath his rage filled her mind. The thought sobered her and she straightened away from the window.

"What is it?" Bryce asked, suddenly concerned at her pensive state.

Ryen looked away, clasping her hands before her. Was she to enter the hall only to see her work lying in ruins on the floor, mugs scattered and broken in the rushes? She feared Bryce's knights could never accept her as one of their own.

"Ryen," he whispered, stepping before her. "Tell me," he urged, lifting a hand to wipe a stray strand of dark hair from her brow.

She wanted to snuggle into the warmth of his body where nothing could touch her love for him, but the thought of her uncertain future stilled her movements. How could she live with him as an enemy, knowing his men hated her? What could the future possibly hold for them? "What will you do with me?" she wondered.

"Do?" His lips turned up in a grin. "I will make you happy. And since it seems you are happiest in bed—" he swept her up into his arms, "—I will allow you full use of it as well!"

Ryen couldn't suppress the laughter that bubbled from her throat.

"But you must eat to keep up your strength," he warned, setting her onto the ground. "I will not tolerate you lying listlessly beneath me."

"Or on top of you," she said playfully, hugging his neck.

"Saucy wench. I should take you now." He stroked her hair, keeping her body pressed closely to his. Very close. He nuzzled her hair with his face and his soft voice reached her ears. "Oh, God. I have never been this happy. Let it last." When she pulled back to study his eyes, she could not tell whether she had imagined the words or not.

He placed her hand upon his arm and continued down the stairs toward the Great Hall. As they turned the corner, a group of maids scattered. Ryen glanced up at Bryce to find him scowling.

At her stare, he murmured, "They should mind their business." He clutched her hand tightly.

"Bryce, will you take me riding?" When he turned startled eyes to her, she continued, "I would like to see your English lands through your eyes, my lord."

He frowned slightly and Ryen thought she saw suspicion etched in the furrows of his brow before he shrugged his large shoulders. "As you wish."

Just before they entered the Great Hall she took a deep breath to prepare herself to face the destruction McFinley had wrought the previous night.

As soon as they stepped through the doors, Ryen's gaze

swiveled to the spot where she had been eating with the peasants. Happiness spread over her. She saw a group of peasants standing before a righted table, their faces aglow with pride.

Everything that had been broken was mended or replaced!

A smile of joy lit Ryen's face. She left Bryce's arm and hurried forward to Polly, who held out her pudgy arms in greeting.

"Oh, my lady!" Polly greeted, clasping Ryen's arms in her hands. "What miracle has allowed ya to stay?"

Ryen stared raptly at the tables. "What happened? Who fixed them?"

"Why, we did, a course!" Kit exclaimed, from beside Polly.

"It's wonderful!" Ryen exclaimed. As everyone began to take their seats, Ryen looked for Bryce, only to find him near the large double doors, speaking with Talbot. His black eyes were focused on her, watching her with an expressionless face. Ryen waited for him to indicate that she should sit beside him. But as Talbot spoke, Bryce's look only darkened.

What have I done to make him so angry? Ryen wondered. She took a step toward him, ready to confront and ease any lie that was being whispered to him. But something called her attention to the front of the room.

Across the great expanse, she could see his whores had their usual seats beside his empty one.

Ryen wilted as doubt rained down upon her, eating away at her happiness. What if Bryce took her with him but seated her with his men, at a place lower than his whores? She stepped back to the peasants' table, watching Bryce.

Polly prattled away beside her about the pudding she planned to make on the morrow.

Kit stood on her other side, speaking of how they had worked through the night to repair the table.

Will I sit with his men if it pleases him? she asked herself As she stared at him, his powerful presence filled her. Yes. I will do anything he asks to please him, to have him smile at me. She imagined him approaching her, his strong legs eating up the distance between them, and taking her to the chair beside him. Displacing one of his whores—with another, a small voice inside her accused.

Then, he was coming and Ryen felt a shiver race along her spine. She was shuddering, not beneath his anger, but at the sight of his body. It seemed to flow across the room like a river, marvelous in its symmetry. Ryen felt her desire spark as her eyes scanned the current of his movement. Her lips parted slightly as she felt the warmth begin to spread over her body. He was so powerful, so handsome! He could sweep her away with a mere glance from those raging eyes.

He halted just before her. She gaped, not knowing what to do or what to say.

Suddenly, his intense gaze shifted to Polly. "You did an admirable job repairing the table," he said.

"Thank you, m'lord," Polly replied pensively.

The peasants began to eat again, studying him intently behind lowered gazes.

How he intimidates them! Ryen thought, and wondered if he realized just how frightening he could be. Something filled her as she stared at his rugged profile. A possessiveness seized her, tugging at the corners of her lips. When Bryce turned back to her, his gaze was softer, kinder somehow.

But suddenly his powerful glance slipped past her and his brow furrowed. "What are you staring at, woman?" he demanded gruffly.

Ryen turned to see Kit watching him with large, curious eyes. As Bryce's dark look bore into her, Kit gasped, "Gaw!" and lowered her head, stuffing a piece of bread into her mouth.

Bryce's back straightened. "What is it?" he repeated.

The timbre of his angry voice shook Ryen and she felt dread slither up her spine like a snake.

Bryce's gaze swept the table, his mood darkening as he saw the peasants staring at him with the same expectant look.

He turned back to Kit, pounding a clenched fist on the table. "Tell me!"

The peasants shot furtive glances at one another. Some of them looked as though they were about to flee.

"You don't know?" Ryen wondered. "Talbot didn't tell you?"

"He told me that McFinley destroyed your hard work and that there was a swordfight. Needed a little exercise, eh, Angel? I'm glad you didn't kill him. I would hate to have to replace such a skilled knight."

"She should have killed the cur," Polly retorted.

Bryce's cold glare froze her to the spot.

"He struck Lady Ryen," Polly said.

Bryce's eyes locked on Ryen for a moment and she saw the uncontrollable anger that swept him like a hot blaze.

Bryce whirled, his gaze searing across the expanse of the hall, pegging McFinley in his chair.

Ryen held out a restraining hand.

But in that second, Bryce had flown across the room faster than a wolf and lunged for McFinley's throat. He had toppled McFinley to the floor, large hands locked around his neck, before Ryen could reach them.

"Bryce!" she screamed, pulling at his arms. "No!"

Bryce squeezed his hands tighter and McFinley fought, bucking and clawing at the grip around his throat.

"Bryce!" Ryen shouted, pulling at Bryce's wrists. "Stop!" She bent her face into his view. "It is *my* right! He struck me!" Her heart racing, she pulled at his fingers and arms trying to free McFinley, but they were locked in a death grip. "Please."

Bryce's hands suddenly went slack. Ryen heard McFinley gasp for air as she raised her eyes to Bryce. He was staring at her, dark eyes peering into her soul. "It is your right," he said, and stood rigidly.

She was on her knees before him, McFinley gasping beside her. Ryen could feel Bryce's pent-up anger, as if he were going to erupt at any moment. She looked at McFinley. Bryce would have killed him, might still kill him, because he had struck her. She felt responsible for his life. How many men had she watched die in battle? Why should she care if one more Englishman was killed or not? But she did care. She cared because something in her had changed. She cared for Bryce's people as though they were her own, even the ones who despised her.

McFinley turned his gaze to Ryen. She could see the fear in his eyes. She had bested him and she had spared his life. Now, he found his life in her hands once again.

Ryen stood looking down at McFinley. "Rise."

He averted his eyes, rubbing his neck for a long moment. Finally he climbed to his feet.

Ryen watched as his shoulders passed her head. She had not remembered him being so tall. "You will serve the peasants at the noon meal."

His eyebrows furrowed. "You cannot give me an order. If you choose to strike me, that is your right."

"Your judgment is my right," Ryen replied confidently. "Now, kneel."

McFinley glanced at Bryce. "I will not take orders from *her!*"

"Kneel," Ryen commanded.

"You will do as she says," Bryce answered tightly. "Or face *my* judgment."

McFinley tightened his jaw and went down on one knee before Ryen.

"Now," she proclaimed. "Pledge your loyalty—"

McFinley glanced sharply up at her, his eyes glaring defiance.

"—to your lord, Bryce Princeton," Ryen finished.

McFinley locked gazes with Bryce in surprise before lowering his eyes. "M'lord," he said solemnly, "I do pledge my loyalty, devotion, and admiration to you, on my honor as a knight. If in any way you are hurt, be it of the spirit or of the flesh, I will be wounded also."

The quiet spread thin throughout the room until finally McFinley glanced up.

Bryce reached out his hand and clasped McFinley's. "Rise, McFinley," he commanded.

Ryen felt the tension in her shoulders lessen and she let out an inaudible sigh at the sight of the two men hand in hand. A grin spread over her lips.

McFinley mirrored her smile of relief as he stood.

Bryce's closed fist connected with McFinley's chin and the man spun once before plummeting to the floor.

Ryen gasped, putting her hands to her mouth.

"Never insult me again," Bryce growled. "And be thankful that Angel is more forgiving than I." Bryce turned his back and strode from the room.

Ryen stood gaping at McFinley. Then she raced after Bryce. Her slippered feet skidded in the doorway as she searched first left and then right. She spotted him down the hall.

"Bryce!" she called, and ran after him.

He slowed and finally stopped, his spine straightening.

As Ryen ran to him, she heard his words. They were wrenched from his body by a forge of remorse. "Why didn't you tell me?"

Ryen blinked, stunned that she had caused him agony. "It was over. I saw no reason . . ."

There was a long moment of silence before Bryce said, "I cannot take you riding, Ryen." The words were as cold as the floor upon which she stood.

A great weight crushed her heart. His rigid shoulders were like a wall against her. The silence stretched between them, an impassable abyss.

"I will not allow them to harm you," he said, before storming off down the hall.

Ryen watched until he had vanished around the corner. She

stood for a long moment staring after him. The hallway stretched out before her, the ceiling high, making her feel tiny.

Ryen lowered her head. It took her a moment to realize that she was alone. For the first time since she'd been at Dark Castle, she was free. A weight lifted from her shoulders. At least he trusted her enough to wander without guards. She glanced up at the hallway before her at the sunlight that danced on the walls. She wanted to be outside so badly that she almost ran to the door.

She paused in the archway, staring out at the opening before her. The stone walls that surrounded the inner ward of Dark Castle rose stories above her head. Guards paced the battlements and walkways that ran along the walls.

Ryen stepped outside into the sun. Warmth washed over her entire body and she turned her face up toward the origin of the heat. She inhaled the fresh air, then stepped forward. As she did, she slipped in the mud and almost fell, but regained her balance. She carefully picked up her skirts to avoid the puddles. She walked around the inner ward, past the kitchens. As she approached what looked like a small alleyway between the kitchen and a building that she guessed was the barracks, a voice from the shadows called to her.

"M'lady?"

Ryen paused, shivers of alarm creeping up her spine. She peered into the shadows, trying to discern the man's outline. Vignon stepped into the light.

She felt every nerve in her body tense. What did he want?

He immediately stepped back into the darkness and she followed him into the alleyway. "What are you doing here, Vignon?" she demanded in a whisper.

"Call me Jonathan Wells," he murmured. "I am here on the command of King Charles."

Ryen was speechless. His words held no trace of a French accent. He even had an English inflection. Tingles shot up her spine. He spoke the language flawlessly . . . as if he'd been born here. She thought back to her first meal, when she'd sat opposite him. He had fought for his food with a vengeance. He fit in perfectly. Almost too perfectly. She did not trust him.

"We cannot be seen together."

"I don't understand," she said.

His eyes darted about the walls. "We cannot speak here. I will contact you," he said. "But remember: I am Jonathan Wells." Suddenly, his head tilted and he stood absolutely still.

Then Ryen heard it. Whistling. She turned to gaze in the direction the sound had come from. She opened her mouth to speak, but when she turned back to him, Vignon was gone.

Thirty-nine

Birds sang happily, their cheerful song filling the morning sky as they flew from tree to tree in their constant search for food. In the distance, the low rumble of surging water echoed through the forest. The air was heavy with dampness. Bryce noticed none of it as he stared straight ahead into the greenery before him. He was sitting with his back to a large tree that rose majestically to the sky. His knees were bent and his wrists rested on them, hands drooping over his legs like the tree's large branches.

Again and again his mind returned to Ryen and her large, trusting eyes, her soft, pliable lips, her womanly body. It was hard as well as painful to imagine her as a warrior, because that was where his trouble lay. He had seen the death and destruction she could cause . . . *had* caused. Had she changed? Did he really want her to?

He recalled their lovemaking of the night before. He had never experienced such exquisite passion. She had matched him thrust for thrust, never tiring. Just the thought of it was enough to send a surge of lust pounding through his veins that was so powerful it threatened to overcome his sensibilities.

And yet his knights treated her roughly, badly. The thought of McFinley striking her, causing a flaw to her skin, causing her pain, brought a sudden and swift anger that had not faded during all these hours. He wanted Ryen with him at Dark Castle. But was that asking too much of her? Would *he* be willing to give up his home, his lands, his country and king to be at Ryen's side, as he was asking her to do?

He bowed his head, raking his hands through his ebony hair. Yes, he thought. I would be willing to go to France to be with her. God help me, but I would give up everything for her. Will she do the same for me?

She already has. She has been labeled "traitor" by her people because of me. What does she have in France to go back to?

A fiancé. The thought of another man kissing her lips, touching her face, enraged him. I have nothing to fear, he told himself. For whatever reasons, she has chosen my bed rather than return to France and her fiancé's arms.

And now, she was not the problem; it was his soldiers, who looked at her and saw the Angel of Death when there was a passionate woman capable of showing them kindness and tolerance. Could he subject her to their brutality and their anger? Was there no place for them to live in peace?

Bryce tensed at the crunch of footsteps trampling the fallen leaves behind him. Slowly his hand reached for his sword, which lay at his side.

"I thought I might find you here," a voice called out.

Bryce released his sword handle. "I usually come here to be *alone.*"

Grey sat down heavily beside him, chuckling. "Should I take that as a hint, brother?"

"I need to think," he replied.

Grey lifted his nose to the air, inhaling its scent. When he lowered his head, he said cheerfully, "I am willing to guess that your problems center around a very headstrong French-woman."

Bryce snorted. "It must have taken you all day to figure that out."

"At least your humor does not wane."

"My men do not approve of her," Bryce said.

"And?"

"And I plan to keep her at Dark Castle."

Grey picked up a branch from the forest floor and began stripping the smaller twigs to make a single stick. "Then I believe you have a battle on your hands."

Bryce's fists clenched. "I will destroy any man who stands against me."

Grey chortled. "Most of your men will not stand against you. You are respected and admired. After all, she is a very comely wench. Any man could easily fall under her spell."

Bryce's eyes flashed. "The Prince of Darkness does not fall under spells."

"And what of Bryce Princeton?"

"It is not a spell," Bryce insisted. "She enflames my very soul when I am with her. Haunts my thoughts and my dreams with her eyes and—"

"It sounds like a spell to me."

Bryce shrugged and grumbled, "So be it. But the people will say that the Prince of Darkness tamed the Angel of Death."

"Maybe. And maybe it will be the other way around."

Bryce shifted his suddenly rigid back. "You are trying my patience, Grey."

Grey waved a hand. "Regardless, that is not the battle I was speaking of. What do you think Count Dumas will do when he believes you are holding her against her will?"

Bryce frowned, anger tightening his jaw. God's blood, he thought, she is causing me another problem. "She will not be held against her will."

Grey tapped the stick against his thigh. "Let's assume she wants to stay."

"There is no assumption about it."

"Still . . . put yourself in her place. To stay willingly in England would be to prove to all of France that she is indeed a traitor."

Bryce stiffened.

"That is a lot to ask of anyone . . . even if it is for love," Grey murmured.

Bryce glanced at him, frowning deeply. Doubts descended in his mind, plaguing him like a festering wound.

A soft snicker sounded in Ryen's ears. Instantly she woke, reaching for her sword. Highwaymen! she thought. Or worse. But her sword was not there. Then she remembered where she was. Bryce had not returned the whole day and she had continued her tour of his castle. It was late when she had wandered into the stables to look at the horses and sat down in one of the stalls with a large war horse, thinking of her beautiful white steed. She must have fallen asleep.

She stood and reached out in the darkness, blindly feeling for the wall. Her hands brushed the wood of the stall, then she felt her way around the horse to the door. Her fingers skimmed the wooden frame until she found the bolt. She drew it back, opened the door, and stepped out.

When she was out of the stables, she cut across the inner ward quickly, moving past the kitchens and, pausing at the entrance to the castle, saw that the portcullis was lowered. She yawned and stretched her arms far above her head, looking up into the sky. The stars were twinkling high overhead and the moon stared down at her like a slitted eye. It was so dark! She wondered how long she had slept. Had she truly been *that* tired? Well, Bryce hadn't allowed her much time to rest last night.

Grinning at the memory, she continued on. The hallways were dim except for an occasional torch. She began to ascend the stairs to her room.

Mumbling reached her ears as she approached the second floor. Polly and Kit were standing in the doorway to her room, wringing their hands and looking fearful. Bryce was in there; she knew by the tension that straightened the servants' shoulders. Then, she heard his voice. He sounded angry and something else. Afraid?

Her brow furrowed as she hurried forward, past Kit and then Polly, who gasped at seeing her.

"Find her," Bryce commanded, "and bring her back. I don't care what it takes." He was leaning out the window, his hands grasping the ledge.

Talbot stood two steps behind Bryce, his back to Ryen. "But Prince, we've been searching all night. It's too dark to see."

Ryen stopped just inside the room to gaze in confusion at the two men.

"I don't care," Bryce snapped, pounding the ledge with his fist. "She's out there somewhere, and I want her back."

"What's wrong? Who are you searching for?" Ryen wondered.

Bryce turned. "Ryen!" he gasped as if he could not believe his own eyes.

"Can I help?" she asked.

"Are you—hurt?" Bryce demanded, a strange huskiness in his tone.

"Me? No," she replied, frowning. She watched as the relief on his face was replaced by furrowing brows and wary eyes.

"Out," he commanded.

Polly and Kit disappeared into the hallway, followed by Talbot. Ryen straightened indignantly. She had offered help and he chose to ignore her. She moved in Talbot's footsteps.

"Not you, Angel," he whispered, his voice caressing her ears.

Ryen stopped, glancing over her shoulder at him, her hair brushing her cheek.

The door closed. His black hose was like a second skin, accenting his powerful strides as he approached her. She could see the tension in his shoulders, the way they were set stiffly. His fists were clenched. "Where have you been?" he asked. His words were strangely clipped.

Ryen turned to face him fully. "The stables," she replied. "You have beautiful stallions."

"You were there all day?" he wondered dubiously.

She felt the silent accusation even as the low timbre of his voice sent ripples down her body. "No. I wished to see your castle, and you were not here to escort me."

He paused just before her, his eyes boring into hers, searching for something. Then they shifted to her soft hair. He raised his hand, and for a moment, Ryen thought he was going to touch her. She gasped in anticipation of his hot stroke.

Bryce pulled his hand back and in his fingers was a piece of straw. Together they stared at it.

Suddenly his arms were around her, crushing her tightly to him, so hard that she could barely breathe.

"Oh, Angel," he whispered.

Ryen could have sworn she felt his body tremble, but then he pulled back to look into her eyes. Ryen's knees grew weak as the intensity in his ebony depths warmed her and chased away the night chill and the doubt. Then, she saw the dark rings lining his eyes. She lifted a hand to his cheek. "You were looking for me."

"I'd forgotten how cold a bed can be," he replied.

Ryen sighed in contentment as she stared at his handsome face, his chiseled beauty, his mysterious eyes.

"You had many people worried, Ryen. No one knew where you had gone."

"I'm sorry. I didn't realize how tired I was . . ."

"I believed Count Dumas had somehow returned for you."

Her hand lowered from his cheek and she studied his worry through admonishing eyes. "And did you think I would willingly go?"

Bryce turned away from her. "I am not sure how much you miss France."

Ryen stepped up behind him. The fire from the candles cast a white hue over his ivory tunic. She gently laid a hand upon his shoulder and felt the warmth of his body soak into her palm. "Bryce," she whispered, "it is true, I *do* miss France. Yet if I were to be separated from you, my longing would be unequaled."

Slowly Bryce turned to her. His eyes shone in happiness as he took her into his arms. "You may have the run of my castle, Angel."

Ryen smiled into his chest. "I know."

"On one condition," Bryce added. When Ryen raised questioning eyes to him, he continued, "Never leave me."

Ryen grinned, feeling his arms grow heavy around her shoulders. "That is not a hard promise. I *remember* how cold a bed can be."

Bryce crushed Ryen in his embrace, then dipped his head and kissed her. She responded with a passion born of love and desire. His hands wandered across her breasts and down the sides of her body.

He loved her again, slowly and thoroughly, tantalizing her until the earth shattered and they rode together on a cloud of passion.

Ryen listened to Bryce's steady breathing, relishing the comfortable weight of his arms across her shoulders. His smell, the scent of clean air, and a vague scent of something wild surrounded her. It was on the sheets, in the pillows. Ryen loved it.

Yet even in the safety of his arms, Ryen's mind was not at peace. Her thoughts were violated by images of Vignon. A French spy, in Dark Castle! I should tell Bryce, she thought. What if he wants to cause Bryce harm? What am I thinking? Betray my country?

Carefully, Ryen slid out from beneath Bryce's arms and walked to the window. The land below her was dark and vacant. She crossed her arms against the chill breeze that suddenly engulfed her.

She felt her duty weigh heavily on her shoulders, pulling

her away from Bryce. Yet her people had scorned and ridiculed her. Her brothers were dead. Her father had turned his back on her. Still, she wished she could see her father. Make amends with him, look into his eyes and see respect. Something she would never see now.

Still, her honor demanded that she remain silent about Vignon. After all, Bryce was the enemy.

But was he?

The flame of hope she carefully protected in her heart leapt higher. Dare I trust him? Can he *love* me? Can he truly think I am beautiful? Or is he deceiving me again?

Doubt plagued her as she thought back to the agony she had experienced at believing he was dead. Again she pictured him perched on the window ledge. Every muscle in his body coiled, ready for action. She reached out a hand and ran it along the sill.

"Angel?"

Ryen jumped, hearing his voice so close to her ear. She could feel the heat of his body, the power. Then, his arms wrapped around her waist and he pulled her against his chest. He had no clothing on and she gasped at the heat that radiated from his sleek body. He laughed low in his throat and she relaxed back against him.

For a moment they stood that way, gazing out over the black land. Then his voice came to her on a breeze. "You are not happy here."

Ryen twisted in his arms to look at him. "Why do you say such a thing?"

"You leave my bed in the middle of the night. Do I not please you?" he asked, his voice earnest.

Ryen grinned as she turned and faced him. She placed her palms against his broad chest. "Oh, Bryce." His eyes were unreadable in the darkness, his lips black in the night.

Ryen lifted up on her toes and pressed her mouth to his. She gently ran her tongue over his lips until they separated and his tongue clashed with hers. She felt his passion growing as he pulled her closer.

Suddenly, he stepped back and gazed down at her, his brow furrowed. "Why did you leave my side? What troubles you, my Angel?"

Some loyalty would not allow her to reveal the spy. Instead, she replied, "It's foolish, really. But I have always wondered how you escaped De Bouriez Castle when I was sure you had died."

A soft chuckle reached her ears and he tugged her toward the bed. "Dress," he commanded.

"What?" Ryen stammered.

"We ride," he replied, pulling on his breeches.

The night's darkness filtered through the clouds, combing the land with trails of darker shadow. Ryen rode behind Bryce's stallion on the second most beautiful horse in his stables, a white mare. They galloped past the sleeping village and the silent farmland to the forest, Ryen admiring Bryce's mastery of the animal, his strong thighs pressed into the dark side of the horse, the way he seemed to command without any tug of the reins.

He led her to an impassable wall of trees. Here, Bryce dismounted and Ryen followed his lead. Grinning, he took her hand in his and led her toward the trees, commanding, "Leave the horses."

The branches and leaves seemed to part magically before him as he moved into the foliage. Ryen listened to the crickets, and somewhere an owl hooted. The bushes and small trees were growing so closely together that Ryen could not see more than two feet in any direction. Finally, they stepped out into a clearing and Ryen gasped at the sight that greeted her. Awash in a magical light, a glittering waterfall cascaded over a sheer one-hundred-foot cliff, its water gleaming and sparkling as it tumbled into the churning white water below.

"Oh, Bryce," Ryen whispered in awe.

He moved up behind her, his long, tanned arm stretched upward before him. "See the rock next to the waterfall?"

Halfway up the cliff, Ryen spotted the brown, flattened ledge and nodded.

"Keep watching," Bryce said, and disappeared silently into the forest.

Ryen approached the water until she came to the bank, her eyes remaining on the ledge Bryce had pointed out. It was far above her head, a flat rock, protruding slightly from the falls.

Ryen's gaze shifted to the water as it tumbled over the slope, then followed the waves down the sheer drop until they crashed against the water pooled in a glistening lake below. Her mind flashed back to the time she had almost been swept over the edge of another falls. A shudder slid up her spine. But somehow, in the moonlight, it seemed different . . . somehow magical. She looked back at the rock. It had not changed.

Ryen's mind dwelt on the waterfall that had claimed Runt's body. Bryce had let his son go to save her life. Why hadn't she realized then how much Bryce meant to her?

She glanced anxiously over her shoulder at the silent forest behind her. Where was Bryce? Then a movement caught her eye and she looked up at the rock. Bryce stood there, his splendid body glowing in the moonlight. He spread his arms out to the side as if worshipping the black sky.

She stepped forward, her eyes riveted on Bryce as he raised his arms and bent his knees. Her heart skipped a beat as fear clamped a cold hand around her.

She could not move, could not breathe. Then, like a graceful cat, he leapt, diving head first like a spear toward the shimmering pool.

"No!" Ryen finally screamed, hearing only a small splash as his body pierced the turbulent water. "No!"

She searched the pond for him, but the surface was unbroken. "Bryce!" Ryen ran forward, moving toward the falls, cutting the water with her body as she waded in. The black liquid rose from her ankles to her waist and then to her shoulders. She began to swim, searching the water and shore with her eyes as she moved. She could barely breathe for the terror that gripped her chest. Over and over again she saw the brackish moat below her window at De Bouriez Castle. All those weeks of gazing at it had carved the image into her memory. All those days of hoping and praying that Bryce was alive. And now, as she pictured Bryce's body lying broken on the rocks, she found herself praying again.

Something slithered about her waist and for a moment she panicked, fighting the grip of death, afraid she would not reach Bryce in time to save him. A soft chuckle came from behind her. "You have not learned yet?" he wondered.

Bryce pulled her trembling body to him, his powerful legs treading water, keeping them both afloat.

Ryen wrapped her arms about his thick neck, relieved in one breath, wanting to strangle him in the next.

"I have been swimming in these waters since I was a child. I learned to dive from the highest cliff. Learned to expand my lungs so I could stay below water for as long as I needed to," Bryce whispered, a hint of light laughter in his tone.

Ryen could only watch his lips as they caressed each word. Suddenly, she felt the length of his solid body against her, felt the blood pound through her veins like molten fire.

"I had no idea what agony my disappearances caused you, or I would have returned," he murmured. His lips brushed her neck and he lifted a hand to push her hair back from her shoulder.

Ryen's arms wrapped languidly around his back, wanting the warmth, wanting his strength.

With a powerful kick, Bryce sent them toward the shore. Ryen's feet just briefly touched ground when he swooped her up in his arms and carried her swiftly inland. He slid her against the length of his body slowly, never taking his eyes from hers. His eyes were dark with passion, glittering like two black coins.

Ryen felt the heat blazing from his wet skin. She opened her mouth to sigh, but before she could utter a sound, his lips took possession of her own. She leaned her head back, responding with all her being to the demands of this god of darkness. She pressed her body closer to his and felt the warmth of him, the essence of heaven and the fires of hell. She felt his hands lightly stroking her back with feathery touches that sent currents of flame up her spine.

Her hands caressed the power in every muscle of his back, his chest, his stomach. But what amazed her the most was not his strength. It was the moonlight that seemed to radiate from his body, as if he had swallowed the radiance of the moon and it had formed a halo around his figure. He *was* a god.

His hand closed over her breast and she arched toward him.

He was wondrously gentle, yet as wild as an April whirl-wind as he crushed her body to him. He lifted the tunic over her head to reveal her glorious breasts. They were copper in the waning moonlight and his lips descended over the peaks eagerly. She saw a flash of white teeth as he teased and ca-ressed her. With silken caresses his hand moved down her breeches to her hip.

Ryen pulled his head closer to her heart, wanting more of his touches. She bent her lips over his dark hair, fluttering kisses over his head. She felt her breeches drop away, and when he stepped back she saw his eyes brush over her naked-ness.

Impatiently, she put a hand against his chest and gently shoved him. He stumbled a few steps away from her until his back hit a tree. Ryen pursued him.

He reached out to her, but she caught his strong wrists in her hands.

She leaned her entire body into his, pressing her lips to his startled ones. Instantly his surprise gave way to passion and desire, and the kiss deepened sending ecstasy swirling through Ryen. She felt her breasts pressed against his strong chest and couldn't resist trailing a path of light kisses over his jaw, down his neck, down to his chest. When her tongue circled one of his nipples she heard him sigh deeply. She moved her mouth down over his stomach, reaching around to cup his buttocks.

His hands dropped to his sides and he groaned in pleasure. She planted slow kisses down to his manhood, marveling that it grew as her lips neared. She pulled slightly away and raised a hand to caress him. She had no sooner touched his warm flesh when he grabbed her arms and raised her up to his lips. His kiss buffeted her like the winds before a savage storm.

His manhood pressed firmly into her lower stomach and Ryen groaned, shifting her hips in response, wanting him inside her, needing him.

Bryce lifted her leg to his hip and Ryen felt the pressure move to her womanhood. She gripped his shoulders and lifting her other leg, wrapped her slim thighs around him. He took the invitation, plunging deep inside her with one mighty thrust. She moaned as he took possession of her body. She met the cadence of his thrusts and felt passion rising in her like the sun. Finally it shattered into a million glowing stars, and for one moment she had a glimpse of heaven.

When she opened her eyes, he was gazing at her.

A smile tugged at the corners of his lips before his hips began to move again and his face contorted in ecstasy. "Ryen," he groaned softly, pulling her closer to him. "My Angel."

Forty

The next morning, Bryce and Ryen returned to the castle. Ryen sat before Bryce on his horse, his strong arms around her as he held the reins. The white mare trailed Bryce's stallion. When they reached the inner ward, Bryce slung his leg from the horse and caught Ryen around the waist, easing her from the animal. For a moment, they stood face to face, sharing the secrets of the night before in their heated expressions. Ryen's lips slowly turned up into a grin.

Bryce's face lit with a warmth that was foreign to the Prince of Darkness. He took her hand and began to walk into the castle.

A miller who had come from town and was unloading his wares paused to follow them with his eyes. Two knights halted as they walked by to stare after their lord and his enemy.

"Prince!" Talbot called, as they entered the castle. When Bryce did not stop, Talbot was forced to hurry to catch up with him. "There is a matter of the harvest you must see to."

"It can wait," Bryce said, staring raptly at Ryen.

Talbot halted his steps. Never had Prince declined to see to the proper running of his estates and his people.

Bryce led Ryen to the Great Hall. When they entered, Ryen faltered. Where would he lead her to sit? Ryen's gaze swept the table where the peasants sat and noticed that the wild-looking people were now at that table. There were seven of them seated in a row. Was that a good sign? she wondered.

Then her eyes were drawn by Bryce's empty chair at the front of the room, a frown creasing her brow. Lotte and Elli sat on either side of his chair. Would he choose to sit beside them?

Finally, Bryce moved forward. Hope beat in Ryen's heart, along with desperation. What will I do if he chooses to sit beside his whores? she wondered, absently massaging her starved stomach. What will I do if he places Lotte above me?

Murmuring broke out around the room as they strolled toward the peasants' table.

Her heart raced as he stood looking over the table for a moment. She took her usual chair. Bryce's gaze shifted to Polly, who sat beside Ryen.

Immediately, the old maid rose and stepped aside. Ryen watched her walk down the table to the extra place they always set.

When Ryen turned back to Bryce, he was taking Polly's seat. "Later you will eat at my table, by my side," he said.

Ryen nodded slightly, numb with happiness.

Bryce stared at the food before him for a moment. He turned his gaze to the peasant beside him. "Take another chair."

Immediately the man scrambled from his seat and Talbot, who had followed them, replaced him at Bryce's side.

Contentedly, Bryce's eyes scanned the table until he came to Grey. He raised an eyebrow and chuckled low in his throat, shaking his head.

Grey shrugged. "The food's better."

The bowls were placed before them and Bryce picked up his trencher.

"M'lord," Talbot said, stopping Bryce before the trencher reached his mouth. Dark eyes focused on Talbot and he continued, "They know not what to do."

Ryen and Bryce turned together, following Talbot's stare. His soldiers sat, whispering among themselves, casting speculative glances at Ryen's table.

Bryce's gaze swiveled to Ryen.

"I will have another cauldron made," Ryen offered. "It won't take long."

Bryce nodded, then announced, "Let them eat what we eat."

Ryen nodded to Kit and the girl jumped up and ran to the kitchens.

Bryce raised the trencher to his mouth, glancing at Grey. "You have not been wrong yet." He shoved the trencher into his mouth. "Ah!" he cried, and spat the pudding from his mouth. "God's blood! It's hot!"

"Of course, m'lord," Ryen answered, with laughter in her voice. "Here. Allow me." She removed the trencher from his hand and dipped it beneath the pudding, scooping up some food. She carefully wiped the excess off on the side of the bowl and brought the bread to her lips. She blew gently on the pudding until it cooled and finally moved the trencher to his lips.

A grin curved his mouth as he opened it for her, taking the bread into his mouth. Subtly he drew his tongue along one of her fingers.

Ryen blanched and quickly looked around to see if the others had noticed, but no one was watching them. When she turned back to him, her smile was sly and seductive.

"Prince," Talbot exclaimed. "I have not tasted food this good since . . . well, since before I was in your service!"

"Aye," Bryce replied quietly, never taking his eyes from Ryen. "The best."

After the meal, Ryen noticed that Bryce's mood turned somber. He was quiet and pensive, thoughtful. He escorted Ryen into the hallway and stopped, turning to her. "There is something I do every month on this day."

Ryen took in the slight droop of his shoulders, and the way he averted his eyes. When he did look at her, she was startled at the sadness in his eyes, the pain hidden behind his scowling brows. It pulled at Ryen's heart and she asked, "What is it?"

Bryce seemed to be studying her, every detail of her face, every aspect of her soul. Finally, he said, "Four months ago, on this day, Runt died. I go to honor his memory."

Even though his voice was strong, she felt the agony that emanated from his body. She knew that she could help him just by being there, by staying with him through his tortured memorial. "I want to go with you."

He blanched as if in disbelief, as if she had said something sacrilegious. She saw it coming. He was going to say no.

Then something happened. His expression changed from one of almost horror to one of gratitude. Bryce held out his hand to her.

Ryen put her palm against his. Silently he led her through the hallway and down a drafty corridor. Many of the servants scurried out of his way after giving Bryce a respectful bow or curtsy. It was reassuring to be at his side. He exuded an air of power that was reflected in every reverent movement of the servants.

As they walked, the corridor became sparse and empty. The darkness was cut only by the firelight from the torches on the wall. Bryce moved toward two wooden doors that were open, welcoming.

A large altar carved of gold and silver stood at the front of the room, a cross hanging suspended above it. Three polished wooden pews lined each side of the chapel. Only one man was sitting there, his back to them, his head bowed. A monk was lighting candles on the altar.

As Bryce moved down the middle of the aisle, something made Ryen turn her head toward the reverent man. He looked up and Ryen froze, almost tripping over her dress.

It was Vignon!

She quickly turned her head away from him and went down on one knee to cover for her clumsiness.

Bryce chuckled darkly. "You cannot tell me this is the god that the Angel of Death prays to."

Baffled, Ryen stood, raising her eyes to him. She tried desperately to hide the nervousness that seized her stomach. "And I suppose the Prince of Darkness worships another?"

Bryce's lip curled in a half-grin, but he did not answer her.

Ryen found her hands trembling. She clasped them as the monk turned, his face hidden beneath the hood of his cloak. He approached them, descending the two steps from the altar. "My lord," he whispered, "it is not complete yet."

"It does not matter," Bryce said, and continued toward the side of the church.

Ryen quickly followed him to a wooden door. Bryce swung it aside and held it open for her. The stairway that stretched downward before them was dark, and Ryen could not see past the first two steps. Bryce took a torch from beside the doorway. As they descended, the circle of light wavered around them. Ryen glanced back, half expecting to see Vignon poised in the doorway with a dagger, but the door swung shut and blackness closed off Ryen's view behind her. She reached out for Bryce's arm, afraid she would tumble down the steep stairway. They plunged through the darkness for a long time until Ryen's foot hit level ground. As she peered down the corridor that stretched before them, she felt trapped, as though the narrow walls were closing in on them. It was like a mausoleum. Torches glowed on the wall, casting an eerie glow in this tomb.

Bryce forged on, and as Ryen moved, she saw small plaques along the wall. She hesitated at one, a golden plaque inscribed in English. Ryen puzzled out the words: *Herein . . . rests . . . Lord Princeton*.

Bryce stepped up beside her, his shoulder brushing her hair.

When Ryen turned to glance at him, his features fluttered in darkness, then in light, as the torch he held above his head flickered. As he looked at the plaque, she saw his eyes narrow with a long-forgotten memory. "It is my grandfather," he stated, quietly. "He died defending our land. Stabbed in the back. The land fell to my father, who was twelve at the time."

Ryen's gaze shot back to the golden plaque. His family was buried here. Suddenly Ryen felt cold and unwelcome. She glanced at the walls and swore they trembled as if they were going to come crashing down around her shoulders. She stepped back, hugging her elbows.

Bryce gently took her hand and raised it to his lips. "They would have liked you," he reassured her. He guided her deeper into the gloom, into the quiet.

Not three steps away, he turned into an alcove. On the floor before them stood a rock about chest high. The bottom part of the stone had been expertly chiseled into a pair of armor legs, as if it were the start of a fine suit of plate mail.

Bryce stepped forward and dropped to one knee before the small, unfinished statue.

It was for Runt! It was a memorial to his son.

Bryce bent his head. "I miss him so much," he murmured, so softly that she barely heard him. His voice echoed quietly in the tomblike cave.

Her heart twisted. She cast a doubtful glance at the cold walls, the dark ceiling, the graves marked by plaques. "Oh, Bryce," Ryen groaned. She placed a delicate hand against his shoulder. "Then honor his memory, his spirit. Do not place this memorial in this darkness and this quiet. He was a boy. Surely he played in the stables or ran outdoors, splashing in the puddles."

Bryce did not speak or turn to her. In the flickering torchlight she saw his back stiffen and straighten, his long black hair washing over his shoulders in waves.

She was an intruder here. She could not tell him how to honor his son. "I'm sorry, Bryce. I spoke out of turn. He was your son and you should place the statue wherever you feel it should be."

"You are right," he said, and stood, towering above her.

Ryen nodded, turning to leave the alcove.

"He loved the gardens." His words stopped her and she turned back to him. "He used to miss meals because he was wielding his wooden sword, cutting down make-believe dragons, which turned out to be Kit's favorite flowers. He once brought me a frog the size of my fist from the pond. He had been warned by my servants to stay out of the gardens, away from the flowers and the trees and the pond. But he never listened." Bryce looked at her and Ryen saw determination sparkle in his dark eyes. "No one shall ever keep him from the gardens again."

His eyes came into focus, and he dropped them to Ryen. They glowed with a different kind of love. She gasped as she recognized the look—it was the one that she had longed for all her life. The look her father had bestowed on her brothers. Respect.

Bryce took both her hands into his and pressed each against his lips. "Thank you."

At midday, Bryce had shown Ryen the armory. They were watching the skilled armorer beat a strip of metal to form a sword when Talbot entered. He informed Bryce that they were leaving to survey the lands.

"I'll be right there," Bryce said. As Talbot left, he turned to Ryen.

"May I accompany you?" she wondered.

Bryce glanced at the armorer, and although his head was bowed over his work, Bryce knew the man heard every word that was said. Bryce took one of Ryen's hands and led her to the door. "It would be better if you stayed behind," Bryce murmured. At Ryen's crestfallen look, he lifted one of her hands and pressed it against his lips. "You know there is nothing I would like more than to have you by my side. But this time I must deny myself the privilege."

Ryen nodded, trying desperately not to look as disappointed as she felt.

"It will only take four days, and I promise you when I return I will make up every minute that I am away."

"Four days?" Ryen whispered in anguish.

Bryce nodded, pulling her against him.

She could hear the beat of his heart as she pressed her head against his chest. When she looked up into his eyes, she saw her anguish mirrored there. He lowered his lips to hers and the kiss was hungry and desperate.

Then Bryce stepped away from her, not releasing her hands. Finally, with a wistful grin, he let her hands go and departed.

Ryen stared out over the forests and plowed land, thinking about their night together. She remembered his hot touch, his eyes as they clouded over with desire, the feel of his soft hair as the wet curls clung to her fingers. She sighed, missing him already, and pushed herself from the window ledge. Four days, she thought wistfully. How long these four days will be without him.

Her feet hit the stone floor and she began to move down the quiet hall. Her hair hung over her shoulders as she stared at the floor. She watched her feet move beneath her blue dress, back and forth, peeking from under the satin material and then disappearing with each step she took. Her mind dwelled for a long time on Bryce; his power over her was unequaled. She looked for him around every corner, in every room. A small smile tugged at her lips.

That's when she heard it. At first, she thought it was her imagination. The way her steps seemed to echo twice in the hallway was odd. It was almost as if . . .

. . . she were being followed. Ryen stopped, every nerve alert for footfalls or the rustle of clothing. A second after she halted, one more footstep fell. Ryen froze, wanting to turn and glance over her shoulder, but knowing that if she did, she would give away her advantage. So she continued on, turning corners and strolling casually through the castle. Listening with heightened awareness, she heard the sound again. As she paused to study a tapestry, the footfalls halted. As she moved, she developed a certain respect for her pursuer. Whoever it was had done this before. He, or she, was matching her steps exactly, only a fragment of a second behind each of hers. And he was quiet. She could not even hear the rustle of clothing. Whoever it was was not wearing armor.

Ryen stopped again, feigning interest in a suit of armor that stood at the side of the hallway. She wondered briefly if it was Vignon, waiting for the right opportunity to approach her. But she could not discount that it might be one of Bryce's men wanting to kill her. For a moment, her mind flashed back to Andre's tent and the soldier who had tried to slit her throat. She glanced instinctively down to her arm, where the scar from the attack was hidden beneath her long sleeves. She vowed she would never let that happen again.

Growing irritated at the game, Ryen stepped around a corner and quickly opened and closed a door, then pressed herself flat against the wall, waiting for the person to show himself.

If he wants to kill me, let him try, Ryen thought. She heard the light fall of footsteps as they neared her hiding spot. Then they stopped. Startled, she braced herself for discovery. The seconds stretched on . . . and on. No one rounded the corner.

Had she been imagining things? She took a deep breath and pushed herself from the wall, turning the corner.

Grey! Ryen gasped at finding him leaning casually against the wall, his arms crossed over his chest. Ryen reared back and slowly, as they stared at each other, her anger rose. "Why are you following me?" she demanded.

After a moment, a slow grin spread over his lips.

His smile only infuriated Ryen and her brows scowled lower. "I asked you a question."

"I heard you," he replied nonchalantly.

Her eyes raked over him, looking for some kind of weapon. His breeches were black and stained with mud; his torn tunic was in worse condition, the edges ragged. The collar was lined with fur. She could see no weapon and this only baffled her. She raised her eyes to his. For a long moment they stared at each other, her cold, angry eyes meeting his amused ones.

"I'm doing someone a favor," he finally answered.

"Are you trying to kill me?"

His lips opened, showing stained teeth as he smiled full out, but his words held none of the humor in his grin. "If I were, you would be dead."

Somehow, she believed him. Grey did not have the power that coursed through every vein in Bryce's body, yet he had an air of wisdom about him.

Ryen observed him through slitted eyes. "Who is this someone?"

"I don't think he would appreciate your knowledge of this."

"No? Well, I don't appreciate being spied on," she retorted. "And I don't think Bryce will find it amusing, either."

"You're right. He wouldn't find it amusing at all," Grey commented with a glimmer in his eye.

Ryen scowled at him. She was sure there was a hidden meaning to his words, but she couldn't decipher it. "Stop following me," she ordered, and stormed down the hall.

A fierce wind slammed open the shutters on the window and Ryen ran to them, pushing the wooden shutters closed. The cold wind whipped relentlessly, its chill whistling through cracks in the moldings.

Ryen sighed and leaned against the wood. She had returned to her room to choose fabric for some dresses Polly insisted on making for her, and now the material was strewn all over the bed. Ryen gazed at them again. They were beautiful, but hardly her style. Where there was silk for a beautiful dress, there should be leather for a pair of boots. Ryen sighed. The only reward would be Bryce's face when he saw her and the feel of his hands on her skin when he removed them.

Ryen sat down on the bed, her legs crossed, and picked up the quill and paper that Polly had left on the table at her request. As she placed the paper on the bed, carefully smoothing out the edges, she began to compose in her mind the letter to Count Dumas explaining that she was staying at Dark Castle of her own accord.

The quill flew elegantly over the paper. She began with a simple introduction and wasted no time in getting to the heart of the matter. She paused in her writing and stroked her chin with the large feather.

Her eyes were drawn by Bryce's image upon the tapestry. She placed the quill and paper on the bed and walked to the woven picture, staring at the precise accuracy of the embroidered eyes. The tapestry seemed to capture his look, his mood.

The door swung open and Ryen turned. The smile that had begun to form when she'd thought it was Bryce vanished. A protective wall slammed down, cutting off her heart from the rest of her senses. Lotte could only be here to hurt her. "Get out," Ryen commanded, an icy jealousy racing across her shoulders and tensing her body.

Lotte grinned. "Such a pleasant way to greet a stranger."

"You are not a stranger," Ryen retorted.

Lotte surveyed the room, her brown eyes growing dreamy. "The things I could have done with this room. I would have sewn a brighter blanket for the bed, hung more tapestries to keep this room warmer . . . and mirrors. Definitely mirrors." Lotte's eyes swept the room until they came to the tapestry. "I would have gotten rid of *that*." She pointed to it.

"What do you want?" Ryen demanded, outrage flashing through her heart. She loved the tapestry, woven with such careful detail that the images were brought to life.

"Why, I thought we could be friends."

Ryen's eyes narrowed. Never, her mind screamed. There was something about the woman that made Ryen's skin crawl.

Lotte's eyes moved to the bed, and slowly she approached it. "Such fine, *fine* cloth. Silk, isn't it?"

Ryen did not answer, but watched as Lotte picked up the material and rubbed it against her cheek. Ryen snapped, "Put it down." The thought of touching the once precious silk now made Ryen's stomach churn.

Lotte carelessly dropped the material. "I suppose you think you're special?" Lotte asked. "Well, you're not. He's taken me in every room of this castle. Including here." Lotte nodded at the bed.

Ryen's cheeks flushed.

"All these fabrics and jewels he bestows on you mean nothing." She turned to Ryen, eyes slitted with loathing. "You will never have his heart, for it is wild. As wild as a wolf's." Her gaze swept over Ryen's form. "And you are not woman enough to tame a wolf."

"Get out," Ryen commanded. "Get out before I strangle you."

"Don't you have any loyalty?" Lotte demanded. "How can you enjoy your enemy's kisses so much, knowing your brother is locked in the dungeon?"

"My brothers are dead!" Ryen shouted.

"Dead?" Lotte stared at Ryen, her brow creased with confusion. Then she burst out laughing. "Who told you that?" she cackled. "Prince?"

Ryen's jaw clenched with her fierce anger. "Do not laugh at me."

Immediately Lotte ceased her snickering and shot a hateful glance at Ryen. "You simple fool. One of your brothers survived the battle."

Stunned, Ryen could only stare for a long moment. Finally, she announced, "I don't believe you," but the tremble in her voice belied the words.

"See for yourself."

"And what should I do?" Ryen asked sarcastically. "Ask the jailer?"

"I'll distract him. The keys are on the wall before the hallway," Lotte said. When Ryen's eyes narrowed dubiously, she continued, "I know. I've been down there before. How do you think I know your brother lives?"

Doubt festered in Ryen's mind. She should turn her back on the vindictive woman. All Lotte wanted was to destroy what she and Bryce had. Still, if Lucien or Andre were alive . . .

A grin slid across Lotte's lips like a snake. "Can you live without knowing for sure?"

Indecision plagued her. It was a trap, she was sure. Why else would Lotte concoct such a story? But . . . there was the nagging doubt. What if . . . what *if* . . .

Ryen marched past her. "Let's go." Ryen was out the door, through the hallway, and down the stairs. Her heart beat in her ears, blocking out all noises. Why would Bryce lie to her? It was ridiculous. He had no reason. Andre and Lucien couldn't be in the dungeon. Why was she even doing this? Then she stopped cold. Where was the dungeon?

Lotte brushed past her with a knowing snicker. "Your brother is in the eighth cell."

Ryen followed Lotte down stone steps into the darkness that was the dungeon. She hid in the shadows of the corridor, her cupped hand protecting her only light—a single candle. Her eyes tried to see into the blackness of the hallway opposite her where the cells were, but it was so dark she could see nothing. She heard Lotte's soft voice cooing to the guard, his snort, and a low curse. Then all was quiet.

Ryen snuck forward to peek around the corner. The guard was standing, his back to her, his head bent. Ryen saw Lotte's skirt between the man's spread legs.

Ryen hurried by, the shimmering circle of light she walked in cutting the black of the dungeon like an ax. She paused and reached around the corner to feel for the keys. Her hand brushed them and they jangled slightly. She pulled back, waiting for the guard to reply. But there was no call of alarm, no shout of "Who goes there?" Her heart pounded in her chest as she again reached around to the keys. Quickly she grabbed them and pulled them to her bosom, stilling any jangling.

Ryen waited for a noise, but the only sounds she could hear were the murmurs of love talk. Then those voices faded away as Lotte led the guard away.

Ryen moved away from the wall and walked into the dungeon. The stench of urine and decay assaulted her and she stumbled back, putting a hand to her nose. After a moment she reached out with her hand and it disappeared in the blackness beyond the candle's flickering light. Her fingers brushed damp, cold stone. She pulled back quickly at the slimy feel of the wet wall.

Taking a deep breath and squeezing the iron keys in her palm, she moved forward.

Ryen passed seven doors and slowed when she approached the eighth. Her heart pounded as she saw the outline of the door. She stood before it, unable to see within. How was she to know if . . . if one of her brothers was behind this door? Or whether it was a trap?

Then there was movement from within. She saw the shadow cross near the door through the small barred window. Ryen tensed. Who was it? She had to know.

"Prince? Is that you, you bastard?"

Lucien. Oh, God, it was Lucien! she thought, as she fumbled to fit the keys into the lock. Her hands trembled uncontrollably, but finally she slipped the key into the hole.

Lucien, her mind repeated. He was alive!

"Who's there?"

Ryen flung open the door and quickly stepped into the room. "It's Ryen," she gasped, searching the darkness of the cell for any sign of her brother.

A mass hit her hard in the side and she was knocked onto her back, the weight pinning her to the cold floor.

"So," Lucien sneered, so close to her ear that Ryen almost

wept for joy. "You are no ghost." His hand closed over her wrist and slid up to her shoulder. "Soft flesh? Who are you?"

The candle had fallen to the floor. Still burning, it cast his blue eyes in an orange glow. Before she could reply, Lucien continued. "Are you one of his *sluts?*"

"No," Ryen gasped.

"It's been a long time," Lucien whispered.

Ryen felt his legs move between her thighs, pushing her knees apart. Horror and outrage crashed over her and she shifted her weight, pressing her thighs together, trying to push him from her. "No. I am Ryen!"

He smashed an arm into her throat. "My sister is dead, wench. Be still. This will not take long."

He doesn't know me, she thought, as she lashed out wildly. Under the barrage, Lucien ducked his head in her shoulder, steeling himself against her attack.

"God's blood, but you fight like Ryen," Lucien murmured to himself, but he reached down to pull up her skirt.

Tears came to Ryen's eyes and she stopped her fight. *"Please,* Lucien," she whispered.

Lucien froze for a long moment. Ryen's harsh gasps echoed in the small cell. "I remember the last time I saw my sister cry. She was six. Our mother had died that morning."

"I cried all day," Ryen murmured. "I remember the snow. It was the first time that year."

Ryen watched his features change. The wildness disappeared from his sunken eyes. The anger melted from his face.

"Ryen," he whispered. He quickly sat up, horrified at what he was about to do. "Oh, God." He buried his face in his hands.

"No, Lucien. Please. You would not have harmed me," Ryen soothed, and knelt beside her brother.

"Do you have any idea what I was going to do to you?"

"But you didn't," Ryen insisted.

Lucien rammed his fist into the dirt wall. "Curse him. He told me you were dead."

Ryen sat back on her heels. She steeled herself against the pain that was rising in her throat.

"Ryen?"

She looked up to find Lucien studying her face.

"Did he touch you?"

Ryen averted her gaze to the flickering candle. "We have to get out of here."

"I'll kill the bastard!" Lucien roared.

"Lucien, hush." Ryen glanced at the door, then back at her brother. She knew the guard would be returning any moment. "I will find some way to help you escape."

"Escape?" Lucien demanded. "I'm leaving with you now!"

"You can't. I have to see you safely through the castle and—"

"Just give me a weapon!"

"Lucien, please," Ryen begged, casting a worried look at the door. "I don't have a weapon. But I will get one and I will be back."

"I will smash that guard's head and take his sword," Lucien said.

"You're too weak. You could *never* overpower him." Ryen rose. She recovered the candle and moved quickly to the door. She checked the hallway, then paused to glance back at Lucien.

He was kneeling in the dirt, his face flickering in and out of shadow, his once glorious hair knotted and dirty. "Let me go with you," he begged.

Her heart twisted. No matter how much she wanted to free him, she knew the wisest decision was to find a sword and come back to the dungeon. "Know that I will return as soon as possible."

Ryen departed the cell, shutting the door behind her.

Forty-one

In the hallway outside her room, Ryen paused. Her senses were numb; her mind kept repeating, he's alive—Lucien's alive. Then a sharp stab of pain would slice across her heart. Bryce had lied! Just as she had begun to hope, to trust him again.

"You're beautiful." His voice, dreamlike and caring, filled her mind.

Why did he lie to her? Why? Ryen covered her mouth with her fingertips and leaned her head against the wooden door.

When she reached for the handle of the door, she found that her hands were trembling. What was she going to do? She knew she had to free Lucien. She could not bear to see him locked up in the dungeon. You gave Bryce your word, an inner voice said. You told him you would not leave him. But he lied to me! What am I going to do?

Ryen straightened. She could not break her word to Bryce. But she would free Lucien. She had to see him away from Dark Castle and Bryce. Then she would deal with Bryce's anger. With the decision made, she needed only one thing—a sword for Lucien.

She raised her eyes from the cold stone floor to the wooden door before her. Ryen was moving to open it when a glint caught her eye. She turned her head to see the two suits of plate mail down the hall . . .

* * *

She peered around the dark corner of the dungeon at the guard who was cleaning his nails with the sharp tip of a dagger. He was balancing precariously on two legs of the wooden chair he sat in, his feet resting comfortably on top of a table. Ryen glanced across the hall and into the darkness beyond. Lucien awaited her. He was depending on her. She took a deep breath and, hiding the sword she had removed from the suit of armor in the folds of her blue dress, stepped out into the dim torchlight.

The guard glanced up as she approached. His feet hit the floor at the same time the two legs of the chair did. He tossed the dagger onto the table and stood. "What do you want?"

Ryen saw his large hands resting on the table before him, the dagger between them. Her eyes shifted from the weapon to his eyes. She stepped forward, forcing a smile to her trembling lips. "I—I think you have something I want," Ryen answered.

His eyes raked over her. The large guard's dark, burly brows slumped over his narrowing eyes. "Who are you?"

She took another step forward. Close enough. She drew the weapon with lightning-fast reflexes, placing it near the guard's throat. "Step around the table," she commanded.

The guard's dark eyes turned from amused disbelief to anger. "I do not take commands from a woman." His hand moved for the dagger.

Before his palm closed over the hilt, Ryen shoved the point of the sword against the man's Adam's apple, halting his movement. "Then this will be the first time you do," she answered. "Move out from behind the table, or I will slit your throat."

The guard did not hesitate this time. He emerged from the cover of his table.

"You will release Lucien De Bouriez," Ryen told him.

He hesitated for a moment as if debating between death and Bryce's wrath.

Ryen hit his arm with the flat side of the sword. "Move," she urged, "or I will make your death a most painful one."

The guard's shoulders slumped and he turned, retrieving a torch from the wall before he headed into the dark hallway. Ryen kept the sword point to his back as he paused before Lucien's cell door. The guard opened the lock and turned to give her a scathing look before throwing the door wide.

Ryen called "Lucien!" as her brother emerged from the darkened pit of his imprisonment.

Lucien glanced at her, his eyes glittering in the feeble light, and then his gaze pierced the guard. His lip curled and he snatched the sword from Ryen's hand. Lucien backhanded the guard and the torch fell to the floor.

"Put him in the cell," Ryen ordered, but Lucien went after him with a vengeance, pounding him in his face with clenched fists and in his stomach with booted feet. With each blow, his lip curled tighter, his sneer growing into a feral snarl. He reared back his head and spat his hatred into the guard's face, continuing to rain blow after blow on the helpless man.

Appalled at her brother's mindless savagery, Ryen grabbed Lucien's arm. "Leave him alone," she called.

Lucien elbowed her away before turning on her. "You defend him?" he demanded.

Ryen stared at him, aghast at how quickly he had turned on her. "We don't have time to delay!" She turned and headed for the entrance to the dungeon.

After a moment, she heard Lucien's footsteps behind her. She paused at the bottom of the stairs, waiting for him in the flickering torchlight.

Lucien stepped into the small circle of brightness and Ryen felt relief in her heart. Yet even as joy filled her to see him free again and out of the dampness of the dungeon, uneasiness gripped her, for there was a wildness about him that was new. His dark blue orbs darted anxiously back and forth. His fingers were curved like claws ready to curl into a fist at the slightest provocation. He cast quick, furtive glances over his shoulders as he moved, as if he were prey fearing a hunter's strike. He is only being cautious, she told herself.

"You know this castle well," Lucien remarked.

Ryen moved forward, up the stairs, but Lucien grabbed her arm, halting her. He moved past her, climbing the stairs and paused. Ryen joined him, whispering, "The only way out is through the inner ward."

"Which way?" Lucien asked.

"Down the hall and out the main doors," Ryen murmured.

"No back entrance?"

"Not that I know of," she replied.

"Stay here," Lucien commanded.

Ryen opened her mouth to object, but he was already making his way down the hall. Anger rose inside her as she watched his back. He still treated her as a child! Even though it was she who had gotten him out of the dungeon. He disappeared around a corner and Ryen sagged back against the wall.

"You shouldn't do this," a voice whispered in the darkness.

Ryen whirled, searching the shadowed stairway behind her. She felt panic rise in her throat, closing off her cry of alarm.

"You shouldn't betray his trust," the voice continued.

Then Ryen recognized the tone. Grey. He stepped out of the darkness of the hallway and into the flickering light thrown by the torches. He was still following her! Where there should have been anger, Ryen felt only fear. He would try to stop her from freeing Lucien.

Grey stood before her, accusal darkening his eyes.

"Stay out of this," Ryen ordered. She didn't want to see him hurt.

Grey's lips twitched into a humorless grin.

Ryen stepped backward, down the hallway, following Lucien's path. Before she could blink, his hand shot out to seize her wrist.

"I'm asking you again not to betray his trust," Grey said.

Ryen yanked her arm free. "He lied to me!" she whispered savagely. Her agonized, indecisive gaze met his and Ryen was surprised to see her emotions mirrored in Grey's eyes.

Suddenly, Ryen caught a flash of a blade above his head. "No!" Ryen screamed as she watched Lucien bring the weapon down upon Grey's head.

Grey's eyes rolled and he collapsed to the ground.

Ryen bent to help, but Lucien grabbed her arm and pulled her down the hallway.

"I circled back," he was saying, "and I saw you struggling with him."

Ryen tried to pull free, but Lucien's hold on her wrist was strong. She glanced back at Grey lying sprawled on the floor, but had only a glimpse of him before Lucien turned the corner and made his way to the great door.

Ryen stopped struggling. She had to get Lucien free, and then she would see to Grey. Lucien released her when she stopped fighting. There they paused only long enough to glance out into the courtyard.

The sun was setting in the distance, bathing the sky in a deep red. Ryen's heart was hammering in her chest. She wanted desperately to return to Grey and make sure he was all right. But Lucien had to be free. She would not allow her brother to rot in the dungeon. She quickly scanned the darkening yard. There was no one in sight and she gave a silent prayer of thanks. Through the open inner ward gate, she could see that the outer ward's gates were also open.

A prickling of warning shot up Ryen's spine. If all the peasants were gone, as the empty courtyard was proof, the gates should have been closed.

Lucien grabbed her arm and pulled her out into the inner ward. Two horses stood before them as if awaiting their arrival.

Ryen stopped, pulling Lucien to a halt. She glanced around at the vacant walls of the castle. No guards walked the battlements. Her eyes swiveled to the gatehouse, which seemed strangely empty. "It's a trap," she announced.

Lucien followed her looks with his own. "The hell with their traps! We're getting out of here now," he hissed urgently. He pulled her to the horses and he quickly mounted one.

Ryen moved forward, prepared to bid him farewell. When he glanced down at her, she saw rage in his deep blue eyes.

"What are you waiting for? Mount," Lucien whispered urgently.

Ryen drew herself up proudly. "I can't leave."

"What?" Lucien cried.

"I gave my word."

"Your word? To whom?"

Ryen tried to swallow in a suddenly dry throat. "I gave my word to the Prince of Darkness that I would not leave."

"What?!" he roared. "Your word means nothing beneath his deceit."

"My word is my honor. I cannot break it."

Lucien's horse pranced, sensing his anger. His deep blue eyes burned with a fury that Ryen had never seen before. He jerked the horse around to face her. "I will not leave without you."

Ryen gasped. She had assumed he would go without an argument. "You must!" Ryen begged. "This is your only chance, Lucien."

"I will not leave you here, with *him*."

"He will throw you in the dungeon again! Please, Lucien."

Lucien's bearded jaw tightened. "He told me you were dead!"

Ryen looked away. "He told me you were dead, also."

Lucien moved to dismount. "Then I will cut him down."

"No!" Ryen shouted, and moved immediately to the other horse. She pulled her dress up over her knees so she could mount.

Lucien straightened on the animal. His lip curled before he yanked savagely on the reins and rode for the gates.

Ryen spared a last look at Dark Castle. She hoped someone would find Grey quickly, that he would be all right. Then she thought on her promise. She had given Bryce her word. But more important than her word was that no harm befell . . . Lucien, yes, of course. Who else could she have been worried about? He was in no condition to face the Prince of Darkness in his weakened state. She had a loyalty to her brother as kin, a loyalty to France and to King Charles. She had no loyalty to Bryce . . . only her heart ached when she thought of him. I trusted you, Bryce, she thought. But you lied to me. I cannot forgive you for that.

Ryen spurred her horse, riding toward the gates into the setting sun.

Standing in the outer gatehouse, watching the two riders through a vertical slitted window as they fled from the castle, Polly stood shaking her head. She caressed one of the bridles she held tightly in her hands.

"Don't feel so bad," a voice from behind her snickered. "Now, you have only one thing to do and you will not have to spend any time in the dungeon." Lotte moved past Polly to glance out the window. "Everything is going perfectly."

Polly turned to leave the small room.

"Oh," Lotte called. When Polly paused, Lotte continued, "If I catch you warming yourself by the kitchen fire again, you will have a month of chores added to your tasks."

Forty-two

Bryce could not get Ryen out of his mind. Every tree's bark hid her smile; the blue of the sky was but a twinkle in her eye; the moon's brightness paled in the light of her glow. He wanted to see her so badly that he had ridden back two days early, leaving his exhausted men to make camp somewhere far behind him. Only Talbot had ridden with him.

As they approached the tall gates of Dark Castle, the image of Ryen promised warmth on the chill night. Suddenly, the hair on the back of Bryce's neck stood straight. Only half of his soldiers walked the walls. Bryce spurred his mount, racing the already exhausted beast into his castle. As he dismounted, one of the guards came rushing up to him.

"What's happened?" Bryce demanded, fighting down the feeling of doom that slithered up his spine.

"It's Lady Ryen. She's gone," the knight answered.

Bryce's frown deepened.

"Gone?" Talbot asked, dismounting beside Bryce.

"Aye," the guard replied, his brow creased in concern and fear. "She is not in the castle."

"How long has she been missing?" Bryce queried, his level tone hiding the pounding of his heart.

The man shuffled his feet nervously.

"Answer me, damn it," Bryce growled.

"She's been gone since late last eve," the knight said.

Bryce swung himself up into the saddle.

"M'lord, she helped a prisoner to escape!"

Bryce froze, every muscle in his body tensing. The knuckles of his hands turned white as they clutched the reins of the horse. His dark eyes burned Talbot to the spot. "Find her."

Polly's hands kneaded her apron. She stood staring at Bryce's hands clenched behind his back as he glared out of the window into the darkness.

"How did this happen?"

His voice caused her to jump.

"M'lord?" Polly asked, her voice trembling.

"Do not play games with me, Polly," Bryce murmured. "I know you two have become close. I want to know what she said before she left."

Polly hesitated. Her hands had begun to shake. "She was very upset, m'lord."

"Why?"

"I don't know. But she said she hated ya 'n would rather die than face ya again."

Bryce did not move. His body was ice. "Where did she go?"

"Ta France, m'lord. She was goin' home." Polly hesitated. She didn't want to say the next words, but the promise of the dungeon made her add, "Ta her true love, Count Dumas."

Bryce turned to face her, and for the first time Polly saw the agony in his eyes. When he spoke, his voice was soft and broken. "How did she find out about her brother?"

"I don't know, m'lord," Polly answered.

He straightened to his full height, until he towered over the plump maid. Then he pushed past her and quit his chambers, leaving Polly standing in the wake of his loneliness and remorse.

Polly's whole body shook as tremors of terror raced along her spine. Just below her fear hid misery. What am I doin' ta them? she asked herself for the thousandth time. Condemning them to a life of anguish and bitterness? They were enemies, she reasoned, pacing the bedroom. They didn't belong together anyway. And the dungeon was a very cold place.

Ryen and Lucien traveled with little sleep and no food. But as they rested on the second day, Ryen felt numb. She didn't hear the rumblings of her stomach. She didn't feel the soreness throughout her body from countless hours of hard riding.

She and Lucien had barely exchanged two words during their journey. She wondered if he even knew where he was going. Ryen raised her tired, aching eyes to her brother.

He still carried with him the filth of the dungeon, reeked of urine and sweat. She briefly wondered why he hadn't washed in the stream they'd happened upon a day ago. But the thought of the stream brought aching, tender memories of Bryce's glorious naked body, glistening in the moonlight, poised far above the falls.

Her chest tightened and tears rose in her eyes. She missed him. And she hated herself for being so weak. He had lied to her! Ryen closed her eyes tightly against the torment that his image brought to her heart.

It was not only the ache in her heart that hurt, but the agony of her soul. She had told Bryce she would stay at Dark Castle. And when she left with Lucien, she had forsaken her honor. She fought down the feeling that she should return to Dark Castle and keep her word. But, as she swiveled her eyes to Lucien who was squatting, mumbling incoherently as he gazed blankly at the ground, she could see the weariness in his slumped shoulders. Lucien needed her here with him.

Again Ryen dropped her head. Her honor was at stake. If she did not return, how could she hope to ever see herself as a true knight? She lived every hour of her life by the Code of Chivalry. And now she was shattering the very foundation upon which it was built.

"Ryen."

She jumped and her eyes came to focus on her brother. His dirty brows drew together as he studied her face.

"We must get food," he finally announced. "And new horses. These are tired and well ridden." His eyes bore into her and Ryen looked away, nodding. "Are you ill?" Lucien asked.

Ryen glanced back at the way they had just come, back toward Dark Castle. "No," she murmured.

After a moment, he took her hand, helping her to her feet, and led the way through the bushes to the horses.

Bryce thundered into town with a garrison of soldiers. He dismounted before his horse had completely stopped and walked toward the stables where an older man stood before the wooden door.

"Are you sure it was her?" he asked.

"Aye, m'lord," the old man answered, scratching his chest. "She took a loaf of bread and two horses, then headed down the road."

Bryce studied the old man's haggard face and his sharp eyes saw the slight swelling and purplish coloring of a bruise beneath one of the man's wrinkled eyes. "You tried to stop her, didn't you?"

The peasant dropped his eyes. "Aye."

"I warned you to stay out of her way. Was she hurt?"

"No, m'lord."

"Good." Bryce whirled, returning to his steed. He climbed into the saddle, his dark eyes stormy as he glared in the direction Ryen had fled. It was a large area to search, many roads they could have taken. But he would find her. She would not slip through his fingers.

He glanced at one of the men in his garrison. "Ride to Dark Castle. Tell the Wolf Pack they are needed with all due speed."

"Yes, m'lord," the man replied, and turned his horse around.

If anyone could track her, they could.

It wasn't until the following night that the Wolf Pack arrived on horseback. Bryce was pacing before the wooden door of the stables like a caged lion.

Night dismounted, followed by Grey. They approached Bryce and he halted immediately, his hands on his hips.

"What took so long?" Bryce snapped as they neared.

A slight breeze ruffled Night's fur cape, but the two men did not move nor answer.

Bryce growled, dragging a hand through his dark hair. He began to pace again. He was feeling the strain of his determination. He hadn't eaten in a full day, hadn't slept all night. "I need your help," he told his two friends.

"She was last seen here?" Grey wondered.

"A day ago," Bryce answered, nodding.

Night glanced at the ground, his eyes studying the dirt path that merged with the street. "A day is a long time. Many tracks have covered hers. The wind has blown over it—"

"I don't want to hear that," Bryce growled. "Find her."

"We will begin here," Grey replied.

The two men of the Wolf Pack turned away and headed back to their horses.

Bryce reached out and seized Grey's shoulder. Grey turned to look at him and saw the desperation in his eyes. "You must find her."

"We will do all we can, brother," Grey answered. "My honor is at stake as well." As he moved toward his horse, he pulled a hood down over his face. It was the face of a wolf.

Ryen shivered and hugged her arms. Lucien had driven the horses relentlessly for two days. Now, as she sat huddled beneath an elm tree near a slow-moving brook, Ryen watched her brother through worried eyes. He had refused to light a fire even though it was cold enough to see their breath.

Lucien stood on a small hill, his dark shape outlined by twinkling stars. During the day, he had continued to mumble to himself, his eyes rolling into his head. They had stopped then, and rested only on Ryen's insistence that she was tired.

She shivered again as she watched him. He appeared normal now, but all her reasoning told her that something was wrong. Dreadfully wrong. Ryen pulled her knees into her chest. They would freeze to death out in the open if they did not start a fire.

Suddenly, she heard a noise. Her head shot up, her eyes piercing the darkness. Nothing. No movement. No sound. She turned to Lucien. He had not moved. Perhaps it is my nerves, she thought. She tried to relax, rolling her shoulders to loosen them.

Lucien stood and turned to her. His gaze was hard, his lips set in a thin line. As he approached her, his footsteps came down hard on the earth.

Ryen rose to her feet as he came to a halt before her.

"There are some things that trouble me, Sister," Lucien said.

Ryen heard the curtness in his voice and did not answer.

"I find it peculiar that you were not in the dungeon, as I was," he continued, then paused for an answer.

Ryen stared at his darkly ringed, red-streaked eyes, his gaunt face, his clenched jaw. She was afraid to say anything for fear of enflaming his anger further.

Suddenly, he reached out and seized a handful of the rich velvet material of her skirt. "No prisoner wears such clothing."

Instinctively Ryen jerked away, pulling her skirt from his hand.

His teeth were clenched, snipping the end of each word. "You slept with him, didn't you?"

His statement shocked her and she took a step away from him.

"She told me you did, but I didn't believe her. Not until now. It all makes sense. Why you're dressed the way you are. Why you weren't in the dungeon." Lucien took a step closer. "Why you didn't want to leave."

"I gave my word!" Ryen hollered.

"She called you a French slut."

Ryen took another step away from Lucien and her back slammed into the tree. Her fears of what she had become rose in her mind again. Bryce's slut. He had labeled her that on their first night together. And now his words rang true. "Who called me that?"

"His dark-haired whore," Lucien replied bitterly. "Who better to see?"

Days of agony rose inside of her, nights of loneliness. "Oh, Lucien," Ryen whispered, tears filling her eyes. "I thought he loved me."

"Loved?" He spat the word as if it were poison. "And you embraced him willingly."

Guilt and remorse rose inside her. She turned away from her brother. "Yes," she whimpered.

"Then you are truly a traitor."

There was a calm in his voice that frightened Ryen, and as she turned to look at him, she heard the silent hiss of the sword being pulled from his belt. Ryen stared at him in disbelief, unable to move as he pointed the tip of the weapon at her throat.

"You deserve death!" he sneered.

One of the horses whinnied nervously, and all at once the forest seemed to come alive.

Lucien pulled his arm back for the final thrust. She twisted and the sword whirled past her, slamming into the bark of the elm tree.

Branches reached out to seize her arms and wrists. Shadows moved about her as if they, too, were alive. Lucien was lost from her view, swallowed by a sea of darkness.

A hand covered her mouth, cutting off any sound.

She felt a rush of power as she lashed out with her knee, catching her captor off guard. She heard a groan as the hand fell from her mouth and wrist. Ryen tore her other arm free and paused, searching the forest for Lucien. Dark shapes seemed to dance before the reflection of the stars in the water of the brook.

A face rose before her and she gasped, stumbling back. Through the shadowy light, she saw a hairy face, teeth pointed to white fangs and eyes red like a demon's. Ryen turned and fled.

Behind her she heard angry shouts. She dashed through the bushes, her heart pounding wildly, the wind roaring in her ears. Bare branches slapped at her face as she crashed through them. Unable to see for the darkness, Ryen pushed blindly on, her hands outstretched to try to feel what was in front of her only moments before her feet landed on the uneven ground beneath the bushes.

It's not real, she told herself, and slowed her steps. It could not be real. Then, over the mad beat of her heart and the rush of blood in her ears, a howl broke the silence of the night. Heavy running footsteps snapped branches and crushed leaves behind her. She broke into a run, turning her head to look over her shoulder, but could see only the darkness. When she spun to face forward, she saw the shadow of the tree too late. Her feet slid in the leaves and she caught herself on the cold bark of the tree. As she turned to head away from the barrier, her dress snagged on the branches of the bushes near her feet.

He bore down upon her like a devil, seizing her wrist in a steely grip. Ryen fought blindly against his strength, but he proved too powerful, stilling her vain struggle by grabbing her other wrist. She looked up into his eyes, which were red like fire. With a gasp, she stumbled back into the trees. He threw back his head and a howl tore from his throat.

The man who had captured her was no man at all, but an animal! It propelled her back toward her camp. She stumbled and fell, but he grabbed her arm, his fingers biting into her flesh, and yanked her to her feet.

A campfire loomed just beyond the trees they were rapidly approaching. The flickering of the flames cast eerie shadows on the trees of the forest.

Her captor yanked her through the foliage and Ryen felt a branch slice her skin. Her other cuts suddenly flared to life and her body ached from exhaustion.

Ryen raised her eyes to the beast that held her wrist as he emerged from the forest and the firelight washed over him. His face was covered with fur, his nose shaped like the muzzle of a beast. It was a wolf, Ryen realized. A wolf that walked like a man! She had heard such fairy tales but had never believed them until now. She tried to pull her hand free, but her movement only succeeded in turning the man-wolf's glare upon her.

"Bring her," a voice called from near the firelight.

The man-wolf pulled her closer to the fire, where she found herself surrounded by seven similar creatures.

One of them placed his hand on his muzzle and raised it up. The wolf-face slid away and Ryen gasped. It was the man who she had eaten beside at Bryce's table, the one who had followed her! He was all right! Then, it dawned on her. The Wolf Pack!

At the same time, the realization struck that they were returning her to Bryce.

Ryen quickly backed away until she bumped into a wall of flesh. She couldn't suppress a whimper as she was spun around to face the man.

Bryce held her at arm's length, the fire reflecting in his black eyes as he scowled at her. They went from her wild hair to her torn dress.

She steeled herself against the sadness that reared its head inside her at his hateful stare.

Then his gaze shifted to Grey. There was no sound as they contemplated each other. Bryce finally nodded and said, "Bring the man to my castle."

Grey dipped his head slightly.

Ryen felt Bryce's hand clamp over her arm, and he turned her away.

His steps were large and surefooted, and Ryen had to struggle to keep up with him. His fingers dug into her flesh as he pulled her along.

"What will you do to Lucien?" Ryen asked.

"You should be more concerned about what I will do to you," Bryce answered sharply.

"Me?" Ryen wondered aloud.

Bryce stopped suddenly and Ryen slammed into his back. She stepped away as he whirled on her. "Yes, *you*. Did you think I would not find you? Did you think there was *any-where* you could run that I would not come after you? Even to France and your lover Count Dumas."

"We are not lovers—" Ryen stated.

"Enough!" Bryce shouted, glaring at her. "I will not hear any more of your lies."

"My lies?" Frustration and hurt overwhelmed Ryen. Her eyes burned as she scowled at Bryce. "And what of *yours?* "

He straightened. "I have never lied to you or in any way led you to believe a falsehood!"

Tears flooded her eyes. "What about under the 'truth pow-der'?" He *had* lied to her, then. He called her beautiful . . . and it had been the foulest of lies, whispered from vengeful lips.

Bryce gazed at her calmly, his expression like the quiet that settles the air before a storm.

"Yes. I lied to you then. But you were my enemy. I have *not* lied to you since."

She raised her quivering chin. "You told me Lucien was dead!"

"The Lucien you knew *is* dead," he answered.

"And how do you know my brother so well?" she retorted sharply.

"I've seen his look before. The madness in his eyes, in his words. I was afraid he would hurt even his sister."

His words startled her into silence. Bryce was right. Lucien had been about to kill her. She felt her body tremble.

Bryce reached out to her. "Angel."

She pulled violently away. No. He wanted her to believe he was only trying to protect her. Another lie. He could have trusted her with the truth, even sought her help with Lucien. Instead, he had chosen to manipulate her. He had used her, twisted her feelings and emotions to suit him.

Bryce had ripped out her heart and split it in half. Now, he wanted her to take it back so he could hurt her again. She didn't want it. "Don't touch me. We were enemies then and we are now," she whispered.

Bryce dropped his hands. "So be it," he murmured.

Forty-three

They moved through the night, Ryen in front of Bryce on his war horse. As they rode, Bryce watched her head bob before him and knew she was asleep.

They were enemies again. The thought drove a wedge into his heart. Somehow they had built a bridge over the abyss of their differences, of their loyalties. They had been happy. Bryce had seen how her eyes glowed when she looked upon him, how her lips curved up in happiness. But now their bridge built from joy and companionship was being swallowed by pride and honor.

For the first time in his life, the word was bitter to him. *Honor.* He had killed for less. Now, he wished he had never heard the word, had never taken his oath to become a knight . . . all for the sake of a woman.

He clenched his teeth. Damn, he thought. How in heaven's name had she found out? Had she been touring his castle and decided to take a stroll in the dungeon? Ridiculous. The dungeon would have been the last place she would go. So, someone must have told her. But who?

The question plagued him for the duration of the journey. They stopped to rest once and Bryce watched Ryen clean her face by a stream. She winced as her fingers brushed over a small cut on her cheek. Bryce felt her pain throughout his body and stepped forward to help, but then stopped. She did not want his help. She did not want *him.* She wanted Dumas.

They had arrived at Dark Castle at sunset without speaking

a word to each other. The fading rays of red splashed their backs and painted the tall, square towers of Dark Castle in a bloody crimson.

Bryce escorted Ryen to his room. He paused in the doorway and watched her walk to the center of the room, where she stopped. Her back straightened and he thought she would speak. But she did not, and Bryce was forced to shut the door on her.

He stared at the dark wood for a long moment. He should take the ransom and send her back to her lover. He knew that was what she wanted. But he couldn't. He couldn't give her to another man. He would rather have her rot in his dungeons.

Bryce locked the door and turned away.

Ryen was awakened from a troubled sleep by a creak of floorboards. She shot up, her eyes wide, her hand searching for her sword that should have been within easy grasp.

A hand clamped over her mouth.

"Quiet," the voice murmured.

Ryen's eyes followed the arm up to the shoulder and then to his face. Vignon was seated on the bed, a tray of fruit in his lap.

An irrational fear closed her throat. A thousand questions raced through her mind, but she could not seem to utter one of them.

He dropped his hand, whispering, "You may not have a lot of time. There is a rumor he will return you to France."

Ryen was momentarily stunned. France, her mind kept repeating.

Vignon pressed a small vial into her hand. "I cannot get close enough to Prince to do it. You must."

Ryen's eyes dropped to the cold cylinder resting in her palm and the clear liquid inside. The cold from the vial seeped into her skin and made her shiver.

"Pour it over his food, or in his ale. He will be dead after one taste."

A shiver shot up her spine. Ryen's fist closed around the vial tightly, her hand suddenly trembling.

Vignon rose, placing the tray on the table. "Do not delay. You may not be here long."

Ryen could not tear her eyes from the vial of death. She had never killed a man who was weaponless, with something he could not defend himself against. It seemed . . . wrong. "I can't," she whispered.

Vignon's cold eyes turned to her, the shadow of a scowl creasing his brow.

Guilt spilled over her and Ryen protested, "He will not see me, let alone eat with me."

Vignon shrugged. "Change his mind. You are a woman."

Ryen gaped at him, anger slowly seeping into her eyes. "I am a knight."

"Then find a sword and run him through. Either way will yield the desired result." He moved silently to the door.

Ryen glanced down at the vial she held cupped in her hand. There was only a small amount of the liquid in the tube. For it to be able to kill a man as strong as Bryce seemed inconceivable.

She raised her eyes to the door. Vignon's dark eyes narrowed, and for a moment, seemed to flash white in the candlelight. "Remember your duty to your king and country. All else is meaningless in war," he hissed, before exiting the room.

Ryen's gaze fell to her clenched fist. She was to kill Bryce. For her country, for her king, she was to poison him.

The thought of Bryce's strong, vibrant body broken and still on the cold stones of the floor haunted her thoughts. Suddenly, she felt so light-headed that she almost dropped the vial. With both hands she clasped the cylinder to her chest.

Bryce used me, she told herself. Used me until I was blind to the truth. Lied to me. Protected me like I was a helpless woman unable to make my own decisions. I hate him.

There was an empty ache in her chest where her heart had been.

He should die for what he has done to me, she thought.

She sat at the window, watching the sun peek over the horizon. She shivered in the gusty, chill wind, but somehow she could not turn away from the hope of a new day. The wind sneaked into her muddied blue velvet dress through a tear in her gown and puffed the material from her body, caressing her naked skin until it slipped out through the bottom of her gown. Ryen trembled in the kiss of the icy breeze.

"Stand away from the window."

His voice shocked her, but she did not budge. How long had he been standing in the doorway watching her? she wondered.

"Where is my brother?" Ryen demanded, without shifting her gaze from the rising sun.

"Where prisoners are kept."

"Why am I not there?"

The silence rose between them like a stone wall, built on stubbornness and pride.

Another breeze swirled about Ryen, lifting the ends of her hair before settling them back around her shoulders.

"I said to stand away from the window."

Ryen raised her chin, defiantly thrusting it toward the glowing orb of the sun. She wanted to look at him, to see his defeat at her small victory. But she did not trust her feelings. Not where Bryce was concerned. She was afraid her victory would turn into defeat when her body turned traitor and desired his touch.

Suddenly, she was shoved back against the wall, Bryce's large hand about her thin throat. Surprised eyes met angry ones. "Why do you defy me? You know I can snap your neck with one squeeze."

She recognized a way out of her inner agony, an avenue that she had not considered, did not have the courage to take herself. Ryen's face softened, the angry, defiant lines melting into pools of tormented grief. "Why don't you?"

Ryen saw terror replace his anger as he stared into her eyes. His gaze took in every curve of her face, every pool of shadow that rested against her skin. She knew he needed to be goaded to kill her, but the words that had come to her lips so easily before could not be spoken from her dry mouth.

Suddenly, his lips slanted over hers and Ryen had to part them under his brutal hunger. His tongue thrust into her mouth and Ryen felt the passion inside her drown under rising tears. I hate him, she thought. And her hands shoved at his chest. But as his hands touched her face, moving in sweet caresses over her cheeks and through her hair, she felt her resolve weaken. As she opened her lips to his kiss, she knew her defeat was complete. She did not hate him; she loved him. She loved him so much that she would rather die than be separated from him. The sob escaped her throat where words could not.

She felt him pull slightly away but could not open her eyes for the tears. Ryen could feel his breath on her lips and her throat closed. He would use her again. Lie to her. Tell her she was beautiful. She knew it, yet she didn't care. She wanted to feel his warm hands on her skin, his kisses. To pretend he thought she was beautiful . . . that he *loved* her.

His hand dropped from her neck and she felt him withdraw. The cold breeze surrounded her trembling body again.

Ryen opened her teary eyes and found him beside her, closing the wooden shutters, closing out the cold. But her shaking would not subside.

When he turned his gaze back to her, his face was void of emotion. Dark eyes regarded her with a calculated coldness. Ryen's knees trembled and she knew she could not hold up under his scrutiny much longer. She was leaning heavily on the wall, silently begging him to leave.

"Prepare to break your fast," he commanded. In two strides his powerful legs took him across the room until he

stood at the door. "And do not open those windows again."
The door closed behind him and Ryen slid down the wall
until she had buried her head in her arms, her hair covering
them like a blanket.

The vial she had tucked into her chemise dug into her
skin, stabbing at her like a silent accusation. For her king . . .

Bryce stared at the door for a long moment without really
seeing it. His eyes were focused on the scene he expected
to find on the opposite side. A feast fit for a king, mountains
of bread, meat pies, lampreys, meats of all sorts—venison,
ox, chicken, and goose, and puddings, pear tarts—the best
Polly could make.

Ryen would be eating until her stomach was full, stuffing
the food into her small, delicate mouth with eager hands. He
would join her for the meal, feasting on her with his eyes.
He had already made up his mind. If she did indeed love
this other man and she was not happy at Dark Castle, he
would allow her to leave.

Bryce shoved open the door.

The food was piled high, as he had imagined; its smell
wafted to him on tendrils of steam. But Ryen was not there.
His brows furrowed as his eyes scanned the room for her.
When he spotted her sitting on the floor near the window,
his scowl deepened. Her head was bent to her knees, her
long, dark hair falling over them to the floor.

He took a step toward her. Ryen lifted her head and Bryce
saw the sadness lining her dull blue eyes. His heart twisted.
Her eyes had been so vibrant, so full of life. But now she
could not stand to be near him. His kiss had made her sob.
She would rather be kissed by Dumas, he thought.

Anger crashed over him at the thought of a young, tall,
fair-haired man holding Ryen. Bryce turned his back on her,
his fists clenching. He walked to the table of food and stared
at it. He had no hunger left.

"You should eat," he commented.

He heard nothing for a long moment. And then, just as he

was preparing to turn and confront her, he heard the soft rustle of her dress, the quiet swoosh of her skirt and the delicate padding of her footsteps as she approached.

"What shall I eat?" she asked. Her words were as listless as her lackluster eyes.

Bryce glanced at her to see if she was being sarcastic, but she was not looking at him; her eyes were focused on the table. Bryce studied her profile, her soft hair highlighted by the cold morning's filtered sun, her smooth, silken skin, her long, feathery lashes and full, pouty lips. "Perhaps some bread?" He reached out to pick up a small loaf and handed it to her.

Ryen took it without looking at him. Bryce watched as she placed a piece into her mouth and chewed almost absently. He turned away from her, unable to watch her sadness or experience her coldness.

"Will you not eat?" she wondered.

Her words startled him and he turned to see those blue eyes penetrating his thoughts, searching his soul. He felt his chest ache and tighten. She uses that look as a child uses tears, he reminded himself.

Ryen raised a loaf of bread to him.

Bryce narrowed his eyes. "I think not, Angel," he replied coldly.

Slowly, her offered hand lowered and a crestfallen look descended over her face.

Bryce steeled himself against her hurt look and gazed at her with angry eyes. She was nothing to him, he told himself, even as his body ached with wanting. His mind refused to acknowledge her shapely form, but the torn gown revealing more skin than was decent drew his gaze nonetheless.

Ryen turned to the table, picking up a mug and filling it with ale. She heard his soft footsteps and knew he had moved away from her. Ryen felt for the vial in her waist cloth. The image of Bryce dead filled her mind, and her hand began to tremble. She glanced over her shoulder to see Bryce standing, his back to her, staring at the tapestry. She removed the vial and uncorked it.

The liquid edged toward the lip of the vial as she held it poised over the ale.

She stood that way for a long moment, staring into the mug. Before a drop could fall, Ryen withdrew her hand, corked the vial, and replaced it.

She could not do it. God help me, she thought. But I cannot hurt him. Not even for my country. Ryen sighed, thinking he probably wouldn't have taken it anyway.

Ryen picked up the mug and approached.

When he set those dark eyes upon her, she froze. They were accusing and distrustful.

"Ale?" she asked.

His eyes narrowed slightly and she felt his gaze rake over her body. Then he took the cup, never taking his eyes off her. He lifted the mug to his lips and paused once before draining it!

Ryen's face paled and she staggered away. She could have killed him! The thought made her stomach churn, and for a moment she had trouble catching her breath.

Bryce drew himself up to his full height, a wall slamming down around him. "I have something to tell you that I think will make you very happy," he said, in a strangely restrained voice.

Ryen hated to hope, but she felt her heart begin to soar.

"I am taking you back to France," Bryce said.

Ryen's jaw dropped, her surprise written in her wide eyes and slackened shoulders.

"Back to your fiancé," Bryce finished.

His voice was cold and without feeling. It carved out Ryen's heart and hopes as swiftly as if it were a knife. As she stared into his dark eyes she wondered how she could have been so fooled by him. Unable to bear his anger and disdain, Ryen dropped her gaze. She watched his feet as he turned and moved to the door.

Ryen glanced up one final time to see his stiff back and broad shoulders as he closed the door. She stood frozen, staring blankly. He was bringing her back. Bryce did not want her. No more than her father did. *He never loved me. Only desired . . .*

The bile rose in her throat. Never loved. Her chest constricted as if all the air had been sucked from her.

The nights they had spent together had been wonderful. She had been so happy in the warmth of his arms. But their memory was tainted. It had all been a lie. He had used her. Humiliated her. And the worst thing was that as much as she wanted to hurt him, to give him some of the agony he was inflicting upon her, she knew she would not kill him.

Ryen removed the vial and stared at it for a long time. Then she threw it out the window.

Forty-four

It was agony, knowing she was in his castle. Once he'd seen she was safe, the rage he had experienced when he had first found her missing evaporated, leaving him with a relief so great that he had almost trembled. But now, as he sat alone behind a large table, in the room where he usually kept track of the harvest, his mood darkened. He was staring at a painted picture of a wolf that hung over the door. If he'd truly been as wild as the Wolf Pack, he'd have taken her and then slit her throat. It would have been easier.

But now . . . the thought of that flawless white neck, that stubborn jaw, plagued him. He could never hurt her. Yet he had. He had kept her from the man she loved.

His head drooped. He only wanted her to be happy. But he could not even accomplish that. He had to let her go.

Bryce raised his weary eyes and saw Grey strolling toward him. His usual furs had been shed in favor of one of Bryce's cotton white tunics and a pair of black leggings. Bryce looked away from his friend, ignoring his change of clothing.

"Have you heard anything from Count Dumas since we sent his messenger back?" Bryce asked.

Grey's eyes narrowed as he sat on a corner of the table. He shook his head. "Nothing."

Bryce sat back in his chair.

"Bryce," Grey said quietly, "I have known you for many years. And in all this time you have never kept anything from me. So I ask you now, brother to brother, what does this woman, this Angel of Death, mean to you?"

Bryce stared hard at Grey. He wondered why he was asking this pointed question, why he was getting involved in his private affairs. Usually, the Wolf Pack asked little but knew everything. Finally his thoughts turned to Grey's question. He saw Ryen in his mind's eye, saw her stubborn jaw clenched with rage, imagined her bright eyes filled with hot anger. "It doesn't matter," he murmured, the image vivid and agonizing.

"Doesn't matter?" Grey repeated. Then a slow smile slid over his lips. "If you truly believe that, then you are more blind than that beggar who stands outside your gatehouse."

"Honor dictates I return her to France."

"Honor," Grey snorted, waving a dismissing hand. "Your grand solution to everything. Let me tell you something. Honor has no place in the matters of the heart."

"This is not a matter of the heart," Bryce retorted.

"Still denying it? Then forget her," Grey dared. "Throw her in the dungeons and don't think on it."

Bryce grunted. If only it were that easy. If he could only wipe away the haunting image of those large sapphire eyes, the curve of her lips, the soft touch of her hands.

"Bryce, you cannot send her back to France. She has no place there," Grey said.

"It seems preferable to what she has here," Bryce grunted.

"Then death would be preferable."

"Don't speak in riddles, Grey."

"Her brother was trying to run her through when we came upon them."

Outrage roared through Bryce's body, bringing him to his feet. "Are you sure?"

Grey nodded once. "His sword was at her throat," Grey stated. "I am sure."

Bryce came around the table so fast that the breeze sent papers fluttering to the floor. "I'll kill him," Bryce promised.

Grey's hand slammed on his shoulder and Bryce halted, whipping around to pin Grey to the spot with his fevered gaze. "And killing him would settle your problems?"

Bryce angrily shrugged Grey's hand from his shoulder. He glanced longingly at the door, his look so hot that it threatened to melt the iron handle. Finally he turned and paced to one side of the room, his fists clenched with anger.

"You care for the wench. Admit it, Bryce," Grey encouraged. "It would make things a lot easier."

"She left me. I will never admit I care for her."

"She left you for kin. You'd do the same for one of us."

Bryce threw him a dark look. "Her brother is dangerous. I was trying to protect her!"

"She is a knight. She needs no protecting."

"God's blood!" Bryce exploded, "She is a woman, too."

"You have won the woman," Grey answered softly. "It is the knight you must be concerned about."

"I have not won the woman. She loves another," Bryce murmured.

"Then why did she write this missive?" Grey tossed a piece of paper onto the desk.

Bryce stared at it for a long moment before picking it up. He cast a speculative glance at Grey before scanning the paper.

"I had one of your men translate it," Grey said, shrugging sheepishly. "She was going to stay."

Bryce frowned at the paper. It was true. She had begun the letter to Dumas announcing her intentions of remaining in England with him. If that was so, how could she love this Count Dumas? Something was wrong. Something did not make sense.

Polly was happy to hear that Ryen was finally coming down to eat. Rumors were running rampant. Some said Lord Prince-

418 *Laurel O'Donnell*

ton had killed her and was keeping her corpse locked up in his room, others that he was starving the truth out of her.

Polly was waiting anxiously near the tables she had assembled with Lady Ryen when finally she spotted her. Polly took a step toward her but stopped cold when she saw that Ryen was being led by one guard and followed by another. Ryen was as white as a ghost, as if the life had been drained from her. She was placed at the soldiers' table, across from Talbot.

Polly watched her during the meal. Her eyes were cast downward and she sat silently, not eating. When Polly turned angry eyes to Bryce, she saw that he, too, sat stoically, the food before him untouched. Through his hard, emotionless face, Polly saw the anguish that touched the corners of his eyes, the pain that turned his lips into a sneer.

What have I done? Polly silently demanded.

It was then that she saw Grey approaching her. At first, Polly was sure he would pass her by, but as his steps took him closer and closer, she knew he was coming for her. She sat heavily in her chair. Grey did indeed stop before her.

When all conversation ceased around them, Grey's sharp eyes scanned the faces of the peasants who were all turned to him. He turned back to Polly. "Lord Princeton wants to see you."

Polly shuddered, casting her glance at her lord. He was staring at her, those dark eyes penetrating her skin as if he could see into her mind.

He knew. She was sure of it.

"After the meal, in the judgment room," Grey finished, and turned, moving to his seat.

Polly knew her sentence had been ordered. Her only defense now was his mercy!

Later that night, Polly shoved aside her dread and hesitantly pushed open the door. "M'lord?" she called.

The room was cast in a red glow, lit by the setting sun

streaming in from the high windows. Polly gasped, for it appeared that the judgment chair on which Bryce sat was glowing.

He was lost in the blackness of the shadow cast from the back of his chair.

Polly stepped forward, carefully closing the door behind her. "M'lord," she said, and suddenly had the urge to flee under his deadly gaze. "I—I have somethin' ta confess."

The silence rang in her ears like the echo of his voice until she was forced to speak to quiet the bells. "I lied ta ya, m'lord." He still didn't move or speak, and Polly wondered if he had heard her. She stepped closer. "But I *had* ta. She was threatenin' me. I was not sure what ta—"

"Stop rambling, woman, and say what you've come to say!" His voice rumbled through the room like a drumbeat.

"Lady Ryen was not returning ta her lover in France. Ta be quite honest, m'lord, we never talked of lovers."

Bryce was absolutely still; Polly couldn't even see him breathing. She panicked. "My lord. Ya have ta understand why I did it. I never meant ta hurt ya, and I would never harm a hair on Lady Ryen's lovely head. I knew no matter what the cost ta me, I could not keep the two of ya apart. Ya belong together." Polly's hands rang her apron, twisting it tightly. Bryce was still silent and Polly was forced to continue. "*I* was the one who gave Lady Ryen the dagger! The bread was as hard as a brick, and she was such a thin thing, so sickly. I never intended her to escape with it . . . That witch found out somehow, and she said I'd end up in the dungeon! Well, I couldna very well—"

"Did you tell Ryen about her brother?"

Bryce's voice shocked her into silence. When she couldn't find the words to answer, he rose up slowly out of his chair. The fiery sunlight splashed over his hair and shoulders. His face was still in shadow, but Polly saw the bunched muscles of his tensed arms. Anger emanated from his tight body and

Polly knew he would kill her. She fell to her knees. "Please, m'lord," she begged, "I meant no harm."

"Do not try my patience. Did you tell Ryen about her brother?"

"I did not tell 'er a thing! I just brought the horses!" Polly trembled. "She made me do it. She said—"

Bryce approached her. "I could kill you right now for this."

"Lotte made me do it! She threatened ta tell ya of the dagger!"

"Lotte?" Bryce's brows knit.

Polly raised clutched hands to Bryce as if to a god. "Please! Please give me another chance! I'll do anything! I'll never—"

"Talbot!"

Polly wept, unable to hold back her fear. "I beg of ya, m'lord. Please. Give me life so I can make it up ta ya."

"Talbot!" Bryce hollered, before turning his deadly gaze on Polly. "Do you think that my ears are deaf to my people? Did you think I would not listen to you?"

"M—McFinley," Polly gasped. "Ya almost killed 'im."

Bryce shut his mouth tightly into a thin line of anger. "He hurt Ryen. You were trying to help her."

The door banged open and Talbot raced in, breathless. "Prince?"

"Find Lotte," Bryce commanded in a dark voice. "And bring her here."

The door opened slowly. The light from the hallway fell across the floor, a white sliver growing wider, slicing the blackness of the room like a dagger. Bryce watched from his judgment chair as Lotte's form, black against the white light, appeared in the doorway.

"My Prince?" she cooed, sure that he had summoned her to take her back.

"Come in, Lotte," he replied quietly.

"It's so dark. Perhaps a candle—"

"No. Come in. Now."

Lotte hesitated. A silent alarm went off somewhere inside her. Finally she entered; the door closed behind her casting the room into the night's pale blue light. Shadows arced from the walls toward Lotte as she passed in and out of them, approaching Bryce.

"Prince," she said finally. "I knew you would call for me. I knew you would return to me." He remained silent and Lotte's anxiety grew. Something was wrong. Had he found out? No, she told herself. That was impossible. She had the situation firmly in hand.

"Lotte," he sneered. "You thought that with Ryen gone I would return to *you."*

Excitement shot up Lotte's spine. "Oh, yes. I've waited so long, m'lord. I knew that you would tire of that French tart before long. I can bear you another son! I can please you in many ways. Together—"

In her excitement, Lotte did not notice the fierce anger that slowly brought Bryce out of his chair, clenched his fists. "You fool. Don't you know that I would have followed Ryen to *hell* to return her to my side. You could *never* take her place in my heart."

Lotte was so shocked that she stood, dumbstruck.

"All your plans and your conniving to rid Dark Castle of Ryen have come to no good. I have seen through your plans and discovered the truth."

"Truth? Conniving? Surely you don't believe—"

"SILENCE!" His voice boomed throughout the judgment room, his anger shaking the rafters high above their heads. "You will never come between us again. *Never."*

Lotte stared at him in disbelief "You don't know what you are saying. She doesn't love you." Her desperation was growing and she took a step forward.

"I gave you a chance to remain at Dark Castle, but you

have rejected my suggestions, instead causing me pain as I have never experienced before."

"My lord, I would never harm you."

Bryce straightened, anger tightening every muscle in his body. "From this day forth you are banished from Dark Castle."

"No," Lotte gasped, eyes wide with horror. "You cannot . . . I have done *everything* for you. Everything. Including bearing your son."

Bryce's eyes narrowed at the mention of Runt. "That is why you are not dead." Bryce paused. "Talbot."

Talbot materialized from the shadows, Polly at his side.

Lotte's mouth dropped at seeing Polly. "You traitor!" she cried. "How could you do this to me?"

"See that Lotte leaves Dark Castle," Bryce commanded.

"Aye, m'lord," Talbot replied, stepping beside her.

"Prince, *no*. I love you. *No!*" Lotte stretched out her open hands to him.

It was Talbot who grasped one of her arms and dragged her toward the door.

"Do not shadow Dark Castle with your presence again. If you are found on my lands you will be quartered," Bryce said.

"Nooooo!" Lotte sobbed, as Talbot dragged her from the room.

Forty-five

Dark, dark hair waving in a soft breeze. Black eyes staring at her, calling to her with a hypnotic power. The corners of his sensual mouth turned up in a devilish grin. The scar on his cheek looking white against his bronzed skin. He was leaning against a wall, his right leg, bent at the knee, crossed over his left ankle. The wind ruffled his glossy hair and his ebony eyes caressed her skin, their gaze sweeping slowly over her breasts, her hips, her legs. Then they shifted, rising to meet hers. She saw the whispered words reflected in those eyes. "You're beautiful."

Beautiful.

He tilted his head back, robust laughter issuing from his open mouth.

Ryen sat up in bed, her body soaked with a layer of perspiration, her face moist with tears. She realized suddenly that she was trembling all over and could not stop.

He was taking her back to France. Ryen pulled the blanket up to her neck and hugged herself. She turned to stare at the tapestry. Bryce had rehung the elaborate weaving before he had left. She gazed at the horned man, staring at the image of Bryce. Why had he kept her brother's life a secret? Was it some game he played with her? A deception? Just like when he had said that she was beautiful?

She was drawn to the image on the tapestry and she rose out of bed, moving toward it. In his dark eyes she saw a cold and mesmerizing look that could consume people alive, make them believe what he wanted them to. It was all a lie. He had seduced her into believing his words again, believing that he cared for her, just as he had at De Bouriez Castle.

The thought should have enraged her, but Ryen found it impossible to call up any anger. Sadness overwhelmed her senses. Sadness, and a pain so great that it threatened to rip out her very soul.

With a groan, Ryen seized the tapestry and tore it from the wall, throwing it to the floor. She stared at it for a long moment. She could see his eye, his watchful gaze, among the crumpled fabric. Her heart lay in the folds of the tapestry. She would never see Bryce again. Good, she thought, as a sob welled in her throat. He will never have the chance to laugh at me.

Her heart ached and her chest constricted until tears filled her vision. Ryen shook her head, refusing to give in to the agony that was tearing her apart. Instead, she turned her back on the tapestry and busied herself with dressing in a very plain brown velvet dress. She had no sooner finished than there was a knock at her door. Ryen turned to find Vignon on the threshold.

Startled, Ryen shot off the bed. He slithered into the room and she forced her eyes to settle on the silver tray he held in his slim hands, but it was impossible to still the pounding of her heart or the feeling of cold terror that snaked its way up her spine.

"Your food," he said, and moved to the table beside the bed, sliding the tray onto it. "Did you do it?"

"No. I haven't had a chance," Ryen lied, thinking of the ale Bryce had drunk. Guilt overwhelmed her and she had to turn away from him.

Vignon swiveled his head to regard her with his cold eyes. "Rest easy. For it is done."

Ryen froze as shivers crept up her spine. "Done?" she asked, suddenly breathless.

"Yes. His wine will taste most bitter at this, his last meal," Vignon said with laughter in his voice.

Ryen stood absolutely motionless. "Good," she finally murmured.

Vignon moved past her to the door where he paused. "Our work is finished, m'lady," he said, before exiting the room.

Ryen shivered slightly. She stared at the tray, trying to convince herself that Vignon had actually been in her room. Her ears refused to acknowledge his words. Yet Ryen could not shake the feeling of doom that enfolded her like a giant hand. She moved to the bed, her mind replaying the fateful words ". . . it is done." They hung in the air like a premonition of ruin.

It would be only moments before Bryce took a sip of wine, and then only seconds before his life ended. Panic surged inside her and she stood, unable to move. Finally, she paced toward the door and then back to the bed, her hands anxiously massaging each other. Perhaps he had already taken a sip and was in the throes of death.

"No," Ryen cried, and surged toward the door.

She came up short just before her fist closed over the handle. How could she betray her country by saving Bryce's life?

The image of Bryce's beautiful, powerful, mysterious body lying broken and still on the cold stone floor rose before her eyes. "No," she whimpered. She thought she had watched him die once before, and the pain she'd experienced had been unbearable. God help her, but she loved him. She loved him more than honor, more than chivalry, more than the disgrace and hate that saving him would bring her. She couldn't let him die. Not for Lucien, not for France.

She stifled a sob and threw the door open.

Talbot, who was bent over, lacing his boots, looked up and straightened upon seeing her.

Ryen could not waste time. She had to get past him. She

couldn't be too late. Her pulse raced as she forced herself to walk to him.

"What—?" Talbot began.

Ryen brought her knee up into his groin. Talbot doubled over, gasping, and Ryen hauled her skirts up to race down the hall toward the stairway, all the while praying that she would reach Bryce in time.

She leapt down the last two steps to the main floor. She straightened cautiously, glancing first left toward the Great Hall, then right.

Not ten paces away stood Vignon looking bemusedly at her.

He'll try to stop me. The words raced through her mind and she crouched to flee toward the Great Hall.

Vignon's gaze slowly turned into a frown as realization hit him. Disbelief flashed in his eyes as he stepped toward her.

Ryen lifted her skirts and fled down the corridor. Her lungs ached with the exertion it took to run full out. Ryen heard the soft padding of his footsteps as he chased her, but she pushed the thought of capture from her mind. She had to stop Bryce. He couldn't die!

Her arms pumping, she rounded the open doorway, entering the Great Hall at a run. She saw him immediately, seated and turned in his chair, a head taller than the man he was speaking with on his right. He was raising the cup!

No, she thought. Oh, God, no!

She was more than halfway into the room when he turned to her, the cup at his lips. Distantly she heard the shouts of angry voices and the cold sound of metal sliding against metal . . . swords!

In desperation she lunged across the table, bringing her hand back, and knocked the cup from his grasp. It crashed to the ground, spilling red wine on Runt's empty chair. She watched it drip over the side onto the floor before turning her gaze to Bryce. His dark eyes were locked on her, brows drawn together in disapproving anger, then rising in stunned surprise.

Reality crashed down around her as mumbled voices of outrage and hate exploded throughout the room. There was a growl from beside her and she was shoved back from Bryce into hands that bruised her arms as they held and shook her. She felt a dagger press into her back; the sharp edge of a sword blade was shoved beneath her chin. The press of bodies was suffocating, like a wall sealing off her view of Bryce. Her arms were pulled back painfully until she whimpered.

"No!" The command cut through the noise and silence engulfed the large room, except for the barking of the dogs that echoed in every corner.

The pressure of the blade beneath her chin forced Ryen's head up. She closed her eyes tightly, fighting down the panic and uncertainty. Had Bryce drunk the wine?

When she opened her eyes, Bryce stood before her. His black eyes gazed down at her in confusion for a moment before his hand shot out, shoving the blade from her neck.

Ryen lowered her chin as angry grumbles sounded around her.

"She tried to kill you," one of the men exclaimed.

"No, she did not," Bryce said with conviction.

Her lip quivered as she choked, *"Poison."*

As the impact of her announcement hit him, Bryce whirled to his empty seat.

The wine was pooling beneath the table where a hound was eagerly lapping at it. A second dog was trying to walk away, but its hind legs slid out from beneath it, then it fell over, its eyes rolling into its head. The first hound suddenly went into convulsions.

Murmurings spread throughout the room as the second of the two dogs died.

Bryce's gaze slammed back to Ryen's.

"Bryce," Ryen gasped, "did you drink?"

The silence filled the hall with expectation. Ryen could not breathe, dared not take a breath.

"No," he answered.

When his lips formed the word she had prayed for, she collapsed into the arms that held her. Relief flooded her heart, a relief so great she wanted to cry out in joy, to throw her arms around Bryce and hug him until the pain of worry faded.

But the hands of his men held her back and kept her from crumpling to the floor.

Bryce's eyes were intense. "How did you know?" he finally asked.

Ryen's relief vanished; her face turned ashen and unreadable. Her only thought had been to save Bryce. She had not thought of the consequences, had not cared. But now her actions rose before her like an accusation. As much as she loved Bryce, now that he was safe, she knew she could not betray France. "I cannot tell you."

Bryce's eyes narrowed slightly as one of the men condemned her. "She did it!"

Bryce's hand closed brutally over her upper arm and he pulled her away from his men into his hold. He towed her past the prying and angry eyes of his people and hauled her up the stairs and down the corridor to his room.

The door slammed behind them and Ryen turned to face him. Her shoulders slumped forward, her eyes wide. She looked fragile, somehow—vulnerable.

"Who did it?" he demanded, trying to keep his voice level against the feelings he felt roaring through his body.

Ryen shook her head, unable to speak. Soft curls fell rebelliously from her long braid, and Bryce had the urge to catch one of them in his open palm. He chased the feeling away with a frown. "You would make me punish you for keeping the traitor's name from me?"

Ryen looked at him with those large blue eyes and Bryce could see the disbelief in their liquid depths.

"No," he said, angry with himself for even suggesting a punishment to her. He could never harm her. And that was his downfall. Cursing, Bryce turned from her. "Why did you save my life? To humiliate me with your silence?"

"Why did you save my life at Agincourt?" her weak, soft voice came from behind him.

He whirled toward her. "Because I—I—" He stopped cold. He had almost said it. Almost told her the disease that ate away at his mind and soul tormented his days and haunted his nights. "It is not the same! How can you . . . *compare* . . ." His voice trailed off as he observed her in a new light, even though she stood in the shadows near the wall. "It was the honorable thing to do." Grey's words rose in his mind: "You have won the woman. It is the knight you must be concerned about." "You did it for honor. Because I saved your life, you felt obligated . . ."

"No!" she objected.

He took a step toward her, his fists clenched. "Tell me his name. I want his name." Cold anger filled his voice. She had not saved him because she cared for him. All she cared about was honor.

Ryen lifted that haughty little chin. The light from the windows sparkled in her eyes and Bryce saw the tears glittering like precious gems.

"Tell me," he insisted, stopping just before her.

Ryen's uplifted chin quivered.

Bryce raised his hands, and while other people would have cowered, she stood her ground. He placed his hands on her shoulders, unable to resist the urge to touch her. He backed her into the wall, his hands sliding from her shoulders down the soft velvet of her dress to her arms as he pressed himself into her. Her sweet breath was hot on his lips. "Tell me," he whispered.

When she didn't reply, he pressed his mouth against hers,

urging her soft lips to open to him with gentle but insistent strokes of his tongue. Then he plunged into her mouth, tasting the sweet victory. The longing in his loins grew and he knew that if she did not tell him, he would gladly take her.

"Oh, Bryce, Bryce," Ryen murmured into his kiss.

He felt her arms flutter up his back.

"Tell me," he groaned, pressing kisses into her throat. At first he thought it was a sigh, the way her throat quivered; then her body shook. Yes, he thought, our bodies still react as one.

He lifted his mouth to claim her lips again. As his cheek moved over hers, he felt the moisture, could taste the salty tears on her lips.

Startled, he pulled back to gaze down at her face. His heart broke, shattering into a thousand pieces.

Her large blue eyes were red and swollen from her tears. They streaked down her face in tiny rivulets.

Bryce reached out with his forefinger and caught one. The drop shimmered on the tip of his finger like a precious gem. He rubbed it reverently between his thumb and forefinger, staring at it with fascination and awe until it disappeared into his skin. He raised perplexed eyes to her.

"Please don't make me tell you," she gasped.

"He will try again," Bryce said flatly.

Ryen buried her face in her palms, her shoulders shaking fiercely. "I can't," she wept. "I want to. God help me, I *want* to. But I can't betray my vows."

So, it was honor again. Even as he thought this, he didn't care. All he wanted was to stop her pain. Bryce reached out to her, placing a heavy hand on her shoulder. A French spy, then, he thought, in Dark Castle. But somehow, it didn't matter. Ryen was all that concerned him. His touch seemed to comfort her and her sobs lessened. "Ryen," he said kindly. My love, he thought.

She raised her tear-reddened eyes to him. "I can't forsake my country and be loyal to you, too," she cried.

Grief, guilt, and anguish flooded through him at once, and he stepped back from her. How can I ask her to? Bryce thought. Would I not do the same, were I in her place? I must help her. But how? There must be some way, some way to satisfy honor without sending her away from me. We are knights, for the love of God. We should be able to . . .

Suddenly, Bryce's eyes lit. Resolution squared his shoulders and he proclaimed, "Sir Ryen De Bouriez, I challenge you to a joust. If you win, you will be set free. Free to return to your beloved France."

She opened her mouth as if to speak, but Bryce hurriedly continued, "However, if I win, you must happily remain at Dark Castle and pledge your loyalty to me—by becoming my wife."

"Wife?" Ryen gasped.

"Do you accept my challenge?"

Stunned, Ryen did not move or speak.

"Well?" he urged.

She nodded, her soft curls bouncing eagerly.

"I must warn you, I will do everything in my power to defeat you," he added.

She did not reply, only stared at him with swollen eyes that were strangely bright. Bryce frowned and turned his back to her. He exited the room.

Talbot awaited him in the hallway, his arms crossed over his chest.

Bryce saw the triumphant look in his eye. "You caught Wells," he said.

Talbot nodded. "Of course. Your feeling about him was correct, as usual."

Bryce agreed with a dip of his head before turning to continue down the hallway.

"Prince," Talbot called, halting his movement. "She saved your life."

"So it would seem."

"Wells was in the crowd at the Great Hall. He was found

with a dagger. He could have slipped through the men and killed her. So it seems you saved her life as well."

The thought of a dagger in Ryen's back brought cold chills to his body. "I owe more to that woman than just a debt of honor," Bryce stated quietly. "I was blind not to have seen it before."

Forty-Six

The sky was as gray as worn armor and a fine spray of mist blanketed the ground, permeating the air with moisture. The field was strangely silent as Bryce rode out, his horse trudging through the wet earth. The grassy area around the field was empty, and there were no cheers or hisses filling the air.

Bryce maneuvered his horse toward Talbot, who had agreed to act as his squire. He did not want an audience for this contest. It was between him and Ryen.

He reined up his horse beside Talbot and glanced across the field. Grey was lounging against the wooden fence at the far end of the field. He had consented to squire Ryen, and Bryce wondered if it was because he had asked Grey to do it or out of curiosity to see who would win.

Cursing, Bryce pulled his shield down over his eyes. Rain splattered his face through the small slit in his visor. He heard the dull *clink* every time a drop hit his plate armor. *If I hurt her, I will never forgive myself, but I cannot lose.* His war horse, Hades, snorted beneath him. The animal was skittish today. Bryce tried to hold him still, yet the beast circled and paced, giving Bryce extra time to study Ryen.

She sat atop the horse, dressed in full plate mail. The animal she rode was as still as its rider. Bryce swore he could see the blinding blue of her eyes even from this distance.

He tried to view her as just another knight, as an opponent, but every time he tried he imagined her large, tearful eyes gazing miserably at him and felt her body shake with a sob.

Doubt festered in his mind. I have never lost a joust, he told himself. And I will not lose this one. But is it right to over-power her and force her to marry me? She did agree! Was it only because she would never lose face by turning down a challenge? This is the only way to settle our differences! The knightly way, the honorable way. But she is not just a warrior . . . she is a woman.

Bryce recalled the very first time he had seen her. He remembered her blue eyes shining through that white mist like the flames of a campfire, remembered his initial shock and dismay at finding his adversary to be a woman. Now, as he stared across the field, he watched her through a fine mist of rain, and even though he did not have chains around his wrists, he felt a heavy weight on his shoulders. He had to win. And yet he had to be careful not to harm her. There had been a time when all he'd wanted was to kill her. Now all he wanted was to wed her.

Angry at not being able to control his wandering thoughts, he grabbed for the jousting pole that Talbot handed to him. Grey gave the signal to begin and Bryce rounded his horse, spurring him on. He bent low in his saddle, pointing the tip at her chest. They raced at each other, coming closer and closer, their horses breathing hotly with the effort of the charge, their hooves kicking up mud in big clumps. They both held their poles firmly at their sides, the deadly tips pointing at each other's heart.

Suddenly, Bryce felt Hades stumble. He swung his pole forward, needing both his hands on the reins to right his steed. For a split second, fear seized him. Her lance was positioned exactly for his chest and he was off balance. He was an easy target.

Bryce braced for the impact . . . but it never came. At the last moment, Ryen raised her lance, missing him completely. The two knights passed and Bryce straightened in his saddle, steadying his horse. With my disadvantage she could have easily unhorsed me, he thought. Why didn't she? He looked over his shoulder in time to see Ryen round her animal and come at him again. Bryce responded, turning his horse to face her and urging the animal forward with a hard kick. As they charged at each other again, Bryce leveled his lance and lowered his body over the horse's neck. Hit her in the stomach, he thought. She's light enough and it will knock her off easily.

The horses raced ever closer to one another. Bryce saw the tip of her lance coming toward him. Suddenly he knew his weight behind the impact of his lance would be too much for her. In his mind's eye, he saw his lance strike her, the wood splinter, and a stray piece pierce her visor. He had seen one man die of such a wound. Panic seized him and he knocked her lance aside with his arm, turning his own away from her.

He raised his visor and turned to face her, shoving his lance to the ground. "Yield to me!" he shouted across the field.

That haughty little chin rose, and in response, she reached for another lance and reeled her steed toward his. Bryce muttered a curse and jerked Hades toward her, weaponless.

Before Ryen reached him, she threw the lance down and reined in her horse, bringing it to a halt.

Bryce stopped Hades not five feet from her.

"You challenged me and now you refuse to fight?" she demanded.

Through the slit of her visor, Bryce could see her blue eyes flashing with fury. "I could not bear to see you hurt," he answered. "It is not worth my pride or my honor."

Ryen's horse whinnied nervously and pranced. "But is it worth *my* honor?" she queried hotly.

Bryce tried desperately to see past the anger that tightened her grip on the reins and clenched her jaw, but all he could see was the fierce rage that lit her deep blue eyes.

Ryen watched Bryce through the feeling of pain and betrayal that gripped her. "You lied to me about my brother!" Ryen yelled.

"I—I couldn't tell you!" he shouted back, helpless.

Sadness gripped her. He didn't trust her enough to tell her. "Pick up your lance," she said.

"He was mad, dangerous! He could have harmed you."

"You told me he was dead." Her voice was tight with sorrow.

"I'm sorry I lied to you," he whispered.

She stared at him for a long moment. She wanted desperately to throw down her weapon and run to him, to feel his embrace. To be his wife. But she knew she couldn't do that. If she did, she would be betraying Lucien, her king, and her country. But mostly, she would be betraying what she was. A warrior. How could she toss aside all that she'd worked for? All that she'd fought to achieve? If she did, she could not respect herself, and she certainly couldn't ask Bryce to. "Are you afraid to fight me? Are you afraid of defeat?" she taunted.

Bryce's gaze bit into hers. "Don't do this."

But she had to; she had no choice. She could not forsake her vows of honor. And if he won, then her vow to him would be the stronger. "Fight me, Prince of Darkness. Face the Angel of Death," she called. "Or are you a coward?"

Bryce knew he was many things, but a coward was not one of them. He spurred his horse to the other side of the field, steeling his feelings. He had never lost a joust. He would not lose this one. He ripped the lance from Talbot's hand and turned Hades to face her.

His eyes narrowed as they came to rest upon her. She had removed her helmet. Her hair shone glorious and wild, defiantly vibrant beneath the light rain. Her large eyes glared across the field at him. Even at this distance, she enflamed his soul. He felt desire course through him, tensing every muscle into rebellion. He growled low in his throat. Damn her, he thought. She attempts to distract me.

Then she spurred her horse. Bryce matched her movement.

The thunder of the horses' hooves pounded in Bryce's ears as they moved toward each other. The tip of her lance was held even and steady.

Bryce forced his mind to focus on victory. He had to hit her in the stomach. He bent low over his mount, centering the pole in his hand. His eyes held on his target.

Ryen's hair waved behind her in the wind. For a moment, he pictured his hand running over the length of it, caressing its softness.

By the time he realized that her subtle trick had worked, it was too late. His lance struck her arm just as he felt an impact smash into his side. Pain roared in his head as he flew from Hades and he saw the sky above him for an instant before his body crashed to the earth. Stunned, he lay still for a long moment, staring at the gray sky. He, the Prince of Darkness, thrown from his horse in a joust! This must be a horrible nightmare. Then a throbbing in his side brought him back to reality. He groaned and pushed himself onto his good side. Somehow, he managed to pull his helmet from his head.

She won, he thought, stunned. No one had ever defeated him. The little vixen had tricked him and won. Her victory brought a sudden sobriety to him. He pushed himself from the ground, looking for her atop her mount. Instead, the sight that greeted him brought a wave of cold chills to his body.

Ryen was lying in the grass not ten feet from him.

Bryce rose, cradling his side, which had suddenly gone numb. He took a hesitant step forward. She wasn't moving. Images of her lying in the mud at the Battle of Agincourt flashed through his mind. "No," he whispered, the agonized gasp wrenched from a suddenly tight throat.

His steps increased in length and urgency until he was running and he skidded to a halt in the wet grass and gazed at her. She can't be hurt. I will never forgive myself. "Ryen," he groaned, fear etched in his dark eyes. He dropped to one knee beside her, his gaze sweeping anxiously over her body. There was no blood, unlike at Agincourt. She was all right.

He knew it the moment her large eyes turned up to him. He knew it the moment she pressed the dagger against his throat.

He was so startled that for a long moment he could not move, did not breathe. The treacherous little wench, he thought. And I was worried for her safety. Two can play at that game.

Gasping for breath, Bryce doubled over, holding his ribs. There was pain spearing through his body from the impact of the lance, but he had experienced the agony in battle before and knew the results would be only dark bruises.

The dagger was immediately replaced by caring hands and Bryce knew he had won. He seized the wrist of her dagger hand and drew her close, crushing her in an embrace so powerful that it threatened to break her ribs. "I learn quickly, Angel," he murmured into her ear.

He felt the outrage surge through her body, felt her push against his embrace, but he did not let go.

"You knew I would come to your aid," he said with admiration in his voice. "You knew my only weakness would be you." Her impudent silence was answer enough for him and he chuckled as she increased her struggle. "And I guessed your only weakness would be me."

"You arrogant—" Ryen shoved against his chest.

When he glanced down at her, there was sorrow in his dark eyes. "I never meant to hurt you. But I could not risk losing you."

Suddenly she wrenched away from him. Disbelief flashed through her bright blue eyes, then suspicion. "Sword!" she called, replacing the dagger in her belt. "I thought you were returning me to France," she snarled, as Grey ran up and handed her a sword.

Bryce tried to ignore the glint of amusement that lit Grey's face as he backed away. "If I had wanted you returned to France, I would have taken the gold and let Dumas have you."

"One bag of gold," Ryen murmured, and swung the blade. Bryce ducked as the blade swooshed over his head. Had that been disappointment in her voice? Bryce's throaty chuckle reached her ears. "Angel, there were more than two carts full in the courtyard."

Shock rounded her eyes as she stared at him, the sword held at the ready beside her head.

"You did not think I would let you go for one tiny bag of gold, did you?"

Talbot rushed to Bryce's side and handed him his sword. Bryce stared at it for a long moment before lifting it from Talbot's hands.

"Two carts?" she gasped.

Still, Bryce did not raise his sword to her. "Don't you know what you mean to me? My life was complete in those days we were together. Those days when you were happy with me. I want that happiness again. For you and for me. Somewhere . . . somehow . . . you became more to me than my enemy, more than France. You became my Angel." Bryce stared into her large blue eyes. They had softened, and for a moment he dared to hope. Would she give up everything for him? Would she lay down her weapon to be his wife?

For a long moment, nothing happened. Then he saw her fingers tighten around the handle of the blade. It was only instinct that saved him from her blow as he raised his own weapon and blocked her swing.

The swords rang out through the battlefield.

"Do not make me fight you. I do not want that, Ryen," he stated between the crossed weapons. "I want you willing."

"Willing?" she echoed.

"Willing to spend your life with me. Willing to be my wife."

"You want *me?*" she asked in disbelief, yanking her weapon back.

"I have wanted you since the first day I saw you," Bryce stated. He saw the conflict in her until her brows crashed together and he had to block another swing.

"I will not yield to you," she ground out between clenched teeth.

"Then I have no choice," Bryce said. He swung mightily, meaning to knock the sword from her hands, but Ryen blocked the blow, using two hands to hold her weapon. The blades crossed and he stared at her between the sharp edges of their swords. "You cannot possibly win under my strength." He forced the weapons closer and closer until their lips were almost touching. "Believe what I say, Angel. I love you with all my heart."

She faltered and he easily pushed forward, brushing her lips with his. He could have won, he had no doubt, but it was far more pleasurable to feel the warmth of her soft lips than the taste of victory. His body trembled with wanting, not just physical, but the need for her at his side, with him always.

When he pulled slightly away, he saw her eyes darken with desire. "If you yield, you swear fealty to *me*," he stated quietly. "It means forsaking your family, your country, to remain at my side. You would never be able to return to France. Would you give that up for me?"

Her lips moved and he could have sworn they had whispered an affirmation. But in the next moment she was shoving him away. He fell onto his back and barely had time to roll out of the way before her sword arced to the ground. "Do you think I betray my vows so easily?"

He pushed himself to his feet.

"You must defeat me first, Prince of Darkness," she challenged. "Then and only then can I swear fealty to you."

Bryce's eyes narrowed and his spine stiffened as he drew himself up straighter. "As you wish," he answered. He raised his arm, swinging the blade. Ryen deflected the blow and countered with an arc toward his side. Bryce stepped back and dodged, spinning to attack again.

The blade slammed down above Ryen's head and she parried with a mighty swing.

She is an admirable opponent, Bryce thought. Yet even as

I enjoy the swordplay, I must bring this to an end. He attacked Ryen relentlessly, driving her further and further back under a barrage of powerful swings and blows. But Ryen was quick, easily dodging or deflecting his attacks.

Finally, with a loud growl of frustration, Bryce swung his blade. Ryen's sword was knocked loose from her hand and the blade spun into the air. She slipped in the mud and went down to her knee.

Bryce paused for a long moment, breathing heavily. Her head was down, her long hair wet with rain, falling to the ground. He stepped forward and calmly put the tip of his sword beneath her lovely neck. With the slightest hint of pressure, he forced her head up until her eyes locked with his.

He could read no emotion in those deep blue eyes. "Yield to me, my Angel," he whispered.

She moved her body slightly and did not say a word. Then a small smile slid over her lips and she replied, "I can think of no one better to spend the rest of my life with, no one I love more."

His face exploded with joy and a smile that threatened to clear up the gray skies. He lowered his sword and took her chin in his hand to study every detail of her face, her rain-moistened skin, her mist-kissed lips, and those sapphire eyes that had captured his heart. "You are everything I could possibly want. I have been a fool not to recognize my happiness for what it is. I love you, Angel." His gloved fingers traced her cheeks from her soft hairline to her lips. "You are so beautiful."

Ryen's mouth dropped open. "You think I'm beautiful?"

"More than all of England."

"Then . . . when you were my prisoner . . . under the truth powder—"

Bryce grinned, a boyish, shy smile that filled Ryen's heart completely. "It was the only truthful thing I told you that day." He was drawing closer to kiss her when he felt something press against his ribs. He glanced down to see a small dagger in her hand resting against the gap in his armor.

He pulled back sharply to gaze into her eyes once more.

"We'll never know," she whispered.

He frowned as she lowered the weapon. "Know what?" he asked.

"Who's the better warrior," she murmured, and leaned forward to press her lips against his.

Bryce framed her head with his hands, pulling her to her feet without breaking the kiss. She had yielded . . . she had yielded of her own accord! The better warrior, he thought. But the kiss deepened and he pulled her closer against him.

Then he scooped her up into his arms and spun her around in the misty rain, joyous laughter bubbling from his throat.

Epilogue

France

Darkness descended over the hillside, covering it like a blanket. The flickering lights of campfires dotted the darkness. In a thicket not far from the camp, a hooded figure huddled in the shadows thrown by giant trees.

Jean Claude De Bouriez stepped into the thicket under the watchful gaze of the silent figure. He glanced about the small clearing and stood motionless for a long moment.

Then the hooded figure moved into the moonlight, its pale glow washing over him, making his robe glow. Jean Claude's head turned. He stared hard, perusing the figure from head to toe.

Slowly a slender hand emerged from the folds of the robe and pushed back the hood. Dark hair tumbled riotously from the confines of the material. Ryen De Bouriez, now Ryen Princeton, stood proudly and somewhat uncertainly before her father, trying to see into his unreadable eyes. She did not move forward, but waited cautiously. "You wanted to see me?"

"Ryen," he gasped, and she heard the pain that gripped his voice.

Ryen's heart coiled tightly and she stepped closer. "We've brought Lucien back."

Jean Claude nodded. "Yes. He's safely in camp," he replied. "He is determined to return to England for you."

Ryen shook her head. "Do not let him."

Jean Claude looked away from her toward the bright moon. "Ryen. I thought you were dead. I—I cursed myself . . ."

Anguish twisted Ryen's heart. "Father—"

He shook his head. "Then the ransom came to Dumas. Oh, Ryen. I was wrong. I never should have betrothed you to him. I did not realize what I had done until I thought you were gone."

Ryen stepped toward him.

"Please," Jean Claude said, holding up his hand and bowing his head. "Let me finish. I will never see you again. You will not be able to return to France. I must disavow you, Ryen."

Ryen raised her chin. "I understand."

Jean Claude shook his head sadly. "I will not see my grandchildren grow and become fine warriors. Most important, I will not see your happiness." He lifted his head to her and Ryen saw the tears glisten in his eyes. "I want you to be happy, little one. I have failed you."

"No, Father," Ryen stressed. "You have made me strong."

"I have hurt you," he insisted. When Ryen shook her head, he added quickly, "Do not deny it is so. I have seen the agony in your eyes."

"Do you see agony now?" she wondered.

"No," he replied in a sigh. Hesitantly, he reached out and took her hand in his own. "My child."

Ryen watched the play of emotions over his features. Sorrow crept its way into the somber scowl he wore; regret rent his brows into a furrow. Finally these emotions dissolved and acceptance speckled his relaxed features. He suddenly looked old. Old and tired.

Tears glistened in her eyes. She would never see him again and she wanted to say so much. Tell him how much she would miss him.

"You love him." It was half statement, half question.

"With all my heart," Ryen replied.

Jean Claude nodded. "As I did your mother."

He nodded his head and a sad smile twitched the corner of his lip, longing filling his eyes. But there was something else there, too. Beneath the pain and the acceptance, Ryen saw it. It was the same look he had bestowed on Lucien and Andre so long ago. As he gazed down at her, his eyes glowed, a slight grin on his lips. Pride puffed up his chest. "You are a fine knight, Ryen," he said sincerely. "You always have been."

Tears welled in Ryen's eyes and she threw her arms around his strong shoulders. For a moment, she enjoyed the feeling of his embrace. "I love you, Father," she whispered finally.

She felt him squeeze her tightly.

"Ryen," a voice from behind her called softly.

She stepped away from her father and turned. Another hooded figure, taller and broader than she, stood waiting in the shadows. Ryen saw the glint of a sword beneath the robe he wore.

"We must go."

Ryen nodded at Bryce and turned back to her father. His hands dropped to his side, but she caught one of them and held it tightly. When she stepped back, he did not release her hand. Only when she had taken another step did he relinquish his grip on her.

Ryen took one more step backward, watching her father, trying to memorize his face. Then she turned and walked into the shadows where Bryce waited. Her head was bowed for a long moment, and when she looked up at him, he nodded and gently touched her cheek. Then he reached around her to pull the hood over her head. He grasped her hand tightly. "Our war is finished, Angel," Bryce whispered.

Together, the Angel of Death and the Prince of Darkness disappeared into the shadows of the night . . .

Taylor-made Romance from Zebra Books

WHISPERED KISSES   (0-8217-3830-5, $4.99/$5.99)
Beautiful Texas heiress Laura Leigh Webster never imagined
that her biggest worry on her African safari would be the handsome Jace Elliot, her tour guide. Laura's guardian, Lord Chad-
wick Hamilton, warns her of Jace's dangerous past; she simply
cannot resist the lure of his strong arms and the passion of his
Whispered Kisses.

KISS OF THE NIGHT WIND   (0-8217-5279-0, $5.99/$6.99)
Carrie Sue Strover thought she was leaving trouble behind her
when she deserted her brother's outlaw gang to live her life as
schoolmarm Carolyn Starns. On her journey, her stagecoach
was attacked and she was rescued by handsome T.J. Rogue. T.J.
plots to have Carrie lead him to her brother's cohorts who murdered his family. T.J., however, soon succumbs to the beautiful
runaway's charms and loving caresses.

FORTUNE'S FLAMES   (0-8217-3825-9, $4.99/$5.99)
Impatient to begin her journey back home to New Orleans,
beautiful Maren James was furious when Captain Hawk delayed
the voyage by searching for stowaways. Impatience gave way
to uncontrollable desire once the handsome captain searched
her cabin. He was looking for illegal passengers; what he found
was wild passion with a woman he knew was unlike all those
he had known before!

PASSIONS WILD AND FREE   (0-8217-5275-8, $5.99/$6.99)
After seeing her family and home destroyed by the cruel and
hateful Epson gang, Randee Hollis swore revenge. She knew
she found the perfect man to help her—gunslinger Marsh
Logan. Not only strong and brave, Marsh had the ebony hair
and light blue eyes to make Randee forget her hate and seek
the love and passion that only he could give her.